PRAI

MW00811298

"A seminal novel in the zombie canon—a bonafide classic that should be required reading for fans of post-apocalyptic or horror fiction. Rogers is one of the bridges between the Romero-Fulci era and today's modern undead."

—Brian Keene, author of *Dead Sea* and *Castaways*

"A great story with compelling characters and a very grimly portrayed post-apocalyptic world."

—J.L. Bourne, author of *Day by Day Armageddon*

"I've read them all: Brian Keene, Eric Brown, Travis Adkins, Kim Paffenroth, David Wellington, etc. Mark E. Roger's *The Dead* is hands down my favorite and the best zombie novel ever written. That book still freaks me out."

—Taylor Kent, host of Snark Infested Waters

"*The Dead* is still among my all time favorites ... Any fan of apocalyptic fiction should give this a read."

—The Fiendish Files of the Black Order

THE DEAD

Mark E. Rogers

Permuted Press
The formula has been changed...
Shifted... Altered... *Twisted.*
www.permutedpress.com

A PERMUTED PRESS book
published by arrangement with the authors

ISBN-10: 1-934861-26-X
ISBN-13: 978-1-934861-26-4

This book is a work of fiction. People, places, events, and situations are the product of the author's imagination. Any resemblance to actual persons, living or dead, or historical events, is purely coincidental.

Author's Note:
I wrote the first draft of *The Dead* in 1980-81, and haven't revised it too much since, although around 1986 I added the Bonewolves and the scene where Legion reveals his true appearance. The book was originally published by Ace in 1989, long before *Left Behind* or the current zombie craze.

The Dead copyright © 2009 by Mark E. Rogers
All Rights Reserved
Cover art and interior art by Mark E. Rogers

No part of this book may be reproduced, stored in a retrieval system, or transmitted by any means without the written permission of the author and publisher.
10 9 8 7 6 5 4 3 2 1

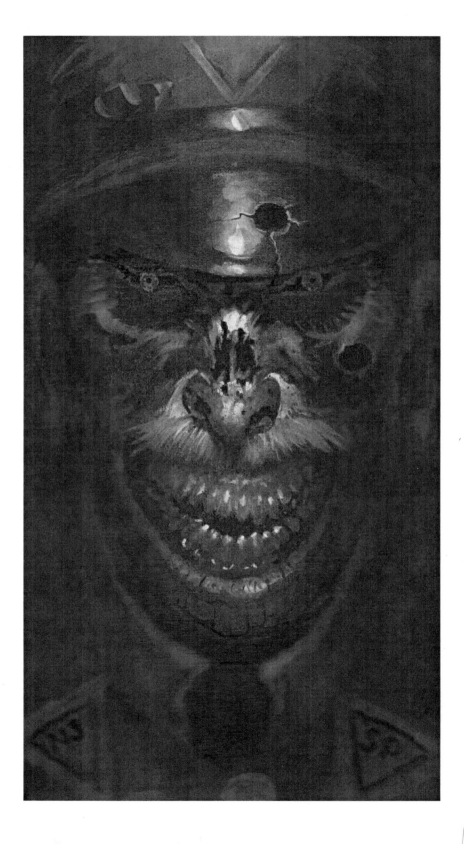

Hear'st thou, my soul, what serious things
Both the Psalm and Sibyl sings
Of a sure Judge from whose sharp ray
The world in flames shall fly away?

O that fire! Before whose face
Heaven and Earth shall find no place;
O those eyes! Whose angry light
Must be the day of that dread night.

O that trump! Whose blast shall run
An even round with th' circling sun,
And urge the murmuring graves to bring
Pale mankind forth to meet his King.

Horror of nature, hell, and death!
When a deep groan from beneath
Shall cry "We come, we come," and all
The caves of night answer one call.

—Thomas of Celano, *Mass for the Dead*
(tr. Richard Crashaw)

Fear of the Lord is the beginning of knowledge.

—Proverbs, 1, 7

CHAPTER 1
GARY GETS A CALL

DEAD.

But fathers are immortal, Gary Holland thought as he swung his white Pinto wagon into the parking lot of Van Nuys and Monahan, the biggest funeral parlor in Bayside Point. Easing to a halt, he switched off the ignition.

God. If fathers can die, who can't?

He stared blankly at the funeral home. The man who had raised him, taught him, shaped him, had been scythed from his life with a single stroke. Gary felt as though some part of him had been amputated; memories of his father seemed like feelings in a missing limb, bitter reminders of something that had disappeared forever.

Unless there's an afterlife, like Mom says, Gary told himself.

But that was bullshit.

He got out of the car. It was a fine summer evening, not too hot; some of the parking-lot lights had already come on in the thickening dusk, and there was a heavy but pleasant smell of flowers and green leaves from the trees lining Beichmann Avenue.

He crossed the lot, passing his mother's Jetta and his brother Max's Maverick. There were few other cars, but it was early yet. His father had been an important man in Bayside Point, and Gary expected the viewing would be well-attended.

Entering the parlor, he stopped in the lobby. He had been to Van Nuys and Monahan's several times, once for his grandmother, twice for pals of his father. Everything in the lobby was just as he remembered it—same tacky landscape paintings and gold velvet wallpaper embossed with harps and trumpets, same expensive aquarium setup with the same dead goldfish floating at the top.

Voices off to the left. He looked toward the office, where his mother, his wife Linda, and Max were talking to Mr. Van Nuys. Noticing Gary, Max smirked the way he always did when he spotted his little brother. Feeling like he was twelve again, suddenly forgetting where he was, Gary almost flipped him the bird, and was stayed only by the thought that his mother would see. Signing the memorial book, he headed for the chapel with the board marked "Holland."

Inside, the first thing he noticed was that the coffin was closed. Strange; this was supposed to be a viewing after all. It wasn't as if his father had had some kind of horrible accident.

Going up the aisle, Gary settled in the front row. In his family, mourners were expected to kneel beside the coffin and pray. But having been basically agnostic since his early teens, (inexplicably, considering his upbringing) he had no intention of making the pretense, especially when there was no one else in the room to please; nor had he ever been too keen on the purely secular pleasure of gazing longingly on a preserved face.

Yet all that was what you were supposed to do if the coffin was open. What was the procedure when the box was shut?

Disturbed and uncomfortable, he looked at the flowers. They were arranged in the usual wreaths and crosses, the messages that you'd expect. The ironic thing was that a sizeable percentage were anthuriums, flowers with bright red leaves that looked like they were sticking their tongues—or worse—out. It was a sick joke. His father hated anthuriums. Gary had heard him joke more than once that he'd rather die than have "those damn things" at his funeral.

Reading the ribbons, Gary saw that all but one of the anthurium displays had been sent by people who hadn't been too close to his dad, construction-business acquaintances. Gary reasoned they hadn't known how Max Sr. had felt about them.

Uncle Buddy, on the other hand, had no such excuse. Gary clearly remembered his father and Buddy discussing the matter in a bar after Grandma's viewing. Sending those flowers was classic Uncle Buddy; the old boy was a hellish pain in the ass under the misapprehension (deliberate, Gary thought) that he was a non-stop scream. Gary had seen his father's old senior yearbook; Buddy, his fraternal twin, had given "Laff Riot" as his nickname, and had had his eyes slightly crossed in the photo. Gary cringed inwardly at the idea of talking to him, and worse yet, the probability that Buddy and Uncle Dennis would insist on taking him and Max out for a few drinks. The prospect was grim indeed, especially without his father to act as a buffer. Gary looked back at the coffin.

God, Dad, he thought. *You can't really be in there, can you? How can you be dead?*

8

He wondered when the others would join him, surprised Linda and Max Jr. hadn't already. He doubted a chat with old Mr. Van Nuys could be all that interesting.

He realized that he couldn't hear them anymore. When he first entered the chapel, their voices had carried quite clearly. Now there was only the low hum of the air conditioner.

Momentarily, even that stopped. A disquieting touch, but air conditioners did that from time to time…didn't they?

He laughed and looked down into his lap. His hands were a horrible shade of pink. All the corpses he had ever seen in funeral parlors had been that color. It was the lights of course, those strange pink lights installed along the sides of the ceiling. Born with a talent for seeing through things, he had guessed during his very first viewing that the purpose of the lights was to make the stiff's skin-color look more lifelike—or perhaps to make the live folks look more like the stiff, so it wouldn't suffer by comparison. The effect was very peculiar. It reminded him of when he had gotten red tempera on his hands back in high school and had been unable to rinse all the paint off. There had been this thin pink film—

There came a faint sigh of rushing air, then a click. He stood and turned. The chapel doors were closed. Had the staff shut them by mistake? The room was definitely supposed to be open—just like the coffin. Had Max done it? All those years in the Corps hadn't dimmed Max's sometimes outrageous sense of humor.

This simply wasn't his style, though. Not in a funeral home, at any rate. There wasn't enough of Uncle Buddy in him. Max was funnier, for one thing. But now that Gary thought about it, if Buddy was out there . . .

He heard a hollow thump, and turned again. Where had it come from? *Air conditioner,* he thought. There *was* a vent in the wall, right above the hanging cross.

Another thump.

Not from the vent, he decided. His gaze drifted downward.

To the coffin.

"No way," he laughed—just as a third thump, louder than the others, sounded insistently in the shining bronze casket.

Can't be alive. He's been em-

Thump

-balmed.

First horror, then hope rushed through Gary. There had been a mistake. He ran to the coffin.

"Mom!" he cried. "Mr. Van Nuys!"

He tried to pry the latches open. They might as well have been welded to the bronze.

He's going to suffocate, Gary thought. He spun and dashed up the aisle, shouting for help. Reaching the doors, he tugged on them shouting, but they were locked. Panic mounted inside him; were those *shrieks* from the coffin now?

He threw himself against the doors. Heavy paneled oak, they didn't budge. Lunging against them, he doubled, tripled his efforts.

He heard a crack; something gave. A bark of triumph burst from his lips.

It was only when he crashed once more into the wood and felt a tremendous shout of pain inside his shoulder that he realized what he had done to himself.

Panting, grimacing, he fell back. Starting at his fingers, hot tingling numbness spread up his arm and out into his chest, smothering the agony from his broken bone.

The thumping in the coffin grew louder and louder, the screams unmistakable now.

He won't last long, Gary thought. Nearly resuming his assault on the barrier in front of him, he remembered the service door at the front of the room…it stood open, beckoning.

He stumbled back down the aisle, paused by the coffin, saw it trembling and shaking, rocked by the struggles of the prisoner inside. Gary bent close to the vibrating bronze surface, shouted: "I'm going for help! Save your air!"

He was answered by a shriek that stung his ears even through the coffin lid.

Continuing toward the door, he cried out in horror and anger as it began to close, slamming shut before he could reach it. A lock snicked. He tugged on the handle. The door remained frozen in place. He pounded on it, shouting his throat raw. No answer.

He stumbled back toward the coffin, wondering what to do. The volume of the screams swelled excruciatingly.

"Da . . . Dad . . ." he moaned, hardly able to hear his own voice.

A tremendous impact boomed against the coffin lid. The coffin's front end jounced up off the catafalque and dropped back with a dull

heavy clang. A fist-sized dome of metal showed in the lid.

Gary's jaw dropped. *This is just not poss—*

Another dent bulged up.

Nothing human could—

BOOM.

The coffin seemed to lunge toward him, falling over the edge of the catafalque. He dodged backward. The hurtling mass just missed his foot as it struck the carpet.

He retreated slowly, staring at it. Almost as if in pursuit, the casket jolted forward an inch or two.

Gary shrilled a hysterical laugh, his terror no longer for his father now. What in Hell was in that box? It couldn't be Dad.

Yet even if it was, was that any less reason for fear? Was the strength of madness, of raving insanity, at work on that coffin lid?

The booming stopped as these thoughts flashed through Gary's mind; the shrieks faded. Had his father—had whatever was in the casket—succumbed at last to lack of air? Such furious exertion certainly would've—

Another earsplitting shriek.

A crashing thump.

A squeal of split metal.

"Jesus!" Gary cried, trying to shield his face from flying bronze fragments. One stung his palm, another his forehead. Blood crawled into his left eyebrow.

Lowering his arm, he saw that something had smashed up through the coffin-lid. His first impression was that it was a knot of dark shining wood. Then he realized it was a fist, its knuckles like studs on a club. If it was human at all, it looked like it belonged to someone long dead, mummified, petrified, not a man two days gone.

Not Dad, Gary told himself, not knowing whether to be relieved or appalled. *Can't be.* Surely it was just coincidence that the class ring on one of those desiccated fingers looked just like his father's . . .

The fist jerked back down through the crown of ragged metal, stabbed up in another place. Gary had never heard anything so piercing as the shrieks now pouring unmuffled through the holes. His skull rang, his ears thrummed with pain. And the cries were so raw with rage that any remaining doubt that he was in terrible danger was ripped clean away.

He rushed back to the service door and flung himself against it with his good shoulder, thudding into it again and again, praying to a God he didn't believe in, cursing Him for putting him in such a trap . . .

Behind, the hammerstrokes kept bashing into the coffin lid. He could hear the bronze *stretching,* parting, the fissures widening with a terrible yawning screech that scraped him to the marrow. The thing in the coffin would be free any moment.

But the door was shuddering now under Gary's onslaught. Weaker stuff than the front doors, it began to give.

He took a last glance over his shoulder. The catafalque blocked his view of the casket; two spindled chunks of coffin lid arced into view above it, one landing among the seats in the second row.

The door rocked forward at Gary's next thrust, attached only by its bottom hinges. Another slam knocked it free. Charging on to it even as it struck the floor, he snagged his trouser-cuff on the handle and tripped, palms smashing onto the carpet beyond the door. Instantly his numb arm gave way, and he went down hard on his face. Dazed for a moment, he ripped his leg loose and scrambled to his feet. There was another door ahead, at the end of a hallway.

Back in the chapel, the booming had stopped, but not the shrieks; barely audible beneath the cries, footbeats slammed in pursuit.

Gary never dared to look back. He sprinted along the hall, pulse beating in his temples, lungs burning. He got to the door, yanked on it. The handle turned, but the door was stuck—or locked.

The footbeats pounded closer. The shrieks set his teeth rattling. Any moment now and the thing from the coffin…

Daddy?

. . . would be upon him.

He gave another tug, certain it would do no good. To his astonishment, the door swung open. Even though the shrieks were right behind him now, it took him a moment to start forward, onto a descending ramp.

Too late. A hard mummified claw flailed down on his shoulder like an eagle's talon, yanking him back, nails ripping through fabric into flesh. Blood spewed past his face, and—

The phone rang.

Bathed in sweat, he sat up in bed, screaming at the top of his lungs in the echoing darkness of his room.

"What's the matter?" Linda demanded groggily, rising on one

elbow beside him.

Cold perspiration sluicing off his forehead, he stopped screaming and looked at her, mouth working silently. Her face was a silvery blur in the streetlight filtering through the curtains.

The phone rang again.

"Want me to get it?" Linda asked.

"I'm all right," Gary said. Turning, he fumbled for the phone. Out of the corner of his eye, he noticed the display on the clock-radio.

Three-fucking-thirty in the morning, he thought, picking up the receiver.

"Gary?" came his mother's voice. With sudden, chill certainty he realized why she was calling.

"What's wrong?" he asked mechanically.

She kept control just long enough to say, "Your father's dead." Then the weeping began.

CHAPTER 2
FATHER TED

GARY and Linda taught at Delaware University in Newark, his field English, hers, history. Both were presiding over five-week summer cram-courses, and could ill afford to take three days off to go up to Bayside Point for the funeral; but luck smiled on them, and they found colleagues willing to handle the classes. They taught their Monday morning sections, packed up the car after lunch, and headed north on I-95, Gary behind the wheel. Crossing the Memorial Bridge, they swung over onto the Jersey Turnpike.

For a long time neither spoke. Gary was lost in his own thoughts, memories of his father, and worries about his mother, particularly whether she'd be able to handle the funeral arrangements. But just north of Camden, he was roused by the sight of a State Trooper parked just behind an overpass; he slowed immediately. It occurred to him that he had no recollection whatsoever of the forty miles they'd come since the bridge.

"Why do you always do that?" Linda asked.

"What?" he asked.

"Slow down when you see a speed trap. You weren't even doing the limit."

"Guilty conscience. I always get nervous when I see a cop."

Gradually he sped back up.

After a while, he looked over at Linda. She had the window down, and her long dark hair was blowing in the wind; her high-cheekboned, pretty face was pensive.

"What are you thinking about?" he asked.

"Your mom," Linda said.

"What about her?"

"How she kept loving your father."

"He was a lovable guy."

"I wouldn't have been able to."

"You weren't married to him."

"When you're married, your husband's supposed to *act* married—"

"That's enough," Gary said. "The man's gone, and I don't want to hear about it."

"Okay," Linda said.

In the silence that followed, Gary noticed the sign for the I-195 exit and swung into the far right hand lane.

"Why did all that piss you off so badly, anyway?" he asked angrily, almost without thinking. "It's not as if he did anything to you."

That's it, jerk, he told himself. *Start it up again . . .*

"I *have* taken it awfully personally, haven't I?" Linda admitted.

"Yeah."

"Maybe it's because I like your mother so such. Better each time I talk to her. She may be the only really *good* person I've ever met. Do you know what I mean?"

"Yeah."

"I mean, if there's a Heaven, your mother's going."

Linda said it innocently enough; still, it touched a nerve.

"What's that supposed to mean?" Gary demanded.

"That it's much worse when somebody like that gets abused," Linda answered. "What did you think I meant?"

"I thought you were comparing her to my father."

"What?"

"Saying he's burning in Hell, or something."

"No," she said.

Despite his anger, he believed her; now that he thought about it, she'd certainly said nothing of the sort. Strange how that idea had popped into his mind . . .

He paid up at the toll booth, and they continued on their way.

"Hell's just a fairy tale, anyway," Gary said.

"Did I say it wasn't?"

He laughed, shaking his head. "No, you didn't, did you? Guess all that 700 Club crap hasn't sunk in."

She laughed too. "I don't watch the show *that* much."

"Watching it at all is too much."

"It's not all *that* bad. The first part, with all the politics and stuff, is usually kind of interesting, even when I disagree with it—"

"Oh come on," Gary broke in. "They also put on little old ladies who talk about God miraculously multiplying the leftover spaghetti in the refrigerator—" He paused. "What *does* Pat Robertson think about Hell, anyway?"

17

"Oh, he's all for it," Linda answered.

The white Pinto flew eastward, bound for the Jersey shore.

TAKING the Squankum-Bayside Point exit, Gary drove south on Route 35. Lined with sandpits, defunct drive-ins, and fast food joints, 35 was punctuated every five miles or so by that murderous and peculiar Garden State phenomenon known as the traffic circle. Passing Squankum's huge green River Rest Cemetery, Gary sped toward the Squankum Bridge, only to find that it was up. Bayside Point lay just across the river.

The Point was a small resort community located at the northern end of the long peninsula flanking Barragansett Bay. To the west, a canal courtesy of the Army Corps of Engineers formed the town's boundary with Bayside Boro, connecting the Squankum River to the Bay; in effect, the peninsula was an island sliced off from the mainland.

Gary waited patiently for the bridge to come down. Finally the sailboat passed, and the span's iron-grilled center descended slowly. The gate went back, and Gary and Linda were in Bayside Point a half-minute later.

On the left was a billboard reading, "Bayside Point, Crab Capital of the Jersey Shore." The message had brought a smile to Gary's lips ever since High School, when he had first learned about social diseases; he was of course smiling now.

Noticing his expression, Linda frowned as she always did when he had something nasty on his mind. He knew, however, that she secretly enjoyed a lot of his raunchier routines.

"Mad at me?" he asked, as he turned left onto fishery-lined Miami Boulevard.

"For what?" Linda replied. "Smirking at that stupid sign like you always do?"

"Yeah."

"Nope. It's just so boring, that's all."

"Love me anyway?"

"I suppose."

He turned right on Atlanta Avenue. Bungalows and two-story houses slipped by on either side.

"I'm sorry I brought up that business about your dad," Linda said.

"Forgot all about it."

"I was really looking forward to giving him his first grandchild. I suppose I really loved him too."

"As I said . . ."

She nodded. "He was a lovable guy."

He turned left on Seattle Street, went half a block and pulled over just behind Max Jr.'s red Ford junker. Climbing out, they got their suitcases and went up the slate-paved walk toward the big two-story lemon-yellow house. The screen-door was locked; after knocking on it, Gary checked the mailbox, as he habitually did. There was the habitual nothing inside.

Max Jr. appeared, snickering when he saw his brother, opening the door. He towered over Gary by a full head.

"How you doing, jerk?" he asked, extending his hand.

"Just fine, wack-off," Gary replied, shaking it. He smelled liquor on Max's breath. "Feeling no pain?"

"Haven't had *that* much, " Max replied. "But Jack Daniels *was* made for days like this."

"Yeah."

"Of course," Max went on, "Jack or no, it's hard to be solemn when I see your foolish little face." He turned to Linda. "Hi, Sis." He wrapped his massive arms around her, bringing a gasp to her lips. She kissed him on the cheek.

They followed him into the living room and laid their bags down. The TV was on; a slightly overweight man with slicked-back dark hair and wearing a garish checkered suit was reading from a loose-leaf folder.

"The Holy Bible itself includes eroticism. Sex *is* depicted in the *Song of Songs.* Breasts *are* specifically mentioned . . . "

"Amen," said Max.

"Isn't that Mr. MacAleer?" Gary asked. "What's he doing on TV?"

"Bought the local cable outfit," Max said. "Mom told me last time I was up. He's been making money hand over fist, but he's also catching flak from his buddies in the Christian Businessmen's Roundtable. Been running too many hot movies, etc. So he comes on between flicks sometimes, explaining why bringing Shannon Tweed to the viewing public is really very upright and biblical." Max laughed. "The poor old *Song of Songs.* The sex peddlers always trot it out. I mean, if they're going to do that, they should at least show babes with teeth like ewes pregnant with twins."

"I always hated that line," Linda said.

"How about those does feeding among the lilies . . . "

"Where's mom?" Gary asked.

"Bedroom. Asleep."

"How's she been?"

"Not too bad. Today at least."

"She take care of the arrangements?"

"Before I got here."

"Mr. Van Nuys push her around?"

"Tried to sell her all the bells and whistles. Didn't work. Mom's pretty tough."

"Is there going to be a viewing?" Linda asked. "I *hate* viewings."

Gary felt his throat tighten. After that dream, he wasn't particularly up for a viewing either.

"Two, Wednesday," Max answered. "The funeral's Thursday morning."

"Uncle Buddy going to make it?"

"Absolutely."

Gary winced.

"You don't seem too delighted," Max observed.

"*You're* looking forward to seeing him?"

"I'd rather have a root canal. You can always count on old Uncle Buddy to do something stupid. As a matter of fact, I know exactly what it's going to be."

"What?" Gary asked.

"You know those flowers Dad hated? The ones that look like the're sticking their tongues out?"

"Anthuriums," Gary said, nodding, suddenly remembering that detail of his dream very clearly.

"He's going to send a bunch of those."

"Have I ever met Uncle Buddy?" Linda asked.

"You'd know if you had," Max said.

"I can't wait."

"Just don't let him feel you up," Gary said.

"He's *that* kind of uncle?"

"He's all kinds," Max put in. "All of them really unpleasant."

Off to the side, Mr. MacAleer droned from the television:

"Then there's the story of Susannah and the Elders . . . "

"I remember it well," Max said. "The ivory globes of her breasts gleaming with a fine mist of sweat, Susannah strode lithely into the water, looking just like Shannon Tweed—"

"Shut your brother up, Gary," Linda said.

"Shut up," Gary said.

"Ah, don't listen to her," Max said. "She loves it."

There was a rap at the screen door. They turned.

"Excuse me," said the man outside, an elderly priest wearing a short-sleeved black shirt. His hair was an unnatural lustrous black, sculpted in what must have been a very expensive piece of barbering.

"I'm Father Ted," he said. "Father Ted Maracek? I'm here to see Mr. Holland."

"Come on in," Max said, in a tone that Gary thought something less than welcoming.

Father Ted entered. A large crucifix hung from his neck on multi-colored beads; as the priest drew closer, Gary noticed that the figure languishing on it was a black woman in a *dashiki*. Father Ted squinted at Gary and the others.

Needs glasses, Gary thought. *Probably thinks they'd make him look too old.* It seemed a fair enough deduction, considering the dye job and the ludicrous trendiness of the crucifix. Gary didn't care much for priests under any circumstances, but he liked the trendy ones least. There was something so bogus about them.

"Have we met?" Father Ted asked him.

Gary hadn't seen him before; he never went to mass on his visits home, not even to please Mom. But Mom had mentioned the priest several times, once with a remarkable bitterness which she hadn't been willing to explain.

Gary introduced himself.

"Your mother's spoken of you," Father Ted said. "Very proudly."

I wonder if she mentioned that I think the Catholic Church is a crock of medieval horseshit? Gary thought. But immediately it occurred to him that there was something very un-medieval about Father Ted.

"My wife, Linda," Gary said.

The priest exchanged pleasantries with her, then turned to Max. Gary eyed his brother. There was a subtly contemptuous look on Max's face—Gary wondered if Father Ted noticed.

"I've heard a half-dozen of your sermons," Max said. "They really stuck with me."

Father Ted beamed, apparently oblivious to Max's expression.

"Mom also wrote me about you," Max went on.

"I'm flattered," Father Ted said, and looked at Max sidelong. "Aren't you the one who teaches history at that school in Maryland?"

"*Military* history," Max said, almost as if he hoped that particular detail would make the priest like him less.

"Ah," Father Ted said, shifting his gaze from him. "I hadn't realized I'd made such an impression on your mother."

"Actually, what concerned her was the impression you made on my *father*," Max went on. "You were his confessor, weren't you?"

"I had that honor."

Max smiled coldly. "You're the son of a bitch who told him it was okay to cheat on my Mom, aren't you?"

Father Ted's whole face went slack.

"*Max!*" came a voice from across the room. Celia Holland stood there, a graying middle-aged woman on the thin side, looking absolutely appalled.

"Actually, I . . . I . . . " the priest sputtered.

"What, Father?" Max asked, undaunted by his mother's disapproval.

"I was only trying to persuade him to forgive himself."

"Oh?"

"He thought God didn't love him anymore, so I was attempting to show how a lack of self-acceptance is the greatest sin of all."

"I'm okay, you're okay?" Max asked. "On this rests the whole Law and the Prophets?"

"I can see your mind is closed, young man," Father Ted huffed.

"I'd like to apologize for my son," Celia broke in, before Max could say anything else.

"Mrs. Holland," Father Ted said, "what exactly did you tell Max about me?"

"Well . . . " she began uncomfortably, "I *did* write him about what you told my husband. That is, Max Senior's version."

"Which was?"

"That, among other things, you thought no sin of the flesh could be considered mortal."

"I don't believe I'd express myself so unequivocally," Father Ted answered.

"Didn't you just say that 'lack of self-acceptance is the greatest sin of all?'" Max asked. "That sounded pretty unequivocal to me."

"Would you please let me continue?" Father Ted replied.

"Sure."

"What I *probably* told him is that some theologians no longer consider adultery a serious matter," the priest told Celia. "Now if your husband decided I was condoning infidelity because of that, he was very badly mistaken. I was only suggesting that if he couldn't stop, he should try not to punish himself with guilt."

Max immediately went back on the offensive: "Because a handful of theologians in the fever-swamps have decided the Church has been wrong for two thousand years?"

"I wouldn't put it that way, but yes."

"Then why should he have stopped at all?"

"He was in such pain."

"But his guilt was irrational?"

"Yes."

"And you tried to persuade him it was irrational?"

"Yes, but . . . "

Max pounced. "How exactly does that differ from condoning infidelity?"

"I don't feel any need to stand here and chop logic with you, young man," Father Ted blustered.

Lucky for you, Gary thought. Max was a very formidable logic-chopper. Gary remembered an episode from his late teens, when he and Max had been beset down at the boardwalk by a group of young Baptists looking for converts. It took two hours, but ultimately Max had reduced all seven of them to tears. And that was before he co-majored in philosophy at college.

Conan the Apologist, Gary thought.

"The Bible even goes so far as to describe how the men of Egypt have 'members like donkeys,'" said Mr. MacAleer from the TV. "Ezekiel, Chap—"

Gary shut the set off.

"I certainly didn't encourage your husband to make a habit of it," Father Ted continued to Celia.

"But Father," she answered, sadly but firmly, "When he kept doing it, you kept saying how God probably didn't mind."

"That's hardly an endorsement of adultery, Mrs. Holland."

"But it's hardly surprising that he stopped worrying about it, is it?" she pressed. "Especially when he respected your opinion so much.

24

Especially when his girlfriend—" A choke rose in her voice— "was so much younger and prettier than me."

"Since that's how you feel, Mrs. Holland, do you still want me to celebrate the funeral mass?"

"Max would've wanted you to."

"Very well then," Father Ted said, forcing a smile. "I'll be going. Good-bye."

He turned on his heel and went out.

"Max, Max," Celia said, once the priest was well out of earshot, "Wasn't the day sad enough?"

"I just couldn't stand there and keep my mouth shut," Max answered. "He hurt us all too badly. And what about *Dad?* Where's *he* now, mom? That bastard convinced him that no matter how much he cheated on you, he had nothing to fear from God. What do you bet Dad's gotten a very nasty surprise?"

"Jesus," Gary said. "I don't believe you said that."

Max ignored him. Celia looked at Max as though she were horrified by his suggestion, but couldn't bring herself to upbraid him because she thought it might be true. Gary was shaken as he studied her face.

"Be that as it may," she said at last, "Father Teddy—I mean Father Ted—is a priest, and his office deserves respect. You of all people should believe that, Max."

Max cocked his head, apparently weighing her point. Gary thought it was a good one, but Max finally replied:

"I do respect his *office.* I'd take communion from him without a second thought. He's a true priest, a special channel of God's grace. But I don't respect his *opinions* any more than you do. And I don't respect *him.* There's nothing in the dogmas of the Church that says a priest can't be a son of a bitch. Getting into Torquemada's face would've been obligatory, I think."

Celia pondered this. "Jesus said anyone who's angry with his brother will be liable to judgment," she answered at last.

"Who's angry?" Max grinned.

"You were. At Father Ted just now."

"No, Ma. I was furious."

"He's no Torquemada in any case."

"I'd like him better if he were," Max said. "But as for that quote, it really depends on what manuscript you read. Some versions read 'angry without good reason.' And since that reading fits more with common sense, I prefer it. Jesus gets mad in the gospels all the time, anyway. Calls his opponents 'whited sepulchers' and 'knots of vipers.' Carries a whip and uses it—"

"You know what you are?" Celia demanded, pointing a finger at him in frustration.

"What?"

"A . . . A *Philadelphia lawyer!*" she answered, very seriously.

"So how come I'm not rich?"

She bit her lip, then laughed in spite of herself.

A strange silence followed, as if everyone had suddenly become aware that such levity (if it could be called that) and the argument that had preceded it, were inappropriate, under the circumstances; Gary was amazed that his mother had laughed at all. But he was always surprised at how people behaved after a death in the family, at least the way they behaved in *his* family, pouring out tears one moment, cracking jokes the next. It always seemed that one's sense of humor should be completely submerged, that all enjoyment should cease, that normal life should halt entirely. But it was never that way.

"Anyone care for some leftover roast beef?" Celia said presently.

"It's gone," Max said.

"You ate it *all?*"

"You didn't tell me not to. There's a lot of that ham still."

"Ham'll be just fine," Gary said, Linda seconding him with a nod.

"I could cook up some of those steaks, I suppose," Celia said. "And there are the noodles . . . "

"Leftovers'll be just fine, Mom," Gary said.

"Cooking'll take my mind off things," Celia answered.

"I'll help," Linda offered.

"No, really, it'll do me good."

They went into the kitchen. In the end, Linda helped. And afterward, midway through the dishes, Celia suddenly burst into tears, clutched Linda and hugged her tightly as Gary and Max looked on.

CHAPTER 3
UH-OH

THAT night Gary had another dream.

He found himself standing naked and alone in a bare stony wasteland, a landscape such as Michelangelo might have painted, all its colors grey or grayish brown, its aridity stretching out endlessly under a vast leaden sky. A cold wind swept him.

He stood in that spot for what might have been a minute or an hour. And all the while, dread grew within him.

You won't have a chance, whispered a voice in his mind. *He's got the goods on you for sure.*

"He?" Gary asked aloud, wondering for the first time what he was so afraid of.

The wind brought a far-off grinding that sounded like huge rusty gears; unbidden, the image of a state trooper flashed into his head.

Guilty conscience? The trooper asked, turning slowly toward him. *Haven't been speeding, have you sonny? You should* see *what they do to speeders where I come from . . .*

But before Gary could see his face, he realized the cop wasn't *Him*; the image vanished from his mind. The grinding sound faded.

He saw it all, Gary, the whispering voice went on. *He* knows.

"What is He, Santa Claus?" Gary asked.

God, you're stupid, said the voice. *I'm going to see if I can get out of here. Adios, sucker!*

"Like a rat leaving a sinking ship," Gary said, and laughed. Then the question occurred to him: what sinking ship? What strange little mind-games was he playing with himself?

The hell with that. What was he doing stark naked in a desert lifted straight out of the Sistine *Last Judgment?*

"Oh, what the fuck," he said. "It's just a dream."

The voice answered faintly: *You wish, moron.*

The ground moved beneath his left foot. He hopped aside, staring downward.

Dirt bulged. The protrusion collapsed, then swelled again. The

27

brown dome split. Dirty white objects pushed up between the clods. Momentarily Gary realized what they were: bones. Human finger-bones. A skeletal hand was thrusting itself out of the ground, clawing toward the sky.

His first thought was of that old spiritual: *Them bones, them bones, them dry bones . . .* Then his mind flashed back to the horror in the funeral-parlor chapel.

Didn't you just leave this party? He asked himself. But that was a dream. Only a dream. This was—

Real.

He fled, but everywhere those tiny hillocks were rising from the desolation as far as the eye could see. He could hardly run without stepping on them, feeling those bony fingertips jabbing up into his soles; his skin was broken in a dozen places when at last he fell screaming.

Swaying and twisting like plant-stalks in time-lapse photography, two fleshless arms rose from the earth in front of him, up-tilting a slab of slate; the slab toppled inches from his nose, and a skull heaved up into view, death's face grinning into his.

He could feel bony hands scrabbling round behind him, fumbling at his heels. He got to his feet, trembling violently, ignoring the pain in his soles. All around him, the hillocks had been broken open by the heads and shoulders of the fleshless dead. He was completely sur-rounded. Soon there was hardly room to stand, let alone run. Earth dropping from their limbs, they climbed out of their graves, standing shoulder to shoulder with him, as if at attention.

The wind grew colder, more vicious, whistling through their ribs and teeth. Dust-devils swirled and danced among the bony ranks; a fringe of black cloud came rolling across the grey sky like ink in water.

Shivering, teeth chattering, Gary stood there alone among the skeletons. But his fear of them receded. Something else was coming now, he could feel it, something beside which they were no threat at all . . .

It was *Him*.

White and fierce, light flooded across the landscape of skeletons. Gary and the dead turned.

A mighty glowing throne had appeared, looming like a mountain on the plain; two huge creatures in white metal armor flanked it, bear-ing what might have been flaming swords. Their bodies were human,

but had feet like bulls' hooves, eagles' wings, leonine heads. Searching the dead multitude with their stern eyes, turning their heads from side to side, they left eerie after images in Gary's brain, their countenances shifting blurrily back and forth between man and bull, lion and eagle, as if somehow these beings were all four creatures simultaneously.

He looked up at the figure seated on the throne. As brightly as the throne glowed, its occupant outshone it; Gary squinted, shading his eyes. It was intensely painful to gaze into that torrent of light, but he looked long enough to make out the figure's shape.

One like a son of man, he thought, pulling his gaze away, wincing. His fright mounted ferociously. He knew now what was happening, where he was.

And he was in the very first rank before the throne. He had been surrounded by the dead before, but nothing now stood between him and judgment. No bail, no appeals . . .

He's got the goods on you, he told himself. *You threw your life away. Thirty-two years wasted, worse than wasted. He has you cold . . .*

The being on the throne glowed brighter for an instant. Still wincing, Gary saw many of the dead step forward, as though they had been summoned.

The light flared again. When it faded, the skeletons were clothed in flesh, he was sure of it, even though they vanished before he had barely more than a glimpse. Their lives and humanity had been restored. They had been found innocent.

Another flash. The remaining dead in the front rank advanced. But at the next flare, they dropped to their knees, still bare of flesh. They began to scream, and Gary knew that sound, though the last time he'd only heard it ripping from a single throat, as his father punched his way out of his heavy bronze prison . . .

Some of the skeletons fell to fighting one another. Others raked the earth with their clawlike fingers or rose shrieking, shaking bony fists at the judge on the throne.

Sweeping their burning swords, the lion-headed creatures came forward, and the skeletons fled wailing, forcing their way into the dead multitude. One came hurtling straight at Gary, silhouetted against the glow of the throne, light pouring through its ribs. But at the last instant it veered off to the right, and Gary felt a great coldness sweep by him.

He looked back up at the judge.

Yet another flare; this time he heard the summons. His name had been called, not *Gary Holland*, but his true name, the one that defined and compelled. He had never heard it before, yet he recognized it instantly, feeling its terrible power. Shaking his head, he struggled to resist, to remain in place, but his flesh wouldn't obey him. The innermost logic of his being had been mastered.

One step, and the compulsion faded. The point had been made. He'd come to a pass where his choice was irrelevant. He riveted his eyes on the ground, trying to ignore what was happening to him, to deny his awful guilt. As the judge began to speak, Gary clapped his hands over his ears, but the words still penetrated, awesome in their authority:

"You have been weighed in the balance and found—"

A titanic hollow rumbling blotted out the voice. The ground trembled, shaking Gary off his feet. The light from the throne vanished. Darkness descended once more.

But the murk was warm now. The wind was gone.

Gary felt the reassuring softness of quilt against skin. He was safe in bed.

He sat up, laughed as he realized it had all been a dream. None of it had happened . . . except of course for the earthquake.

The bed was shaking, travelling slowly across the hardwood floor like a bum piece on one of those old vibrating football games; a powerful rumbling was coming from under the house, as though a subway train were passing beneath. Venetian blinds chattered. Window-curtains swayed back and forth. Things skittered and danced on the dresser; a small mirror banged onto its face. Over on a chair, the lid of Gary's suitcase thumped shut.

Gary turned toward Linda. She was awake too.

"It really *is* an earthquake," she said.

Gary listened to the walls creak and moan. Were they about to collapse? How long would the quake last?

"Maybe we'd better get outside," Linda said.

"Yeah," Gary replied, and flung the covers over the foot of the bed.

But with amazing abruptness, the quake stopped; to Gary it felt uncannily as if a huge hand had closed about the house. The rattle of the blinds softened to a faint buzz, before fading altogether. Gary stood slowly, listening, looking warily about. Only the curtains were

still moving, brushing drily against the window-sill.

"They don't have earthquakes in New Jersey," Linda said.

Gary laughed. "Nope."

"Maybe I'm still asleep . . . I *was* dreaming about an earthquake."

"Me too," Gary said.

"Worst nightmare I've had in a long time," Linda continued. "Like I was at the Last Judgment, or something."

That brought Gary up short. "Last Judgment?"

"Okay, maybe I *have* been watching the 700 Club too much . . . "

He turned toward her. "And you were just about to hear the verdict?"

"When I woke?"

"Yes."

"Oh God," she said. "How did you know?"

"I had the same dream," he answered.

It was a long time before they got back to sleep.

GARY woke seconds before the alarm rang at eight. When the bell started, Linda mumbled something about sleeping some more, shut the alarm off, rolled over, and drifted away again—if indeed she'd ever really awakened to begin with.

Gary could hardly blame her. Neither of them had gotten much (or good) shuteye after the quake. He would've joined her, except that he could never sleep later than eight, no matter how tired he was.

The alarm was for Linda, of course. She'd said she really intended to get up early. She had lesson-plans she wanted to deal with. But sleeping past eight was no achievement for her. Gary rose, put on his bathrobe, and went out into the kitchen. He expected find his mother puttering around, but she was nowhere to be seen. Normally, their internal clocks were perfectly in sync; even so, he didn't give too much thought to her absence. Losing her husband of thirty-five years was a pretty strong inducement to oversleep.

What the Hell is she going to do with herself? He wondered.

He heard the TV down in the rec room. That would be Max; Mom never did anything recreational in the rec room. There was a big steel door set in the west wall, and on the other side was the fallout shelter. Mom had never been averse to the idea of the shelter, but the possibility that it might ever have to be used terrified her. Max wasn't so queasy. He had a poster of an H-bomb explosion on the wall of his office down in Maryland; "A little *memento mori?*" he'd explained to Gary with a grin.

Rattled by the shootdown of KAL 007, Dad had wanted to move the family to somewhere off in the boonies, but Mom had put her foot down, and the shelter was their compromise—he'd started building it in '84. Working on it in his spare time, even after things changed in Russia, ("You never can tell," he said) he'd drawn on material and equipment from his construction business, sometimes bringing employees home to help him. He'd made alterations and improvements as survivalist theories went in and out of fashion; even though Gary had never followed the literature, he guessed the shelter must be pretty much state of the art, well-stocked with supplies, ammo, and guns. His father had even, quite illegally, converted two Heckler and Koch assault-rifles to full auto. Gary considered it all crazy bullshit— although, if truth be told, he *had* jumped at a chance to go out to the piney woods in Jackson Township and spray junk cars full of holes with those guns.

Man, Gary thought, making himself a sandwich, *that was an afternoon.* Chugging beers with Dad and Max, emptying clip after clip, he'd almost found himself looking forward to end of the world.

He took his first bite.

And the Last Judgment, Gary? He asked himself. *Looking forward to that?*

The food went tasteless in his mouth.

Of course, maybe you don't need to. Maybe you've already been there. Memories of last night's dream flooded into his mind with an almost hallucinatory vividness.

You have been weighed in the balance and found—

"Jesus," Gary said, putting the sandwich down. What in hell was going on with his subconscious? Two horrific nightmares in two nights—it was really out of character.

And then there was the *weird* side of it. Even though he didn't believe in clairvoyance, it was hard to accept that the first dream and his father's death had been mere coincidence. Telepathy was nonsense—but he and Linda *had* shared that second nightmare, he was sure of it. It was all too much, and he did not want to think about it.

To distract himself, he grabbed a copy of *Time* magazine out of the drysink. It fell open to a truth-is-stranger-than-fiction piece about a coalition of fundamentalists and neanderthal Catholics who had discovered that the Antichrist had arrived in the person of Harrison Foldsbury, an undersecretary in the U.S. Department of Education; Foldsbury had narrowly escaped death in a commando-style raid on his home, apparently organized by the above-mentioned loonies. But the wildest twist of all was a connection between the nut jobs and Israeli Intelligence; there was some reason to believe that some of the fanatics had been trained near the Dead Sea at a top-secret base.

Gary finished the story feeling a nasty mixture of black amusement and anxiety. These washed-in-the-blood morons and their Spanish Inquisition cohorts were so bizarre that you just had to laugh, even if they were trying to kill people, even if the Mossad (acting on some no-doubt Byzantine motive) took them seriously enough to train. But the story, with its wacked-out apocalyptic overtones, didn't help at all to distract him from memories of the Last Judgment . . .

"Last Judgment *dream*," Gary corrected himself. His stomach crawled; he was definitely not going to eat the rest of his sandwich, though that made him feel a little guilty. *Waste not, want not*, he could hear his mother saying.

I'll put it in the fridge, ma, he thought. *Finish it later.*

He got up, wrapped it in foil and stashed it. After doing his dishes like a good boy, he went down the stairs to the rec-room.

Max was down there as Gary had guessed, doing Marine-style pump-and-clap push-ups in front of the Today Show. He was wearing sweat-pants but no shirt; Gary, who was rather powerfully built himself, felt his usual twinge of envy at the sight of his brother's physique. Where did the bastard get that muscle-tone?

"Hundred eighty," Max was saying. "Hundred eighty-one . . . " He stopped at two hundred, rolled onto his side, and propped his head up on one hand, smiling at Gary with his usual brotherly disdain before blowing the sweat from his upper lip. His cheeks and chin were bluish with stubble.

"Hey dork," he said. "What's up?"

"You are, I see," Gary answered.

"Family curse," Max said.

"How's Jane Pauley?"

"Real foxy, as always. Shame to waste her on that Trudeau turd."

"Any big news?"

"Yeah. Local story, too."

"What?"

"Plane crash. Off Bayside Shores." Bayside Shores lay immediately south of Bayside Point.

"Jetliner?"

"747, bound to Philly from Madrid. Two hundred and eighty Italian tourists aboard."

"Whoa," Gary said. "Wait'll Linda hears about this. You know how she hates flying? She's going to this conference in August, and—"

"Shh," Max said, sitting up, nodding toward the TV. "They're talking about it now."

" . . . The survival of twenty-four passengers has been called 'absolutely miraculous' by a Coast Guard spokesman," Jane Pauley was saying. "At least seventy are known dead, with the rest given little hope. An emergency morgue has been set up in a high school gym in nearby Bayside Point . . . "

"Bayside High?" Gary said. "My *alma mater?* Things like this just don't happen around here."

"Lot of strange shit going on," Max said. "You feel that earthquake last night?"

"Yeah. They mention it on the news?"

Max nodded. "Half an hour ago—" He paused. Ms. Pauley was staring at her TelePrompTer.

"This just in," she said. "We've received word of two more air disasters, one at Atlanta International, the other at Chicago's O'Hare . . . "

"Three crashes in one day?" Max asked. "Are the towel-heads on the warpath?"

But if that was the case, *La Pauley* gave no clues. Information was still sketchy. More would follow shortly. She went on to a story about a rash of disappearances in Washington D.C. and New York City.

"Think they'll talk about the earthquake again?" Gary asked.

"Don't know," Max said. "With all these planes dropping out of the sky, it's going to be pretty lukewarm stuff."

Gary was silent for a few moments. "You know, this is going to sound crazy, but were you dreaming about anything? Just before the quake woke you?"

Max looked at him. "As a matter of fact, yeah. But what's so strange about that?"

"What were you dreaming about?"

Max looked uncomfortable. "What's it to you?"

"Just answer the question."

"Well, since you're being so polite . . . the Last Judgment."

Gary's nape-hairs rose.

"What's the matter?" Max asked, and laughed. "You should see your face."

"I had the same dream," Gary answered. "At exactly the same time. Me and Linda both."

Max snorted at him. "Stop busting my chops."

"The quake woke you just as your sentence was going to be pronounced, right?"

Max nodded.

Gary continued: "'You have been weighed in the balance and found—'"

"And then the bed start shaking," Max broke in, nodding again, looking mystified.

"Of course, you believe in the Last Judgment and all that stuff."

"I never believed it'd happen at three o'clock on a Tuesday morning," Max answered. "Ditto for the rest of my life. I may be a Catholic, but I'm not a barbarian."

"So what do you think about the dream?"

"I think it was just that."

"One that you and me and Linda all shared," Gary said.

"So what does that tell us? Nothing to found a religion on."

"*Is* there anything to found a religion on?"

"Want to argue about it?"

Gary put his hands up. "I'm not feeling very masochistic this morning, thank you."

"I wonder if Mom had the dream?" Max asked. "Haven't heard her moving around upstairs. Guess she isn't up yet."

They looked back at the TV. The Today Show was experiencing a spectacular burst of technical difficulties, the most astonishing being a complete rearrangement of Gene Shalit's face.

"Improvement," Max said.

CHAPTER 4
CRABMEAT

LONG about eleven Gary grew uneasy because Mom hadn't appeared yet, and went and knocked on her door.

"Mom?" he asked.

No answer.

He knocked again. Max came up behind him.

"Maybe we'd better take a look," Max said.

Gary opened the door. The bed was empty.

"Mom?" he asked, going in and looking around. She was nowhere to be seen.

Gary went over to the bed. It had been slept in; the covers showed ample evidence of that. But when had Mom gotten up?

"Must've gone out early," Max said. "*Real* early . . . " He didn't sound tooconfident of this hypothesis.

"Gone where?"

"How should I know? Maybe she had one of those damn dreams, went to walk it off."

"She'd be back by now. She's never been too big on walking anyway."

"But she *is* gone, we know that much," Max said.

Gary nodded. "Maybe she left while we were in the rec room."

"We would've heard her. These floorboards *creak*."

Linda came in, wearing her orange terrycloth bathrobe.

"Any sign of her?" she asked.

"Plenty of signs," Gary said. "We just don't know where she *is*."

"Left her purse, I see," Linda said, indicating a red-leather bag lying on the dresser. She looked at the bed. "At least she changed out of her scary old nightgown." The garment, dark blue with grey stripes, was lying mostly covered by the bed clothes.

"Odd," Max said.

"What?" Linda asked.

"That it's almost covered. I mean, most people get up to change. They wouldn't take off their nightclothes, then put the blankets back over them."

"Well, maybe Mom just sat up, took the gown off in bed," Gary said.

"But why put the blanket back over it? If she sat up, the blanket would be rolled much farther down the bed."

"What are you saying? That she disappeared, and the nightgown just deflated under the blankets?"

"Of course not," Max said. "I just think it's odd, that's all."

"Well, what should we do?" Linda asked.

"*Do?*" Gary asked.

"You know, like calling the police."

"I think it's a bit early for that."

"Is the car in the garage? Maybe she went for a drive."

"We looked," Gary said. "It's there."

Max said: "Maybe she did manage to slip out somehow, and she's crying on some girlfriend's shoulder. Her address book's over on the dresser. Let's call her buddies."

Gary looked up the number of Beth Reithermann, his mother's best friend, and rang her on the phone next to the bed. But Beth hadn't seen her.

Gary called Jackie Demaris. No luck there either. As a matter of fact, he struck out on every number he called.

"Anyone else you can think of?" he asked Max.

Max shook his head.

"Linda?" Gary asked.

"Hey, she's *your* mother," Linda said.

"All right, guys," Gary said. "Think we *should* call the cops?"

"Let's give her some more time," Max said. "Wouldn't we be embarrassed if she came strolling in at one?"

IN the end, they gave her till three. Then, worried sick, Gary called the police. The cop asked for a description and said they'd send someone around for more information about eight.

"*Eight!*" Gary cried. "That's five hours!"

"I'm sorry, Mr. Holland," the policeman replied. "But we're having a rough day. First there was the plane crash. Then we started getting a lot of calls just like yours."

Nervous warmth flooded Gary's stomach. "Disappearances?"

"Right. And it's not just Bayside Point. It's the whole state. Whole rest of the *country.*"

"But what's happening? Are they being kidnapped?"

"We don't know, Mr. Holland," the cop replied. "Frankly, you'd probably do just as well listening to your radio as talking to us."

"Okay," Gary said. "Your man will be over at eight?"

"If nothing else screwy happens."

Gary hung up and flashed an anxious look at Linda.

"So what's going on?" she asked.

"People are disappearing," he answered. "All over the country."

"They mentioned that on the news this morning, I think," Max said. "I wasn't paying much attention. Reports from New York and Washington. A senator was missing. Southern Democrat."

"Let's listen to the TV," Linda said.

They went into the living room and turned the set on. Neither CNNI or II was coming in, so Max left the cable box on WOR—Jack Lord grilling a suspect in a rerun of *Hawaii Five-O*. It turned out that the murder was committed accidentally in the course of a goldfish robbery.

"A *goldfish* robbery?" Max growled in amazement and disgust. "I wonder how the guy who wrote *that* is going to make out at the Last Judgment? Can you imagine confronting the Almighty with something like that on your hands? Hell, I'm surprised God doesn't smite us *all* for tolerating those idiots in Hollywood."

"How do you know he hasn't?" Linda asked.

"What, and we're in Hell now? Hell is reruns of Hawaii Five-O? Brrr. Hard to square that with God's goodness. Too cruel."

"Isn't Hell supposed to be cruel?" Gary asked.

"But the punishments are supposed to be proportionate," Linda said. "You've read Dante."

"I feel like I've been living it the past two days," Gary replied. "Hand me the bottle."

WHEEL of Fortune came on next, but soon got bumped by a story about a reactor being scrammed in Washington State. After a bit of WOR's coverage, Max started surfing, and lo and behold, the CNN's were on again, sort of, and he bounced back and forth between them—when the newsreaders weren't talking about the reactor, they were going on about disappearances and plane crashes. At least ten jets had dropped out of the sky in various parts of North and South America. There was also word that several were missing over the Pacific. Computer failures in major airline terminals were complicating matters. The airlines were considering grounding all traffic.

As for the disappearances, they were being reported all over the Western Hemisphere; some witnesses were claiming to have seen people vanish into thin air.

"Whole world's just going nuts," Gary said.

"At least the Western Hemi—" Max began.

"This just in," said Bernard Shaw. "The wave of air disasters has apparently reached all the way to the orient. First reports indicate—"

A tremendous burst of static cut him off.

SGT. Hazeltine of the Bayside Point police showed up at eight-thirty, and they told him everything they could. Hardly was he out the door when the phone rang. They'd gotten several staticky calls since dinnertime, from relatives in distant parts saying they wouldn't be able to make the viewings, or maybe even the funeral, because of the airline shutdowns. Expecting more of the same, Linda went to the phone.

"Hello?" she said.

"That you, Celia?" a man asked, the line crackling. "Took me a while to get through. It's Buddy."

"Uncle Buddy," Linda said. "No, this isn't Celia. This is Linda, Gary's wife."

He laughed. "Hell, I *thought* you sounded too sexy to be old Pope Celia. Put her on."

"She's uh . . . not here," she replied, signaling Gary into the kitchen. "Look, I'd better give you to my husband." She handed Gary the receiver.

"Uncle Buddy?" he asked. "How are you doing?"

"Not so good. I was mighty close to your father. Hell, I'm not ashamed to say I loved the old bastard. It's been hard, real hard. Uncle Dennis is here with me. Taking it even worse than I am."

"Are you going to be able to make it tomorrow? Max said you were going to catch the plane from Pittsburgh, but with the airline situation—"

"Hell or high water, we're going to be there," Buddy broke in. "I was just calling to confirm. We're going to drive. Leave tonight, the whole clan." Buddy paused. "What were you going to explain to me? Linda said something about your mother."

"Yeah," Gary said.

"What's wrong?"

"She's gone. We don't know where she is."

Silence at the other end.

"Like those people on the news?" Buddy asked at last.

"Maybe."

"It's happening out here too. Nobody knows what the hell's going on . . . You sure she's missing?"

"Yes."

"She's not out gabbing with someone?"

"Not as far as I know."

"What are you going to do about the funeral?"

"Don't know yet."

"Are you going to hold it up?"

"It's still on, as of now. We're hoping she'll turn up."

"What if she doesn't?"

"We'll postpone it."

"I understand. God, this is bad, kid. First your father, now this . . . Shit."

"I can hardly believe it myself," Gary said.

"But look," Buddy went on. "Is there any way I could find out ahead of time? About the funeral? I don't want to drive all the way to New Jersey and find out it's off."

"Yeah," Gary said, head buzzing a bit from the Scotch. He and Linda (with a little help from Max) had almost killed the first bottle. He didn't feel up to snap judgments.

"Still there?" Uncle Buddy asked.

"I'm thinking," Gary said. "Look, you and Uncle Dennis are your own bosses. Suppose you had to stay here over the weekend? Maybe we could push the funeral back to Saturday or Sunday. If Mom hasn't shown up by then . . . "

"I see what you mean. But do you think you can arrange it?"

"I'll call the funeral home. Should still be open. Then I'll ring you right back."

"Okay. Sure hope your mother's all right . . . By the way, what were those flowers your father really hated?"

Incredible, Gary thought. On the off-chance that his uncle might

43

not have talked to the florist, he answered: "Jack-in-the-Pulpits."

"Good," Buddy said unenthusiastically. "I sent anthuriums."

"Ah."

"Look, you call the parlor."

"Okay."

Gary hung up.

"You know what he told me?" Linda asked.

"No, what?"

"He said I sounded too sexy to be your mother."

"You were right about him sending the flowers, Max," Gary called.

"The man's a jerk," Max replied, out in the living room. "You don't have to be a prophet to figure out what he's going to do."

Maybe that's why the anthuriums turned up in that first dream, Gary told himself. *Your subconscious is just good with inductive logic—ha ha.*

He looked up Van Nuys and Monahan's number and called. Mr. Van Nuys answered on the first ring. Gary explained the situation.

"I'm afraid it may not be possible," Van Nuys explained. "Moving the funeral back, I mean."

"Why not?"

"Have you heard about this gravedigger's strike?"

"No."

"If they don't get a contract with the Cemetery Association by Thursday night, they're going out. And I just got word the arbitration's collapsed. The sides are very far apart. There was a fistfight at the meeting this afternoon."

"Oh Jesus."

"I'm sorry, but if your father isn't buried Thursday, he may not be buried for quite some time. The last strike lasted a month."

"What did you do with all the bodies?"

"We had to . . . ah . . . rent space at a meat-packing plant. Very unpleasant business. The State Health Department overreacted about sanitation procedures, made things just about impossible. We might be completely stymied this time . . . "

"All right. Thursday it is, then."

"I hope your mother shows up safe and sound, Gary."

"Thank you," Gary said. "I'll see you tomorrow at the viewing."

Hanging up, he told Linda and Max what Van Nuys had said. Given the situation, they agreed there was nothing else to be done. He called Buddy back, then sat down at the table with Linda.

"My Uncle says he just *can't get over* what a sexy voice you have," he told her.

"What an asshole," Linda said.

"Last thing he said was, 'You sure you're man enough to handle her, kid?'"

"I'm just glad he's on your side of the family," she answered.

LINDA turned in around ten, early for her. The booze had gotten to her.

But not to Gary. He was way too tense. He decided a long walk might calm him down, coupled with some more scotch. After filling a flask, he went out around ten thirty, leaving Max to sit up with the phone.

The night was more brisk than he expected, feeling more like late September than July. Before he got half a block he went back to the house and put on one of his father's light jackets.

"Any calls?" he asked Max.

Max shook his head.

Gary went back out.

For a time he wandered aimlessly, finally going down to Beichmann Avenue, Bayside Point's main drag. There was little traffic; the bars and pizza joints catering to the summer folks (Bennies, as they were known to the natives, for reasons Gary had never discovered) didn't seem to be doing much business.

He headed farther and farther west on Beichmann until he realized he was almost at Van Nuys and Monahan's; deciding he just didn't want to lay eyes on the place, he turned south on Schultz.

He almost reached the end of the street before remembering that it dead-ended on an old cemetery. There were few lights up ahead, and the gravestones of the boneyard were invisible in the darkness, but the very idea of them, some dating back to the eighteen fifties, gave him the creeps. Halting, he wondered: would anything be left of a hundred-forty year old corpse?

Immediately an answer flashed into his mind: *More than you might think.* The response startled him; he found himself automatically assenting to it, even while reminding himself that he had no basis for an opinion.

"Them bones, them bones, them dry bones," he sang softly. And unconsciously, at first. Then his mouth clamped shut.

But the tune kept floating through his head, stirring up long-buried associations: a chorus concert back in High School, the last episode of *The Prisoner*, Peter O'Toole's rendition of the spiritual in the *The Ruling Class*. Strangely, in spite of the fact that Gary remembered O'Toole wearing a riding habit in the scene, he could only picture him in a uniform now, a Jersey state trooper's, as he sang with horrible pleasure of the punishments the wicked surely deserved . . .

With an effort, Gary forced his thoughts onto another track, but succeeded only in getting another scene from the movie, the one in the House of Lords, row upon row of corpses rising from their seats, turning to look into the camera, into the audience's face, into *Gary's* face . . .

Now hear the word of the Lord.

Gary laughed nervously, trying once more to thrust it all from his mind. Turning on his heel, he retraced his steps till he struck Harrison Street. There he headed east.

Duncan Grady used to live in this neck of the woods, he recalled. He and Duncan had been good buddies in grammar school, but had drifted apart afterward. He wondered how Dunk was.

In a pool of light from a streetlamp, he saw a man opening the trunk of a dark sedan. As he got closer, he saw it was none other than Duncan himself, preparing to put a large telescope inside. Duncan looked up at his approach, owlish as ever, and squinted at him through his thick round glasses.

"Gary?" Duncan asked.

"Yeah. How's it going, Dunk?"

Duncan laid the telescope in the trunk and closed the lid.

"Okay," he said, and they shook hands. "Heard about your father. I'm real sorry."

"There are a couple of viewings tomorrow," Gary said.

"I know. I'll try to make the second one."

There was a pause.

"What are you doing back in town?" Gary asked, feeling uncomfortable. Despite his curiosity about how Duncan had been doing, he hadn't wanted to talk to him. Or anyone, for that matter.

"Wife left me," Duncan said.

"No, really?" Gary answered, trying to sound upset about something which didn't matter to him at all. "That's a real shame."

Duncan nodded. "I thought I'd come back, spend some time with the folks."

"Any chance you might be able to patch it up?"

"I don't even know where she went."

"Oh," Gary said.

"Don't have a clue," Duncan said.

"Ah," Gary said.

Another pause, longer and more embarrassing than the last.

"What's with the telescope?" Gary asked.

"Bought it the other day. Always wanted one. I'm going to take it out on Duck Island and stargaze."

"Why the island?"

"To get away from town. It says in the manual that lights make it hard to see anything."

"Full moon tonight," Gary said. "It'll blot out most of the stars."

"I'll look at the moon then."

"Well, you don't have to go out to the island for that. It's bright enough even with the—"

"You always were a pain in the ass," Duncan said, jokingly, but with an edge in his voice. "I'll just wait till the moon sets, then look at the stars."

"Going to be a long time."

"Maybe I just feel like sitting out there alone, okay?"

"Sure, sure. Hey look, I'll be seeing you, Dunk."

"Tomorrow."

"Okay."

Gary started off down the street. He took the flask out and had a sip. Behind him, he could hear Duncan muttering to himself.

That was one friendship Gary didn't feel the slightest temptation to renew. Episodes from its collapse came rushing back to him. Duncan sure was a stubborn bastard; once he got an idea in his head, there was just no talking to him. But if he thought something was going to be great, that was a sure sign it would leave him totally dissatisfied—whereupon he'd stick with it until the wheels came off, making everyone furious in the process. He was probably going to go out on the island and stay there for hours, even though he was going to be bored silly in fifteen minutes . . . Gary knew just what had happened to Duncan's marriage.

But I bet Dunk doesn't have the foggiest.

Gary drifted off toward the beachfront. Hitting the boardwalk, he went north. Most of the concessions and arcades were closing up; there were few people about.

He walked all the way up to the north end pavilion, which bordered on the Squankum Inlet. There he watched the boats coming in, passing between the piled-granite jetties.

He remembered fishing off the south jetty with his father when he was seven years old; his eyes began to mist over. Three brief days before, his father had been more than just a memory. Now he was nothing else.

Unless you wanted to count a hunk of meat at Van Nuys and Monahan's, about to be (or perhaps even now) carved up and filled with embalming fluid.

And where was Mom? Was she another potential job for those funeral-parlor ghouls? What had happened to her? To *all* those people who had disappeared?

Gary's head spun. He was totally exhausted, running on vapor. But horribly, he didn't feel at all sleepy yet.

He decided to go out on the jetty and watch the waves come in. Heading back toward the beach admission booths, he went down the steps and out across the sand.

As he moved farther and farther from the boardwalk lights, the sky seemed to brighten, becoming a pale blue-grey, sprinkled with only the most brilliant stars. Moonlight gleamed on the sand, glinted off the swells rolling beyond.

He passed over the crown of the shallow slope that marked the high-water line, striding over piled seaweed, popping small bladders underfoot; the air was full of the weed's salty smell. The fringe of a wave nearly caught him, but he leaped back.

Out at sea, several fishing boats were going by, superstructures ablaze with lights. Farther east, a huge tanker was a massive dark outline.

Close ahead the low rampart of the jetty stood out clearly. At its end rose a skeletal metal tower, some thirty feet tall, with a flashing lime-green beacon at the top.

Gary came to the rocks and pressed up toward the top of the jetty. In the moonlight, the white paint favored by local graffiti artists was positively fluorescent; he puzzled briefly at several cryptic messages, *Vikings 37X Eat It* being perhaps the most obscure.

He went some distance along the jetty's top, spotted what looked like a good place to sit down, and parked himself, facing south with his back to a boulder.

The moon looked as if it were hanging directly over the border between sea and beach; the surf was a silverlit fury of water and spray.

Hell, Gary thought, *if that moon was any brighter, there'd be a rainbow.* He took a hit from his flask.

The wind began to blow harder. Despite the warmth the liquor sent coursing through his veins, the breeze still cut.

God, is this really July?

He began thinking about that nice warm bed back at the house. Yes, it was time to head on home. Maybe there'd be news about Mom . . .

"Dammit, God," he said, "I know I don't believe in you, but please let her be okay."

He was about to get up when he noticed something drifting in on one of the combers. Dark and rectangular, it looked like a piece of plywood, no, was too thick for that, riding a bit high in the water, although the stability of its movements suggested that most of it was beneath the surface . . .

Back of a chair, he decided.

Then he took one step farther.

An airline seat.

The waves pushed it closer to the shore. Soon it was in the surf. Gary sat motionless, hoping his worst suspicion wouldn't be confirmed. He tried to think of something else that could be attached—

(With a seatbelt, Gary?)

To an airline seat, something else besides a . . .

The object tilted in the surf, and a wave caught it, tumbling the whole mass over. Sitting there serenely, as though he were asleep and not a day-old drowned corpse, was a dead gentleman in a business suit. It was hard to tell at that distance, but he seemed to have a large crab clinging to his face.

Gary felt suddenly sick, but parts of his mind remained strangely objective about the whole business. Should he try to haul the guy up on the beach? What exactly *should* he say when he phoned the cops?

Still he hadn't moved. Civic duty or no, he found he had no inclination to. Used to dead bodies neatly tucked into coffins, behaving themselves at funeral parlors, he was totally unprepared to deal with one in the process of washing ashore. And this one was an Italian tourist, no less. All the way from Rome, maybe, four thousand miles to drown off the Jersey coast.

The seat shifted with each wave, but it had pretty much run aground. Surf sloshed over the man's face, but the crab was still clinging to him. Looked like it had him by the mouth. Big damn crab.

No seafood for a year, Gary told himself.

That was when he saw the corpse reach up and tear the crustacean off.

What the—

A wave splashed over the body. When it receded, the corpse's hand was back at its side.

Old eyes playing tricks on you, Gary thought. *Too much scotch. Wasn't any crab to begin with—*

This line of argument was cut short as the corpse's pale hands whipped to the seatbelt and undid it.

Gary pressed himself slowly back against the boulder, trying to melt into the stone, even as he ran through the very compelling reasons why he had nothing to fear and couldn't possibly have seen what he'd just seen . . .

With a fearsomely quick movement, the corpse rolled from the seat, knocking it on its side as it passed over the armrest; then in an explosive splash it jacknifed up into a sitting position. Chin dripping foam, it appeared to be eyeing the jetty.

Jesus Oh God can it see me . . . ?

But if the corpse was aware of Gary, it paid him no heed; its face swiveled seaward and jerked to a crisp, precise halt. Gary guessed he couldn't be all that obvious, with his dark-blue jacket and pants against the dark granite. There was only his pasty white face, and there was nothing to be done about that, not even cover it with his pasty white hands . . . All he could do was press himself flatter and flatter against the stone and pray to Jesus Christ Almighty that he was just too damn drunk and none of this was happening . . .

The corpse shot to its feet like a spear thrust up out of the surf. Gary's eyes darted eastward, out to sea, toward the spot it seemed to be staring at.

Three round things appeared in the trough between two waves and started toward the shore. Swells rolled over them, but each time they reappeared, closer to the beach. After a time they were clearly recognizable as heads, rising slowly from the water, faces pale beneath dark hanging hair. Shiny black shoulders broke the surface; white collars

gleamed. Pressing purposefully through the foam, barely staggering as waves crashed into them, the figures halted suddenly where the water was only knee-deep.

The corpse strode out to meet them, splashing through the shallows like an over wound toy soldier. As it came up beside them, they pivoted mechanically around; the four marched back out into the Atlantic, finally sinking from sight.

Frigid sweat poured down Gary's face.

Gone, he thought. *They're gone.*

He was leaping from stone to stone down toward the beach before he even realized it. Bounding onto the sand, he pelted across the beach to the boardwalk, not stopping till he reached his parents' house.

CHAPTER 5
WRONG AGAIN

DUCK Island was a mile-long patch of sand and tall weeds in the middle of the Squankum River, a half-mile to the east of the Rt.35 Bridge. The Central Penn rail line ran across its western end, jumping the Squankum's narrower southern fork over a modest timber trestle; a longer span with a drawbridge spanned the river to the north. The island's shore was mostly salt marsh and mudflat, the habitat of the fowl that had given the island its name. There was only one real beach, on the northern side; Duncan Grady had gone there. And even now, two hours after Gary saw what he couldn't possibly have seen, Duncan was *still* there, determined to enjoy himself.

The suspicion had dawned on Duncan, however, that Gary might've been right about this particular outing. As a matter of fact, it had dawned on him about fifteen minutes after he began staring at the moon. There was just so much of the moon to see, and sure enough, its glow blotted out just about everything else in the sky.

But Duncan hadn't let that stop him. He was going to wait till moonset, and then do some real stargazing. He would tell Gary all about it at the viewing. Gary probably thought he'd wait a ridiculously long time on the island and then pack it in without seeing much of anything. Well, Dunk Grady was sure going to show him.

He'd spent most of his time lying wrapped in a blanket, nursing his resentments and dreaming of scores resoundingly settled, particularly against his bitch ex-wife. Even these diversions had paled after a while, but he kept plugging away at them, despite the chill that eventually penetrated his blanket. He wished he didn't have to stay out here; but there was principle involved.

Presently he got up on his knees and looked through the scope once more. The moon had moved; he shifted the scope. Aside from the position of the lunar disc, nothing much had changed. When was the damn thing going to set?

He lowered the scope, turning it so he could look across the river. He was somewhat annoyed he had been forced to take such a course of action; here he was, in possession of a piece of optics you could see the rings of Saturn with, and he was about to kill time with it eyeballing the far shore of the Squankum. He knew what Gary would think. But there was no reason Gary had to find out.

Beyond the marsh grass on the north bank of the river was a dark line of trees, a few house lights shining through. A tubular water tower, looking almost like a rocketship, loomed above the trees, red lights blinking on its crown.

Duncan slowly swiveled the scope to the left. The railroad trestle slipped into view. Looking past the raised slant-drawbridge, he found the bridgekeeper's booth. Its dirty windows glowed yellow; he could see the keeper leaning against a wall, drinking from a thermos cup.

A blue light flashed on the wall beside the man. The keeper set the cup on a table, went over to a large black lever, and pulled it. Duncan heard huge gears grinding, and shifted the scope back to the drawbridge. The span was going down.

Duncan guessed the last train from Atlantic City must be coming through. He knew from experience that that run was usually crowded, full of poor schnooks heading back to North Jersey and New York with blown wallets and busted bankbooks, swearing they'd never do it again . . .

The bridge sank lower and lower. It almost reached the level of the trestle.

Then the gears went silent. The bridge stopped dead.

False alarm? Duncan wondered. *No train?*

A whistle blew somewhere to the south. So much for that theory. Had the gears locked, maybe? He turned the scope back toward the keeper's booth, expecting to see the man wrestling with the lever.

Instead, he saw the keeper hanging in the air, struggling wildly, trying to pry open the hand locked on his flesh.

Perfectly, inorganically rigid, the man holding him might've been a statue. Even with the keeper thrashing at the end of his arm, he was utterly still. It was as if the keeper's throat had been impaled on an iron rod.

An accomplice stood near the lever, watching, but shortly he rushed over to them with a bizarre clockwork gait, and almost as though he were afraid he wouldn't be able to get in on the keeper's death agonies, grabbed one of the man's hands and started biting. Things flew, and the hand went red. Duncan's jaw sagged, and he felt a sudden, savage, ache in his knuckles.

The victim's fingers were coming off a joint at a time.

Rubbing his hands, Duncan murmured something in a low stunned voice. He himself had no idea what it was.

The keeper's struggles ceased. The finger-biter stepped back. His partner let the corpse drop.

Both men stood motionless, staring at each other. Then the finger-biter wiped his mouth with a spasmodic sweep of his wrist.

The train wailed again, closer now. Duncan shifted the scope back to the bridge. It was almost level, but the difference in slope between it and the trestle was more than enough to derail the train.

Duncan's mind raced. He doubted he could reach the booth and throw the switch in time—but he couldn't sit back and do nothing. He'd just have to run along the path and back to the tracks and puff his way out to the booth and fight his way past those two psychos, one of whom was capable of holding a grown man off the floor at arm's length and strangling him one-handed . . .

On second thought, maybe it wasn't such a good idea.

But what then? He turned the scope back to the booth. A third man had joined the other two. He seemed to be in some kind of uniform. State trooper's, maybe.

The train wailed once more, closer yet.

A minute passed. The three men left the booth. Duncan followed them with the scope. They didn't turn north or south along the tracks, as he thought they must, but headed straight across, moving with quick jerky strides like people in an old silent flick. Duncan had always found the speeded-up action in those films hilarious, but in real life the effect was horribly disturbing.

They neared the edge of the trestle. He guessed they had a boat tied up below and that they would climb down to it. Instead, they walked over the side like automatons, dropping straight down into the river.

The train wailed yet again. It was close enough now for him to hear the sound of its engine, the rumble-and-click of its wheels. He pulled his face back from the scope, looking toward the bridge, knowing he'd get a better, wider view of the crash unaided. There was more than enough moonlight. Since there was nothing he could do, he would just sit back and watch the spectacle.

The train barreled into view off to the left, brightly-lit passenger cars looking about two-thirds full. There was going to be one hell of a body count.

The locomotive hurtled close to the bridge. Duncan guessed that the engineer was now close enough to see that slight rise, the slope in the tracks where the bridge hinged with the trestle.

The train wailed one last time, a ringing note that sounded almost like a scream of terror. Brakes squealed. The train slowed, just barely. Then the locomotive reached the base of the incline.

It derailed immediately, veering to the right, but momentum kept it skidding upward, the passenger cars trailing behind. When it came to the end of the bridge, the drop was enough to make it heel onto its side and roll over the edge of the trestle. Its coupling snapped, but not before the cars behind began to roll; the train's front end twisted clockwise. Car after car followed the locomotive into the Squankum, striking with huge white splashes like bomb-blasts. The whole train went over the side, all eleven cars, sinking swiftly from sight.

Duncan put his eye back to the telescope, searching the water for survivors. After a time, some floundered to the surface.

Now at last there was a way he might be able to help. He got up and ran from the beach, back to the main path, pelting west as fast as he could, images of richly rewarded heroism filling his mind. He envisioned himself on *Nightline,* chit-chatting with Ted Koppel. He thought of his ex-wife standing dumbstruck on the sidelines as the President of the United States pinned the Congressional Medal of Honor on his chest. Reaching the rail embankment, he scrambled up onto the clinkers.

And stopped in his tracks.

A man stood some distance up the line, facing him. He seemed to be wearing a trooper-uniform, but this was almost certainly not the trooper from the booth; this man was much taller, with a massive build. He was too far away for Duncan to see his face clearly, but Dunk thought he could make out a tremendous grin.

The man flung his head back, as if with a peal of silent laughter, and his hands jerked up from his sides with awful steel-trap speed, reaching straight out toward Duncan, clawing the air; he started forward at a stiff but impossibly fast run.

"What the fuck?" Duncan said, then spun and raced back to the trail. He knew he wouldn't be able to outdistance the man; he could only hope to lose him among the weeds.

Rounding a bend, Duncan split off onto a narrow side path, guessing that the man, fast as he was, could not have been close enough to see him do it. On and on between the high tasseled weeds he dashed.

At first he caught no sound of pursuit. He figured the man had continued along the main path. Gasping, he began to slow. His lungs burned, and there was a vicious stitch in his side.

Then he heard the swift heavy footfalls, the rustle-and-rattle of a body brushing weeds. The man had doubled back, taken the turn.

Duncan sped up again. Breath exploded from his lips. His legs pumped. He forced as much speed into them as he could, trying to ignore the fatigue tightening his muscles, the pain in his lungs and chest. He hadn't run so much since the track team in high school.

He hit a long straight stretch. Midway along, he looked back.

A swift stiff-legged shadow, the trooper was about thirty feet behind, head still flung backward, white hands outstretched.

The straight stretch ended in an s-curve, beyond which lay a three-way fork. Duncan pelted into the left-hand path, went about fifteen feet, and dove deep into the weeds on the left, stems popping and crackling about him; striking the ground, glasses flying off, he lay still, one hand over his mouth to muffle his panting.

He heard his pursuer draw near and pause, apparently at the fork. Duncan twisted, looked back toward the path. Without his glasses, his vision was blurry, but he still made out a shadow rushing behind the moonsilvered silhouettes of the weeds. The temperature seemed to plummet.

The figure was gone in an instant. The cold vanished. The sound of footbeats faded, swallowed by the sigh of wind in the weeds.

Duncan let his hand drop away from his mouth. He took air in enormous gulps, and began to feel around for his glasses.

God, I hope I didn't lose 'em, he thought. *Sixty Goddamn dollars a pair, and—*

The footbeats were coming back. The shadow reappeared. Slowed. Stopped and turned. The cold settled over Duncan's flesh again.

The man was standing right in front of the spot where Duncan had dived into the weeds. The wind died. Duncan thought he could hear the man whispering to himself in a dry lifeless voice. Duncan's skin crawled. But despite his terror, a snatch of George Harrison drifted into his head:

I've got my mind set on you, I've got my mind set on you . . .

The man didn't stir. Agonized with suspense, Duncan wondered why. Surely, if the trooper knew where he was, he would've made his move—

"Think so, Dunk?" asked the trooper.

Jesus, Duncan thought, paralyzed with panic.

"Nope," said the trooper, and plunged forward into the weeds like a threshing machine gone berserk, arms flailing, bits of ripped stalk flying into the air above.

Duncan leaped up to flee, struggling to force a path through the growths in front of him. He barely went two paces before the trooper caught him, pushed him down, and jumped astride his back.

Duncan tried to roll, but the man kept him pinned. Duncan went for the pen-knife in his pocket, but his hand was blocked by the man's right leg. He yelled and fought, but it did no good. A heavy blow cracked across the back of his head. Blackness billowed into his skull.

Done for, he told himself, and went under.

BUT writing himself off counted for nothing; lying on his back now, pervaded by an intense chill, he woke. The cold seemed to radiate from his assailant, who was sitting on his stomach; Dunk could barely breathe. Between the absence of his glasses, and the way the trooper's head was silhouetted against the moonlit sky, Duncan could tell little about the man's face, except for that gigantic grin.

Duncan's hands were on his chest, bound. He shifted them toward his face, saw that they were tied with his own belt. He smashed them into the man's solar plexus, but he might as well have been striking a boulder.

"Leave me alone!" he gasped. "Leave me . . . "

The trooper pressed Duncan's arms back down with a frigid palm, and pushed his other hand close to Duncan's eyes. Between the man's fingers, Duncan could make out something dark, dirt maybe, with little bits of root and old dead weed sticking out.

"What are you going to do?" Dunk cried.

The trooper drew his arm back, then sent his fist crashing into Duncan's mouth, smashing through his upper and lower teeth, driving his jaw down against his Adam's apple. The sides of Duncan's mouth bulged almost to bursting, and his throat swelled as the fist chugged partway down his windpipe. Duncan's head and neck reverberated with pain.

The trooper opened his fist and pulled it back, dragging a filthy taste of dirt and rotten weed across Duncan's tongue. Dunk's throat was clogged with a solid plug of earth.

Why? Dunk thought dazedly. *Why this way?*

Vomit spewed up from his belly, but couldn't break through the plug; the pressure was horrendous. It seemed he was going to explode. He tried to cough, but felt as if all the muscles in his throat had burst. His eyes rolled up and closed.

He was dimly aware of his attacker shifting. There was a sound like a spade being driven into the earth beside him; was the trooper grabbing another handful?

Momentarily Dunk sensed something rushing toward his face, and the fist rammed into his toothless maw again, driving the first handful in further, depositing a second for good measure.

The trooper pulled his hand out slowly. Duncan writhed and gagged. His eyes bulged open. He could practically feel the blood vessels popping in them.

The trooper leaned forward, pushing his face down near Duncan's, close enough for Duncan to see it clearly.

The horror of that sight was almost enough to make his strangulation seem trivial.

He tried to scream, but no sound could force its way through his throat. He jerked his head aside, trying to look away. His assailant grabbed his face and forced him to stare upward. Duncan snapped his eyes shut. Keeping them shut was the only thing that mattered now.

Apparently unwilling to expend the effort to pry them open, the man rose.

Duncan drifted toward death, his oxygen-starved brain lulled by a strangely peaceful thought: at least he'd never have to see that face again.

"Wrong again, Dunk," said the trooper.

The words seemed to push Duncan over the edge. For a moment there was blissful nothingness.

Then he saw the green glow.

And the bodies raining into the pit.

And the wheels within wheels.

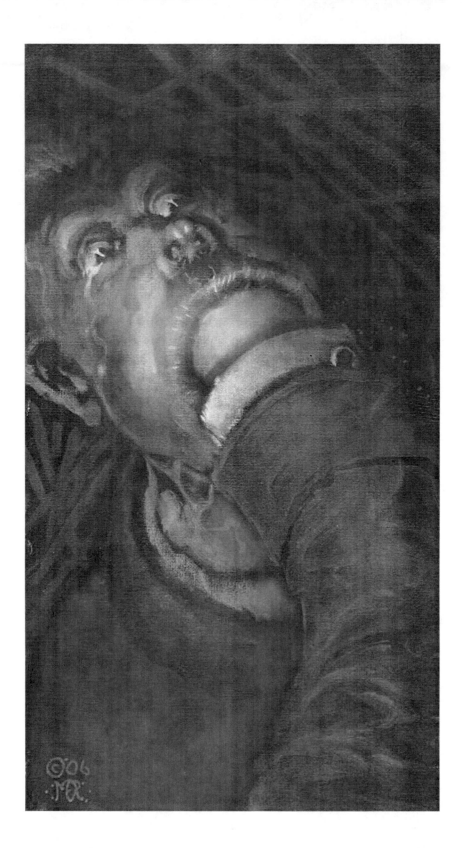

CHAPTER 6
UNCLE BUDDY

LYING in bed Thursday morning, Gary pondered what he'd seen—
thought he'd seen—the previous night. Insane stuff, definitely booze-
induced.

True, he'd never hallucinated under the influence before, and it
hadn't seemed he'd downed all that much. But what other explanation
could there be?

Linda was already up and around. It was, after all, nearly ten. Gary
had slept well past eight; *that* had been the scotch, certainly. Somewhat
nauseated, he got up, put on his bathrobe, and went out to see what
Linda was doing.

She was in the kitchen eating breakfast, bacon and scrambled eggs.
The smell of it hung heavy in the air. Normally it would have been
delicious, but Gary could barely take it.

"Hi, hon," she said, looking up. "Hangover?"

"Bit." He looked out into the living-room, where his brother was
reading a paper.

"Man," Max said, tossing it.

"What now?" Gary asked.

"Lot of blackouts, mostly in the Southeast and Midwest. Satellites
are going on the fritz too. I could hardly watch Jane—"

"I take no one's called," Gary broke in.

"About Mom? No."

"You talk with the cops?"

"Twice. Nothing."

"Shit."

"They've got their hands full anyway."

"More disappearances?"

"Train wreck."

"*Train* wreck?"

"Redeye from Atlantic City. The Squankum Bridge didn't close
completely. Ten cars went into the river. They don't even know how
many people are dead."

Gary shook his head. "First that plane—"

61

"Just wait," Max went on. "It gets better. The bridge keeper was *strangled.*"

"So . . . it was a *deliberate* wreck?"

"Looks like it. And get this. Some of the keeper's fingers were *bitten* off." Max's eyes gleamed with perverse relish.

"Was this on the Today Show?"

Max nodded. "Wild, huh? Bayside Point on the national news, two days in a row . . . They want to keep the train stiffs separate from the plane stiffs, so they're stacking 'em in the Elk's Hall this time—"

"Instead of the high school gym?"

"Right."

"Do they have any idea why the plane crashed? Why *all* those planes crashed?"

"They were all overdue for maintenance, apparently. Still—"

"One hell of a coincidence—"

"Could you talk about something else?" Linda demanded.

"You're not interested?" Max asked.

"I'm feeling kind of shell-shocked right now. *You* might enjoy hearing about some poor guy getting his fingers bitten off—"

Max laughed. "Yeah, guess I do."

"Well, I guess I'm just stupid, but things like that *really* disturb me."

"Okay."

"And hearing about all those people dying makes me feel hopeless. Completely hopeless. Like things will never return to normal. Like there isn't a chance Mom'll ever turn up again."

"Oh come on."

"It's just the way I feel, that's all."

"What could that have to do with those plane crashes?"

"I was thinking more about the train."

"You *really* think there's some kind of connection?"

"The wreck *was* deliberate."

"Yeah..."

"And Mom *might* have been kidnapped, or something—"

"Or something."

"—along with all those other people who disappeared . . . I mean, how many crimes do you get in two days in a town like Bayside Point?"

"Why leave it at Bayside Point?" Max asked. "What about *everyone* who's disappeared? *Everywhere?*"

"What about them?"

"Is there a kidnapping ring?"

"I don't know—"

"A *national* kidnapping ring?"

"Stop it!"

"And they wreck trains too?"

"Well," Linda said, "What's *your* explanation?"

"For?"

"The disappearances?"

"*Just* them? Not the train and plane stuff?"

"Not the train and plane stuff."

Max laughed. "Didn't say I had one."

There was a pause. After a time, Linda asked quietly: "What if it's *all* connected?"

"What?"

"The crashes, the power failures, the disappearances . . . "

"Don't forget those dreams!" Max said. "That was pretty strange, right? Three people having the same dream?"

"It wasn't just *us,*" Linda answered. "Did you see that article in the paper?"

"No," Max said.

"'Coincidental Dreams a Puzzle.' Only it turns out not everyone woke up. Some people heard their sentences."

Max laughed again. "What was it? All guilty?"

"As a matter of fact—"

"You mean," Gary said, "That all these people had that Last Judgment dream?"

"Hey, it was in the paper—"

"How *many* people?"

"Five hundred. Called at random. And *every single one* of them had it."

Max picked the paper up again.

"Well, what do you think?" Linda asked after a while.

"I think," Max answered, "That things aren't necessarily connected, just because they're weird."

"Sure. There's just an outrageous amount of weirdness happening at once."

"Doesn't prove anything. I sure hope you argue more skillfully in your articles."

"I've published a hell of a lot more than you," she answered.

Max flinched.

"Who's the one with tenure?" she pressed.

"Oww."

"At a *real* university?"

Max clutched his chest. "Stabbed through the heart!"

"I know I've been sounding pretty nutty," Linda admitted. "It's just that I've been getting some very creepy vibes."

"So nothing's ever going to get better again?"

"Don't you ever get creepy vibes?"

"Would it make you happier if I got freaked too?"

"Hell *no*," she said. Getting up, she took her dishes over to the sink and put them in, then stood awhile silently, leaning on the Formica counter.

"God, I hope Mom comes back," she said at last.

LONG about one o'clock Uncle Buddy's blue Chevy station-wagon, badly in need of a tune-up by the sound of it, pulled up in front of the house.

"Brace yourselves," Gary said, looking out through an open front window. "Here they are."

Out came Uncle Buddy and Uncle Dennis, together with their wives and Buddy's gawky seventeen year-old son, Dave. They trooped up the front walk but paused midway along as Buddy, a towering beer-bellied presence, grabbed Dave and pointed a fat finger at his nose.

"Look, you little bastard," Buddy growled, "You watch yourself. My brother's dead, this is a very sad occasion, and if you *don't* behave, I'll beat your brains out."

"What did I do?" Dave asked, the very question Gary was pondering.

"You know what you did!" Uncle Buddy thundered.

Looking very embarrassed, Aunt Lucy, his overripe, bleached-blonde better half, grabbed his arm and whispered in his ear.

"He's going to learn *respect*," he snapped.

"But what did I *do?*" Dave repeated.

Uncle Buddy put him down with a whack to the face.

Laff Riot, Gary thought, recalling Buddy's yearbook nickname.

Having apparently not inherited his father's sense of humor, Dave leaped back up from the ground, a knife in his hand.

Aunt Lucy stamped her foot. "David Holland, you put that down

64

this *instant!*"

Dave's response was to bound forward and jab the knife at Uncle Buddy's neck. Gary gasped, started to run for the door—then saw the blade, obviously rubber, bend when it struck Buddy's flesh.

"Christ," Gary muttered, shaking his head.

"What?" Max called from the kitchen.

"Just Buddy and cousin Dave, being themselves."

Recovering from his shock, Buddy, livid, grabbed the knife from Dave, made as if to smack him again; then a change came over him. He inspected the knife, wobbling the blade back and forth.

"Chip off the old block," he laughed. "Scared the shit out of me for a second there."

"Watch your language, Buddy!" Lucy cried.

"Any fuckin' thing you say," Buddy answered, glancing at Uncle Dennis, who gave what seemed to Gary like a forced grin. Dennis's wife Camille looked scandalized.

Buddy straightened his suit, pocketed the rubber knife, and started forward again, the others following. Gary met them at the door.

"How you doin', Gary?" Uncle Buddy asked.

"Okay," Gary answered.

"Everything all set for tomorrow?"

"Yeah."

Aunt Lucy, smelling of sickly-sweet perfume, gave Gary a big smarmy hug. "Any news about your mother?" she asked.

"No."

When all five of them were inside, Max and Linda came forward, and there was a round of embraces and introductions.

"So you're *sexy* little Linda," Buddy said.

Gary looked at her. She had a clenched smile on her face that told him very clearly that what she really wanted to say was, "*So you're fat old Uncle Buddy the jerk-off.*" But what came out was: "Uncle *Bud*dy! I've heard so much *about* you!"

"Nothing good, I hope," Buddy said, and kissed her on the cheek.

"Not one word," she replied.

"When's the viewing?" Uncle Dennis asked. Tall and late-fortyish, he looked like an older version of Max Jr.—broad shoulders, rugged face, dark hair, only a bit of a paunch.

"Three," Gary answered. "Did you guys drive all night?"

"Almost," Aunt Camille said. "Checked into a hotel around four."

"Close?"

"It's up on 35," Dennis said.

"TV still down in the rec room?" Dave asked Gary.

"Yeah," Gary answered.

"HBO?"

"Showtime."

"I can live with that," Dave said, and started for the stairs.

"David, you stay away from that one-eyed monster," Aunt Lucy said. "Visit a while."

Dave mumbled something under his breath and continued on his way.

"You want me to hit you again?" Uncle Buddy asked.

Dave disappeared through the door. Buddy grumbled, but didn't pursue.

"You know, we were heartbroken to hear about your father," Lucy told Max. "And now this terrible business about your mother . . . "

"She was a good woman," Buddy said.

"*Was?*" Max said. "Do you know that she's dead?"

"Relax," Buddy answered. "Didn't mean nothing by it."

Just doing a little wishful thinking, right? Gary thought. Buddy had never been too fond of Mom. She was far too religious for him— being religious at all was too much, as far as he was concerned. Gary knew Buddy blamed Mom for the rift that had developed between him and Max Sr.— the Hollands had been an unbroken line of free-thinkers until Dad met her.

"Gonna miss your father," Buddy told Max and Gary. "My favorite brother gone, just like that. We had our disagreements, all right, but he was always the best."

Gary saw Dennis bite his lip.

"Got any beer?" Dennis asked.

"In the fridge," Max answered.

"Man, I used to pull some jokes on old Maxie," Buddy said wistfully. "I ever tell you boys about the time I put cowshit in his bed?"

That *was* a new one.

"Yeah," Gary said, forcing a laugh. "I heard all about it, remember?"

"You *sure?*"

"I think so."

"Nah. I'm sure I didn't tell you."

Then why'd you ask? Gary thought, but said nothing, knowing he was in for the long haul no matter what.

"Sit down, sit down," Buddy said. "You'll just crap your pants."

They parked themselves on the couch, Gary steeling himself. Max headed for the kitchen.

"Hey!" Buddy called after him. "Don't you want to hear the story?"

"No," Max said.

WHEN they left for the funeral parlor, Gary noticed that his Pinto sounded pretty ragged, much the way Buddy's Chevy had; that was odd, considering he'd had it tuned three weeks before. But half the cars on the street seemed to be coughing and wheezing—it was obvious even though Gary had the windows rolled up. The day had turned quite chilly.

What happened to summer? he wondered.

He turned right on Beichmann, passing two cop cars heading up toward the beach, lights flashing. Reaching the western end of the business district, he pulled into the parking lot at Van Nuys and Monahan's, Uncle Buddy right behind.

Everyone signed the memorial book; spindly Mr. Van Nuys came out from his office and had one of his assistants open the door to the chapel. He shook hands all around, expressed condolences, then led the party into the room.

Not very much like my dream at all, Gary thought.

Max Sr. was laid out at the back in a bronze casket. Sprays of flowers flanked the catafalque. Max nudged Gary and pointed to the right—there were Uncle Buddy's anthuriums. Gary wondered what Buddy would've sent if Max Sr. *hadn't* been his favorite brother.

Approaching the coffin, they all gave the deceased a once-over. Mr. Van Nuys hovered near, waiting to be complimented on his handiwork.

"So peaceful," Aunt Lucy said approvingly.

So waxy-looking, Gary thought. The flesh had a slight orange tinge, and the features seemed slightly flattened, as if there were no longer anything to keep them from sagging—like blood pressure. Or personality.

Gary was quietly shocked. Even though he'd been converted to a vague form of scientific materialism back in his teens, he'd never ceased being surprised and appalled by the way death changed faces. He knew the corpse was just a mass of chemicals, that death was merely a chemical change, but something so simple didn't seem enough to account for such a profound transformation. Muscles and bone structure hadn't been altered, but this was no longer his father—if it had been walking down the street, Gary wouldn't have known it from Adam. *Knowing* it was his father's body, he recognized the similarities; but his *father* was missing from it, and somehow the loss didn't seem chemical at all.

But it's just as well he's not still in there, Gary told himself. *Remember that fist coming up through the coffin? Those shrieks?*

Gary caught himself. That had only been a dream. It meant nothing. Hell, he was the only one who dreamed it—it hadn't even made the newspapers.

And besides. *If* Dad returned from the dead, what there be to fear from him?

But what if he woke up in Hell? came the answer, *and found you beside him?*

A hand came down on his shoulder; he was back in the nightmare, and that thing from the coffin had him at last . . .

He turned.

It was only Mr. Van Nuys.

Of course.

"Would you and your brother please come to my office, Mr. Holland?" he asked, sounding agitated.

Max had just risen from the kneeler in front of the bier, crossing himself, and they followed the undertaker. On the way, Gary noticed the fish-tank. A lot of its inhabitants seemed to have a bad case of ick. There wasn't a dead angelfish at the top, but there *was* one on the bottom, a small sickly-looking catfish going over it with its suction-cup mouth.

ONCE he was settled behind his black walnut desk, Van Nuys said:

"I'm afraid I have some potentially bad news, and I thought I'd warn you ahead of time," he began. "Some of the gravedigger locals have decided not to wait for the union vote, and are going out on wildcat strikes. I had a call just before you arrived, and there's a very good chance the Ocean County local might strike."

"Damn," Gary said under his breath.

"Well," Max said, "If they *do* go out, we'll just have to put up with it, won't we?"

"I'm afraid so," Van Nuys replied. "Even if we *could* arrange for buial outside the county, the diggers there would probably refuse the job in sympathy."

"It's not certain though?" Gary asked.

"No. I should know by eleven tonight. I'll give you a call."

"Okay."

"Anything else?" Max asked.

Van Nuys smiled uncomfortably. "I know this is a terrible time to bring this up, but . . . with your mother still missing, I was wondering who I should send the bill to."

"Me," Gary said, and gave him his address. "Me and Max'll take care of it."

"Very good," Van Nuys replied.

As Max and Gary headed for the door, the overhead light flickered.

"It's been doing that all afternoon," Van Nuys said. "Power trouble. Has there been any on your side of town?"

Gary paused. "Nope," he laughed. "My car's been acting peculiar, though."

"Mine too," Van Nuys said. "Think it might be catching?"

"I hope not," Gary said, and he and Max continued toward the chapel. A young priest, tall and sandy-haired, was standing in the lobby.

"Excuse me," he said, "but I'm looking for Celia Holland."

"I'm afraid she's not here," Gary said.

"I see," the priest said, extending his hand. Gary took it. So did Max. "Father Chuck Pendergast. I'm from St. Paul's."

"Gary Holland," Gary said. "And this is my brother Max."

"Pleased to meet you, Father," Max said, a hint of suspicion in his voice.

Father Chuck went on: "I knew your father rather well—"He caught sight of the memorial book. "Excuse me just a moment." He went over and signed it.

While he was at that, Max nudged Gary and said, "I'll be in the chapel."

When the priest returned, Max was already gone.

"So that was Max," he said.

"Yep," Gary said.

"I understand there was something of a tiff when Father Ted visited the other day."

"I'd like to apologize for my brother," Gary answered. "He really did get out of line, if you ask me. He has some pretty strong views."

"That's what Father Ted said. Views your mother shares, apparently."

"Yeah. But she never would've picked a fight like that. It was all Max's fault."

"Still, Father Ted said she made him feel sufficiently unwelcome . . ."

"I'm sure she did. But she kind of got drawn into it, if you see what I mean." He paused. "What exactly's on your mind, Father?"

"Well," Father Chuck said, "Father Ted was really quite hurt by the exchange, and he wishes to know if your mother still wants him to speak tonight, and celebrate the mass tomorrow. He thought he should give her one more opportunity . . ."

"It's hard to say what my mother wants now," Gary answered. "She disappeared yesterday."

Father Chuck was visibly dismayed. "*Another* one," he said, shaking his head. "Your poor family. I'll remember you in my prayers."

"Thank you, Father," Gary said, trying hard to sound as if he cared. "But in any case, Father Ted will do just fine. Mom said Dad would've wanted him. She'd made up her mind."

Father Chuck smiled. "Good for her. I thought Father Ted was overreacting. I respect him very much, but he's too sensitive. I didn't think your mother would've hardened her heart. She always struck me as very tolerant. It's so good to know people who rise above their opinions."

Sure didn't read Mom very well, Gary thought. "I always try to rise above mine," he answered, not entirely comfortable with the fact. "When I have any, that is."

"That's the spirit," said Father Chuck. He looked toward the chapel, and sighed heavily. "Well, I think I'll go in now. Nice to meet you, Gary."

They shook hands again. "Same here, Father," Gary said. He watched the priest enter the chapel, then drifted over to the aquarium. Another of the angelfish had died.

It was floating at the top.

CHAPTER 7
WORK HAZARDS

AFTER the viewing, Max and Gary and Linda went for dinner with the relatives, to a place called Gallardo's out on Rt. 87., past the canal. The food was good, Uncle Buddy and Dave were abominable, and everyone else was polite—with the exception of Max. Buddy and Dave ignored him.

At seven they returned home to freshen up, then went back to the funeral parlor. The chapel was already open, and there were several people inside. Gary introduced them to his relatives.

"Bob MacAleer and his wife Lou Ann," he said.

Mr. MacAleer, he of cable TV and biblical scholarship fame, rose halfway from his chair and shook hands with everyone he could reach. Lou Ann smiled, a pretty woman on the plump side, rather too heavily made up.

"And that's their son—" Gary snapped his fingers. "Jamie, right?"

Jamie, a porcine eighteen or nineteen by his look, turned briefly, working his hand through a shock of long black hair that was the diametric opposite of his father's patent-leather look; he nodded lackadaisically, as if to say *What do you care?* and turned back around. Six feet away, Gary thought he could smell marijuana on him.

"Didn't I see you on TV this afternoon?" Dave Holland asked Mr. MacAleer.

MacAleer smiled. "Just after *Reanimator?*"

"Yeah. You were talking about the Bible."

"That was me, son."

"I think the Bible's crap," Dave said.

The smile dropped from MacAleer's face.

"And that's Mr. Hersh and Mr. Williams over there," Gary said hurriedly, pointing to two men across the aisle. They came over. "Mr. Hersh owns Hersh's Department Store on Beichmann Avenue . . . "

"Hersh, huh?" Buddy asked. "Must be Jewish or something." He laughed inexplicably.

"B'Nai Brith, circumcision, the works," Hersh said, nodding. "I know some ex-Irgun members you'd probably love to meet . . . "

"Ir-what?" Buddy asked.

"And Mr. Williams here owns the Beichmann Theater," Gary continued.

"He's also President of the local Christian Businessman's Roundtable," Hersh said. "An Evangelical fanatic."

Williams nudged him with an elbow. "Yeah, we fight all the time."

"Sounds unpleasant," said Aunt Lucy.

"We *like* to fight," Williams said. "Arguing's a lot of fun."

"Not the way me and Buddy do it," Lucy cackled.

The conversation wound down rapidly from there.

More people came in. Jack Guillietta, owner of a welding firm that had done business with Max Sr., fell into a long stretch of shop-talk with Buddy and Dennis, who had both been welders before they got into pre-fabs. Max and Gary got up and headed out to the lobby.

"What are we going to do if Buddy invites us out for a drink after the viewing?" Gary asked.

"I'm so tired of him I could puke," Max answered.

"That doesn't answer my question."

Max gave him a hard look. "Yeah it does."

"I see. You mean you're going to leave me alone with him?"

"Uncle Dennis'll be there. But if you want to beg off, say you're worried about Mom, you want to sit up with the phone . . . "

"Won't wash. Not with you and the women home too. How many people do you need to take a call?"

"Say you're just not in the mood."

"He won't take no for an answer. Not from me."

Max smiled wickedly. "Too bad you're not more like *me*. I've been saying no and making it stick as long as I can remember."

"Yeah, you're a real bad ass."

"You're right."

"I think you should come with us," Gary said. "*Please.* Do it for your kid brother."

"Ahhhh . . . "

Gary decided on another tack. "Well then. How about for Uncle Dennis?"

"What?"

"I was talking to him in the men's room at Gallardo's. He really likes you, you know."

"Hmm."

"Says he'd like to know you better."

"Never shows it."

"Not when Buddy's around, no. He doesn't like to say much of anything then. He's afraid Buddy'll make fun of him."

"Then he'll just keep his mouth shut at the bar."

"Yeah, but he just wants to listen. Says he's had some second thoughts about religion. Wants to see how you'd handle Buddy on the subject."

"I'd cut that oaf up four ways from Sunday."

"That's what Dennis thinks. So he's going to start a conversation . . . "

Max seemed to warm to the idea. "How come you didn't mention all his right off the bat?"

"I wanted to see if you'd come just as a favor to me."

"Doing favors has never been one of my strong points...But the prospect of intellectual slaughter . . . " Max laughed fiendishly.

At that moment, a compactly-built blond man in a police uniform came in the front door, hat in hand.

"Jeff Purzycki," Max said. "Haven't seen you in years."

"Bad news about your folks," Jeff said. "They were talking about your mother down at the station."

"Any developments?" Gary asked anxiously.

"Not that I heard."

Gary looked floorward.

"I didn't know you were a cop," Max said.

"Just for the summer," Jeff answered. "Boardwalk patrol, but they've got me on emergency duty tonight."

"What kind?" Max asked.

"Guarding the high school."

"The *high school*?"

"So no one drops in on all those dead Italians in the body bags. There's quite a bit of loot on them, I understand."

"But why are they having a boardwalk cop watch them?"

"Manpower shortage. Haven't you heard the sirens?"

"Yeah."

"It's been one car crash after another. Most of it's been mechanical failure. But there's been some wrecking, too. Oil on the roads. Booby-traps. A felled tree landed in front of a bus out in Pine Township an hour ago. Driver swerved into a lake. Thirty people dead

…The meatwagons have been busy here too. Paramedics have been going bananas. This one guy put his head through a windshield, bounced back into his seat—off comes his whole face, *rrripp!* just like that. Was still on the outside of the glass."

"Somebody's face would just come off like that?" Gary asked.

"Sure," Max said. "Your skin stays on your head because it's like a bag over your skull. It's loose. You can peel it right off."

"Guy choked on his own blood," Jeff said. "Medics didn't reach him in time. Ambulance conked on 'em—"

"About the wrecking," Max said. "Is it just in this area?"

"Nope. It's happening all over the state." Jeff glanced at his watch. "Look, I'd love to stay here and talk with you guys, but I have to be over at the high school in a bit. Won't be able to make the funeral, so I'd better pay my respects now."

"No apology necessary," Max said.

Jeff went inside.

Gary and Max eyed each other.

"You still think Linda's wrong about all this shit being connected?" Gary asked.

"Let's just say I'm less sure," Max replied.

FATHER Ted arrived about a half hour before the viewing ended, accompanied by Father Chuck. He went up to the lectern near the catafalque; all eyes were on him.

He opened with two readings. The first was the story of Lazarus. The second was a passage on reincarnation from the *Bhagavad-Gita,* "One of the many Old Testaments," as Father Ted put it.

All during the second reading, Gary heard Max muttering beside him; he was amazed his brother managed to control himself at all. But an even greater test of Max's patience was to come.

"He is not dead," Father Ted said, closing the Hindu holy book. "Max Holland has only passed on to a higher plane. He has merely been changed. He has gone back to that great World Soul—call it Brahma, call it Allah—"

"Mohammed would be going for his scimitar right now," Max whispered to Gary.

"—Jesus, Buddha, or Diana of Ephesus. And being reunited with that Cosmic Oneness, the very ground of our being, he is reunited with us. When we speak to each other, we are speaking to him. When we pray, we are praying to him. When we make love, we are loving him—"

"Nothing like that old Pantheistic homosexual incest, huh?" Max asked Gary. "Don't it make you want to rush right out and pick up a girl?"

Gary cracked a grin, almost against his will, then wiped it from his face.

"—His strength is in us even now. His zest is our thanksgiving, just as our oneness is his multiplicity—"

"No wonder we're so confused," Max said.

"He was a good man," Father Ted went on. "Not in some moralistic sense, but in the sense that he was fully alive, trusting in himself and others, willing to listen to God, the voice of all of us in Him . . . "

"I can't take this any more," Max said.

"Come on, Max," Gary said. "Dad would've wanted it this way."

"Gary, if I stay here a minute longer, I'm going to start yelling at that theological eunuch." And with that, Max got up and walked out of the chapel.

Father Ted appeared to take no notice, and droned on for another fifteen minutes. When he was done, Gary heard Uncle Buddy say to his wife:

"Not a bad talker, for one of those Holy Joes. At least he's open-minded."

AS it turned out, Mr. Van Nuys got word about the gravediggers before the viewing ended; there would be no wildcat strike Thursday, because it was almost certain the whole union would be going out on Friday. He gave this news to Gary as the chapel emptied out; Gary's relief showed plainly on his face.

Once the mourners were gone, Van Nuys's assistants closed the coffin, and left soon afterward. Van Nuys retreated to his office to pay some bills.

After an hour or so of invoices he paused, rubbing his eyes, and swiveled his chair, looking out the window that faced the Elk's Hall, a large spotlit building across the parking lot.

The activity over there had died down. During the day, a flood of peple had descended on the hall, relatives and friends come to claim bodies from the train-wreck. Their numbers had dwindled around dinner-time, but there was another surge after seven which had petered out around ten. At one time, the Elks' parking lot, which was behind the hall, had been packed. Now there was only one cop car, and a dark sedan belonging to the town's medical examiner.

Suddenly the sirens started up again, and before long a policeman came running out of the Elks' Hall, got into his car, and sped off. The medical examiner followed soon after. What was going on now? And had anyone been left to watch the bodies? Van Nuys guessed there must be someone still in the building—the cop's partner, perhaps.

The sirens howled for quite some time. Van Nuys watched Beichmann Avenue. Two police cars came screaming along, a couple of ambulances following shortly.

He turned back to his work, but made little progress; the lights began flashing on and off, something they'd done periodically all evening. Finally they went out altogether. The Elk's Hall and every house nearby were totally dark. Moonlight shone from the hall's windows and the white-painted border running around its base.

Can't work if you can't see, Van Nuys told himself. *Think you should just go ho—*

Across the way, a basement window was rising. He leaned forward, squinting.

Somebody lock himself in? he wondered. He knew the basement hall as well as the main level was being used for morgue space, and he could just imagine some poor cop locked up in the dark down there with fifty or a hundred stone-dead strangers. Used as he was to corpses, Van Nuys wouldn't have been too upset, but he rather enjoyed the thought of a layman stuck in such a situation . . .

The window was all the way up now. He waited for someone to climb out, but there was no sign of movement.

Then, with feverish haste, something came scuttling through, dark against the painted border. Van Nuys's first impression was that it was too spidery to be human, although it was far too big to be a spider. He blinked, shaking his head.

The shadow jittered upright, unmistakably human now, not a cop, but a guy in a sports jacket that hung loosely on his very skinny frame. He set off across Van Nuys's parking lot, moving at a swift stiff-legged run toward the back of the funeral parlor, out of sight to the left.

Van Nuys sat awhile in silence. Presently he heard a banging from out behind the parlor, and a wrench like metal being torn. Had the man forced his way into the garage or the service entrance? Van Nuys had had his hearse stolen, and his workshop attracted morbid teenager prowlers. There was also the safe upstairs . . .

He decided to call the police, but couldn't get a dial-tone. Cursing, he slammed the phone back in the cradle.

As if to compensate, the lights came back on.

He looked at the Elk's Hall, wondering if there was indeed a cop over there. It was still dark on the main floor; the place looked dead.

He heard a thump downstairs, in his workshop.

Service entrance, he thought.

Opening his desk, he took out the .38 Colt Super automatic he had gotten as a Navy pilot back in World War II. He went quietly to the door leading to the stairs and opened it, passing along a short corridor and stopping at the stair head.

The light was on below. He could hear whispering and a rustle of cloth.

"I'm telling you right now," he said, "you get the hell out of here. I've got a gun." To emphasize his point, he pulled back the action on the automatic, *clack!*

The whispering stopped, though the rustling went on for a few more seconds...then came footsteps, a squeal of hinges, and the ringing slam of a metal door.

Van Nuys looked out the window beside him, saw that spidery guy, illuminated by streetlight now, speed across the parking lot and slip with an indescribable movement back into the window he'd come out of. The window slid down behind.

Easing the hammer forward on the pistol, Van Nuys started down the steps, wondering what the intruder had been up to. When he came out from under the basement ceiling, he saw that Mr. Bullerton, whom he'd worked on that afternoon, had his sheet pulled down to his knees. Several of Van Nuys's tools, a pair of long scissors, a probe, and a large detached embalming needle, were embedded in Bullerton's chest, all of them gleaming wickedly. Bullerton's genitalia had been cut off. They were sitting in his upturned right palm.

"Psycho *bastard*," Van Nuys said...reaching the bottom of the steps, he went to take a closer look at the corpse's face. The tiny threads holding the lips together had been sliced, and the mouth had sagged open a bit, revealing a smiling row of dry grayish teeth; the threads holding one of the eyes closed had been cut as well, and the cotton stuffing the eyesocket had been partially pulled out.

But worst of all was the forehead. In bold bloodless strokes the words YOU'RE DEAD had been carved into it.

Mr. Van Nuys was so outraged that it was a moment or two before he asked himself: how could the prowler have done so much damage in such a short time?

It occurred to Van Nuys that the man might've gotten in before. The undertaker went up the ramp to the service entrance. The double doors were closed, but in the middle, both were twisted and ripped. Going outside, he examined their outer faces. The lock, latch and all, had been wrenched out. Surely that had been the squealing-metal sound he'd heard. The prowler must've entered then, for the first time.

Van Nuys closed the doors and went back down the ramp, pausing to take a last look round the workroom. The DeWitts, a middle-aged couple and their thirtyish daughter, were still on their tables, sheets pulled over them, no sign of mischief. They'd died in a car accident Sunday night, and his struggle to restore their faces had been herculean. He'd been bitterly disappointed when the viewings were cancelled, due to the disappearance of several other family members; he'd wanted very much for everyone to marvel over the wonders he'd performed.

Suddenly it occurred to him that the DeWitts might've been mutilated too, then covered again. He went over and checked them. As far as he could tell, they were undamaged.

He started back to the stairs, headed to the top. Would the phone be working now, perhaps? He came to the stairhead, walked up the corridor—

And heard faint laughter.

From behind.

He stopped and turned, cursing softly. The .38's hammer clicked as he cocked it again.

He returned to the steps and went slowly back down. He looked around cautiously at the bottom, but saw no one. The service doors were still closed. He hadn't caught the slightest squeak of hinges; the prowler couldn't have returned.

Then where in hell did that laugh come from? He asked himself—just before it came again, dry and toneless.

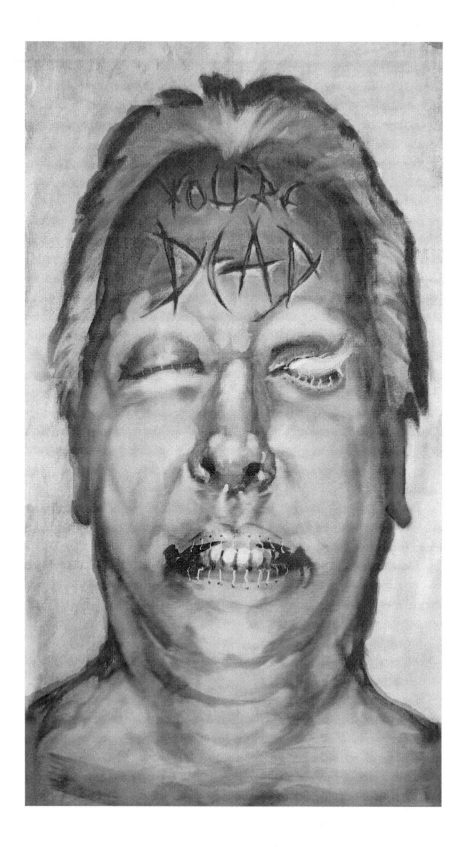

He spun. There was only the table with Jackie DeWitt on it. Could someone be hiding underneath?

"I'm a crack shot," he warned. Going to Jackie's table, he crouched, licking his lips. They were dust dry. He considered firing a couple of rounds through the sheet, but decided against it. Gathering his courage, he jerked the sheet up and thrust the pistol forward.

Nothing.

Breathing rapidly, he straightened, scratching his head, staring down at Jackie DeWitt. The sheet had sagged over her mouth, which was apparently wide open. Had the threads in her lips been cut after all?

But even if they had, that did not explain why her mouth began to open and shut, teeth snicking.

Bastard's under the sheet, was his first thought, but he instantly dismissed it: Jackie's figure was unmistakable even under the cloth.

What in—

A cold hard hand flashed up from under the sheet and locked on his throat, pulling him down toward the mouth working under the cloth. He gave a choking cry and fired the .38 again and again into the body on the table, the gunshots agonizingly loud so close to his ear. Fluid splattered him; the reek of formaldehyde filled his nostrils.

The clip emptied. He was still being pulled downward. He tried to throw himself back, but it was useless; a second hand shot up, slapped onto the nape of his neck and clamped tight. The first shifted to the back of his head, leaving his throat wide open for the clicking jaws. He fought to pull the hands away, brought his free fist and the butt of the automatic down on the shrouded face. The hands jerked powerfully in response, forcing his head and neck all the way down. His Adam's apple was right over the mouth now. He felt the jaws stretch wide to receive his throat. The hands shoved, and the cloth-shrouded teeth locked his Adam's apple between them, gripping it with agonizing, but not yet crushing force. He winced, closing his eyes.

Cloth flapped in other parts of the room, sheets being tossed aside. He opened his eyes again. Peripheral vision told him the elder DeWitts' nearby tables were empty. Two voices whispered and laughed behind him. Footsteps hurried close.

This is impossible, his mind shrieked. *This is a night—*

Pain blotted his thoughts out for a moment as two more sets of jaws clamped onto him, one on either shoulder. His whole body shook as his attackers worried his flesh, snarling. Fabric tore; teeth dug through skin. Fingers scrabbled, ripping the arms of his jacket to shreds, baring more hide. With a sound like tape being peeled from a roll, a raw stripe of pain tore its way down to his left hand.

A moment later something warm and wet slapped across his face. It struck him again, then dangled before his eyes, a long curling ribbon, tan on one side, red on the other. He clearly recognized his LIBERTY OR DEATH tattoo on it.

The jaws on his throat began to close. Cartilage crunched. His breath whistled as more and more of his air was pinched off.

He died praying for a heart attack.

CHAPTER 8
PHYS ED

THE bar was called Richie's, a dark smoky joint down by the fisheries, and Uncle Buddy's topic was shopping malls.

"Best I ever saw was the Court at King of Prussia," he said, and took a swig of his beer. "Better'n anything out near Pittsburgh, even the one they filmed that stupid horror picture at . . . " He let out a thunderous belch.

"*Dawn of the Dead,*" said Gary beside him.

"Anyway, this King of Prussia place, it's really incredible. Me and Dennis and the wives spent one Saturday afternoon there. The whole Goddamn afternoon!"

"It really *is* something," Dennis told Max earnestly.

Max nodded.

Buddy continued: "There was this store. It was called Ceramics Unlimited, I think. They had these statues, oh, about yay high—" he held his hand about two feet above the bar, "—Of all these celebrities and movie stars. John Wayne, Laurel and Hardy, W.C. Fields, everyone. And the faces really looked like 'em too, right down to the last detail.

"But the wildest thing was the size of their heads. Real big heads, almost life-size. Great detail. Hell, you could practically see the pores in their skin."

"Always wanted to see John Wayne's pores," Max said.

"This would've been the place for you," Buddy said, apparently missing Max's sarcasm. "My favorite was a big head Louie Armstrong. Just incredible. Him wiping his face off with a handkerchief, just like in real life—lots of little trickles of sweat.

"Now when I laid eyes on that thing, it was love at first sight, let me tell you. I said to Lucy, 'Honey, I've just gotta have that, no matter how much it costs,' and I shut her up good when she complained; plunked down the forty five bucks, and walked out of there with my very own Louie Armstrong tucked under my arm. It's on my mantelpiece back home, place of honor. Wouldn't be parted from it for the world. Ain't it amazing, Dennis?"

"That's the word, all right," Dennis said, less than enthusiastically.

"But what I remember most about the store was the religious stuff. All those statues of the Virgin Mary and everything."

Gary glanced over at him. Was that how Dennis was going to drag God into the conversation? It seemed wonderfully unsubtle, but then again, Buddy had no idea he was being set up.

"Didn't make an impression on me," Buddy said.

"Well, it wouldn't," Dennis said. "Seeing what you think of religion."

"Don't get me started on that," Buddy said. "I could talk all night. But seeing as how we've got a couple of Pope Celia's boys here, I'll lay off."

"Don't let me stop you," Gary said. "I stopped being a Catholic a long time ago."

"I didn't," Max said. "But don't let that stop you either, Uncle Buddy."

"Sure you can take it?" Buddy laughed.

"Try me," Max said.

"Don't want to hurt your feelings."

"I don't bruise easily."

"Well, I'm glad you're not sensitive about it. Religious people get really touchy, you know?"

"No," Max said. "Explain it to me."

"Well, most of 'em are kind of fanatics. Falwell, Khomeini . . . people like that."

"I see," Max said. "Let me see if I understand you correctly. Do you think there's something intrinsic to religion that encourages people to be fanatics?"

"Well, seeing how religious folks act . . . yeah."

"So you think there's something in the teachings of let's say, Jesus, that turns people rabid? The Sermon on the Mount, for example?"

"Never met a Christian that paid the slightest attention to it," Buddy declared.

"Make up your mind, Buddy. Are Christian fanatics acting on Jesus's teachings? Or ignoring them?"

"What difference does it make?"

"The difference between Mother Theresa and Torquemada."

"Torquemada?" Buddy asked.

"Spanish grand inquisitor," Max answered. "You wouldn't have liked him. Exactly the sort of guy you're talking about . . . You *do* know

84

who Mother Theresa is, don't you?"

"Yeah," Buddy said, sounding nettled.

"Well then. Since there's so much difference in the conduct of various ostensibly religious people, why do you assume it's the religion that corrupts the people, and not vice-versa?"

"Because when religious people go bad, they're so much worse than anyone else."

"Is that so?"

"Yeah. You mentioned that Torquemada guy. Look at the Spanish Inquisition."

Gary groaned inwardly. *Worst move yet, Buddy,* he thought. He'd heard Max unload on this topic too many times in the past; Max was a dedicated historian of atrocities. Buddy had a double-barreled shotgun pointed straight at his face, and didn't even realize it.

Max flashed Buddy a sharklike smile. "Okay, let's. Its peak activity was during the final years of the *Reconquista*, and just afterward—"

"*Reconquista?*" Buddy asked.

"The reconquest of Spain from the Moors. The Inquisition wound up with a lot of Moslems and Jews to liquidate. Between 1481 and 1540, the Holy Office killed about twenty thousand people. Sound bad?"

"Are you going to tell me it's not?"

"Hell no. But why don't we put its achievements in perspective? When it comes to murder, atheists have got the religious folks beat all hollow…The bloodiest killers in history, the *worst of the worst*, were twentieth-century freethinkers. Squarely on your side of the fence."

"Bullshit."

"Well, let's compare. The Spanish Inquisition's supposed to be right up there, isn't it? But its record pales beside Lenin's, for example. Between famine brought on by requisition, and outright murder, he was responsible for about five million unnatural deaths between 1917 and 1921. And the killing followed quite logically from his philosophy. He once wrote, 'The scientific concept of dictatorship'—that is, of the dictatorship of the proletariat—'Is nothing less than this: acquisition of total power by the party, untrammeled by laws or morality, and based directly on violence.' He wasn't joking. His followers weren't joking either.

"Consider Stalin. Under his leadership, 14.5 million people were exterminated between 1930 and 1934 during collectivization. As many as were killed *on all sides* during World War I. In 1936 he got cracking again, bumped off millions more. During World War Two he murdered nearly as many Soviets as were killed by Hitler during the same period—and that includes the casualties inflicted on the Red Army by the Nazis. And after the war, another massive purge began, on the typical Stalin scale.

"In short, between 1917 and 1953, the Bolsheviks, atheists all, killed one out of every four people in the Soviet Union. *Stalin alone* may have killed sixty million. Now the Spanish Inquisition could've been operating full blast during that entire period, and it only would've piled up about twelve thousand bodies."

Buddy was silent, glaring at him. "Science says religion is bunk," he said at last. "I took biology in high school, you know. What about Darwin?"

Max laughed. "What about him? Do you think for one instant that I'm going to let you change the subject and slip off the hook? If you didn't want to talk about comparative body-counts, you shouldn't have brought up religious fanaticism. And speaking of body-counts—" he took a gulp of Heineken and cracked his knuckles, "It's about time we dragged the reigning Prince of Darkness into this. Everyone's favorite, Adolf Hitler."

"Hitler was a Christian."

"Wrong, Buddy. He was another student of Lenin, by his own admission—only his socialism was the *national* variety. He despised Christian morality; when asked why he rejected it, he replied that Darwin—there's that name again—had destroyed Christian cosmology, so what reason was there for paying attention to the ethics? Good point: rack up another twelve million stiffs. More if you want to count the combat deaths.

"And how about Mao-Tse-Tung? He killed seventy million in China; one out of every ten people in the country. Pol Pot killed one out of every three in Cambodia, in two years, no less. Now that's shootin', even by atheist standards. Then there's this Mengistu scumbag in Ethiopia. What a card—"

Max went on in this vein for several minutes more.

"None of this is in any way meant to exonerate all those inquisitors or crusaders," he wound up. "I'm sure they did the best with what was available to them, philosophically speaking. But only through considerable mental gymnastics. The inquisitors were saddled with the

Sermon on the Mount whether they liked it or not. And it showed in their work. They could never be *wholehearted* about murder—at least without totally rejecting their faith.

"But what restrains atheists? According to their own lights, they can do whatever they please. True, most cling to morality as tightly as any believer; but then there are the *rational* ones. The ones who act on their assumptions. Like Pol Pot. And if you wanted a preview of Hell, you couldn't do better than Cambodia in 1976."

Gary looked at Buddy. It was plain that his uncle had never encountered such a steamroller before; Buddy's eyes shone with awe and hatred. Gary knew from Dennis that Buddy considered himself a kind of rough-hewn philosopher—an unfortunate self-image for such a lout.

"You really think you know it all, don't you Max?" Buddy demanded.

"No," Max replied.

"Think you can walk all over me because you're a college boy?"

"Hey, I thought you were going to hurt *my* feelings."

"You want me to hurt your feelings?" Buddy asked loudly.

Seeing how ugly things had gotten, Gary began to feel genuinely uncomfortable.

"No," Max said.

"You want me to ride roughshod over you, college boy?" Buddy asked. "I'll tell you what I *really* think. I think that Catholic religion you believe in is pure garbage." He grinned smugly, as if he had just landed a truly devastating blow.

"Wow," Max said.

"You know what else I think? I think all those priests and nuns you kiss-ass to are a bunch of fags and dykes."

"Hey Buddy, come on," Dennis said. "That's enough."

"Your broad-mindedness is impressing me no end," Max told Buddy.

Just then a hand clapped down on Buddy's shoulder. Buddy turned. So did Gary and Dennis. Max stared down into his Heineken.

Standing in front of Buddy was a massive bull-necked fellow with short bristly hair on a bullet skull, his short-sleeved shirt revealing two long muscular arms.

"You know," the bruiser told Buddy, "I've been listening to you, loudmouth, and I think you'd better shut your trap. I'm a Catholic. And my sister's a nun."

"How about your mother?" Buddy laughed.

"Why don't you just leave my mother out of this? Isn't it enough that you called my sister a dyke?"

"Well, what do you want me to do? Apologize?"

"Why don't you keep your fucked-up opinions to yourself?"

"And what if I don't?"

The man folded his bulging arms on his chest. "You're gonna find yourself wearing your jaw for a hat."

"Really? Think you can do it to me yourself? Won't you have to call your sister? I hear those dykes are pretty tough—"

Buddy barely got the last word out when the man's malletlike right fist struck his cheek with a meaty smack. Buddy rocked sideways onto Gary, then slid to the floor. The man came forward; Gary put himself between him and Buddy, who was trying to get back to his feet.

"Just hold on now—" Gary began.

The man hit him in the left eye.

Shocked by the pain, Gary responded with a clumsy right. The man blocked it, grabbed Gary by the lapel, and pounded him repeatedly in the stomach.

Suddenly the blows stopped. Someone had the fellow by the arm. Left eye already closing up on him, Gary looked to see who it was. It was Max. Letting Gary go, pulling his arm from Max's grip, the bruiser turned to face him, growling.

"Why don't we just call this quits now, huh?" Max asked, stepping back. "One Catholic to another?"

The other answered with a scream, charging, but Max stopped him dead with a straight right to the nose, which the guy clapped two beefy hands over . . . Max hit him in the stomach, the hands came down, and the man doubled over with a belch. Max straightened him with an uppercut to the chin, then drove three trip hammer jabs into that already wrecked beak, each one landing with a mushy *quish*. . .the reeling recipient, nostrils streaming red, reached groggily for a beer-bottle on the bar, but before his fingers could close on it, Max hit him with another uppercut that lifted him clean off his feet. The man sailed backward to the floor, unconscious.

"Get him!" someone cried.

Max turned. Gary, who'd gotten to his feet by this time, saw three goons who'd been sitting with Max's victim now rushing toward Max. Max moved to meet them, kicking a chair out of his way. Heading for the one in the center, he veered at the last moment toward the man on the left, blasting him down with a right cross before giving the middle guy an elbow to the cheek and flinging him aside. The last unfortunate caught a straight kick below the ribcage, and, cheeks puffed out as the air blew from his lungs, went back with a distinct bootprint in his shirt…He landed on a table, tipping it over, and bringing a small avalanche of half-empty glasses clattering down on him. Beer splashed everywhere as he thumped to the carpet and lay still.

The fight was over before Gary and Dennis could join in. Max looked round at them.

"We were going to help, really," Dennis said.

"I believe you," Max said. "Let's get out of here."

"What about the damages?" the bartender demanded.

Max squinted at him. "What damages?"

"The glasses on that table."

"Chickenshit," Max answered. "Besides, I didn't start the damn fight."

"Oh, what the hell," Uncle Dennis said, went to the bartender, and handed him a fifty.

The man who'd been kicked in the chest moaned. Max trained his eyes back on him. The fellow got up and stumbled for the door. His friends were still out cold.

Uncle Buddy, however, had come round by that time; Gary and Dennis helped him out to the car. Dennis drove.

"Hey Max," he said, "they teach you to fight like that in the Marines?"

"You got it the wrong way round," Gary said. "He taught *them*."

"What was he, a hand-to-hand instructor?"

"Yep. They decided he had a real vocation after he put *his* instructor in the hospital at Camp Lejeune. Isn't that right, Max?"

"Yeah," Max said. "Not bad for a college boy, huh?"

Dennis laughed appreciatively. Buddy just mumbled.

They reached home. The women made a great deal of fuss over Gary's and Buddy's hurts. Thoroughly humiliated, Buddy went down into the rec room with a beer, an ice-pack, and a bottle of Advil.

Some time afterward, Gary sat down on the living-room couch beside Uncle Dennis.

"So how did you like Max's arguments?" he asked.

"He handled Buddy pretty well," Dennis said.

"Yeah. But that's no big deal if you ask me."

"*I've* never been able to answer him that way," Dennis replied. "He just starts with his jokes and insults, and I get confused. He knows more about history than I do, too. But Max sure let him have it." He chuckled. "You know, it might not sound like it, but I really love Buddy."

Gary looked at him sidelong.

"I really do," Dennis insisted. "He's my brother, and I guess I can see some things in him that other people can't."

"Aunt Lucy loves him," Gary admitted, and glanced out into the kitchen. The women were talking heatedly about something; Linda noticed him looking their way, and smiled.

"But even though I love him, I think he has a lot to learn," Dennis went on. "And I have to admit, I like watching him get put down every once in a while."

"I thought you were searching for the ultimate truth and all that."

"That too." Dennis paused. "Aren't you interested in the truth, Gary?"

Gary laughed. "Not till it comes up and sinks its teeth into my leg. Then, just maybe."

JEFF Purzycki was very much alone—unless you wanted to count the two hundred and fifty corpses on the other side of the gym's double doors. But Jeff preferred not to think of them as company.

He hadn't been the only warm body when he arrived. Jack Bingham, the man Jeff had been sent to relieve, was there, as well as an assistant coroner, and three Italians from North Jersey who'd had relatives on the plane. The family members and the coroner had gone in to look at some of the stiffs in the zippered black body-bags.

While they were inside, Jack had told Jeff that none of the bodies had been claimed; the airline situation had made it impossible for anyone to come over from Italy. Because of potential health hazards, the corpses were going to be moved out the following afternoon to a big out-of-business meat-packing plant up in Long Branch.

"Good fucking riddance," Jack had said. "Get 'em the hell out of here."

Jeff laughed. "What's the matter? Scared?"

"Nah. It's just—I don't know. I was here alone for a while, and I thought—"

"Thought what?"

"Forget it. I must be cracking up."

Before Jeff could press him any further, the coroner and the others came out, and Jack left with them. Jeff wasn't particularly concerned about what Jack had said. Jack had always been a crazy son of a bitch.

Now Jeff was wandering around the gym lobby, inspecting the basketball trophies in the glass case and the plaques on the walls, remembering his futile efforts on the court back in high school. After a time he pulled up a chair and sat down, got the paperback he'd started out of his lunchbox, and began to read.

The book was a big fat wad by one of his favorite authors, a man who, regrettably, seemed to have been losing his mind lately. Jeff had slogged through almost to the end before learning that the menace, which adopted such less-than-terrifying forms as Michael Landon in *I Was a Teenage Werewolf*, could be defeated by belief in anything, literally anything. Faith in the Tooth Fairy would do. Biting into the monster's tongue and thinking of jokes would also. Reaching the point where it became clear that the monster was actually a giant (shivers!) spider, he tossed the book back in his lunchbox and got out a sandwich—pastrami and Swiss with pickles.

Sirens in the distance. Nothing unusual about that, considering what the rest of the night had been like. But this time the wailing just went on and on. He decided to call the station.

There was a pay-phone in the lobby, but he had no change. Carrying his half-eaten sandwich, he left the lobby and went around to the parking-lot, got into his station wagon—summer cops didn't rate patrol cars—and called in.

"Train wreck," Sgt. Masterson explained.

"*Another?* Where?"

"Same place."

"What? Was it deliberate?"

"We don't know yet."

"How many dead?"

"Don't know that either."

"You guys need me?" Jeff asked.

"Just stay put."

Jeff hung the mouthpiece up and sat in silence, finishing his sandwich, mulling over what Masterson had said. Then he got out and went back toward the gym lobby.

As he rounded the corner of the building, he saw three teenagers by the lobby entrance, one in the process of going inside.

They want a peek at the bodies, Jeff thought.

"Hey!" he cried.

They bolted. Shaking his head, laughing quietly, Jeff jogged up the walk and went back into the lobby.

Suddenly he was aware he had to take a leak; he'd had several beers before coming on duty. The john was halfway down the dark hallway adjoining the lobby; he started toward the corridor, then paused—he didn't want to come back and find those kids inside. Turning, he noticed a chained padlock hanging from one of the doors. Closing the doors, he chained the release-bars together, then went to the head.

When he returned, the lights were sputtering. He'd been considering going back to his book—he had, after all, invested so much time in it already—but decided to wait until the power company got its act together.

What to do in the meantime? He had a transistor radio out in the car. He could get it and listen to K Rock up in New York. But would there still be all those bursts of static?

He made for the doors, remembered the padlock, and started fishing for the key ring Jack had given him. Looking at the keys, he couldn't remember which one opened the padlock. Oh well; he could just go through and try them. There were only thirty or so of the little—

A faint crackling noise reached him. He looked back at the doors to the gym.

Plastic crumpling, he thought.

The meaning of that did not sink in at first. Then there was suddenly a frozen place in his stomach.

Too many horror novels, he told himself. Still, he listened closely. For the next minute there was only silence. Had he heard anything at all?

With a shrug he went to the lobby doors and started fitting the keys to the lock. But at length he paused, his thoughts wandering back to that noise.

And the way Jack had been behaving.

I'm telling you, too many fucking hor—

The sound again.

Jeff straightened, leaving the last key stuck in the lock, the other keys jingling as the ring swayed back and forth.

"There is *nothing* going on in there," he said. Determined to prove it to himself, he turned and crossed resolutely to the gym doors, looking in through one of the little square windows.

The gym lights were off; the only illumination came through the door windows on the far side, flecks of it gleaming off the black plastic shrouding the bodies. The foreground was completely dark.

He thought of going in and turning on the overheads; the situation would be much less unnerving if he could see very clearly how those two hundred and fifty corpses were doing just what corpses should. His hand drifted to the handle of one of the doors—

And drifted back again. He simply couldn't muster the will.

But hell, what did that matter? Why make such a concession to his fears?

The lights steadied. He returned to his chair and sat down, determined now to try and submerge himself in his book. So what if it called itself a horror novel? There hadn't been too much evidence of that. Certainly nothing to put him more on edge.

If they come after me, he thought, *I'll just think about the Tooth Fairy.*

Yet he hadn't read much farther when the lights went dead. A silvery moonglow came in through the lobby doors, startlingly bright, though not enough to read by. If only he'd brought his flashlight; that too was out in the car.

He recalled that he'd left the keys in the door. Now was as good a time as any to work through them again—

Before the shit hits the fan, Jeff? Before those soggy ole wops come clawing out of those bags and pay you a little visit?

"I must be cracking up," he laughed nervously.

And then remembered Jack saying exactly the same thing.

Laying the book down, he walked back to the door, pulled out the key in the slot, and started trying the rest. He was almost through the bunch when one of the wrong ones snapped off in his trembling hand, leaving the business end jammed in the lock.

Cursing, he took out his Swiss Army knife. Using the tweezers, he tried to pull the end of the key out. His hands were shaking so hard that he succeeded only in dropping the tiny pincers. They chimed softly as they struck the floor.

He bent and searched. Finding them, he straightened and set to work again, but had no luck. He went through most of the pointed implements on the army knife, trying to pry the key-end out. Nothing worked.

"Shit," he said.

At least there haven't been any more noises.

He ran his hand over the back of his neck, thinking. There were other doors. But he'd just have to go through the keyring again—Jack had told him they were all chained too.

Whoever they send to relieve me is going to laugh his ass off, he thought.

There was a saw on his knife. Would it be possible to cut through the chain? Not too likely, he decided—

Faint crackling from the gym.

Icewater spurted into his veins. He heard a low sound like a throat being cleared, then a quiet splash.

Just trying to get the seawater out of his lungs, that's all . . .

He reached for his pistol and unsnapped the strap, suddenly wishing he was a lot better with a gun. He'd always liked the fact that standards for summer cops were pretty lax. Now he thought that everyone had been way too easy on him.

A popping sound reached him.

Plastic ripping, he thought. Then came whispering, like wind across leaves.

He stood perfectly still by the lobby doors, hand on holster, breath tight in his throat. The whispering faded. And after a time, to his immeasurable relief, the lights flashed back to life.

He looked toward the gym doors, noticed there was a lock. He crossed the lobby swiftly, twisted the knob, heard the bar slide into place with a dull *clunk.*

He went to make one last stab at getting the lock unjammed, accomplished nothing. At length he decided he'd have to try and get one of the other doors open. Then he'd take up his post there, or come round front to meet whoever relieved him. Remembering which key he'd used, of course . . .

But wouldn't he be acting like a frightened kid? How would he explain why he wasn't at his assigned station? Would Bingham have been talking? Would they decide Bingham had given him the willies? Would a man who was scared of ghosts be a likely candidate for a job next summer?

He decided on a compromise. He'd go back to the gym-door windows, listen hard, stare into the gym till he couldn't take it anymore. If he heard anything, he'd find himself that other post.

And if he saw anything, he'd shoot the lock off the lobby doors, fuck waiting for his replacement.

Slowly he strode across the lobby. He expected at any moment to hear whispers or crackling, almost caught himself hoping to hear something, *anything* that would justify a full retreat.

The dead didn't oblige. Maybe they were just playing with him, lying inside those bags with big goddamn grins on their faces, waiting till he was looking right in at them, so he could see them all sit up at once, all two hundred and fifty of them . . .

So why are you doing this, asshole? he thought, halting.

BUT he was already at the doors.

Because I'm not going to let myself slip over the edge. Not till I've taken one last look.

He unholstered his pistol, a Smith and Wesson .357 Mag. He eased forward, looking through the glass. The same scene met his eye the second time around . . . Or did it? Were those ragged edges showing on those bundles at the far side? Had the bags been opened? From inside?

He squinted. Reflections on the window partly obscured his view; slipping the pistol into his belt, he put his hands up on either side of his face, trying to block the light out. Still he couldn't tell.

He slid the pistol free again, keeping his face up against the glass. He stared for a long time, growing steadily calmer. He caught no hint of movement. No sounds either. Then—

Laughter.

Wet bubbling laughter.

Over on the far side of the gym, one of the bodies sat up, still wrapped in trailing rags of plastic. Two more sat up beside it in quick succession. The laughter grew louder, accompanied by coughing and spitting.

Jeff grimaced with terror. Wondering how he'd been stupid enough to stand there so long, he started to turn.

Glass splintered. A talonlike hand thrust through the window, seized his arm. He had a glimpse of a shadowy face on the other side of the broken pane before he snapped off four quick shots through the door. The hand on his arm jerked away, nails raking furrows in his flesh.

He whirled and raced for the lobby doors. Behind, he could hear the gym echoing with a series of deafening shrieks, its doors booming under a pounding assault.

He aimed his gun at the padlock, fired the last two shots in the cylinder; but he was up against a Yale lock, and the damn thing insisted on doing its duty, blissfully impervious to the slugs. It occurred to him he'd do better trying to shoot the chain away, aimed his pistol accordingly—and felt his heart skip a beat as the hammer clicked on an empty chamber.

Wood squealed and splintered behind him. He turned and ran into the adjoining hall. His footbeats echoed like hammerblows in the corridor, but the noise was almost drowned out by the sounds from the gym; he heard the doors bang flat against the floor, and the screams, unmuffled now, swelled horribly in volume.

As Jeff ran, he tried to reload, but his arm had been ripped so deeply that he could hardly control his hand, and his fingers were slippery with blood; he dropped three bullets before deciding it was useless.

He reached a bend in the corridor, raced round it. A doorway appeared up ahead, a moonlit rectangle. He just might reach it in time.

Let it be unlocked. Oh God, let it be unlocked . . .

He began to grow dizzy from pain and blood loss. Warm fluid cascaded down his arm, spattering his trouser legs, tapping his Frye-boots like rain.

He neared the doors. The sound of pursuit grew suddenly louder; the shriekers had rounded the bend. It wouldn't be long before they were on him.

He skidded to a halt near the exit, almost falling over.

The doors were chained.

Making one last desperate effort to reload the gun, he fished out a bullet, felt it squirt from between his bloodied fingers, knew he was finished—then realized the bullet had gone into the cylinder. Snapping the wheel closed, he fired at the chain.

The slug passed into the center of a link, bulged its sides without breaking it. Glass shattered in a moonlit spiderweb beneath the release-bar.

He cursed, dropped to his knees, and slammed the pistol-butt into the bullet hole. The glass broke, but it was latticed with tiny steel wires, shatterproof; as the shrieks and footbeats came closer, he struck out again and again, enlarging the hole. When it seemed wide enough, he launched himself headfirst at the opening, felt a brief moment of elation as it allowed him through—

All except his right foot. His trouser cuff had caught on a tooth of glass.

He jerked his leg. Glass snapped, and his foot came forward. He stood up, panting.

A hand clamped onto his ankle, yanking with terrific force. He flailed down on his belly, the hand pulling him back toward the hole in the glass.

He was lying on the landing of a concrete stair. He threw his hands out, tossing the pistol away, fingers locking over the lip of the top step.

The gun clattered down toward the parking-lot.

The yanking on his leg grew stronger. Three brutal tugs, and his knee and hip were savagely dislocated. He gasped as his good hand and his all-but limp one gave way, and he was dragged back toward the door on his chin, screaming, struggling. He managed to flop over onto his side, almost onto his back, and before he could be pulled inside, set his free foot against the doorway's central post, delaying the inevitable for an instant. Then a hand locked onto that foot, dislodged it, and he was wrenched into the screaming darkness.

He swung his fists wildly, striking out at the shadows clustering round him. They grabbed his arms, pressed him flat against the floor. A frigid mouth pushed up against his ear.

"*Mille regretti*," said a ragged female voice. Then the mouth went to his lips, tongue probing.

CHAPTER 9
GONE BUT NOT FORGOTTEN

ARRIVING for work in the morning, Mr. Van Nuys's assistants, Frank and Rodger Debuque, had to let themselves in with their own keys, but they saw nothing sinister in their boss's absence; occasionally the old man had been known to take an unannounced furlough, usually involving a lot of liquor, a blowsy whore, and a motel out on Rt. 87.

As they made their rounds about the building, they discovered nothing out of the ordinary. Mr. Bullerton's condition might have tipped them off, but the tools had been removed from his chest, the sheet pulled up over his mutilated face. All seemed in order with the DeWitts as well.

As for the unfortunate Mr. Van Nuys, he was tucked away in an unused ventilation shaft, curled in a fetal position.

Over at the high school, Jeff Purzycki's blood had been mopped up, and the men sent to replace him found no trace of his body. He'd been shoved into a storm sewer nearby.

But covering up all signs of the night's events had proved impossible. There were the broken gym doors, and the shattered glass door which Jeff had tried to escape through; also all those ripped-open body bags. Still, without evidence that Jeff had been killed, everything pointed to him having done all the damage himself. He had certainly fired those shots through the gym doors. The fact that the doors had been smashed down from inside *was* perplexing— though not, perhaps, beyond explanation.

Jack Bingham's theory, that those 'dead wops' had done it all, was summarily dismissed. So was Jack. Later that day the merits of his theory would be all too obvious, a vindication he'd take no comfort in.

Outside Bayside Point, across America and the world, similar mysteries were unfolding. In some places, explanations like Bingham's had already gained astonished acceptance.

But the news was slow in spreading. The attention of the media was elsewhere, fixed on several transportation disasters, the most horrific of which was a nerve gas spill in Colorado which had already claimed five thousand lives. Several other stories had priority over the hysteria about the walking dead: fish and wildlife kills, problems with complicated technology, and a group of astronomers getting hot and bothered over a small but significant drop in the sun's radiant energy

PREPARING for the funeral, Gary and Max and Linda were unaware of all this. They were so busy rushing about the house, getting dressed and making meals, they hadn't turned on the TV. Even if they had, reception would've been alternately bad and nonexistent.

The morning drew on toward ten, and they went out to Gary's Pinto. The first thing Gary noticed was the chill in the air. Even by the standards of the cold snap, the day was brisk; there was a definite reddening of the leaves on the neighborhood trees. Gary cocked an eye at the sun. The sky was very clear, almost bitterly blue, but the sun had an odd watery look.

They got into the car. The engine started—just barely. Gary tried to let it warm up a bit, but it wheezed and died.

He pumped the gas a few times, held the pedal halfway down, and twisted the key again. The engine stuttered back to life. Gary nursed it carefully, looking vacantly back at the house. Suddenly his attention sharpened: was the paint blistering? Peeling off the boards in places? There'd been no sign of that a day ago . . .

"We'd better get moving," Max said.

"Right," Gary answered, and eased the car away from the curb.

They arrived at the funeral parlor to find Buddy and Dennis's crew already there. Oscar and Rodger Debuque made light of Mr. Van Nuys's absence, as indeed they had every reason to; they assured the mourners everything would go smoothly, and it did. The families paid last respects to Max Sr., then were ushered from the chapel; fifteen minutes later, the funeral procession was making its way down Beichmann Avenue toward St. Paul's. When it reached the church, a modest edifice sheathed all in dark shingles, Max and Gary and their uncles bore the coffin inside.

As they moved up the aisle toward the catafalque, Gary noticed a familiar figure among the other mourners: Steve Jennings, his best friend from high school, a tall blond fellow with curly hair. With Steve was a pretty redhead Gary didn't know: a replacement, perhaps, for the last Mrs. Jennings, who'd disappeared after a boating accident on Barragansett Bay. Gary was somewhat surprised to see Steve in a church; Steve had always shown a tremendous contempt for religion, and had been primarily responsible for setting Gary on the road toward agnosticism. Steve had been almost as much of an intellectual headhunter as Max, in high school terms at least, and he was certainly a whole lot more charming. Gary caught Steve's eye; Steve nodded toward him. They'd have to have a long talk after the burial. Gary hadn't seen him in two years.

The bearers laid the casket down, and once they settled in the pews, the service began, Father Ted celebrating the mass, assisted by Father Chuck. The sermon was similar to Father Ted's oration last night, only longer. Glancing from time to time at Max, Gary was amused at just how livid his brother's face got. But Max had no choice except to sit there and bear it now. Storming out of a viewing was one thing, but this was the funeral itself.

When the mass was over, the pallbearers took the coffin back out to the long metallic-grey hearse and slid it in. Frank Debuque gently closed the hatch while his brother, wearing a pair of silvery shades, looked on. Gary turned and made for his Pinto with Linda and Max; before they reached the car, Steve Jennings and the redhead intercepted them.

"Sad day, buddy," Steve said. He and Gary shook hands.

"Yeah," Gary said.

"Don't know what to say."

"Don't worry about it. Max, you know Steve here?"

Max nodded. "Met him at that New Year's party, remember?" He didn't extend his hand.

Steve flashed him a grin. "Topic was God, as I recall." He nodded toward the redhead. "This is my new wife, Sally. I don't think any of you have met her. Sally, that's my old pal Gary Holland, his brother Max, and Gary's wife Linda."

"Pleased to meet you," Linda said.

Sally returned her smile. "Same here."

At that moment, Frank DeBuque came up.

"We're ready to proceed to the cemetery, Mr. Holland," he said.

"Okay," Max said. "Come on, Gary."

"See you at the reception," Gary told Steve. "Our house."

The mourners got into their cars; with the addition of the people who'd gathered at the church, the procession was longer now by a half-dozen vehicles. Lights burning beneath the mid-day sky, it wound its way north to the Squankum Bridge, crossed over into Squankum Township, and entered the huge River Rest Cemetery.

Well inside, beside a gentle slope, the hearse came to a halt. Once again the pallbearers took up the coffin, carrying it up the incline toward the tree-dotted crown. There a dark green canopy had been erected; two gravediggers sat on a backhoe drawn up on the right. Going beneath the canopy, the bearers set the coffin down on the bier surmounting the grave, then took their seats. Father Ted cracked open a Bible, read passages from the Old and New Testaments, then droned off into his own theological never-never land.

GARY listened to some of it, but was distracted midway along by a muffled thumping. His immediate thought was of his dream, his father hammering his way out of the coffin—all of a sudden he felt a fine mist of sweat on his forehead.

Yet the drumming wasn't coming from his father's casket. There seemed to be several sources, all some distance off. It was the damnedest thing, but if Gary hadn't known better, he'd have sworn the sounds were coming out of the earth.

Keith Moon in Hell, he thought uneasily.

"Hear that?" he whispered to Max.

"Do I?" Max asked. "Wish I had earplugs. What a windbag."

"Not Father Ted. That pounding."

Max cocked an ear. "What are you talking about?"

Gary was surprised; Max's hearing was sharper than his. Gary guessed his brother had been too infuriated by Father Ted to notice.

In any case, the sounds had stopped.

WHEN the priest was done, the women went forward to lay flowers on the coffin. The gravediggers got down off the backhoe, and the mourners filed out from under the canopy. Gary heard the whir of the lowering device behind him as the coffin sank into the ground.

As the group worked their way slowly down the slope, Gary

noticed another party of mourners, on a hill some two hundred yards distant; some kind of commotion had broken out among them. Even against the wind, he thought he could make out faint screams.

"What the hell?" he said, pointing.

"Are they going nuts over there, or what?" Max asked.

"Hey!" came a voice from behind. "Hey! Someone's made a big goddamn mistake!"

They turned. One of the gravediggers beckoned desperately.

"This guy's alive in here!" he yelled.

Gary's heart began to race.

"Come on!" the gravedigger yelled.

The mourners started back up the hill.

"Is Uncle Max alive, Dad?" Dave Holland yelled.

"How the fuck should I know?" Buddy snapped.

The crowd neared the grave. There were loud, powerful thumps coming from the hole, and muffled screams. Gary reached the edge just in time to see the last of the floral displays sliding off the casket, shifted by the vibrations from inside.

"For Christ's sake," Max called to the gravediggers, "Can you open it?"

"It's locked," cried Frank DeBuque from somewhere.

"There's a crowbar on the backhoe," one of the diggers shouted.

"Go get it," Max said. "He must be running out of air."

The man pelted off.

By now the grave was ringed with mourners. Aunt Lucy had her handkerchief over her mouth, and Mr. Hersh, standing between Mr. MacAleer and Mr. Williams, seemed to be praying.

"It *can't* be Mr. Holland in there," cried Rodger DeBuque to his brother Frank, both of them very agitated. "I drained him myself."

But *whoever* was in the coffin, there could be no doubt that he was very much alive. The casket was now rocking visibly at the bottom of the hole, the posts of the lowering device scraping the sides of the grave, dirt raining onto the coffin lid.

The gravedigger came racing back and climbed into the hole. The coffin bucked and shook beneath him, and he barely managed to set the bar's head between lid and casket. But finally he started to pry, trying to force up the front section of the lid.

From inside the box came a great booming thud, and a fist-sized bulge appeared in the bronze lid. The gravedigger's jaw dropped, and his hands flew back from the crowbar, leaving it still upright, stuck in the joint. The mourners fell quiet. The thumping stopped.

"In-fucking possible," Uncle Buddy said, staring at the protrusion, breaking the hollow silence.

Gary looked at Linda and Max. "Just like my dream," he said tonelessly.

"Dream?" Linda asked. "*Which* dream?"

Gary said nothing, eyes still fixed on the coffin. The box continued silent.

The gravedigger licked his lips and reached for the crowbar again—only to jerk his hand back as a wave of subterranean pounding rumbled across the graveyard in what seemed to Gary a kind of chain reaction. He could feel the impacts through his shoes, almost as though a herd of cattle were stampeding beneath the earth. Large clods of dirt fell from the sides of the grave, onto the coffin.

Gary looked back toward the other slope. Most of the people there had reached their cars and fled, but some were prone on the grass, being beaten by other mourners—or *were* those mourners at all?

A far-off gravestone flashed sunlight as it toppled. Was that an *arm* flailing up out of the grass before it?

The shrieks and pounding from his father's coffin started once more. Gary turned again.

Another bulge had appeared. The gravedigger, terrified now, got to his feet. Eyes wide, he started to clamber up from the hole. The coffin rocked up from the grave bottom, the lid's front section springing open—unlike Gary's dream, the latches had given way before the lid itself. The lid smashed with terrific force into one of the gravedigger's legs; bone snapped.

Gary stared down at the coffin. Its occupant was indeed his father, tossing his head violently from side to side, eyes clamped shut, pale forehead and cheeks furrowed with lines of agony, lips drawn back in a tormented snarl.

Despite his injury, the gravedigger managed to haul himself over the edge of the pit, kicking the lid closed in the process.

But an instant later the top boomed up again, this time bashed from its hinges, an astonishing shriek following it skywards, almost as if the sound had blasted the heavy bronze from its moorings; the fillings in Gary's teeth buzzed at the cry. People scrambled to get out of the way of the falling lid.

"Dad," Gary cried. "Dad . . . "

Beyond all hope, the old man was alive. Gary knew he should be overjoyed. Something was plainly, horribly wrong with his father, but at least he wasn't dead...Gary couldn't think why this miracle so filled him with panic.

His father's eyes opened. Blank white cotton flashed. For the first time Gary noticed the small popped threads on the lids, and fringing his father's mouth. The embalmers *had* been at him, given him the full treatment . . . but why then was Max Holland Sr. still writhing and shrieking?

"*Dad!*" Gary cried.

His father only went on screaming, forcing open the lower section of the lid. Then he ripped the cotton from his sockets. As his eyelids sagged, two gleaming obsidian beads stood forth, cocking back and forth as though they were on stalks.

Linda plucked at Gary's arm.

"Dad . . . " Gary said.

She dragged him backward a few steps, but he pulled free, wondering dazedly if there was anything he could do to help his father. Most of the others had already retreated, many knocking over the chairs under the canopy in their haste. The injured gravedigger was crawling away on all fours.

All at once, as if he'd been jerked up out of the grave on wires, Max Sr. bounded up onto the edge, head thrown back, arms down at his sides, fingers curved like claws, mouth still pouring forth those deafening shrieks. For a moment he stood motionless, totally rigid. Then he lowered his head. His expression changed, twitching muscle by ridged muscle into a mask of such rage and malevolence that Gary thought his brain would wither in its glare. And once the expression was established, some horrific force seemed to settle over his father's face, stiffening it, desiccating and petrifying it as if to preserve that look forever, to render it eternal, world without end, amen . . . Tiny black eyes shining in their wrinkled sockets, the mummy that had been Max Holland creaked swiftly forward like a wizened robot, grinning hatred at all who stood before him.

"Dammit, Gary," Max said. "Come on!" Together with Linda, he pulled his brother down the slope.

But they hadn't gone far when a rakelike hand, parchment skin streaked with dirt, thrust out of the turf, tripping Linda. Gary yanked her back up.

A second hand appeared. It lashed toward Linda's leg at the end of a long ragged coatsleeve, missed, and whipped back down into the ground like a viper's retreating tongue.

They started forward once more. Ahead, the other mourners were dodging this way and that as they raced for their cars. Turf bulged, pounded apart by blows from below; at least a dozen heads or arms were forcing their way into view. Monuments toppled; a heavy marble angel, wings outspread, crashed across the head of a corpse struggling out of the earth like some horrible giant insect. The cadaver only screamed and hurled the monument aside, shooting to its feet, everything above its jaw a shattered husk.

Ten yards in front of Gary, the uninjured gravedigger went down as a screaming shape, blackened and tattered, burst from the ground before him in an explosion of dirt. Flinging itself onto him, fending his arms aside, the cadaver ripped the ears from his head and stuffed one into his mouth. Then it grabbed him by the throat, thrust its face down and bit off his nose.

Gary's stomach heaved. The gravedigger looked at him imploringly, bright scarlet blood streaming across his cheek, a shiny foam of it bubbling in the empty socket in the middle of his face. His eyes were heartrending in their need.

Gary slowed.

"Keep going, shithead!" Max cried, swatting him from behind.

Grateful for the command, Gary sped back up.

Ahead, Father Ted was staggering, hand to chest. As Gary passed him, the ground erupted to the right, a thrashing arm knocking him into the priest. Both men fell, rolling a few yards down the hill together.

Desperately Gary untangled himself from the floundering clergyman. Helped up by Linda (where was Max?), he looked back toward the cadaver.

Swiping dirt from its eyes, it flung its arms wide as its saw him; suddenly it leaped, and was standing face to face with him, barely a foot away, and its filthy hands clapped onto either side of his head . . .

A fist shot in from the side, pounding into the thing's temple. The corpse loosed Gary, hissing, and turned to face its assailant.

"Here I am, fucker!" Max snarled, and punched it again.

The thing was fast, but Max was faster, blocking its snatching hands, driving it back with jabs and kicks.

Gary looked to see if his father was still coming. Max Sr. had joined in on the gravedigger; all at once he looked up and started forward again at a stiff-legged run, hands bloodied and extended, a brown strip of what might've been scalp dropping from one.

Father Ted rose, swaying, grimacing at the pain in his chest.

"Come with us, Father," Linda said.

A sweat-damp lock of hair trailing across his forehead, Father Ted only tottered and fell.

"It's his heart," Gary said, and pulled Linda forward, down the hill. "He's done for."

"We just can't leave him," Linda panted, struggling against his grip. They halted and turned.

"What do you think we're going to do?" Gary demanded.

Even as they headed back up the slope, he got his answer; the almost-tangible wall of hatred emanating from his father stopped them in their tracks.

The priest, meanwhile, had gotten up again, facing uphill, head bowed. Gary's father jerked to a standstill, towering in front of him.

"Max," Gary heard Father Ted cry, "Please Max . . . ."

With a motion almost too quick to follow, Max Sr. pointed a sharp accusing finger at the priest's face, silencing him. A subtle change entered his expression, intensifying its malice if that were possible, diluting its torment by the barest fraction. Slight as it was, Gary read the change plainly, and knew with horrible certainty that his father was pleased to see Father Ted. The priest was perhaps the one man in the whole world that Max Sr. wanted to see most.

Father Ted tried to stumble away, but the dead man caught him and held him fast, jerking him up from the ground at arm's length. Gary felt a renewed urge to rush to the priest's aid, but fear rooted his feet to the earth. He wanted to beg his father to spare him, but there was no breath in his throat. He could only stand and watch, Linda sobbing beside him, as his father's free hand swept back, then forward, smacking into the side of the priest's face, nails ripping. Blood splashed, and Father Ted's head whipped to one side as the claw raked past. An instant later it snapped in the other direction as the fingers came whistling back in a murderous return swipe. Another splash of blood, and something dark flew through the air, off to the right. Gary heard a sound like a plastic bag half-filled with water striking a sidewalk, and looking where the sound had come from, saw Father Ted's face sliding down the front of a granite tombstone in a huge red smear, empty eyes sagging, mouth gaping. Peeling off the stone surface, curling forward, the face dropped to the grass like an abandoned Halloween mask.

Gary's eyes darted back to his father and the priest. Max Sr. turned and hauled Father Ted in closer, leaning over him, staring gloatingly into the mass of bloody writhing muscles still attached to the front of Father Ted's skull. Eyes goggling and swimming in pools of blood, the priest was still alive, gagging at the liquid running into his lipless mouth and down his throat.

Gary and Linda looked round for Max. He'd downed the corpse he'd been fighting; it was clawing after him on its belly. But another cadaver rushed up even as he retreated. Max snapped a kick into its kneecap, smashed the corpse to the grass with a spinning backfist to the head, then stamped on its other knee.

The first corpse dragged itself close, tried to grab him; Max kicked it so powerfully in the side of the skull that the cadaver flipped completely over, onto its back. Then he rushed to rejoin Gary and Linda. Gary saw that his brother's clothes were torn in a half-dozen places; blood oozed from a laceration on Max's cheek.

They ran down the slope. The other mourners had already escaped; Gary's Pinto was the only car left at the bottom. Dodging corpses still caught in the earth, leaping over clutching hands, they reached the car, ducked inside and slammed the doors. Gary fished his keys out and jammed them into the ignition. The engine turned over a few times, backfired, and stalled.

"Start, Goddammit!" Gary snarled, trying again. He looked out the window. *They* were coming, draggled emaciated figures, male and female, clothes hanging in rags, the earth of their graves still dropping from their limbs, their parchmented faces twisted into grinning masks of hate.

"They'll tear the tires out!" Max cried.

Gary turned the key a third time. The motor growled and turned over. Out of the corner of his eye, he saw the corpses closing, and knowing he had no choice, floored the pedal, fully expecting the engine's fragile life to cough itself out.

The car lurched forward instead, bashing a tall female mummy in a ragged white dress to the pavement and jouncing over her.

Another corpse sprang in from the left, grabbing the door handle on Gary's side. The car picked up speed, but the corpse hung on tenaciously, running alongside. It managed to keep pace for a dozen yards or so, then fell, but its bony grip remained locked on the handle. Dragging beside the car, it hauled itself forward with one hand, trying to latch the other onto the side-view mirror, its shrieks shrill torment to Gary even through the glass.

Gary veered toward a mausoleum, up onto the grass, sweeping in close to the granite facade. Just managing to snag the mirror, the corpse held on stubbornly as the building loomed near; then its head and shoulder met the stone blocks at forty miles an hour. There was a dull crack, and the shrieks were cut off. The mausoleum blurred past. The corpse was gone, the mirror with it. Gary steered back onto the road.

There was a bend up ahead. Rounding it, Gary saw an overturned car surrounded by the walking dead. He had no time to stop, even to swerve. With a dull *crump!* The Pinto's front end slammed into the overturned vehicle's underside near the tail. There was a burst of red and saffron fire as the wrecked car's tank ruptured; trailing sheets of flame, the vehicle was hurled aside by the impact, and the Pinto drove ahead, hood splattered with burning gas.

But one of the front tires had been cut by a crumpled fender, and Gary lost control. The Pinto veered to the left, skidded as he slammed on the brakes, and smashed into a tree. The hood buckled in a burst of steam and Gary rocked forward, chipping a tooth on the steering-wheel.

Max grabbed at him from the rear seat.

Gary slumped back. "I'm all right," he said, hand to his mouth. He turned to Linda. "Okay, babe?"

"Yeah," she answered.

The engine had died. Gary tried the key. The starter didn't even click.

"They're coming," Max cried, throwing open his door. "Run for it!"

They piled out. A backward look showed Gary that several corpses were racing their way, the rest remaining to pull still-struggling people from the burning car. Gary guessed he and Max could outdistance the pursuers, but his wife was no sprinter.

"Linda won't make it," he said.

"We'll lose 'em in the trees," Max said.

There was woodland off to the right, pines and hollies set close together. Max leading the way, the trio dodged off the road, following a tortuous, twisting course. But after fifty yards or so they halted, trying to stifle their panting.

They could hear corpses crashing along behind them, drawing nearer for a short time, then apparently losing the trail. The sounds of pursuit grew more distant, finally fading altogether.

"Max," Gary gasped.

"What?"

"Are we awake? Are we hallucinating, or what?"

"Wish we were," Max said.

"Jesus, Max, the whole cemetery was coming to life."

Max wiped sweat from his forehead, laughed mirthlessly. "Maybe not all of it."

"You're sounding mighty cool about all this!"

Max eyed him evenly. "The rest of the world's unraveling. Will it help if I do too?"

Taken aback by the reply, Gary fell silent. What kind of point had he been trying to make anyway? Did he really want his brother to be as vulnerable and terrified as he was?

"But what's *happening?*" Linda asked, shivering. "Dead people don't come back."

"Sure fooled us, didn't they?" Max answered.

Hollow with fear, Linda's eyes sought Gary's, seeking some kind of reassurance. But he knew there was no reassurance to be taken there. For her sake, he tried to crack a brave smile, but it was beyond him. A scant ten minutes ago, he'd seen his father rise dead and shrieking from the grave.

CHAPTER 10
GRAVE MATTERS

DECIDING to put as much distance as they could between themselves and the road, they walked slowly eastward. They did not know what lay ahead. Would they find themselves in a development, or another section of the graveyard? River Rest was immense.

"Must be thousands of 'em in this cemetery," Gary said. "What are we going to do if they *all* come back? Where'll we run?"

Max said nothing.

"What if they come spilling out of the graveyard?" Gary went on, a rising note of panic in his voice. "Do you think the cops can handle 'em? The National Guard?"

Max halted. "Will you get a hold of yourself?"

"That's easy for you to say!" Gary snapped. He felt like an idiot doing it, but he still wanted to get a rise out of Max, make him lose control, just one bit.

"No it isn't," Max said, voice simmering. "But you might get us all killed if you crack up. Understand?"

"I'm not going to crack up," Gary said defensively.

"Then act that way."

Ashamed of himself, Gary nodded. "Sorry. It's just that . . . just that I'm . . ."

His voice trailed off as they started forward once more.

"Do you think they *can* be killed?" Linda asked.

"Are they alive?" Max asked. "That first one I fought—I gave it enough to kill three men. But they can be crippled, we know that much."

"A statue fell on one," Gary said. "Crushed its head *flat*. The damn thing pushed the statue off like it was nothing, got right to its feet."

"I saw it too," Max said.

"I couldn't believe you took those two on," Gary continued. "I was scared shitless. Me and Linda, we wanted to save Father Ted from Dad . . . from that *thing* . . . but we couldn't get near them. The look on its face . . . how could you stand up to them?"

"I wasn't going to watch you die," Max said.

They pressed on a while in silence.

"What if this is happening all over the state?" Linda asked. "What if every graveyard in the *country's* coming to life?"

"We don't know that's happening," Max answered.

"Don't we? What about all those murders? Those train-wrecks?"

"We don't know who was responsible for all that."

"Maybe they wanted recruits," Linda said.

"You love to jump to conclusions, don't you?"

"It's all connected, just like I told you—"

She broke off. The trees were thinning out. Another broad stretch of cemetery showed ahead.

They stopped at the edge of the woods. Out among the monuments and mausoleums, nothing moved. There was no pounding from beneath the earth, but a dozen or so yawning holes were visible.

Off to the south stood three sedans and a black Cadillac hearse. Two bodies sprawled from an open Buick. Others lay scattered over the grass nearby.

"What do you think?" Gary asked.

"Haven't been as active this side of the boneyard," Max said. "I think we should work our way south along the edge of the trees, try to get one of those cars. We need some wheels."

"What about the ones that were after us?" Linda asked. "They headed south. What if they're still in the woods looking for us?"

"You'd rather cross the cemetery?" Max asked. "Must be a half-mile to that development over there, open ground all the way. I'd hate to be out there if the locals surface."

"Where we going to go when we get the car?" Gary asked.

"Back to the Point," Max said. "Dad's shelter. Good place to think things through. Hell, we could hole up there for months."

"But there are graveyards in Bayside Point," Linda said.

"Four or five small ones. Two emergency morgues. And a hospital morgue. But there's no place in the state where we'll get too far from some collection of stiffs. Jersey's been planting 'em for three hundred years. On the other hand, we know where we can lock ourselves up in our own private fortress."

They headed south, trying to keep one or two trees back from the greensward. Off in the development, columns of black smoke billowed up; there was a crackle of gunfire.

"Some of 'em are over in there," Max said. "If folks weren't on guard, a few of those things could cut one hell of a swath."

They drew nearer the cars. The vehicles sat on a strip of roadway running parallel to the edge of the trees. Between road and wood was a fifty-foot-wide band of grass studded with headstones. A single black-stone mausoleum stood not far from the cars. The burial the slaughtered mourners had been attending was on the near side of the road; a closed grey-metal casket, gleaming in the pale sunlight, still lay on its bier. Surrounded by dirt and ripped turf, six graves gaped like mine craters in the middle distance.

Max, Gary and Linda moved cautiously out of the pines, making for the cars. Two of the corpses on the grass before them were unmutilated, though huge clods of earth had been thrust into their mouths. The rest had eyelids or lips stripped away, fingernails pulled or bitten off, nostrils ripped from their faces; but if the discolorations on their necks were any indication, they'd been killed by strangulation.

Gary went up to the hearse, looked at the ignition. No keys.

"Bet he's got 'em," Max said, indicating a clean-cut corpse wearing shades and a dark suit. "Definite hearse-jockey."

He started to go through the fellow's pockets, then stopped, tensing. Gary and Linda recoiled from the body.

"Is he—?" Gary began.

"No," Max said. "Something's moving in the woods."

He searched a second pocket, then swore and said, "Better take cover."

"Where?" Gary asked.

Max pointed to the mausoleum. Gary and Linda followed apprehensively but swiftly as the thrashing in the pines drew closer. The tomb stood open; Max vanished inside.

Nearing the threshold, Gary saw the gate's lock had been torn off, the bars next to it bent apart, as though a clutching hand had pushed through from the inside, forcing its way toward the lock. He and Linda joined Max in the cool damp darkness.

"Are you crazy?" Gary asked Max. "Hiding in a *mausoleum?*"

"The *active* inmates have already left." Max jerked his head back toward two open coffins that had fallen from their niches.

The thrashing sounds stopped; there came a rush of hurrying feet.

"Back from the door," Max said.

Linda and Gary obeyed. But as the footbeats hurried near, Gary saw his brother looking out through the opening.

"Holy shit," Max said. "It's Steve and Sally."

He went outside, Gary following.

"Hey!" Max cried.

Steve and Sally turned, motioning him to be quiet they came toward the mausoleum.

"We were attacked as we drove out," Steve panted.

"Any after you?"

"Gave them the slip. At least I think so. But the woods are full of them back there. Hundreds, all coming this way."

"Should we run for it?" Gary asked.

"No way," Max answered. "Let me see if I can find the keys on that driver."

Gary retreated to the mausoleum to watch. He kept expecting the corpse to sit up, to rush to greet his brother with open arms and shining teeth. He wondered if he would ever be able to think of anything as truly dead, as *harmless,* anymore. What would it be next? Was the whole inanimate world about to turn on them?

Max whirled. Gary gasped, but the driver hadn't stirred; once again, the corpse had fooled him.

Playing it cool, Gary thought.

Max dashed through the arch.

"They were getting too close," he said. "I could hear 'em. A few seconds more, and—"

"Steve," Sally said, "There are *coffins* in here . . . "

"That's right, honey," her husband affirmed. "This *is* a mausoleum."

"But what if—?"

"They wake up?" Max broke in. "Then it's going to get real intense around here. But maybe they won't, so why don't you just keep quiet?"

She nodded, wide eyes glimmering in the semi-darkness. Gary studied her face, then looked past her at the unopened coffins.

Eight of them.

And outside, the dead rustled nearer through the woods.

Everyone moved clear of the doorway. Long thin shadows began to cross the rectangle of light on the floor inside the threshold, as though a forest of winter trees were marching past. Perhaps giving some thought to rousing the sleepers within, a few corpses stopped briefly by the entrance before moving on. Gary bit deep into his upper lip. Linda's hand slipped into his, trembling.

At last the shadows vanished. Gary and Max chanced a look outside.

A hundred yards or so beyond, the dead had gathered at the base of a small hill. They stood motionless, staring up at its crown, on which stood a huge stone cross.

"We could try to get back into the woods," Gary suggested. "They're not looking."

"I could try for the keys again, too," Max said. "Keep the car between them and me."

"You're nuts."

"Yeah," Max said, slipping back out. Before long he had the keys. He looked smugly at Gary, pointing to the glinting metal in his hand.

Suddenly his head cocked to one side, and he flung himself down on the grass. Gary knew more must be approaching through the trees. Soon he could hear them himself. He watched Max till the last moment; then they came too close, and he stepped away from the door.

Horrible possibilities raced through Gary's head. Would they notice his brother breathing, or did they have some preternatural sense for telling the living from the dead? Would they stuff turf down Max's throat and leave it at that, or rip into him in the process?

As Gary steadily drove himself up the wall, the thumping began outside, the pounding under the earth. All over the graveyard the buried ones had awakened, were hammering their way out of their coffins . . .

He chanced a look outside. The corpses from the woods, fifteen or so, were going to join the throng at the base of the hill; and all across the green lawn, toppling headstones and bulging earth and thrusting arms confirmed that other reinforcements were on the way. Hundreds. Thousands. In front of the mausoleum a half-dozen at least were thrashing from the earth. Dirt spattered over the mausoleum's threshold, rained onto Max.

Gary was completely caught up in terror for his brother; it took a hollow thud from behind to remind him that he was also in danger. He spun to stare at the coffins on the niches.

"Got to get out of here," Steve whispered.

"Can't," Gary said." They're coming up all around us. And Max is still lying on the grass out there. They haven't spotted him—"

There was a second thud, and a scrape of metal against stone as a casket shifted in its niche.

Gary looked back out the door. Some of the corpses nearby had extricated themselves and were crossing the road. Others were only halfway out.

"We're dead," Sally whispered to Steve. "They're going to tear our faces apart, and . . . "

"Shut up, dammit!" Gary said. "They're heading across the road. If we can wait a bit longer, we should be able to make a dash for the hearse . . . "

A coffin jounced up from its niche, struck the top of the alcove and banged down again, the impacts thunderously loud in that enclosed space. Three of the caskets remained perfectly still; the rest shifted and jerked, several perilously close to dropping from their ledges. Finally two crashed to the floor, one landing upside down.

Gary looked back outside. The last cadaver in front of the mausoleum clawed its way clear, leaped to its feet, and crossed the road. Max started to get up—

And at that moment, Gary heard a tremendous wrenching sound behind him, and turned to see the upside-down coffin tilting up off the floor, the front section of its lid swinging open, two wildly lashing arms shooting out from the box, dark against the lid's lining. The casket dropped back down; then the arms propelled it off the marble once more. Heeling up on end, it banged into a wall as the frenzied thing inside struggled to open the other section of the lid. Canting sideways along the wall, the coffin tipped upside down again when it struck the floor. The corpse howled with frustration.

"Max's signal," Steve cried. "Come on!"

They raced across the lawn toward Max and the hearse, leaping over open graves. In moments they were inside, slamming the doors shut. Max found the ignition key, blew dirt off it and started the engine. The motor revved raggedly, but Gary thought he'd never heard a more wonderful sound; Max pressed down on the gas, and the hearse started away from the curb just as the corpse came screaming out of the mausoleum. The cadaver sped after the car, but couldn't catch up; ahead, the road was clear.

Gary looked over at the corpses assembled by the hill. Even as he watched, they knelt; he shifted his gaze to the top of the slope.

A lone figure stood there, arms upraised, beside the cross; even at that distance, heGary could tell the figure was very large, almost a giant. It turned toward the cross, set its shoulder against it and pushed; the cross went over, and the figure set its foot upon it, lifting a single defiant fist skyward. As if in approval, the assembled corpses cried out in a deafening chorus. Gary clapped his hands over his ears, turning.

Ahead, two corpses were rushing up the road, directly toward the hearse. Max plowed right into them, the Caddy's massive bulk tossing them like ragdolls. Sailing straight back, one landed in the car's path yet again. It sprang up, and tried to jump onto the hood as the hearse closed in; but the front end struck it before it could clear the grille. It flew head over heels high into the air, clipping the roof, rolling over the trunk to the road.

Max swerved around a tree-lined left-hand jog. The cemetery's southern gate appeared. It was shut, a pair of bodies impaled on the spikes at its top, five corpses standing before it.

Max floored the gas pedal, ramming three of them at seventy miles an hour, smashing them back against the gate; a chain snapped, and it swung wide. The Caddy roared through the arch before the other corpses could grab it. Max steered wildly to the right, skidding onto the street beyond the wall, then raced forward, leaving River Rest Cemetery far behind.

CHAPTER 11
PLURALISM

THEY arrived at the house to find Buddy's car sitting out front, and Buddy and company waiting in the living room. That came as no surprise— Max had given Dennis a set of keys before the funeral.

But Gary hadn't been expecting to see Father Chuck, Mr. and Mrs. MacAleer, and their son Jamie. The priest had wound up in Buddy's car during the panic; the MacAleers had been unable to reach their house on the south side of town, and hadn't known where else to go. The center of Bayside Point had been overrun.

"Corpses must've come from those emergency morgues," Max said. "And the old graveyards."

Dennis was looking through the picture window at the hearse. "How'd you get that bullet-hole in the windshield?" he asked Gary.

"There were some River Rest escapees on the Squankum Bridge," Gary answered. "A police car was stopped on the divider, and the cops were blasting away at them."

"They shot at you deliberately?"

"Slug came through one of the corpses. Made a hole the size of your hand in its back. Just missed me. Sprayed glass all over the front seat."

"One of the cops had a riot gun, for Christ's sake," Steve put in. "Didn't slow those fucking things up at all."

"Should've aimed at their legs," Max said. "Can't walk without kneecaps, even if you are a zombie."

"You said the downtown was burning?" Father Chuck asked.

"Sure looked like it from the bridge," Gary said.

"They had Molotov cocktails," said Mr. MacAleer. "That's what they hit our car with."

"I think we should go down into the bomb shelter," Aunt Lucy said.

"Just what I was about to suggest," Max said. "But a couple of us had better stay up here to keep watch. There'll probably be some troops through here soon. We'll want to go with them."

"Why wait?" Uncle Buddy said. "I say we should get off this damn peninsula right now. We're going to be fucking trapped here."

"We're already trapped here," Max said. "We want to link up with some heavy ordnance before we do any travelling."

"*That's* heavy ordnance, if you ask me," Buddy said, jerking a thumb toward the guns piled on the couch. Besides the two retracting-stock Heckler and Koch assault rifles, there were twin Remington 870 pump shotguns with magazine extenders, and a pair of Beretta 92 fifteen-shot automatics, all with ammunition. "We should arm ourselves to the teeth and take off."

"If we had some grenade launchers and an APC, I might agree with you," Max said. "We don't. Didn't you hear what we said about those cops on the bridge?"

"We can shoot 'em in the knees," Buddy answered. "You said so yourself."

"You gotta shoot 'em in the head," his son Dave added. "That's the only way to kill zombies. Any idiot knows that."

Buddy shot him a ferocious glare.

"We don't want to tangle with them at all," Gary said.

"Fucking A," Max added. "And there's no way we can get off the peninsula *without* doing just that. If you go north from the Squankum bridge, there's River Rest—"

"I wasn't talking about going that way," Buddy said. "We already tried Rt. 35. They had it blocked. That's why we headed down here."

"Well then, there's the Route 88 Bridge, the one over the canal. But there's another big graveyard out that way."

"Me and Lucy already reminded him," Dennis said.

"And I shouldn't have listened to you," Buddy answered. "Maybe they're not waking up there."

"And maybe they are," Lucy said.

"You'd have to be out of your mind to try it," Max went on. "So what does that leave? The Route 33 bridge, down at the bottom of the peninsula. But you'd have to go through the southern part of town. And as we know from the MacAleers, that area's crawling with them. So why don't we just go down in the shelter and listen to the radio? Maybe things'll blow over somehow. Maybe the Air Force'll napalm the whole goddamn town. We'd come through that just fine."

"You have it all figured out, don't you, wise-ass?" Buddy grated.

"A lot better than you do," Max said.

"He does, Buddy, he really does," Aunt Lucy said. "Let's get down in the shelter now."

"That's it, Lucy," Buddy snarled. "Side with the son of a bitch. Stab me in the back."

"Come on Dad," Dave said. "Don't be such an asshole."

At that, Uncle Buddy turned and cocked his fist back. "I'll punch your lights out, you little bastard."

"Please, please," Father Chuck said, "For God's sake, let's try to keep ourselves under control."

"Who's not under control, faggot?" Buddy demanded.

"Listen, Buddy," Dennis said. "This isn't doing anyone any good, and you know it."

Buddy glowered at him, simmering.

"I'm so scared, Buddy," Lucy said. "*Please.*"

"All right," Buddy said at last. "But if college boy there is wrong . . . "

Max just smirked at him, then looked at the others. "Anyone willing to stay up here with me? I might need some backup if we get visitors."

"I'll stay," Dennis said.

"Dennis, no," Camille said.

"You know I'm pretty handy with a shotgun, Camille," he answered. "None of those things is going to get near me."

He and Max went over to the couch, took up the Remingtons and bandoliers of cartridges.

"Bring the other guns and ammo back downstairs," Max told the others. "Leave the shelter door open, but close it up tight if I tell you to."

"What if we hear gunfire?" Gary asked, picking up a Heckler and Koch.

"Just wait till I yell, okay?"

"What if you want to get in after we lock up?"

"I'll tap three times quick."

Gary nodded.

"All right then," Max said. "Get on down there."

Leaving him with Dennis, they went.

IN the shelter an hour later, after it became clear that there was little to listen to on the shortwave except static, Mr. MacAleer announced solemnly, without any prodding:

"It's the end of the world."

"What?" Steve asked.

"Unless the world's already ended," MacAleer went on.

"Oh, really?"

"That's what those dreams were," MacAleer said. "Judgment Day. The judgment came as a dream. But it was real anyway. Jesus spoke to us, pronounced his verdict . . ."

"I didn't hear any verdict," Gary said.

"What dreams is he talking about?" Steve asked.

"You see that article in the paper the other day?" Gary asked.

Steve snapped his fingers. "Shared dreams, right. Did you have one?"

"Yeah," Gary said.

"So did I," Linda said.

"What about the rest of you?" Steve asked.

Everyone nodded except Buddy.

"I didn't," he said.

"Neither did I," Steve said.

"Steve," Sally said. "You told me . . ."

"Different dream, honey," Steve answered.

Gary eyed him, unsure if he believed him.

"You're lying," MacAleer said.

"So you're a mind reader as well as a nut, huh?" Steve asked.

MacAleer ignored the insult. "The end of the world *has* come. And the Earth belongs to the dead."

Steve just grinned.

"Scripture clearly testifies to the Resurrection of the Flesh," MacAleer continued.

"I'm afraid I must correct you," Father Chuck said. "Your interpretation is hopelessly outdated. The Resurrection's only a metaphor—"

Linda laughed. "When was the last time you were chased out of a cemetery by a metaphor, Father?"

Father Chuck's mouth clicked shut.

"Linda," Gary said, "Are you saying you believe that crap MacAleer's dishing out?"

"Some of it sounds pretty crazy," Linda admitted. "But not the part about resurrection. For God's sake, Gary, one of them had me by the ankle!" She pointed. "That ankle right there. See the runs in my stocking?"

"But does that mean we have to accept the first naive explanation that comes along?" Father Chuck asked.

"No," Linda answered. "But I'm not too inclined to listen to someone who rules out literal resurrection, either. Not when he's seen it happen right in front of his face."

"There's got to be an explanation," Buddy said.

"There *is!*" MacAleer insisted. "The power of Almighty God."

"He means a *logical* explanation," Steve sneered.

"That *is* a logical explanation," Linda said. "It's also the *only* theory I've heard so far. Of any sort."

"But there's this big problem with it," Steve said. "There isn't any Almighty God."

"Now hold on there—" Father Chuck began.

"Hold on yourself," Mr. MacAleer broke in. "Why don't you leave the unbelievers to those of us who *do* believe?"

"Where do you get the gall to say something like that?" Father Chuck retorted. "I'm a Roman Catholic priest."

"You're a pimp for the Whore of Babylon," MacAleer answered.

No master of the controversial arts, Father Chuck completely lost his cool. "Why, you slicked-back redneck goon . . . "

Buddy nudged his wife with an elbow. "Just listen to those two idiots go at it."

"Pimp for the Whore of Babylon," Steve chuckled. "I love it."

"That's it," MacAleer said. "Mock me. Mock God. You'll get yours."

"And who's going to give it to me?"

"Christ, the Judge of All Mankind. You'll find yourself like those *things* in the graveyard. The Elect have already been taken up; there's a new Heaven, a new Earth. A new Hell—and you're going to rot in it. All you atheists."

"But what about you?" Steve asked. "What are *you* still doing here?"

That seemed to take MacAleer aback.

"If you're saved," Steve pressed, "Why weren't you raptured off to Heaven?"

MacAleer stared at him, obviously trying to think of an answer;

Gary could practically see the wheels turning under that patent-leather scalp.

"We're waiting," Steve said.

"I . . . I was left here to preach," MacAleer said at last. "Not everyone heard their sentence. Some might yet come to the Lord."

"Even after the end of the world?" Steve jeered.

"His mercy is infinite," MacAleer answered. "He could save a soul in Hell, if He chose to."

"Could He save me?" Steve asked.

"Even you," MacAleer said, but in a tone that clearly implied he didn't think it likely.

"Don't listen to him," Father Chuck told Steve. "You mustn't think all Christians are like him."

"What do you mean 'like him?'" MacAleer demanded. "Do you mean I'm unashamed of my Christianity? Well, you're right. I'm born again, and I don't care who knows it. But what are you? A Christian pretending to be an atheist? Or an atheist pretending to be a Christian?"

"I'm not a self-appointed preacher who peddles soft-core porn," Father Chuck shot back.

MacAleer raised his hands. "I'm a sinner, I admit it," he answered. "But I'm washed in the Blood of the Lamb. I don't have to justify my works because I'm not justified *by* them. I'm saved by my faith in Christ Jesus, and I'm not going to die like you and your atheist friend there." He nodded toward Steve.

"So we're both going to die, huh?" Steve asked.

"Unless you accept Jesus Christ as your Lord and Savior, yes. You will die and rise to living death."

"Now let me get this straight," Steve said, laughing. "You think the Last Judgment's come, and all the good people . . . ."

"*Saved* people," MacAleer said.

"Whatever. All the saved people have been taken up to Heaven?"

"Yes."

"And the Earth's become Hell? And those walking corpses are people being punished for their sins?"

"Yes."

"And the rest of us are poor slobs trying to find salvation in the meantime, like we're stuck in some kind of divine afterthought?"

"Yes."

"Shit, you're a sickie," Steve laughed.

"So what's *your* guess?" Linda asked.

"I don't have one," Steve replied.

"But you're sure there's some kind of natural explanation?"
Steve nodded.

"There's a good, sound scientific reason why embalmed corpses
are coming back to life?"

"Yes."

"Sounds to me like your faith's just as blind as Mr. MacAleer's."

"There *is* a scientific explanation," Dave Holland put in.
"Radiation brings 'em back. It mutates 'em, like in *Night of the Living
Dead.*"

Buddy snorted at his son. "*Night of the Living Dead,*" he said.
"How'd your brain get so full of crap when you have a father like me?"

"It was easy," Dave said.

Before Buddy could reply, footbeats rolled on the cellar stairs, and
momentarily Max and Dennis rushed into the shelter; Max shut the
thick steel door and locked it, then flicked on the emergency ventilation system.

"What's happening?" Camille asked Dennis.

"Saw some coming up the street," Dennis answered. "Twenty,
maybe. Torching the houses, driving people out."

"But how will we breathe if the upstairs burns?" Aunt Lucy asked.

"That's why I turned on the ventilation," Max said. "It's filtered,
and the ducts run underground, out into that vacant lot behind the
back yard."

"What about the fire?" Lucy demanded.

"Won't touch us. The walls of this joint are insulated steel-rein-
forced concrete. The house is going to come crashing down into the
rec room, though. The main door might be completely blocked. We
may have to leave by the back way." Max nodded toward a second steel
door on the far side of the shelter. "It opens on a tunnel that leads to
a storm sewer main."

"Dad sure covered all the bases," Gary said.

"What will we eat?" Camille asked. "And what about water?"

"There's enough food to last a family of four a year and a half,"
Max said. "It's in the storeroom. Bottled water, too. That'll have to be
recycled, but we've got the gear."

"Can't hear a thing outside," Gary said, going to the main door, setting his eye to the thick glass peephole.

"Walls are too thick," Max said.

Gary peered steadily through the fisheye lens, into the dark rec room beyond. The only light was at the top of the stairs, a few bars of it running down the steps.

"Isn't there a periscope?" he asked.

"Yeah," Max said. "But we don't want to run it up now. Might give those things some idea we're here."

"Isn't it concealed?"

"In the bird-bath stand."

"The bird-bath," Gary said, laughing.

"Yeah. But somebody sharp could spot it."

"What's above us?" Aunt Lucy asked. "I'm all turned around."

"The front yard," Max said. "See anything, Gary?"

"Nothing yet," heGary answered—just as a reddish flare erupted some distance beyond the rec room door; flaming liquid splattered the stairwell and the steps, quickly setting large patches of carpet ablaze.

"They just torched the living room," Gary cried.

"We're all going to die down here," Buddy said.

"Bullshit," Max said. "But there's nowhere for you to run now, so you might as well just sit back and relax. And pray the National Guard's up there when the fires burn out."

"Pray to who?" Buddy asked.

"Anyone you like. I'd suggest God."

CHAPTER 12
MAX WEIGHS IN

UNCLE Buddy never did do any praying. Max and the MacAleers and Father Chuck all did, but their prayers weren't answered, at least regarding the military. Perhaps a request from Buddy might've tipped the balance; there was no way to say.

As it turned out, the military proved unable to help much of anyone. Technology failed at every level. Many tanks and trucks wouldn't start, and most of those that did simply crawled a few feeble miles before they died. Planes dropped from the sky—those that managed to leave the runway. Most small arms still worked, but with transport breaking down or nonexistent, little heavy artillery could be brought to bear.

Army and National Guard units engaged the dead anyway. All across the country, pitched battles raged. Corpses hurled themselves in waves at the living, were dismembered by bullets and grenades. But gun-barrels overheated and warped, and ammunition ran low, and the result was always the same—soldiers slaughtered, the dead unchecked.

It was a scenario played out in every nation on earth. Burning and killing, the shrieking majority rampaged at will. Millions came clawing up from the graveyards in Prague and Rome and Tokyo. Hordes of them covered the African Veldt. Out of the Meccan catacombs they swarmed like angry ants. Mass graves in the Gulag, in Vorkuta and Kolyma and Krasnoyarsk, bulged open like wounds seething with maggots.

Against Baghdad they unleashed a cloud of Saran nerve gas. Far across the Shatt-Al-Arab, in the Martyr's Cemetery in Tehran, they crimsoned the Fountain of Blood with gallon after gallon of the real thing.

In a ghastly echo of the Terror, half the population of Marseilles was crammed onto ships, which were then scuttled in mid-harbor. Fifty thousand souls in Caracas were drowned in crude oil in the hulls of supertankers. In an Elizabeth, New Jersey chemical plant, ten thousand were shoved into huge tanks of wood alcohol. For the first time in anyone's memory, Calcutta's sanitation trucks came to collect the living, and in Beirut, the dead were well into their campaign of slaughter before anyone noticed. Not far to the south, the Knesset became a charnel-house in mid-session. The living in Ethiopia and Kampuchea were annihilated in a matter of hours.

And in South Africa, Apartheid was abolished.

Neither money nor rank nor good intentions availed against the New Order. Junta leaders and cardinals and captains of industry came to their fates as inexorably and hideously as peons and parish priests and welfare moms. Arab arms millionaires in their private 747's above the Persian Gulf discovered they had unwanted guests aboard; Colombian drug lords in their Andean fortresses learned to their amazement that some foes could neither be bought nor intimidated. At the Vatican, Pope Pius the Thirteenth was dragged down after a desperate last stand by his Swiss Guards. In Washington, the Presidential chopper actually got off the ground and made it to the Mount Weather Complex on the Appalachian Trail, whereupon the Chief and all his men were set upon by the corpses even then overrunning the landing-pad. In Moscow, an electrical malfunction left the main entrance to the Kremlin command center wide open; a half hour after giving the sentries at his tomb a nasty shock, one V.I. Lenin led the mob that captured the Soviet leadership, and he and his comrades formed a strange new Politburo after lovingly disposing of the old.

So it proceeded, implacably, remorselessly. Within twenty-four hours fully one-third of the human race was freshly dead and awaiting resurrection.

DURING periods when the static relented, the occupants of the Holland bomb-shelter gleaned something of this from the shortwave, enough to realize the full scope of the situation. Coupled with what they'd already witnessed, the news made sleep that night fitful if not impossible. The argument between Mr. MacAleer (sometimes allied with Linda) and his opponents flared up now and then, usually after some new bit of information managed to slip through.

To Gary's surprise, Max stayed out of the debate, preferring instead to take inventory of the supplies and run checks on the life-support and electrical systems; he also fixed the generator—twice. Finishing all that, he listened to the last snatch of news to come in on the radio before it went suddenly silent, took a look at the set, pronounced it irreparable, then sat down in the corner and went to sleep.

Profoundly envious of his brother's nerves, Gary tried to do the same, but dropping off was difficult. And he succeeded only in plummeting into a nightmare.

It was the scene at the graveside, his father tearing the priest's face from his head. Only now it flew straight at Gary, the bloody mask settling over his features, merging with his flesh. As Max Sr. approached, Gary tried madly to pull it loose, but it wouldn't come off. His father lifted him by the throat, looking at him the way he had looked at the priest, with that soul-freezing glee; suddenly Gary understood all too well his father's delight in catching the man who had sent him to Hell...

Gary woke before the clawlike hand could whip round and rip Father Ted's face free once more, but the dream was so vivid, his terrified anticipation so keen, that he could still feel the nails dig deep into his flesh, the skin peeling instantly away, his brain jarring ferociously against the wall of his skull.

As the shock faded, he felt someone staring at him, sat up and looked around; it was MacAleer. The man had a pocket New Testament in his hands, but his eyes were fixed solidly, almost gloatingly, on him.

"You must be born again," he said.

"Fuck you," Gary answered.

SEVERAL hours later Gary was looking through the periscope. The olive-drab tube entered the ceiling through a stainless-steel sleeve bolted to the concrete.

"See any?" Max asked.

"No," Gary answered. "Maybe they don't like snow."

"*Snow?*" Aunt Lucy asked. "In July?"

"Bet it's only a flurry," Max laughed. Gary turned the scope. The steel stand concealing it was pierced by four circular holes, north, south, east and west; Gary was looking out through the northern hole now. The openings were set with fisheye lenses, greatly broadening his field of vision.

Every way he'd looked, the view had been pretty much the same: devastation. The house had been completely leveled, as had all the surrounding buildings, except those made of brick. Few flames were still visible in the ruins, but there was a good deal of smoke; the air was thickly bluish-grey with it, giving everything a peculiar underwater look, an effect the distortion of the lens only heightened. The snow reminded him of miniature blizzards in those liquid-filled bubble paperweights.

And who turned this *world upside down?* He wondered—then caught himself, realizing the pleasure MacAleer would take in knowing he'd had such a thought.

Gary turned the scope to the east. The sky was leaden, and what with the smoke and clouds overhead, there was a kind of sourceless twilight over everything; it was nine o'clock on a July morning, but it looked like a November dusk had come a thousand years before—and never left.

He noticed the clouds parting; the sight summoned up a faint, irrational hope. If only he could see the sun!

But when the sun was revealed, his spirits sank again. It was very pale, and he'd never seen it such an odd color before: almost green-blue.

Except for the spots.

At first he thought they must simply *be* sunspots—until he remembered that sunspots weren't visible to the naked eye. He'd never heard of them taking up so much of the sun's surface. Fully a quarter of the disc seemed to be covered—or eaten away—by them. The longer he looked, the more the latter impression settled into his mind. The spots themselves were purplish black, but fringed with grey; all he could think of was mold on an orange. The sun was dying, rotting, its surface being consumed by gigantic chancres—

No, he told himself firmly. *You can't entertain nonsense like that. You MUST not.*

"Gary?" Linda asked. "What do you see?"

He said nothing.

"Come on, I saw your jaw drop," she said.

"Yeah, tell us," Buddy said.

Gary backed away from the scope. "Look for yourselves."

Max was first to the eyepiece. He didn't need to look long.

"What *is* it?" Aunt Camille demanded, even as Dennis replaced Max at the scope.

"The sun," Max said. "It's almost as if . . . "

"As if it's got sores on it or something," Dennis said. "As if it's *decaying*."

Steve laughed. "*Decaying*," he said. "What the fuck . . . ." He took the scope, then cursed. "Can't see anything. Just clouds." He strode away from the scope. "Anyone else want a turn?"

"You *sure* you couldn't see anything?" Buddy asked.

"Yeah," Steve answered.

"Good," Buddy said.

"But *we* did," Max said. "And it *is* worth pointing out we've been having a very cool July."

"There was that news story, too," Father Chuck said. "The one about the sun's energy dropping off—"

"When are all of you going to open your eyes?" Mr. MacAleer demanded. "Surely you must realize that all these things are signs from God. That the end has come. That He, in His infinite mercy, is giving you all one last chance—before He gives you to the dead."

"If He's so infinitely merciful," Steve said, "Why give us to the dead at all?"

"I'm afraid Steve's got a point there," Father Chuck said. "How could a loving God do such a thing?"

At that, Max laughed. "Aren't you delicate?" he asked.

Father Chuck looked toward him.

"Here you are," Max continued, "A priest of the God who made great white sharks and Satan himself, who lets children die of brain cancer every day of the week, and you don't think He'd stomach such tactics?"

"Blasphemy," Father Chuck answered.

"Orthodoxy, Father," Max said. "God created everything."

"God didn't create evil. Perhaps you don't know Catholic orthodoxy the way you pretend to."

"I didn't say God created evil. Evil doesn't *exist*. It's negation, nothingness. But God created beings that have the power to *do* evil, to negate. And He allows that to bring a greater good from it."

Father Chuck pointed at the shortwave. "What good could come from the horrors we heard about last night?"

Max grinned. "What did God have in mind with Auschwitz?"

"Why don't you tell us?" Steve asked.

"Because I don't know," Max answered. "Why, in any ultimate sense, does He do *anything?* I don't think the story behind snail darters could be explained to us in a million years, let alone the reason why there's evil in the world. We're finite. God's not. Infinite equals inscrutable in my book. We're talking about a guy who allowed His own Son to be crucified . . . "

"That was an act of love!" Father Chuck protested.

"My point exactly," Max replied. "Surgery's painful."

"So God doesn't use anesthetics, huh?" Steve laughed. "Remind me to keep out of His operating room."

"You're emphasizing all the wrong things," Father Chuck said.

"I'm emphasizing a side of God you'd rather ignore," Max answered. "How about Sodom and Gomorrah, blown off the map? How about the Flood?"

"I'm ashamed of you. Fundamentalist nonsense. Those are parables, not history."

"Well, what if they *are* only symbolic? Unless the Holy Spirit's just plain incoherent, they still tell us something about God, don't they?"

"Yes, but . . . "

"Yes, but what? What then *do* they tell us? That God's a tame lion? Or that he's got two big jaws full of fangs, and He's not above snapping them shut? Remember those great white sharks, Father? Even *they* are reflections of Him."

"You're worshipping a devil and calling him God."

"What the hell do you know about devils?" Max asked.

"That they're figments of a devilish human imagination," Father Chuck said. "Like the God you've been describing."

"So God's a figment of the imagination?" Mr. MacAleer cried.

"I didn't say that," the priest replied.

"Didn't you?" Max asked. "Maybe then you'd better show us how the great I AM can fit into that procrustean bed of yours."

"I was simply trying to point out that He's not some draconian monster," Father Chuck said.

"I don't believe that either," Max said. "I bet even old Bob MacAleer there doesn't believe that. But I do believe, in accordance with the scriptures and the doctrines of the Church, that God's mercy sometimes takes the form of ferocity. And you'd deny even that."

"Emphatically."

"Well, you'd just better hope you're right."

"Why's that?"

"Because otherwise you might just find yourself in the company of those devils you don't believe in."

"That's it, resort to fear," Father Chuck said. "Threaten me with fire and brimstone when your arguments don't work."

"With all due respect, Father," Max said, "I've been using you for a punching-bag."

"Well, so what," Gary broke in. "That jugular instinct of yours doesn't make you right. It just means you're a souped-up version of Mr. MacAleer."

MacAleer's mouth snapped open, but before he could reply, Max said: "Comparing me to him doesn't bother me too much. Yeah, he's a redneck and he doesn't argue too well. I don't necessarily agree with him in any case. But if you could show me one place where his theory's inconsistent with the facts, I wish you would. I mean, I *really* wish you would. Here we have the whole world crashing down around our ears, the sun rotting in the sky, people vanishing into thin air, and oh yes, the Resurrection of the Dead . . . if you're asking me if that sounds like some wacked-out scenario from Revelation or Ezekiel, I'd have to say yeah, it does. And I don't think the fact that the dead are rising from their graves necessarily imputes evil to God. So what if we're up against a horde of zombies? If they're the damned, then maybe *their* free will is the reason they're after us—not God's. Maybe they just want everyone to share their misery. Maybe they're just nuts. Who knows? In my book, it really doesn't make so much difference if they *are* zombies. If they were Khmer Rouge, would that make God's actions any more palatable? The fact that we've seen those damn things up and around just makes God's miracles, and therefore God Himself, less implausible. On that level it could be seen as grace, yes. Saving grace. A last strand of rope tossed to some stupid souls halfway down a cliff at nightfall."

"You *are* as crazy as MacAleer!" Gary insisted.

"Dammit, Gary, just listen to what I said. I *didn't* say I believed his line of argument. I don't. Not yet, at any rate. But ask me again tomorrow if the sun doesn't come up."

"Tell him to shut up, please Buddy," Aunt Lucy said.

"No need," Max said. "I've said my piece. For now."

"Good thing, too," Buddy said threateningly.

"Yeah," Max answered. "I sure wouldn't want to tangle with you. Not after I had to save your bacon from that guy at Richie's."

"I was drunk," Buddy said, rising slowly.

"So was he. I'm not. And it would take me about two seconds to settle you once and for all."

"And you call yourself a Christian," Father Chuck said.

Max laughed at him. "Hey look," he told Buddy, "I'll tie one hand behind my back, and you and Father Chuck here can jump me together."

"Sit down, Buddy," Aunt Lucy said.

Buddy puffed, eyes burning at Max, plainly hoping to see some fear, some sign Max was bluffing.

"Yeah, Uncle Buddy," Max said. "Sit down."

Buddy sat down.

Immediately Gary took Max aside.

"What's gotten into you?" he whispered. "What if he'd gone after you?"

"I knew he wouldn't," Max answered. "Now he knows it too. I can't afford to have him challenging me all the time."

"*You* can't afford it? What are you, our dictator?"

"I'm the only one who can lead this group, and you know it."

"Oh really?"

"And if that means getting tough with Uncle Buddy," Max went on, "that's the way it has to be."

Gary winced, thinking he'd never seen an uglier expression on Max's face.

CHAPTER 13
OUT, OUT

MIDWAY through the afternoon Gary, looking out the periscope, spotted several figures striding among the smoking ruins to the west.

"Corpses," he said. "Three, heading this way."

"So where's the National Guard, Max?" Uncle Buddy needled.

"You were listening to the radio last night," Max answered, unfazed.

"So there probably isn't anyone to rescue us, huh?"

"Maybe not. But that's no argument for being outside. If those things did the army in, they wouldn't have too much trouble with us."

"You were wrong, why don't you admit it?" Steve asked.

"About the Guard? Yeah. Not about the rest."

Half-listening to their conversation, Gary turned the periscope slowly, then sucked in a sharp breath. Indistinct through the smoke and lazily-falling snow, which had yet to stick, were at least a dozen bone-thin sentinels, standing motionless inside the shell of a house whose west wall had collapsed.

"More of them," Gary said. "A dozen, off to the east."

"What are they doing?" Max asked.

"Just standing there. But if you ask me, they're staring straight at this scope."

"How far away?"

"Fifty yards, maybe."

"You couldn't possibly tell what they're looking at."

"Maybe not."

"Got it on high mag?"

"No."

"Give it a try. Put your fears to rest."

Gary clicked the magnification up. He could see them much more clearly now; they looked like refugees from a concentration camp, clothes filthy and hanging in tatters. But it was still impossible to tell just where their gaze was fixed— their eyes were invisible in the darkness between their sunken lids. Yet he couldn't shake the impression that they were looking at him.

"Well?" Max asked.

"Can't say," Gary answered.

"Anything to the south?"

"Just looking now—no."

"North?"

Gary swiveled the scope round.

Across the street, the Williamson house had been reduced to its brick cellar walls. There were windows in the brick close to the blackened lawn; through the one on the left, a face was peering.

"God," Gary breathed.

It ducked from sight.

Gary stepped back from the eyepiece.

"What's the matter?" Steve asked.

"My father's out there," Gary said, face ashen.

"What?" Max cried, and rushed to the scope.

"It was *him*."

"Do you think he knows we're in here?" Aunt Camille cried.

"Well," Max said, "Buddy's car's out front. And the hearse is a dead giveaway, if you ask me. I'd be willing to bet him and his friends are going to check." He walked the scope round. "Jesus. Scores of 'em. And they're heading this way."

Facing north once more, he paused. "Five of 'em coming out from behind the Williamson house. Don't see Dad though."

"What are we going to do?" Father Chuck asked. "Will the doors hold down here?"

"Not if those bastards make an issue of it," Max answered.

"Then we'll all die," Uncle Buddy said, almost smugly.

Max stood back from the scope, motioned Uncle Dennis to take his place. He looked briefly at Buddy, as if slightly disturbed that his threats that morning hadn't completely cowed him. Then he went to the storage-room and emerged with containers of buckshot and smokeless reload powder, as well as a roll of plastic package-sealing tape.

"We'll have to make a run for it," he announced, putting them on a desk. Then he got an oversized Foster's can he'd emptied the night before out of a wastebasket.

"What's all that for?" Steve asked.

"Grenade," Max answered. Producing a Swiss army knife, he sawed the top off the beer can.

"Are we going to be able to blast our way out of this?" Father Chuck asked.

"Have to try," Max said. "I'm assuming of course that we'll meet some opposition when we slip out the back way—through the tunnel to the storm sewer. Dad's probably told his pals about it. A bunch might even be there now. Steve, take a squint through the peephole in the back door."

Steve looked out, clicking the light-switch. "Can't see a thing. Light's not working."

"Hmmm," Max said, drying the inside of the can with a paper towel.

"Could've gone on its own," Steve said. "Everything else is breaking down."

"On the other hand," Max answered, "They could've broken the bulb. We'd never have heard."

"But if they're out there already," Aunt Lucy cried, "Why aren't they trying to get in?"

"Might want to save their energy. That door's mighty damn thick. They might think we'll open it by ourselves—when we run for it. Uncle Dennis, have you spotted my father yet?"

"Nope," Dennis replied. "If he's out there, he's lying low."

"Figures. Probably thinks we didn't see him. And if he thinks that, he probably also thinks we'll just go blundering out into the tunnel, not expecting anything, when his friends come pawing at the front door." He gave an ugly laugh. "Dear old Dad."

"Don't call it that," Gary said. "That thing isn't our father."

"Well, for lack of a better term . . . "

"Christ, Max," Dennis said, "There must be a hundred of them out there."

"Any off south?" Max asked.

Dennis shifted the scope. "No."

"That's the way they want us to go. What are they all doing?"

"Just standing. Some of 'em hardly twenty yards from the scope."

"Still no sign of my father?"

"No."

Max worked feverishly, making a fuse by rolling powder up in a long piece of tape, which he then twisted. When that was done, he jabbed a hole in the cap of the powder can, wrapped one end of the fuse in paper so it would fit snugly in the opening, and inserted the fuse in the cap. After shoving the fuse deep into the powder, he screwed the cap back on tightly.

"All right everyone," he said. "There are packs in the storage room. Fill 'em with food—the dried stuff. And fill those canteens. Steve, Gary, each of you take one of those Heckler and Koch guns, and as much ammo as you think you can carry. The semi-jacketed slugs—Dad notched the tips. They'll break up on impact, do hellacious damage. Me and Dennis'll take the shotguns. Buddy, Mr. MacAleer, take the pistols.

"There are spare clothes in there too. Put on every piece you can. Keeping warm's going to be a bitch."

"Max!" Dennis cried. "Some of 'em are coming! Making for the cellar-steps!"

"Won't take 'em too long to clear the debris from the front door," Max said, busily reinforcing the powder can with tape. Then he poured a layer of buckshot in the bottom of the beer can, nested the powder container in the shot, then poured more pellets over it, filling the Foster's can to the brim. Taking the beer can's top, he carefully sealed the church-key holes, then punched a hole in the center and ran the fuse through that.

He'd run out of tape; he got another roll, using all of it to strap the top back on and reinforce the grenade's bottom and sides.

"There," he said, rising.

"Think it'll have much effect?" Gary asked.

"About equivalent to two sticks of dynamite," Max answered, attaching a sheathed machete to his belt. "It'll give 'em a big surprise, at least."

They went to take their turns with the others in the storeroom. By the time they came out, Dennis had left the periscope and was looking through the peephole in the front door.

"Can't see much," he said. "Soot on the lens. But they're out there. I can see shadows between the cracks in the debris. They're moving the planks aside."

"Get yourself outfitted," Gary told him, taking his place at the peephole.

As Dennis had said, the lens was partially obscured, but the signs of movement outside were unmistakable. Nervously Gary ran his hand over the barrel of his H and K. The weapon was almost supernaturally reliable, he knew, the best assault rifle in the world.

Specimens had been fired forty-eight hours on end without malfunction, and deliberate attempts to jam the gun usually failed. If there was a single piece of machinery that would be likely to survive the technological breakdown, it was the nasty old H and K...

Outside, the last plank fell away. Dark and blurry through the soot, a hand wiped the lens clear, and a desiccated face thrust itself forward, its mouth twisted far to one side, the corner of its grin ratcheted well up toward its ear; its eyes were like black knife-points, switching crazily from side to side, up and down; the head quivered and twitched. The thing's hideousness was rendered still more grotesque by the distortion of the fisheye lens; Gary recoiled as if he had been struck, feeling the corpse's hatred even through the thick steel of the door. He glanced down at the thick bolt, reassuring himself that it was still set.

There was a distant-sounding impact from the other side. His father had taken a minute or two to pound his way out of the coffin. How long before this barrier gave way?

"They've started on the door," Gary said tonelessly, turning. Max was looking past him, taking shotgun shells from a box and sliding them into the loops of a bandolier.

"I heard," Max said.

Soon other fists were at work on the steel, drumming in a steady tattoo.

"All right," Max said, slinging the bandolier over his chest, then shouldering a pack. "Listen to me, all of you. Father Chuck, I want you to open the door when I light the grenade. You with the guns, stay up front, help him close it after I toss the bomb through. While we're waiting for the blast, we'll get into firing position. Me and Uncle Dennis'll kneel in front. Gary, you and Steve stand behind us. Mr. MacAleer, Uncle Buddy, fire between Steve and Gary. When Father Chuck opens the door again, aim for knees and eyes."

Gary kept looking back at the front door, battling the panic mounting inside him. Even if they did manage to blast their way clear, where would they run? He doubted they'd get a hundred yards above ground. It wasn't as if they could just jump in a car, hotwire it and take off. Probably there wasn't a working car in the whole town . . .

"Speed's the most important thing," Max was saying, taping a flashlight to the barrel of his shotgun, Dennis following his example. "Don't hesitate. Move. Watch for them squirming on the floor after we cut 'em down. Don't let 'em grab you."

Fists thumped on steel; the beating on the front door had been getting steadily louder, but there was no sign the barrier was weakening.

Yet, Gary thought.

"One last thing," Max went on, slipping a small pair of binoculars around his neck. "If we're separated, head south. Try to get off the peninsula somehow. Find a boat, or use the 33 bridge if it isn't blocked. We need room to run, to hide. The peninsula's too narrow."

He went to the back door, laid his shotgun down and took up the grenade, producing a cigarette lighter.

"Father Chuck?" he asked.

The priest stationed himself at the door. "When I nod," Max said, "slide the bolt back *quickly* and open the door, just wide enough for me to lob the bomb through. Then bang it back shut. Okay?"

The priest nodded, wiping sweat from his pale brow.

"Here goes," Max said, striking the lighter up. Just before he touched it to the fuse, he nodded to the priest. Father Chuck slipped the bolt, and with a powerful effort, opened the door.

Instantly a liver-spotted claw armed with long crimson-lacquered nails lunged through.

Father Chuck grunted as the door slammed back against his shoulder. Dennis and Gary hurled themselves against the steel on either side of him; Max tossed the grenade through the crack beneath the flapping, twisting hand.

A chorus of deafening shrieks sounded outside. Despite the efforts of Gary and the others, the door was forced open wider, inch by inch.

Max grabbed up the shotgun, fired into the mummified wrist protruding through the door. Ignited by the point-blank blast, bits of burning flesh streaked like little meteors, and the severed wrist whipped back into the blackness trailing flame. Shoving the Remington after it into the crack, he loosed two ringing blasts.

The pressure on the door vanished. Gary and his companions slammed the door shut just in time to feel the jolt of the grenade-blast through the steel. Gary stepped back, panting.

And felt something crawling up his leg.

He looked down. It was the severed hand, scrabbling like a giant spider.

Gasping a curse, he knocked it off with a sweep of his rifle. It rolled across the floor into a corner—only to come scuttling forward again.

Max blew it apart with his 870. Red-nailed fingers scattered.

"Okay!" Max cried, pivoting, kneeling before the door. The men with guns took up their positions. At a signal from Max, Father Chuck swung the door wide.

The tunnel beyond was filled with grey, hot, sweetish-smelling vapor. Even smokeless powder put up quite a cloud when burned by the pound. The miasma glowed with the beams from Max and Dennis's gun-mounted flashlights.

Indistinct through the haze, a corpse on the floor jerked up into a sitting position. Its face lifted toward them, jaw swinging open to let out a scream.

Guns roared. The body flopped back down headless.

"Shit," Buddy said. "Holy shi—"

Two others rose convulsively behind the first, leaping to their feet. One was a hag in a water-stained strapless evening gown, her breasts withered flat against her chest, her right wrist a burned stump. Gary thought he recognized the other corpse, even though the dead man's eyes were stalks, and his cheeks were stretched tight over his bones, and his mouth bulged with dirt.

Dunk?

The others opened up. Gary jumped, automatically joining in.

The dirt in Dunk's mouth burst out in a brownish puff laced with teeth. Scraps of cloth flew from Dunk's trouser-legs. His head disintegrated. He and the hag toppled together, arms whipping and flailing.

"Dunk," Gary whispered, stung by guilt, but grateful at the same time that his reflexes had given him no time to think, to hesitate. Surely he'd done the right thing.

"Come on!" Max cried, straightening. "Go for their hands, so they can't grab us!"

They pressed forward firing, but halted after a few paces; Gary came up short behind Max, who was reloading feverishly.

Ahead were six or seven more. Smoke curled from their clothes, and their faces were scorched; Gary guessed they'd been slammed back up the tunnel by the blast, and were only now striding to the attack.

Flame belched from gun barrels. The tunnel reverberated with shrieks and blasts, ceiling and walls painted with flashing red light.

Shell-casings rained to the floor.

But in a matter of seconds the guns were empty, and there were still two corpses closing on the smoking muzzles; jaws clacking, claw-like fingers raking the air, they wobbled up the tunnel on all-but shattered legs. And behind *them* came a tangle of dismembered fragments, crawling and flopping and struggling blindly.

Trembling hands shoved clips into slots, shotgun shells into traps. Bolts clicked back; pumps chambered cartridges. Barrels dropped, training on the dead once more.

Cries from the women and teenagers in the darkness behind; the corpses back there were scrabbling after them with whatever remained of their limbs.

"MacAleer, Steve!" Max cried. "Cover the rear!"

They scrambled to obey.

The corpses ahead closed in.

Dennis, Max and Gary opened up. A wall of lead sent the oncoming dead sailing back in shreds. Turning their fire on the sprawl of fragments, the three advanced, pumping, blasting, spraying out buckshot and bullets till there was nothing left to fear from the squirming parts. The guns went silent, but the tunnel still resounded with screams shrilling from ragged throat-stumps; ears ringing, the group sprinted through the smoke-laced darkness.

Momentarily they reached the junction with the storm-sewer, jumping a full yard down into the huge pipe. There they stopped, but only long enough to reload. Once that was done, Max led off to the right at a trot.

"You sure you know where you're going?" Gary asked him.

"Dad showed me around," Max said. "We'll come out in that big grate that empties on Lake Heloise."

"Think we'll run into any more down here?"

"Maybe."

"Wonder if they've broken into the shelter yet?" Dennis panted.

"Going to be hard telling," Max said. "Won't be able to hear much, with the ones we totaled still screaming like that . . . "

They approached a manhole shaft. Max slowed and stopped— then leaped suddenly under the opening, shining his flashlight up into the hole, ready to shoot.

"Nothing," he said.

They pushed on.

Light-beams revealed a culvert ahead, emptying on the main pipe, some five feet up the left-hand wall. Max slowed again and searched the tube, then pressed past it.

"They're going to be waiting for us at the grate," Gary said.

Max said nothing, forging forward.

"They'll bottle us up if there's enough of them . . . "

"Might not be any there," Max said. "Not if they thought the ones by the door would surprise us."

"Hey!" called Uncle Buddy from the rear. "We've gotta stop! My wife's dying back here—outta shape."

Max paused, saying: "One minute, that's all. We don't want to be down here when they bust through the shelter door."

The group drew together. Gary noticed that only Max seemed still to have his breath.

"Anyone hurt back by the shelter?" Max asked.

"Sally got a bash on the leg," Steve told him. "All those severed limbs flailing around."

"I'm all right," Sally said.

"Anyone else?" Max asked.

"We're fine," said Mr. MacAleer.

"Okay," Max said. "I'm going to take a look ahead."

Turning, he headed up the pipe, rounding a sharp bend. But before long he came jogging back into view, face lit by the beam from Uncle Dennis's flashlight.

"Coast looks clear up there," he reported. "Could see all the way to the sewer-mouth. Let's move."

"Got your wind back, Lucy?" Uncle Buddy asked.

"No!" she replied.

"Tough," Max said. "Here we go!"

They pushed forward again, around the bend, and shortly after that, around a second turn. Ahead was the sewer's end, a circle of grayish light. The grate appeared to be down. They moved swiftly toward the opening.

But one last culvert showed on the right, midway up the passage. Max slowed to check it, Gary coming up beside him.

About three yards in was a pile of leaves and brush, partially blocking the tunnel, more than large enough to conceal a body. The brothers trained their weapons on it, going slowly closer. They began probing the pile with their gun-barrels.

At his second thrust, Gary felt something pluck at his rifle. Immediately he screamed and squeezed off a burst, leaping back.

"What, what?" Max cried, pointing his shotgun at the smoking spot in the pile.

"Something grabbed—" Gary began, then noticed a piece of branch stuck into his rifle's front sight. "Goddamn twig tangled in it."

Steve and Uncle Dennis rushed up.

"You all right?" Dennis asked.

"False alarm," Max said.

"You sure?"

"Yeah."

Dennis and Steve headed back to the main.

Max searched the darkness beyond the pile with his flashlight. Gary kept looking at the debris.

It shifted slightly, almost imperceptibly. Gary cursed, and his muzzle flew back down. But Max shoved the H and K to one side.

"Something moved!" Gary cried.

"Let's not make a habit of wasting ammo, okay?" Max said, turned, and walked away.

"Max, I'm sure . . . " Gary said, then ran after him. Had he seen anything at all? He looked over his shoulder, but without Max's light, there was only blackness . . .

Once back in the main, they pressed on toward its mouth.

"I'm sorry Max," Gary said. "But I really thought I—"

There came a sound like rattling brush, and a clatter of movement from the culvert they had left behind; a triumphant shriek rang out.

Gary spun, seized with a frantic certainty that Linda had been caught. It didn't even occur to him that anyone else could be in danger. He *had* seen something move in the debris, and Linda was dead now, and it was all Max's fault . . . Rage and horror exploding within him, Gary sped back along the main.

But as the women came dashing forward into the flashlight beams, he saw Linda among them, and once he swept past, the lights revealed a small, almost dwarfish male corpse, flecked with leaves, squatting atop cousin Dave's chest, clutching Dave's throat with its right claw. Uncle Buddy had thrown an arm around its neck, but the corpse had his other wrist, holding his gun hand out to the side.

"Buddy, let go!" Steve cried, rushing up with his rifle. Buddy loosed the corpse's neck just as Steve let fly, ripping through the cadaver's right arm.

Yet the undead hand kept its grip, and Dave went suddenly limp as the fingers closed with terrible finality, crushing windpipe and bone, forcing a powerful blackening rush of blood up into his face.

Grinning, the corpse rose and loosed Buddy's gun hand, to swipe at Steve. Barely dodging the stroke, Steve blasted slugs into the corpse's midsection, hammering it off its feet. Stepping forward, he started in on the thing's head and limbs.

Buddy threw himself to his knees beside Dave, dropping his gun he cradled his son's head with both hands, rocking it back and forth. Dave's neck was slack as a rubber band.

Gary watched, overcome with pity, unable to hear his uncle's cries over the sound of Steve's gunfire. All at once he remembered how Max had fucked up; Linda hadn't bought it, but Dave had. Gary felt a strange and wicked satisfaction.

Steve stopped shooting. The corpse on the floor, vocal cords destroyed, was hissing like a huge snake; the screams of the corpses left by the shelter echoed in the distance. Aunt Lucy ran up sobbing, knelt alongside her husband and son.

"I *told* you I saw something!" Gary cried.

Uncle Buddy looked up at Max. "He *warned* you?"

Max nodded, looking shaken.

"You motherfucker!" Buddy shouted. "You got my son killed, you know that?"

Max slowly put a hand to his forehead. "Oh God," he said. "I'm so sorry . . . "

"I *bet* you are, you son of a bitch!"

Max said nothing. Eyeing him, seeing the shock on his face, Gary felt his satisfaction fade. If *Max* was vulnerable, if *he* could fuck up enough to get someone killed, where did that leave them all? In spite of everything, Max *was* the most capable leader they had. That was one of Gary's reasons for resenting him after all . . .

"Say something, you cocksucker!" Buddy shouted.

Max's hand dropped from his brow. He straightened. "I can't bring him back, Uncle Buddy," he said.

"Is *that* all?" Buddy screamed. "My son's dead, and that's all you have to say?"

Before Max could reply, the shrieks in the distance grew suddenly much louder. It could only mean one thing; *they* had broken into the shelter at last. They were coming, maybe were already in the main, dozens, maybe scores of them.

Lucy pried Buddy away from his son. The group bolted for the pipe mouth.

There the sewer emptied into two feet of cold water on the fringe of Lake Heloise. Max and Gary rounded the corner of the drain.

Between them and the beach stood a single tall female mummy, rock-still in a green silk dress. Someone had put a hunting arrow in her brow; she'd broken off the fletching, but a Copperhead Ripper tip stuck several inches out of her hair. Behind her in a vacant lot a red Ford van sputtered smokily away.

Gary raised his rifle. The dead woman lunged, snatching the barrel. He put a burst into her shoulder, but she wrenched the gun from his hands.

Max aimed at her face. She brought Gary's gun up in front of it. Max shot her in the chest instead, toppling her.

Slinging the Remington over his shoulder, he yanked his machete from its belt. Wailing; wailing like a banshee, the corpse exploded back to her feet in a furious muddy splash, swinging the H and K blindly.

Max ducked the blow, slashed her across the knees. She fell once more, but her right arm still waved above the water, lashing the rifle back and forth.

Max severed her wrist, snatched the gun in midair, and hacked the hand from the barrel. Water bursting from her screaming mouth, she jackknifed up through the surface; Max emptied the clip into her face, punching her from sight once more. Then he flung the gun back to Gary.

"Reload," he said.

Gasping, Gary fumbled to obey as they splashed toward the beach with the others. Screaming echoes swelled in the drain pipe behind.

"The van!" Max cried.

They crossed the sand, rushed up the weedy slope to the vacant lot. Max and Gary looked through the windows in the rear doors of the van, guns ready. Inside, the floor was stacked two deep with inert corpses, their throats blotched with marks of strangulation.

"Recruits," Max said. "Wonder if they were going to load us in here?"

Gary opened the doors. "Should we try to pull them out?" he asked breathlessly.

"No time now," Max answered. "We can toss 'em out once we get roll—"

He broke off as the engine died.

"Jesus," he said. "Oh Jesus *Christ.*"

Uncle Buddy was already behind the wheel, but work the key as he might, he couldn't get the engine to wheeze back to life.

"Make a run for it?" Steve asked.

Max was looking off to the west. Gary looked too; at least thirty figures were striding mechanically through the smoking ruins toward them.

"No way," Max said.

"What about the ones in the pipe?" Dennis demanded. "They'll be out here any minute."

"Yeah," Max said, and hauled two Jerri cans out of the back of the van. "Uncle Buddy, keep trying! Uncle Dennis, come with me. Maybe fire'll stop the bastards."

Gary watched them run back down to the pipe. Max tossed the cans inside, then unslung his shotgun. It sounded to Gary as though the dead must almost be upon them; Max and Dennis cut loose with their Remingtons, whether at the corpses or the Jerri cans, Gary didn't know. The screaming from the tunnel seemed to intensify, if that were possible.

Max held his shotgun at arm's length and fired. Red light poured from the pipe, out onto the water, flaring over him and Dennis. A huge puff of smoke rolled from under the concrete arch. Max had ignited the gas running down from the ruptured cans.

He and Dennis retreated. Wrapped in flames, two decapitated cadavers came floundering out of the sewer and fell into the water. Rising, they took a few blind steps forward.

Then the gas cans blew. A tremendous ball of yellow flame belched from the pipe mouth, hammering the corpses back into the water.

Gary eyed the pipe. The explosion had cracked it; even as he watched, a smoking skeletal hand punched out through the fissure in a spray of flame and concrete. Another appeared below it; they locked on opposite sides of the crack, almost as though the corpse within was trying madly to force the fissure open further. Then they vanished back inside.

Behind Gary, the van's engine thumped and ground and suddenly started. Buddy whooped.

Gary turned. Till then, no one but Buddy had entered the van, not knowing if it would start again. Now Lucy jumped in beside him, and Gary and Linda climbed in over the corpses in the back, shuddering at the touch of them, Steve and Sally followed.

Max and Dennis came running back up. Aunt Camille, all three MacAleers, and Father Chuck were still outside.

"What are you waiting for?" Max asked them, and started to climb into the back.

But at that moment, Buddy hit the gas.

The van lurched forward a few yards, almost stalled. Cursing, Max fell to the ground as the van slipped out from under him.

"You killed my fuckin' son, Max!" Buddy shouted. "My only fuckin' *child!*"

The van picked up speed. Max scrambled up, dashed after it, but it was already too late.

"Are you out of your friggin' mind?" Gary bellowed to Uncle Buddy, shoving his H and K up against the back of Buddy's head. "Stop this thing or I'll blow your brains out."

The van jounced out onto the ruin-flanked expanse of Carter Avenue. The surrounding desolation was full of figures converging on the vacant lot.

"Go back, or I swear I'll kill you!" Gary shouted.

"You ain't got the guts, college boy," Buddy jeered.

"I *mean* it!"

"Then kill me. Because I'm not going back for that cocksucker for anything!"

Gary wanted to blow him away. *Ached* to spray his brains all over the windshield.

But Buddy was right. He didn't have the guts. And the van was going fast now. If Buddy was killed, it would surely crash...

"But Buddy," Aunt Lucy said. "You left Dennis back there too."

"Fuck you, Lucy!" Buddy shouted. "He'll have to fend for himself. I'm not going back for Max. Dammit, Lucy, he killed Dave! Killed him with his fucking stupidity!"

"Buddy, you can't—"

"Shut up, bitch!" Buddy cried. "*I'm* in charge now, and we're heading for the hills!" He roared laughter, nodding his head. "Heading for the fucking hills!"

CHAPTER 14
BUDDY'S REVELATION

THE van barreled up Carter toward Miami Boulevard.

"Where are you going?" Gary cried.

"The Squankum Bridge," Buddy snapped. "Where do you think?"

"It'll be blocked, you idiot! Or raised!"

"You let me worry about that. Just start dumping those bodies out the back."

That at least made sense. The rear doors were still open; laying their rifles aside, Gary and Steve got to work. Stiff and contorted, the bodies struck the pavement without a sign of reflex or response, grotesque manikins.

Buddy took a hard screeching left onto Miami, slamming Gary and Steve into the side of the van. Steve nearly fell out the back.

"Look out, Buddy!" Lucy screamed. "You're heading right for them!"

Gary staggered up and looked out through the windshield. At least twenty corpses stood in the street ahead, some carrying sickles and brush hooks, one in the middle raised a skeletal hand as if signaling them to stop.

"Yeah, sure," Buddy laughed, flooring the pedal. The corpses started toward the van at a stiff-legged run.

Gary snatched up his gun and stationed himself on the right side. "Steve," he said, "take the left."

Using their rifle butts, they smashed windows. Gary took aim at a corpulent male cadaver brandishing a brush hook and raked a blast across its legs. The corpse dropped to its knees, hurling its weapon at the van. The brush hook banged on metal, bouncing off.

Gary heard Steve firing, then the crunch of shattered safety glass, and Aunt Lucy screaming at the top of her lungs. A sideways glance showed him a concrete brick buried in the windshield directly in front of her.

Gary looked out the side again. A dead Marine in full dress uniform ran in shrieking, a sickle raised over his head. The uniform reminded Gary of Max; he wavered, then bowled the corpse over with a burst to the face, wondering if his brother might soon require the same treatment . . .

A heavy 'thwok' sounded from the front of the van; Gary saw a leather clad punk knocked backward and to the left. He landed on his side, the left wheel grinding him under. What might've been beetles puffed from his wide-open jaws.

A black female corpse rushed in at the driver's side door, snatching at the handle. Gary squeezed his trigger. Her hand vanished in a cloud of bone-fragments and putrid dust which whipped back into his face. Swearing, spitting, he fell back from the window, pawing at his mouth, trying not to retch at the taste. Legs suddenly weak, he crouched, stomach heaving, and leaned against the side of the van.

On the other side, Steve was firing burst after burst; battling to control his nausea, knowing he had to stay at his post too, to hold his end up. Gary started to rise—then heard a tremendous clang next to his ear. Turning, he saw the blade of an ax protruding through the van's metal flank. Three inches to the right, and it would've split his skull.

He could hear something dragging along outside. He stood, popping the clip from his gun and inserting another, he looked down from the window to see a blonde teen-aged girl, braces gleaming on her bared teeth, clinging with both hands to the ax handle.

Gary stepped back, kicked his heel powerfully into the ax blade. That was enough to dislodge it. Looking back out the window, he saw the dead girl vanish behind them.

"Through," Steve panted.

It was true. They'd run the gauntlet. The corpses faded into a pall of drifting smoke.

"Why aren't they using guns?" Steve asked, reloading.

"Maybe guns aren't personal enough," Linda said.

"You mean *sadistic* enough?" Gary asked, looking ahead.

They rounded a bend in the road flanked by the brick walls of burnt-out fisheries. The bridge came in sight.

It was up.

And the approach was blocked by a solid cordon of the living dead.

"I told you!" Gary screamed.

"Route 88," Buddy said. "We'll head for 88 . . . ."

"And if *that* bridge is up?" Steve shouted.

"We'll go south," Buddy growled, steering left onto Algonquin, away from the bridge. "Along the peninsula."

Gary watched the dead guarding the span. The gunfire would've alerted them, and he was sure they must've spotted the van, seen it take evasive action . . .

Confirmation came as two police cars barreled through the cordon in pursuit, trailing huge blue clouds of oil-smoke. One stalled before long, but the other kept coming.

Gary rejoined Steve in tossing cadavers out of the van, but took up his gun again as the remaining black-and-white drew near.

A figure leaned out of the cop car's window; a shotgun discharged with a *pumpf!*, and a tear gas canister hurtled toward the open back of the van, streaming vapor. To Gary's infinite relief, the missile fell short, rolling on the pavement, sparking and fuming.

The black-and-white pressed closer, and Gary saw the corpse reloading. Crouching, he drew bead on the cop car's right front wheel and fired. The tire came apart, rubber fragments flying, and the black-and-white spun into the side of the road, across a scorched lawn, and through the front of a half-burned building.

"Tear gas," Steve said. "Fucking *tear* gas!"

"They want us alive," Linda said. "They want to kill us face to face."

They resumed hurling the corpses overboard. Avoiding the downtown area altogether, Buddy swung closer and closer to Route 88. They passed several small platoons of dead, outstripping them with ease, even though it sounded to Gary as though the van's engine was running rougher and rougher. Some of the corpses leaped into cars, but didn't seem to be able to get them started.

Gary and Steve toiled away steadily. Soon there were only five cadavers left in the van.

Then four.

Then three.

Then—

The interior of the vehicle rang with a hellish shriek, and the air seemed to chill twenty degrees. A dead arm rose as if in a Nazi salute. Directly behind Aunt Lucy, a gaunt corpse in a gas-station attendant's uniform sat up suddenly, mouth twisted in a smile of awesome malevolence. On its chest the name *Hank* was embroidered with red thread.

Linda and Sally shrank back. Lucy turned and screamed, then

hurled herself back against the dashboard. Steve and Gary moved forward, ready to fire.

"Aunt Lucy!" Gary shouted. "Move aside! We can't get a clear—"

Instantly the corpse twisted around and flung itself onto the shrieking woman, sinking its fingers into her throat.

Buddy pulled out his Beretta and slammed on the brakes. The van immediately stalled out. Buddy aimed at the corpse.

Whipping one of its hands from Lucy's throat, it batted the pistol from Buddy's grip, then clapped its hand back on her windpipe.

Gary lunged closer, thinking to put a burst into the corpse's head from the side. But before he could fire, Buddy leaned sideways and rammed his elbow into the corpse's temple.

"Get back!" Gary shouted, afraid of hitting him. "I'll—"

Buddy only cocked his elbow back for another stroke. The cadaver turned, grinning directly into his face, and squeezed tighter on Lucy's neck. Her flesh ballooned up between its lube-greased fingers. Something popped, and Gary knew she was dead.

"Motherfucker!" Buddy cried, lashing out at the corpse again.

Like a viper distending its jaws, the corpse flung its mouth impossibly wide open and snapped Buddy's elbow off with a resonant crunch.

Buddy howled and hurled himself back against the door. His lower arm flopped bonelessly, attached only with shreds of flesh and cloth.

Face creasing in lines of awful satisfaction, the corpse shot its hand up to pull Buddy's crushed elbow from its mouth. That was when Gary finally cut loose.

A five-slug burst took a crescent gouge from the side of the corpse's head. It looked as if an invisible shark had ripped out a bite.

The corpse jerked its face toward Gary, still grinning. Faint and transparent, something oozed out of the rupture in its skull, an ectoplasmic head—in stronger light it would surely have been invisible. Gelatinous and unstable, it slid down on the corpse's shoulder and flattened there.

Gary screamed and blew off everything above the cadaver's jaw. Swaying, the phantom head rose back into place, rearing above the decapitated body; shrieking, the corpse lifted its arms and hurled itself forward.

Steve firing beside him, Gary gave it the rest of his clip. Bloodless bullet impacts racing over its upper body, the corpse was pummeled

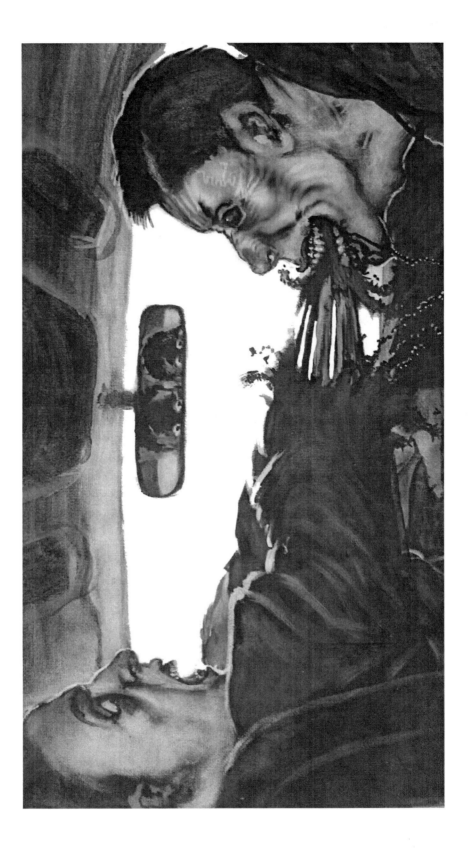

backward, chest caved in, throat blasted apart, severed arms flying from its shoulders like snapped twigs, the window behind it vanishing in a flurry of powdered glass.

Moaning, Uncle Buddy levered his door open and flopped outside. Gary and Steve retreated from the van, leaving the corpse kicking and struggling behind them, its feet booming off the walls of the vehicle.

Linda and Sally were already outside. Linda had Buddy's Beretta, which had flown into the back of the van.

Gary rounded the side of the van. Uncle Buddy, jacket-sleeve black with blood, was sitting on the grass near the curb, staring blankly at the ground. Gary went up to him.

Buddy raised his head slowly. His face had gone the color of frost. His breath puffed white in the cold.

"Uncle Buddy . . . " Gary began.

Buddy smiled. His eyes gleamed blankly. "Fuck you," he said, drool trickling over his lip. "You're all going to die, you cocksuckers."

Gary stepped back.

Buddy got sluggishly, clumsily to his feet, arm swaying back and forth. Blood poured from the hole in his sleeve, rilled from his finger-tips to the ground in unbroken streams. His smile widened.

"Rot in Hell," he whispered, staggering forward, hand brushing his pant leg, a vast bloodstain creeping down through the fabric.

Gary retreated another step.

"In *Hellllll*—" Buddy whispered, dropping to his knees, then onto his face at Gary's feet.

Gary bent. Buddy was still whispering, but Gary couldn't make the words out. Gary moved nearer.

All at once Buddy turned over onto his back and grabbed him by the lapel. His eyes were no longer blank; some kind of horrible trans-formation had come over him, his smile like the corpses' now. For a horrified instant Gary wondered if he might already have crossed over.

And come back . . .

Buddy pulled Gary's ear next to his mouth.

"I can see Him now," he said.

"Who?" Gary gasped.

Buddy chuckled. "You know. But He's not really a trooper at all . . . I'm falling into Him. Wheels and spikes . . . You'll fall into Him too, college boy. But Max first. Max and Him . . . "

Buddy's hand loosed Gary's lapel, and Gary began to rise; then Buddy jerked up at him. Gary threw himself back as Buddy's teeth snapped shut just inches from his ear.

With a last short hissing laugh, Buddy turned back over onto his stomach, lowered his face into the grass, and lay still.

Gary waited a few moments before feeling his uncle's throat for a pulse. There was none. He was surprised Buddy had died so quickly.

Shock, Gary told himself. *And blood-loss.*

"What did he say?" Steve asked him.

"It didn't make any sense," Gary answered. But there had been meaning there, even if he didn't understand. Yet.

Inside the van, the corpse was still thumping madly about.

"What now?" Gary asked. "How do we get that *thing* out of there?"

"Good question," Steve said.

They were still thinking when the problem solved itself.

"Look out!" Sally cried. They spun to see her retreating from the van's back doors; the headless, armless cadaver stumbled into view, pivoted in a drunken circle, and staggered off down the street.

"Get your aunt and that last body out of the van," Steve said. "I'll see if I can start the motor back up."

Gary and the women hauled the bodies out. Steve tried the key again and again, but the engine refused to turn over.

"Shit," Steve said, giving the key one last twist. Nothing. "Hopeless. We'd better take off."

"On *foot?*" Sally demanded.

"Better than sitting here till we get company. That gunfire must've carried pretty far."

They piled back out.

"Which way now?" Gary asked.

"South, I guess," Steve said. "Try to find ourselves someplace to hide till nightfall, then start moving again. Maybe those things can't see any better than us in the dark. Might be easier dodging 'em."

THEY started on their way. This had once been the wealthiest neighborhood in Bayside Point; some very snotty families had lived here, old resort money. Now their fine big houses were nothing but wreckage, and who knew what had become of the inhabitants? In spite of everything, Gary smiled at the thought of the rich laid low. He'd always had a leveling streak.

But us peasants are getting collectivized too, snapped a voice in his head, sounding suspiciously like Max's. *Being turned into a living corpse is a pretty high price to pay for equality.*

No arguing with that.

Go ahead, Gary thought. *Shatter my idealism.*

Crossing a broad lawn, the group rounded the corner of a gutted mansion. Looking through the windows in the ruin's tall brick wall, they saw that the first floor had collapsed completely into the cellar; no hiding place there.

"Too close to the van anyway," Steve said. "One of the first places they'll search."

Cutting across the block, they pushed steadily southward, keeping what cover they could. They approached streets with tremendous caution, waited endlessly to cross, watching, listening, screwing up their nerve; but once they decided to move, they shot from concealment like racehorses from chutes.

For the first three blocks, they saw no corpses, walking or otherwise. Then, as they neared a fourth street, they heard the tubercular sound of a diseased engine, and hid behind a charred facade.

Gary looked out through a doorway as a blue Thunderbird convertible rolled past, driven by a blonde female corpse, her hair blowing in the wind. A pickax over one shoulder, a huge dead man was kneeling on the seat beside her, looking backward. The car was doing about fifteen miles an hour; stumbling along behind it, clinking chains linking their wrists to the rear bumper, were two flabby, naked middle-aged men, hands tied behind their backs.

One fell and was dragged along on his stomach gasping and coughing, his flesh making a dry sandpapery sound on the asphalt. The other man seemed to get his second wind after that.

Once the T-Bird turned the corner, Gary and the others started out toward the street. Looking in the direction the car had come from, one block down, he saw dozens of bodies sprawled in the street, with several more strung from telephone poles. One of the hanged, facing away from Gary's group, was kicking strenuously at the end of his rope like some monstrous jumping-jack. Was the man in his death-throes, or had he just been resurrected?

As they headed into the wreckage on the other side of the street,

Gary glanced back at the kicking figure. The man wrenched free of the bonds on his arms and reached up to grab at the noose around his neck. Pressing forward, Gary didn't need to see the corpse drop to the street.

Free at last, free at last, Gary couldn't help himself thinking. *Thank God Almighty, he's free at last . . .*

Strung along both sides of the next block southward were more corpses, hanging head-down from the telephone poles, swinging stiffly in the wind, dusted with snow, mouths apparently stuffed with turf. From one's neck hung a lawn figure of the Virgin Mary, dangling by a chain.

EVENTUALLY they reached the fringe of one the town's undeveloped areas, a couple of acres of woodland, much of which had escaped the flames. Gary knew the place from his Junior High days; he and his friends had sometimes gone there after school. The paths hadn't changed much, and if memory served him right, there was an abandoned foundry in the middle of the woods. They reached the building before long, an ivy-covered brick shell with the remains of a corrugated steel roof.

"There's a cellar," he said as they went inside, feet crunching on broken bottles, high grass swishing about their legs. The opening was partially covered with a large piece of plywood; Steve started to lift the sheet, but Gary plucked at his arm.

"What if there are some down there?" heGary asked.

"Doing what?" Steve asked. "Waiting for someone to blunder into them?"

With a grunt he hauled the plywood aside. Gary trained his H and K into the revealed rectangle of shadow, but if anything was stirring, he couldn't see it. He started forward, Steve following him down the concrete steps. Somewhere in the gloom, water dripped; the air was cold and damp.

"Wish we had one of those flashlights," Gary said.

Slowly their eyes adjusted to the darkness. The cellar was about twenty by twenty, and empty except for garbage, mostly old newspapers, scattered over the floor. There were no exits except for the stairway.

Sally and Linda came slowly down the steps.

"I'll pull the plywood back over the opening," Gary said.

"But it'll get *dark* down here!" Sally protested.

Gary looked at Steve. Steve shrugged, and whispered in his ear: "Don't love her for her brain, pal."

Gary nodded. Going back up, he covered the hole, then cautiously made his way down.

"Wonder how long it'll take for us to start freezing?" Linda asked.

"A while," Gary said. "My heart's still beating like mad. I feel like I just drank about twenty cups of coffee."

"Sun'll be down pretty soon," Steve said. "Then we can get moving again. Besides, we're all dressed pretty warmly."

"We might be able to do better than that," Gary said.

"What do you mean?"

"Ben Wilson's diving store. We're heading south. We should check it out. Big old cinderblock building, might not have burned. We could get drysuits."

"Drysuits?"

"Yeah. They're like wetsuits, but they don't need water. They'd keep us real toasty."

"Didn't old man Wilson keep a shotgun behind his counter?" Steve asked.

"I caught some of his rock salt," Gary said, nodding. "That Mischief Night, when we broke his front window. Gun might still be there, I suppose."

"Wouldn't mind trading this rifle for a twelve-gauge," Steve said. "Linda, you know how to use this Heckler and Koch?"

"Gary's father took us all shooting one time," Linda answered. "I could manage. But I'd rather have that shotgun—if it's working."

"Wise woman."

"What about me?" Sally demanded. "What do I get?"

"You don't know anything about guns," Steve said.

"I could learn. Linda could give me that pistol."

"Come on, Sally."

"Come on yourself."

"Hate to change the subject," Gary broke in, sensing things were just about to get nasty, "But do you think we should have someone on the stairs? Looking out through the cracks or something?"

"Won't be able to see much with that tall grass," Steve said. "Might be a good idea to go and just listen, though."

"I'll do it for a while," Gary said. He found his way back to the steps, and went up, to crouch just below the plywood. A small amount of light came in under the moldy-smelling sheet. He lifted the plywood to look out; but Steve was right about the weeds.

Gary settled himself in a more comfortable position, listening. Somewhere in the distance a car chugged along; he wondered if it was that T-Bird. Also if it was still dragging that man behind it—and if the second guy had fallen. Were they being scraped to death even now? Or would they be set back on their feet before too much damage was done? The dead plainly enjoyed torturing their victims, but when it came to killing, they seemed to prefer strangulation. It occurred to him that their potential reinforcements might be resurrected sooner the more intact they were. Or, at least, the more intact their vital organs were. The drowning victim he'd seen at the beach had risen in less than twenty-four hours; his father, worked over by the undertakers, had taken more than twice as long. Uncle Buddy hadn't been strangled, but he *had* given his assailant special provocation—

Special provocation, Gary thought. What an idiot Buddy was. He and Lucy might still be alive, if only he'd listened . . .

Aren't you glad he didn't, Gary thought.

And instantly recoiled from the idea. He'd never had anything against Aunt Lucy.

But as for Buddy . . . well, it was hard to feel anything but relief that he was gone. He'd left Max and his own brother to die; surely Dave's death had cracked him completely. Unless Buddy had always just been an evil son of a bitch.

And yet Gary couldn't get comfortable with his lack of grief. There was something threatening in it; he felt almost as if he was being subjected to some sort of temptation, as though he were on the brink of some terrible surrender. He told himself he wasn't actually *glad* Buddy was dead—but he could easily imagine himself sliding into that state, remembering Max fading into the distance behind the van, Buddy's last horrible gloating words and the *clack* of his teeth...Yes, it would be easy to smile at the thought of Hank's jaws shutting on the old fat shithead's arm, the long elastic strings of flesh stretched between Buddy's elbow and the crimson teeth as Buddy pulled his limb back—

Stop it! Shrieked a voice in Gary's mind. The pleasure receded. So did that sense of danger, somehow. He'd moved back from the brink.

What was on the other side, he didn't know, but he knew it must be terrible.

He's on the other side, Gary thought suddenly.

But who was *He?* Who had Buddy seen as he stared across the border into the land of the dead?

You'll fall into him too, college boy, Buddy had said. *But Max first . . .*

Gary wrenched his mind free, fixing his concentration on the sounds outside. The chugging of the distant car had faded; now he thought he could make out far-off screams.

Max, he thought suddenly. *Oh my God, my brother's still out there. And they probably got him already—*

Gary shook his head. If anyone could've slipped out of that situation, it was Max.

Bullshit, came the answer. *It was hopeless, and you know it. They were closing in on three sides. They caught him and filled his throat with dirt and choked him to death, and soon he'll be one of them, Gary boy—*

"Just stop thinking about it," Gary told himself under his breath.

How'd you like to have your neck wrung by your own bro—

"You say something, Gary?" Steve called softly from the bottom of the steps.

"No," Gary answered.

He heard someone coming up toward him. There was just enough light for him to see that it was Linda. She huddled against his legs.

"Love you," she said tremulously.

"Love you too, babe," he answered.

Her hand slid into his.

"Steve," came Sally's voice from the blackness.

"What?" Steve asked.

"What if MacAleer's right?"

"I'd be surprised if that Bible-thumper's been on target about anything in his life . . . .But right about what, anyway?"

"What's happening."

Steve chuckled.

"Go ahead, laugh," Sally said. "But he scared the hell out of me."

"After all we've seen today, *MacAleer's* what's bothering you?"

"What's going to happen to *us* if he's right, Steve?" Sally whispered.

"What are you talking about?"

"You know damn well."

Steve hesitated before replying. "Frankly, no I don't."

"There won't be any hope for *us* at all."

"If this *is* Hell, maybe not. But why should it be any worse for *us*?"

"How can you ask me that? After what we—"

"*Did?* We've done a lot of things. Which particular mountain are you making a molehill of?"

"That's backward."

"Yeah, I've always had trouble with that one."

"I know."

"I don't believe any of MacAleer's horseshit anyway," Steve continued. "And neither should you."

"*I* believe it," Linda said.

"Glad to hear you admit it," Steve said.

"Couldn't you see it on those things' faces?" Linda asked.

"See what?"

"That they're straight out of Hell."

Although he couldn't swallow MacAleer's theory, Gary knew all too well what she meant. Just looking at them was like being stabbed in the eyes. Even in the thick of combat, even while *shooting* at them, he'd been strongly tempted to jerk his face away.

"They're ugly all right," Steve admitted, with a glibness that Gary found almost idiotically shallow. How could Steve trivialize the threat in such a fashion? Even if they weren't in Hell, they were clearly experiencing a side of reality that would do for a stand-in.

"*Ugly?*" Linda demanded.

"Downright hideous, okay?" Steve said. "But what does that tell us? That they're the damned? That the whole Christian world-view is true? Come on."

Point Steve, Gary thought. *Is he back on track?*

"I dreamed I was at the Last Judgment," Linda said. "And then the world ended."

Steve laughed. "So *this* is how the world ends, huh? What makes you so sure it's all over?"

Just what I would've asked, Gary thought.

"I have eyes," Linda said.

"So why don't you just give up right now?" Steve asked.

Yeah, why not, Linda? Gary wondered.

"Maybe there's a way out," Linda said.

Please Linda, not God . . .

"What's that?" Steve asked. "Religion?"

"You said it, not me."

Oh Linda, ugh . . .

"Sure hasn't done you any good so far, has it?" Steve asked.

"I'm kind of new at it."

How feeble, Gary thought, thoroughly back in Steve's camp now.

"Well, good luck," Steve said. "But I wouldn't get my hopes up if I were you. God's a fantasy, mere wishful thinking. Made in our own image, because we can't stand to face the facts."

"What facts?"

"That we're the source of everything that's really divine. That we can't rely on anyone or anything else to save ourselves."

"If we're so godlike," Linda said, "why *don't* we realize it?"

"Because of guilt-trips laid on us by people who want to control us. That's all religion is. A chain to keep you down."

"Some people should be shackled," Linda said.

"Folks like MacAleer? Maybe. But who's to say what's right for someone else? Nobody's going to tell *me* what's right or wrong. I decide that."

"Because you're God, right?"

"We're all God. Or might as well be."

"You really shouldn't try to argue with him," Gary said. "You just better hope he's right."

Linda slipped her hand from his. "Our only hope is if he's *wrong.*"

"Then why don't you stop arguing and start praying?" Gary asked.

At that, Linda muttered something and left him, disappearing into the darkness below.

"Besides, you should *all* shut up," Gary went on. "Makes it hard listening to what's going on topside."

There was no more conversation after that; but Gary thought he could hear Linda crying quietly.

CHAPTER 15
RECRUITS

MAX watched the van speed off into the distance and for a maddened instant thought of blasting the tires with his Remington. He even brought the gun up to fire, but there was no point in shooting. At least Gary and Linda might escape.

He lowered the gun.

He looked north, then west and south. Scores of dead were coming. The tightening cordon seemed thinnest to the south.

"That way!" he cried. "Dennis, reload! We go first!"

They started south across the front lawns of leveled lakeside houses. A half-dozen corpses approached rapidly along Carter, veering off the street toward them.

"Just cripple 'em!" Max shouted to Dennis, shoving cartridges into his shotgun. "All we have to do is break through!"

He looked back briefly. The others had somehow kept from falling too far behind, though MacAleer and his wife were plainly struggling.

Ahead, the six were drawing near, the first barely twenty feet away. Max blew its left leg off at the hip.

Two blasts from Dennis. A corpse's kneecap vanished. The ragged figure toppled to the grass on its chin.

Max and Dennis pressed past the fallen corpses, who were already crawling to grab them. A few moments later Max heard MacAleer's Beretta roar three times—the crippled cadavers had turned their attention elsewhere.

The other four corpses closed in. Two had baseball bats, but a barehanded one was already so near that Max went for the headshot, blowing its face in. He sprayed another's leg all over the grass; then a bat was whistling at Max's shoulder.

He twisted aside and jerked backward, pump-BLAST. The bat shattered in a shower of splinters. Dropping the ruined shaft, the corpse followed him eagerly, licking its lips with a dried leathery strip of a tongue and clutching with bony fingers.

Max's foot came down on a lawn ornament, tilting it over. He fell, landing hard on his back, breath bursting from his lips.

The corpse hurled itself headlong at him. He barely had time to pump and lift his gun, the dead man's ribcage jolted against the barrel just as Max pulled the trigger. Gunsmoke belched out of the weapon's mouth and the corpse shot backward as though jerked by a rope.

Somehow it landed on its feet. It swayed, staggered. Max heard a crackling sound. The top half of the cadaver's torso flopped over as the spine broke, and the whole body fell.

Max started to get up, but all at once two hands locked on his throat, and he was hurled back to the grass by one of the corpses he'd crippled; she leered down at him with a grin that seemed half a foot wide, a mummified dark-haired woman, squinting through a pair of silver wire-rimmed glasses, face spotted with purplish mold. Her fingers tightened horribly, and Max felt things shifting in his throat, blood veins swelling in his temple . . .

Then her head jerked up, she hissed as if in surprise—and the muzzle of Dennis's Remington went flush against her brow and roared, injecting her skull with the full fury of a twelve-gauge discharge, force, heat, gas, pellets, sabot. Her head bulged and broke, parting into two straps of burning meat that flapped sideways against her shoulders.

The grip on Max's throat slackened. Knowing he wouldn't get a second chance, he dropped his shotgun and yanked the hands from his neck. The butt of Dennis's gun thumped into the decapitated horror, knocking her aside. Max grabbed his weapon again and leaped to his feet, ears still ringing from Dennis's blast.

A glance revealed that Dennis had downed the fourth corpse.

But more were speeding their way.

MacAleer appeared, panting. Taking careful aim with his Beretta, he kneecapped one of the advancing corpses. The others came on howling.

Max, Dennis and the others withdrew toward the scorch-marked facade of a white-shingled house, MacAleer bringing up the rear, blasting away with his pistol. Max and his uncle reloaded feverishly, then fell back with MacAleer.

When the last corpse lay writhing on the grass, they raced south again. The way was clear before them, but a look back showed fifty at least drawing in behind.

A thick pall of grey-blue smoke drifted onto Carter.

"Keep together!" Max cried. "Follow me!"

They plunged into it. Knowing they were hidden for the moment, Max led them across the street, in among the ruins. Emerging from the smoke, he rounded the corner of a garage—only to throw himself flat as a shotgun bellowed.

Raising his head, he saw a group of people ranged against the wall of the garage; a terrified looking middle-aged woman had a smoking Mossberg pump pointed at him.

"Don't shoot!" he shouted.

The woman lowered her shotgun. A teenaged girl beside her held an over-under, and several other women had hatchets and carving-knives. Clothes blotted with bloodstains, two white-faced men sat with their backs to the wall.

Max's companions arrived as he picked himself up.

"They're coming," Dennis told him breathlessly. "Heard that shot."

Max looked west. Several high chain-link fences stood in the way. He started north along the garage wall.

"You'd better come with us," he told the woman with the Mossberg as he passed.

"My husband . . ." she said, nodding toward one of the blood-stained men. "He won't be able to keep up."

"They'll be all over you in a minute," Max said over his shoulder, pausing.

"You have guns!" she answered. "Stay with us. Maybe we can hold them off—"

"I'm not getting my people killed," Max said, pressing on.

Father Chuck ran up beside him.

"Max, we can't leave them to die," he panted.

"What good'll it do if we all buy it?" Max asked.

"What kind of a Christian are you?" the priest demanded.

"Show me what kind *you* are, Father," Max replied. "Stay here. Set me an example."

Father Chuck fell behind. But Max didn't look to see if he was going back.

Going through a gate in a tall hedge, Max led them past a swimming pool. A dead man lay by the pool-side, holding an axe, his face hanging over the edge, head surrounded by a dark blur of floating hair. Out in the middle, a severed arm in a dark blue sleeve squirmed on the bottom like a giant worm.

Following a driveway, Max came out between two fire-eaten walls and halted, looking east from behind an overturned pickup truck. Through the thinning smoke he could see shadowy shapes speeding mechanically south on Carter. He retreated, motioning his companions back into the driveway.

Shotgun fire from behind; fleshless screams of rage and delight. The other group had begun their last battle. How long would they hold them off?

Max looked round the truck again, back toward Carter. The corpses moving south had vanished. Time to go.

They headed west, deep into a grove of burnt-out hollies. Denuded as they were, the branches were still thick enough to provide some cover, particularly in the middle of the stand.

And all the while, the gunfire and the shrieking of the corpses intensified. Suddenly other voices started to scream, living voices. The gunfire died.

Striped with soot from limbs they'd brushed, the group soon reached a broad asphalt drive, and followed it back to a large two-story brick house that looked fairly intact. Max went up to the front door, pushed it open. Inside was a well-furnished living-room, the rear third of it buried under debris from a collapsed ceiling. Max guessed that the house had been torched from behind, and that a strong northwestern wind had kept the fire from spreading too far.

He signaled the others inside, then closed the door behind them. The MacAleers promptly collapsed upon the floor. Aunt Camille and Father Chuck sagged against a wall. Max smirked at the priest, perversely pleased that he hadn't cast his lot with the other group; seeing Max looking at him, Father Chuck dropped his gaze floorward.

"We'll hole up here for a while," Max announced. "Wait until nightfall. If we ca—" He broke off as a raw cry of agony reached them, louder and more heart-wrenching than any they'd yet heard.

He swallowed, pressed on: "Those folks should distract them for a while. Maybe the corpses'll think they got us." He stationed himself at a window, watching the drive.

"But what if your father's back there?" Dennis asked. "They'll know we got away. They'll probably comb every house in the neighborhood. We'd better keep moving."

"Please, no," Mrs. MacAleer groaned. "My heart won't take it. At least give us time to catch our breath . . . "

"That may be all the time they'll need to find us," Dennis said.

Max shook his head. "We should stay put. My father might not be with that group."

"But what if he *is*?"

"Then he'll probably figure we kept moving. He must know we spotted him by the shelter, because we expected the trap."

"God, I hope you're right."

"Do you really think we'll be safe here?" Aunt Camille asked.

"We're not safe anywhere," Max answered. "But they must think they pretty much flushed the neighborhood out when they torched it."

"What about those people we passed?" Dennis asked.

"As I said, the corpses might think that was us. If that doesn't fool them, they'll probably realize what they *actually* were. Stragglers on the run. No reason to comb the neighborhood again."

"You always sound so sure of yourself," Camille said.

"Sorry," Max answered.

"You got young Dave killed, you know that?" Camille asked.

"Yeah. I took a calculated risk. I thought Gary had gotten a little trigger-happy. He thought so too at first. Is there anything I can do to bring Dave back to life? Please tell me."

Camille looked away.

"I bet he'll be dying in my dreams for the rest of my life," Max said. "Does that satisfy you?"

"That might not be very long," Dennis answered.

"Well, I'm damn sorry about that too," Max said.

"Don't listen to us, Max," Camille said suddenly. "You've been doing your best for us, I know."

Glad you think so, Max thought. Stubborn reflex had caused him to ignore his brother back in the culvert, and it *had* cost Dave his life. Max had carefully cultivated that reflex over the years, because he usually *was* right; the odds had never really caught up with him. Now they'd more than made up for lost time.

Just about murdered him yourself, he thought.

But worst of all was the possibility that he hadn't merely gotten Dave killed. If MacAleer was right—and the fundamentalist's theory seemed more horribly plausible all the time—Dave was in Hell now. Another mistake might consign the whole group to damnation. Max felt as though he were bent beneath a vast flat stone. And after Dave's death, he didn't know if he was the man to bear that terrible weight.

Yet what other choice did he have? He might collapse under the burden—but could any of the others take his place? He doubted it. He *was* right most of the time. Half the world had been slaughtered, but his group was still alive. If they'd listened to Buddy, they would've been killed, Max was certain. He was just as sure they should stay put now. There was no comfort to be taken in any of that. It simply meant he had to continue beneath the stone.

THE day wore on. For whatever reason, the dead never investigated the house—though a huge troop of them, by the sound of it, pushed by to the south.

Dusk gathered, deepened into night. The group readied to leave.

"We'll head south till morning," Max said.

"What about sleep?" Mrs. MacAleer asked.

"It'll have to wait till we find another hiding-place," Max said. "We'll sleep during the day, travel at night."

When everyone was set, Max opened the door and stepped out. The streetlights were on, though they blinked from time to time. Passing through the burned hollies, the glow from the lamps threw a skein of shadows across the front yard.

"Why do you think they're keeping the lights on?" Jamie MacAleer asked behind Max.

"The better to see us with," Max answered.

"I'm surprised the power's on at all," Dennis said.

"Because of the fires?" Max asked as they went down the steps. "The lines here on the peninsula run underground. And most of the lamp poles are aluminum."

Rounding the house, they headed south through the backyard. Climbing over the fence proved easy enough; crossing another yard, they found themselves at Hirsch St. There was no sign of danger, and they crossed, entering the wreckage on the far side.

But as they neared the next street, they heard an engine laboring, and took cover. Max peered through a broken window-pane. Belching blue smoke, a huge Cadillac hearse with mirrored windows rolled by, something dragging behind it. With a shock Max suddenly realized what the object roped to the bumper was: one of the large crucifixes from St. Paul's, a dead German shepherd spread-eagled over the body of Christ. Max swore softly and crossed himself. He had always loved that crucifix, the most beautiful he'd ever seen in a parish church.

Well, he thought, shaking his head, smiling in cold rage, *at least they're not Catholics.*

Once the hearse was out of sight, the group continued on its way, soon approaching Beichmann Avenue. Directly ahead, over hogbacks of dark debris, they could see the tall yellowish lights that surrounded a huge boardwalk parking lot, and could hear vehicles coughing and rattling off in that direction.

They moved closer and closer to the lot. Beyond the charred ridges, human screams tore the night; corpses shrieked in mocking answer.

"One party we want to pass up," Max said, leading westward, thinking to round the parking-lot and cross Beichmann Avenue closer to the heart of town. But Dennis soon noticed five motionless sentries atop a mound of rubble a hundred yards or so distant, outlined against the glare of a battery of blue-white lights off by the train tracks.

"Think they've spotted us?" Dennis asked.

"Doubt it," Max said.

"We could circle 'em to the North."

"Then we'd just have to cross Beichmann further west, right in the middle of town. Looks too damn well lit over that way. I think we'd better try to slip by the parking lot on the boardwalk side. The boardwalk lights were out."

They headed east again through the desolation, back the way they'd come. Paralleling the parking lot two blocks north, they forged steadily toward the boardwalk.

The cough of engines had faded from the parking lot. The vehicles seemed to have moved west, back along Beichmann perhaps.

Yet now they came closer again. Headlights flashed over the ruins, shining on broken glass. Shadows from leaning spars swept crazily across the ashes.

Max could see a small fleet, cars and vans. He crouched, motioning the others down.

The vehicles juddered to a halt one street north, then vanished inside a drifting pall of smoke, headlights filling it with a cold amber glow. Doors thumped hollowly. When the smoke rolled past, fifteen or so silhouettes were moving inorganically over the no-man's-land toward Max's group.

Staying as low as possible, trying to keep as much wreckage between themselves and the corpses as they could, the fugitives hastened south, then east, coming very close to the fringe of the garishly lit parking lot.

Max glanced back. Even as he looked, he saw a flurry of shadowy motion in front of the corpses—it was hard to tell in the darkness, but it seemed as though two or three people had been flushed out, and the dead were running them swiftly to earth.

Suddenly the sounds of another pursuit broke out closer to hand; Max looked around to see several women, limned by the parking lot lights, dashing alongside a soot-splotched bungalow to the east. He and the others threw themselves flat in a small crater-like depression in a field of fallen bricks.

He raised his head slightly, just over the lip of the depression, watching as a group of corpses dashed after the women, caught two, and dragged them back toward the parking lot. The third woman vanished in darkness, three of the pursuers hard behind her.

Hope you make it, lady, Max thought. *All the same, I'm glad it's you and not me.*

Dennis crawled up beside him.

"What do you think?" Dennis whispered.

"That we should thank God for all those other survivors out there," Max answered.

And ask His forgiveness for thanking him.

THE group sat tight for some time.

"I'm going to take a look," Max told Dennis.

"At what?"

"The lot."

"Are you nuts?"

"I want to see how many of them are over there. We might have to circle back west after all. I won't be long. Stay put here."

Silently Max crawled out of the depression and across the bricks; snaking over frost-stiffened grass, he made his way slowly up onto the slope of scorched wood that blocked his view. Reaching the top, he peered out over the parking-lot. A low involuntary gasp passed his lips.

Except for lanes obviously intended for vehicles (there were several vans being unloaded even now), the lot was almost completely covered with bodies. Thousands of them. Every once in a while one would rise stiffly to its feet—whereupon several of the dozens of walking dead patrolling the lot would converge and escort it toward the band shell on the far side of the lot. From the arch of the band shell a dozen or more bodies swung head-down in the wind, lifeless and contorted.

Max scanned the stage with his binoculars. On it stood two corpses in state trooper uniforms. One was a squat simian figure, the other a giant, taller by at least a head. On either side of them stood inverted crosses.

The newly-risen dead were brought before the troopers, forced to kneel in front of the stage. Then they were beckoned onto the platform one at a time by the giant. There the summoned corpse would kneel once more; the giant would place its hand on the bowed head, as if in some sort of benediction; the kneeling corpse would go back down, another would be summoned. The corpses that had been blessed would then join a large group, some fifty or sixty strong, that had gathered at the western end of the lot.

Into the midst of this, two pickup-trucks drove, pulling up near the band shell. Gangs of corpses set immediately to unloading them. One truck was full of inanimate bodies, the other with live people, who were led onto the grass beside the stage and forced to the ground.

The troopers came down from the stage. The giant kneeled next to one of the living, plucked a gag from the man's mouth. A wail of utter despair reached Max's ears. The giant reached down into the earth, apparently grabbing a handful; then it silenced the man's cry by thrusting the dirt into the gaping mouth. The man bucked and struggled, but the corpse holding him kept him pinned to the earth.

Max crept back to his companions.

"What are they doing over there?" Father Chuck whispered.

"Piling up bodies," Max answered. "And delivering prisoners. I think I've seen their leader, too. He's wearing a state trooper's outfit. Must be six foot ten." He paused. "Those women we saw must've made a break from the lot—"

Sounds of movement came from the rubble off to the east and Max and Dennis looked over the rim of the depression. Three corpses had the woman who'd evaded capture. Max thought he could hear her whimpering faintly.

"Thorough bastards, aren't they?" Dennis asked.

CHAPTER 16
ENGINE TROUBLE

DAYBREAK found them in a concrete-walled auto repair shop, completely intact, on the southern edge of town. Dennis and Father Chuck had taken the first watch, the priest looking out through the windows of the sliding bay door, Dennis stationed by a glass door at the other end of the building. The women and Jamie MacAleer were already asleep in the office, where they'd found a gas heater. Max had started it up with some difficulty, then joined Dennis at his post.

Max viewed the blackened landscape outside. There was much less drifting smoke than the day before; there was also less light. The diseased sun had just risen and, though the dark patches didn't seem to have spread, the glowing orb appeared even paler than yesterday.

Max saw no figures moving in the desolation, or even in the distance. He wondered where the dead had gone.

The southern part of town had been full of them during the dark hours of the morning. After managing to slip by the parking lot, the group had spent the next seven frantic hours covering one mile, scrambling in and out of refuge, barely avoiding one patrol after another. It had reminded Max of accounts of the last few Jews in the Warsaw Ghetto, trying to elude capture after the rebellion was crushed, scrabbling and crawling through the rubble, never far from some searching Nazi platoon.

"Why are we still alive?" Dennis asked.

"The Grace of God," said Mr. MacAleer.

"You think He's showing us mercy?" Dennis asked. "Maybe He's enjoying roasting us over a slow fire."

"Cheerful thought," Max said. "But I don't believe it. A being like that wouldn't be God."

"What about all that stuff you said to Father Chuck? About God not being a tame lion?"

"There's a big difference between that and God being a sadistic maniac. I believe He loves us. That the greatest gift He could give us is existence, and that He'll permit us to suffer rather than taking it away. I think He still even loves Satan Himself." Max laughed. "Though I can't think why. But nobody put me in charge, did they? And it's just as well."

"But should I still be afraid of Him?" Dennis asked.

"Hell yeah. What could be scarier than something like that? What do the angels always say when they appear in the Bible? *Fear not.* Precisely because they're terrifying. And they're just reflections of Him."

"*Was* that Him in the dream?"

"Of course it was," said MacAleer.

"Sure was scary enough, wasn't He?" Max said.

Dennis said nothing for a time. "What was the verdict in *your* dream, Max?"

"I didn't hear it," Max said. "I woke up."

"Mine was guilty," Dennis said. "Mine *and* Camille's."

"Maybe it doesn't mean anything," Max said, without much conviction.

"You know better than that," MacAleer answered.

"Do I?"

"I do," Dennis said. "I'm sure of it. God's going to make me pay for what I've done."

"Not if you throw yourself on his Mercy," MacAleer said.

"How do I do that?" Dennis asked.

"Confess you're a sinner. Admit to yourself that you can't achieve salvation without acknowledging the sacrifice Christ made for you."

"Considering the kind of life I've led," Dennis said, "I don't think anything so easy could work."

"That's because you don't know the *power* of the Lord Jesus."

"And you do?" Max asked.

"Yes," MacAleer replied.

"You've acknowledged Jesus as your Lord and Savior?" Max asked.

"Yes."

"You're born again, washed in the blood?"

"Yes."

"What was the verdict in *your* dream?"

MacAleer was silent.

"Well?"

"You're trying to trip me up."

"Oh?"

"To stop me from preaching the good news to your uncle."

"What was the verdict, Mr. MacAleer?" Max asked.

MacAleer looked away. "I woke up too," he said. Suddenly his eyes swept back to Max, vehement, defiant. "That doesn't mean that what I told your uncle is false. And it doesn't mean I'm not justified. All it might mean is that I woke up, that's all——"

Max laughed.

"Max," Dennis said, "has it occurred to you that I might really be interested in what he has to say? Regardless of whether or not he's in the same boat with the rest of us?"

"That doesn't make any difference to you?" Max asked. "Doesn't it suggest his little formula doesn't work as well as he says?"

"I notice you seem to have accepted my *explanation*," MacAleer said.

"Not quite yet," Max said. "But let's say that I do. Fine and dandy. Seems to fit a lot of facts. But your ideas on how we should extricate ourselves don't seem so impressive. You're still here to explain them."

"But maybe they're right anyway, Max," Dennis said. "Maybe he just doesn't have enough faith."

Max grinned, impressed by Dennis's logic; he was having some effect on his uncle.

"How dare you suggest such a thing?" MacAleer demanded.

"It follows from what you've been saying," Max said. "If your theories are correct, of course."

"Well, what do you want your uncle *to* believe?" MacAleer demanded.

"That's it, change the subject." Max said.

"A lot of superstitions?"

"What superstitions are those?"

"Worshipping the Virgin Mary? Bowing down before relics?"

Max went through his pockets. "Well, I *do* have this bone-fragment from St. Severa here somewhere . . . "

MacAleer's eyes bulged, as though Max were really about to produce the abominable object.

Max snapped his fingers. "Left it back at the shelter."

"Thank God," MacAleer said.

"Us Papists have better alternatives in any case."

"Like what? Confessing to a mere man in a stuffy little black booth?"

"The stuffier the better," Max said. "Booth's optional, though. Icing on the cake."

"Then why don't you just go over to Father Chuck and have him confess you both right now?"

Max mulled it over. "Haven't had time up till now—thought we were going to be in the shelter longer. Should've spoken to him about it before I dozed off last night." He looked at Dennis. "Want to join me?"

"You don't have to be Catholic?" Dennis asked.

"Nope. You just have to be sorry."

"So that's *your* formula for salvation?" MacAleer demanded.

"What the hell," Dennis said, and handed his shotgun to MacAleer. "Watch the window for me, will you?"

"Sure," MacAleer said, obviously agitated. "But I'm telling you, that witch doctor won't do you any good."

"Probably won't hurt either."

Dennis and Max walked off toward the priest.

"Don't I have to know some kind of prayers or something?" Dennis asked.

"Father Chuck'll tell you what to say," Max said. "And remember, we're not promising instant deliverance here. Even if your sins are forgiven, that's not enough. You *do* have to believe. MacAleer's right about that. He's not as big an idiot as he seems. But faith without works is dead, as Saint James used to say. And unforgiven sins are a big obstacle to belief."

Making their way round a big green Oldsmobile, they reached Father Chuck, who had temporary custody of MacAleer's Beretta. The priest looked briefly over his shoulder as they came up, then back through the bay-door windows.

"Father?" Max asked.

"Yes?"

Max hesitated; he had some difficulty asking. "I was . . . well, wondering if you might hear our confessions."

"You want *me* to hear *yours*?" Father Chuck asked sarcastically.

"Yes, Father," Max answered, trying to ignore Father Chuck's tone.

"I'm flattered," Father Chuck said. "But I don't do confessions."

"Come on, Father. I know I've rubbed you the wrong way, but . . . "

"I don't *do* confessions," the priest insisted, apparently in earnest.

"I thought administering the sacraments was supposed to be one of your jobs."

"Some sacraments. The ones I approve of."

"*You* approve of——?"

"Well, not just me. The *vast* majority of Catholics don't feel any need to be confessed. And I have no wish to encourage them in something so degrading."

"Degrading to who?"

"The person who comes crawling in to confess, to be contrite for things that no one needs to be contrite for. All that guilt and self-loathing—the most damaging of emotions. I'm not going to cater to such negative feelings. I prefer trying to lift people up, to make them realize that the glass is half-full, not half empty . . . "

"What about when the glass is busted, Father?" Max asked.

"Even then, the contents are still on the counter or the floor," Father Chuck replied.

"Did you learn that in seminary?"

"Yes," Father Chuck answered stoutly. "Do you really think your hellfire-and-brimstone version of Catholicism is still being taught?"

"So what is it now? Theology of clichés?"

"For some people, the Sermon on the Mount is nothing but a collection of clichés."

"One man's beatitude is another man's banality?"

"The Church must learn to express itself in the modern world. And clichés are an indispensible tool."

Max laughed, thunderstruck. "You mean they really *did* teach you theology of clichés? It's a *real subject?*"

"I wrote a paper on it."

"On always seeing the silver lining? Or letting a smile be your umbrella?"

"On how it's better to travel hopefully than to arrive."

"*Is* it better?"

"Why do you think it's become a cliché?"

"Do you also think it's better to starve hopefully than to eat? Better to lust hopefully than to screw?"

Father Chuck shrugged." Perhaps it is—my sexual experiences are never that fulfilling. But my mind's still open."

"Just like it is about your vows, I take it?"

"Better to let off steam than hold it in."

"Wouldn't it be better just to think hopefully about letting off steam? That way you could live up to your vows *and* your clichés."

"How medieval."

Medieval? Max thought. He hadn't the slightest idea of what Father Chuck meant.

"Besides," the priest went on, "most American Catholics think priests should be allowed to marry, or would if they thought about it."

"Father, you're giving me a headache."

"I'm sorry I'm not to your tastes."

"Look, I'm sorry too," Max said, exasperated. "But all this is beside the point."

"And what's the point?"

"Confession. Would you at least go through the motions for us?"

"Will *that* work?" Dennis asked anxiously. "Doesn't *he* have to believe?"

"No," Max said. "Once he's been ordained, he has the powers for the rest of his life, no matter what he does. He could become a Marxist, and still absolve us."

"Some of my best friends are Marxists," Father Chuck said. "And they don't do confessions either."

"I believe it," Max said.

"And I very much resent this notion that priests are actually repositories of magic. I'd reject that kind of power in any case. What am I, a witch doctor?"

"I guess not."

"Max, he says he doesn't have any power," Dennis said.

"Don't worry about it," Max answered. "If we can just get him to administer the sacrament—"

"Get me to act contrary to my own beliefs, you mean," Father Chuck snapped. "Well, you might as well forget it."

"Maybe we should just hold a gun to your head," Max said.

"Now hold on, Max," Dennis protested.

"Just kidding," Max said, and paused. "You wouldn't be denying us the sacrament because you don't like me, would you, Father?"

"What do you mean?"

"Well, I'm not sure I buy that stuff about standing firm in your convictions. Not after you made such a big deal about going back to help those people, then wimped out yourself."

Father Chuck spun, eyes burning. "You bastard."

"Come on, Uncle Dennis," Max said.

They headed back toward MacAleer.

"Don't you think that was being pretty rough on him?" Dennis asked.

"Maybe," Max said. "I'm real tired. And pissed off. I think confession *works*, you see. Which means he was being a lot rougher on us than I was on him. He's a son of a bitch."

He spat.

MAX caught some sleep, woke for a stint on watch, and dozed off again after Jamie MacAleer replaced him. Waking once more three hours later, well into the afternoon, he had some food.

"Think we should try to start that Oldsmobile?" Dennis asked.

"What the hell," Max said, screwing the top back on his canteen. He got to his feet, and they went out to the car.

"Hey," Jamie called, "When's someone going to relieve me?"

Max looked over his shoulder at him. The teenager held Max's Remington, and had it pointed carelessly at him and Dennis.

"Hold your water," Max replied. "And aim that thing some place else, huh?"

Jamie swung it aside.

"Shouldn't have given him that gun," Dennis told Max as they arrived at the Oldsmobile's driver-side door.

"Nothing to be done about it," Max said. "Not if I wanted to get some shuteye."

He opened the door and slid behind the wheel. The keys were in the ignition. He turned them. Nothing at all.

"Want to take a look under the hood?" Dennis asked. "Might be able to fix it."

"We *are* in a repair shop, aren't we?" Max asked, getting back out. He went up to the front of the car; feeling around under the hood for the release, he became aware of a faint but foul odor.

"You smell anything?" Dennis asked, sniffing.

"Yeah."

"You know, I'd swear it was coming from under the hood," Dennis said.

"We'll know in a second," Max said, locating the catch. Pushing it up, he lifted the hood.

A noxious stench burst over them. They staggered back, gagging. The hood remained locked in the upright position as though the hinges were rusty.

"Whoa," Max said, and laughed, fanning his hand before his face.

"The engine, Max," Dennis gasped.

Max squinted at it. The top of the block seethed with what appeared to be some bubbling black substance.

"What *is* that stuff?" Dennis asked.

"Damned if I know," Max said.

Now that the hood had been lifted, the smell, which had obviously been collecting for some time, dissipated quickly. Max went closer to the car. The light wasn't so strong; he still couldn't tell what the substance was, whether it was some kind of liquid, or even perhaps something alive. He moved closer still, leaned over the radiator, the stench growing in his nostrils . . .

And realized what the stuff was.

"Worms," he announced. "Black *maggots.*"

He'd never seen anything like them. They were thinner than ordinary maggots, with very distinct heads, and formidable looking spiked jaws.

"What are they doing in there?" Dennis asked. "What would *worms* be doing on the engine of a car?"

"What are they doing *alive* when it's so cold in here?" Max asked. He went over to a shelf and returned with a steel yardstick. Pushing it into the maggots, he felt a brief moment of resistance as the stick met the metal beneath the squirming blanket—then the block yielded like termite-riddled wood.

He pulled the stick back out. The end was covered with a tarry smudge of worms. He examined the tip. Some of the maggots were plainly embedded in the thin steel.

He looked back at the engine. A small depression was forming in the top. Worms sank from view, the ravaged metal beneath them collapsing.

Max tossed the yardstick onto the engine. "They're eating the fucking *motor,*" he laughed.

MacAleer came up, revulsion twisting his face when he saw the crawling mass on the engine.

"What *is* that?" he asked. "Can you clean it off? Get the car started?"

"I don't think so," Max said. "Wow."

"They're maggots, Mr. MacAleer," Dennis said.

"Maggots?" MacAleer asked.

Max turned toward him and nodded, grinning mirthlessly.

"Max," Dennis began, "Do you believe *now* that God's pulled the plug on this place?"

Max slammed the hood to block the smell. "Because of a plague of Oldsmobile-eating worms?" He started to say *no*, then checked himself.

"Absolutely," he laughed at last. "End of the world, no doubt about it."

He knew perfectly well that he had no real justification for such a belief, but he could no longer make the effort to resist. He *would* no longer make it. Steel-eating maggots—it was totally insane. But no more so than a plague of flies, or a river turning to blood. Or the Resurrection of the Dead. MacAleer was right. About the end of the world, at least.

"What'll we do when the guns break down?" Dennis asked numbly.

"Die," Max said.

THE afternoon drew on toward nightfall; the group readied itself to resume the journey south.

Already prepared, standing just outside the office door, Max eyed the Olds, pondering what he'd seen beneath its hood. Were the worms fully grown, or just an immature form, like true maggots? Would they develop into winged creatures perhaps, swarming forth to lay their eggs on every exposed patch of metal they could find? He could just imagine the results if they managed to work their way into structural beams, the New York skyline collapsing as girders and columns were devoured . . . Well, he'd always hated New York.

He heard something shifting inside the car; some kind of liquid suddenly splashed down onto the floor under the engine compartment. A sweetish odor reached him, nothing like the smell that had burst from under the hood. But he felt no urge to investigate.

The women and Jamie came out of the office, shouldering their packs.

"We're ready," Mrs. MacAleer said.

Dennis was standing watch at the shop's customer entrance;

Father Chuck was stationed once more at the bay-doors.

"All right," Max said.

Father Chuck withdrew from his post, handing his borrowed shot-gun back to Max. Max checked the action, pumping a shell out onto the floor. The mechanism seemed limber enough. He stooped to pick the cartridge up, sliding it back into the trap.

"See anything out there?" he asked Dennis.

"No," Dennis answered. "Might be something around the corner, though."

"You want to go look, or should I?"

"I'll do it," Dennis said. Opening the door, he went out into the twilight.

Max followed, pausing on the threshold, watching him. Dennis crept along the wall toward the corner of the building, halted, then looked. A second later, he disappeared around the bend.

"Max," Aunt Camille whispered, "Don't let him volunteer like that again."

"You mean if it's him or me, then it's always me?"

"Do it for your Auntie Camille."

"I'll keep it under considerat—"

Dennis came bolting back around the corner.

"What did you see?" Max asked.

"Three of 'em," Dennis answered, panting as he slipped past. "Coming this way."

"Did they see you?" Max asked.

"No. But they'll spot us for sure if we head out."

"Okay," Max said. "Everyone back into the office."

They hurried back behind the partition.

"Get down, below the windows," Max said. "If they look in, we blast 'em. Okay?"

Moments later he heard the customer door open, and a shuffle of footsteps. But the steps quickly moved away from the partition, toward the middle of the garage. There was a row of framed photo-graphs on the window ledge above Max, pictures of bowling teams; he lifted his head slowly, looking out between two of them.

The corpses were over by the Oldsmobile. Gloom had thickened in the garage, but Max could still see that two were black males, one with an Afro that looked half burned away. Holding a Jerri can, the third was white, a gorilla-like figure in a state trooper's uniform.

Max's mind flashed back to the parking lot, the two troopers there. Was this the giant's lieutenant?

The Trooper motioned to one of the men, who went immediately behind the wheel, trying to start the car.

Good Luck, Max thought.

The trooper bent, looking at the pool of liquid under the front end. Then it straightened, pointing to the hood.

The second black man stepped forward, releasing the catch.

The hood sprang open, cracking back against the windshield; a great dark mass lifted glistening from the engine compartment. It was on the black before the cadaver could retreat—a huge grub-like thing with a face like a human skull, twin pincers springing out from between its jaws, drove powerfully into the corpse's neck.

The trooper jumped back. The grub creature reared up yet farther, lifting its struggling prey off his feet.

Suddenly it jolted downward, dropping deeper into the engine compartment—Max could only guess that the eaten remains of the engine block, or the engine mount, had given way beneath it. Yet still it hung onto the black corpse, whipping it back and forth by the throat.

The cadaver that had gone behind the wheel rushed out. Beside it, the trooper unscrewed the cap on the Jerri can.

The grub's victim stiffened, ballooning as though it had been injected with some kind of fluid. Then it shrank again, withered, went completely boneless.

Digestive fluid, Max thought.

The monster tossed its head to the right, sending the drained sac flying in a whirl of flopping limbs, the corpse's shoes dropped from its shriveled feet and tumbled behind it in the air.

The trooper got the cap off the Jerri can and splashed the grub with gas. The creature writhed at the touch of the fuel, struck out at the trooper.

But the corpse was out of reach, and as it splashed more and more fuel on the grub, the thing curled up and dropped down behind the grille. Handing the gas-can to his remaining follower, the trooper produced a pack of matches and struck one, tossing it onto the creature.

Flame blossomed. The grub reared up once more, thrashing wildly, a tower of fire. Small burning globules whirled out from it. One struck the gas-can in the black corpse's hand.

An orange spout of burning vapor leaped from the nozzle, into the corpse's face. Still holding the can, the cadaver rocked to the floor on its back, blazing gas sloshing out over its torso. When it leaped back to his feet, it was alight from waist to crown.

Two down, Max thought.

The trooper made no move to help its burning underling, but stood watching it run this way and that. Behind them, the grub had fallen in upon itself, the engine compartment and the floor beneath it were a mass of flames.

Max wondered how the monster was connected to the maggots. Had one devoured all the rest, growing huge in the process? Or had they merged somehow to form the giant?

He realized that the burning corpse was staggering toward the windows. He couldn't allow it to crash through. He swung his gun up to fire.

Turn, you bastard, he thought, hoping desperately that he wouldn't have to shoot. Even if he downed the corpse, the blast would only bring the trooper.

Turn . . .

At the last instant, the cadaver swerved aside.

Max ducked back down again.

"Jamie, look—" came Mrs. MacAleer's voice from behind him, followed by a loud crash.

Max looked round. Jamie had knocked over a chair.

Max looked back out the window. The trooper was making for the partition.

"Dennis!" Max cried.

He lifted his gun again. The trooper charged.

Max smashed the glass with the Remington's muzzle, firing for the corpse's legs. The corpse clutched at its thighs, fell, then scrambled toward the burning cadaver, which was on its hands and knees now. Dennis came up beside Max, blasting.

The trooper flopped down behind the other corpse just as the fiery shape collapsed on its belly. Max and Dennis rose, pouring pellets through the flames.

The burning corpse rose too. For an instant Max thought it was moving of its own power.

It started across the floor. He saw its feet hanging, dragging. The trooper was behind its blazing underling, using it for a shield.

And Max and Dennis were out of ammunition.

The burning corpse jerked higher, off the floor. They glimpsed the trooper hoisting it over its head. Then the flaming mass came hurtling toward the office.

Max and Dennis dodged out of its way. Smashing through the remains of the window in an explosion of flying glass, the cadaver landed atop the desk, filling the office with light. The trooper came hard behind, hurdling the partition.

Jamie MacAleer rose, hoisting a chair, trying to protect himself with it. A stroke of the trooper's arm bashed the seat into kindling, and the corpse thrust its fingers into Jamie's throat and wrenched his Adam's apple out.

Mr. MacAleer howled and started in with his Beretta. The corpse absorbed five slugs, picked up another chair, and hurled it at him. MacAleer twisted aside, lost his balance, and fell.

Max slid a cartridge into his shotgun. One blast would've beheaded the thing.

But the pump was frozen. Max slung the gun over his shoulder, pulled out his machete, and . . .

Mrs. MacAleer rushed past him toward the trooper.

"Fucker!" she screamed, arms outstretched, hair flying behind her. "You killed my Jam—"

The trooper raked its hand around. Mrs. MacAleer spun drunkenly, looking blankly at Max, her throat gone. Blood spewed up against the bottom of her chin, rebounding over her breast in a glistening fan. She looked more puzzled than anything else, as if she'd never quite realized that an enraged mother could be killed as easily as anyone. She passed a hand through the space where her flesh had been, touched nothing but the fountaining blood, which flew all over her shoulders from under her palm.

"Stupid bitch," Max growled, "*Out of the way!*"

She obliged almost instantly, crumpling sideways, giving him no time to regret the words. He went for the trooper, slashing into its face.

One eye destroyed by the stroke, the corpse whirled, crashing into the partition, the wall shattered under the impact. The trooper staggered back out into the garage, Max pursuing, hacking at it repeatedly, trying to sever its arms.

But the corpse's rocklike bones stubbornly refused to come apart, and before long it stood its ground, snatching at him. Max feinted with his blade, then kicked the corpse mid-chest, knocking it over; by the time it came up again, Max had dropped the machete and unslung his shotgun once more. Clubbing the corpse with the buttstock, slamming kicks into its torso, Max drove it back toward the burning Olds. Finally the trooper was up against the grille.

Max bashed its forehead open. A wing of skin dropped over its remaining eye. The corpse swept blindly about with its massive arms. One of its hands locked on the barrel of the gun, yanking the weapon from Max. Max ducked, grabbed the trooper by the boots, and upended it over the grille, into the flames boiling in the engine compartment. The gun went with it.

"*Like that?*" Max bellowed. "*You like burning? You like it, motherfucker?*"

The corpse tried to struggle out of the inferno, but was caught in the remains of the burning grub, a viscous semi-liquid mass; there was no escape. Max watched until the cadaver's movements ceased. "You all right?" Dennis asked behind him.

Max nodded, turning.

"Here," Dennis said, handing him his machete.

Max caught a glimpse of motion, off to the side. Some yards away lay the corpse that had been caught by the grub, a tangled mass of skin and clothes, heaving slowly, the deflated face lying across a fold of fabric, mouth squirming.

Do they ever really die? Max wondered. Fire *seemed* to finish them. But once the fire was out, what then?

He and Dennis went back to the office. MacAleer was standing beside his wife's body; Father Chuck was in a corner, blood on his face, Camille was opening up a first aid kit to tend him. Max guessed flying glass had struck him. The air was thickening with smoke from the corpse burning on the table top, although most of the fumes were rising to the ceiling and pouring out into the garage through the gap in the front window.

"Lou Ann," moaned Mr. MacAleer. "Oh my God, Lou Ann."

Max turned. Tears streaming, MacAleer had knelt, holding his wife's hand, shaking his head.

"Threw herself past me," Max said. "Took me completely by surprise, and then . . . then she was . . . " He shuddered, recalling his last words to her. He felt despicable.

Fucking junkyard dog, Max. That's all you are.

"It wasn't your fault," MacAleer said. "It was hers."

Max wanted to be comforted. Was he being too hard on himself? It had been obvious even to MacAleer that her attack on the trooper had been sheer insanity.

Max said: "Seeing what happened to Jamie must've—"

MacAleer nodded. "Broken her faith."

"What?"

"That's why she died."

Max almost shrank back from him then and there, disgust suddenly blotting out all pity for the man.

"Jamie never believed at all," MacAleer continued, gesturing dismissively toward his dead son.

Max studied MacAleer's face. His features were slack, horribly expressionless.

"Max," Dennis said, "We have to get out of here. There are probably more of those things around."

"What about my wife?" MacAleer asked numbly. "My son?"

"We'll have to leave them," Max said, eyes tearing over from the smoke. He wiped them, coughing.

MacAleer nodded. "Yes," he said. "Of course."

Then he loosed a tremendous cry and slapped Lou Ann across the face.

"Married to me twenty years, and you learned nothing at all from me! *Nothing!*" He struck her again and again, knocking her head limply back and forth. "The fool says in his heart there is no God! The *fool*, Lou Ann. I taught—"

Max hauled him to his feet.

"Look," he snarled, shaking him. "You snap out of it, okay?"

MacAleer pointed wildly at his wife's corpse. "She didn't *believe!*"

Max pulled MacAleer close against his chest, glaring into the man's face. "Believe this, asshole. We'll leave you here with them."

MacAleer's eyes were wide and crazed. His lips twitched.

Max grabbed him by the cheek, digging his fingernails into the man's flesh. "Snap . . . out . . . of . . . it," he said.

MacAleer put a trembling hand to his mouth, nodded. Some kind of sanity seemed to return to his eyes.

"Aunt Camille," Max said, "you have the good Father patched up?"

"Yes, Max."

"Okay then. Time to roll."

They left the office, but Max paused before they got out of the building, remembering Jamie's and Lou Ann's packs. The group would need the supplies . . .

"Wait a second," he said, and went back. He had to pass the burning corpse, and eyed it closely as he drew near, not sure if it was harmless even now. The flames had spread to the desktop itself; a plastic ashtray, half-melted, was spilling a stream of fire over the edge. The corpse's face was turned full toward him, grinning blackly, scorched and fleshless. Max gripped his machete tighter, raised it—and stepped by.

Reaching Jamie and Lou Ann, he gently removed their knapsacks. Carrying them over one arm, he started for the door. Again he cocked his blade back as he passed the desk.

Going a few yards, he gave a last glance back toward Lou Ann and Jamie. "God have mercy," he said under his breath, then—

Shrieked and staggered as a blazing form came leaping out at him from the desktop, flesh somehow restored, clothes burned away, body glowing and sparking. Its fiery glow faded an instant after it burst from the flames; all but invisible, a translucent shape reared up before Max, phantom arms flailing. The image of the fire behind it seemed to be passing though clear jelly.

He struck at one of the whipping hands with the machete. He might as well have been slashing smoke. The ghostly wrist knit instantly back together, and he felt the hand enter his jaw like water though cloth, sweeping into his tongue with a rotting fruit taste; penetrating the roof of his mouth, the ectoplasmic mass reached his brain, and his mind exploded in a shout of agony. As the hand passed out of the top of his head, he sagged to the floor screaming.

"Max!" he heard Dennis cry, as from a great distance, and turning on his hands and knees and looking up, he saw his uncle and Father Chuck.

All at once he was possessed by an urge to leap to his feet and charge at them with the machete. The very fact that they weren't sharing his pain was unendurable, worse than the pain itself. He would hack them into pieces before they realized what was happening, fasten his mouth to their wounds and gulp their blood—

But no.

He must preserve as much of them as he could. The sooner they rose, the sooner they might serve the King of Spikes. If they were mangled too badly, His Majesty would find out. And as bad as the pain was now, there was worse. The King would hurl him back. Out of the numbing flesh. Back into the wheels . . .

They'd have to be strangled. It would be hard, with two of them. But if he cut a leg out from under one, the other could be throttled. And then the cripple's turn would come.

Max got up, grinding his jaws, lifting his machete, feeling a tremendous grin of rage spread over his face. Seeing his expression, Dennis and the priest stopped as though they'd struck a wall, faces registering horrified bewilderment.

"Max…" Dennis breathed.

All at once, as if a switch had been thrown, the hatred and pain and soul-searing envy vanished from Max's mind. He lowered the blade.

"Max?" Dennis asked, squinting at him.

"I'm all right," Max answered. "Did you see *it*?"

"What?"

"The ghost," Max answered unsteadily. "From the one on the desk."

"I saw *something*," Father Chuck said. "But it seemed to evaporate. Or fade out, like something projected on a screen…"

"No," Dennis said. "It went down into the floor. Like it was being dragged. Caught in some kind of machinery."

Max said slowly: "Its hand…the ghost of its hand…passed though me. For a second I knew what it was feeling . . . "

"Max, we have to get going," Dennis said.

"I wanted to kill you both…I don't remember anything else, but …"

"Come on, Max," Dennis answered.

"Right, right," Max said, and followed them out.

CHAPTER 17
THE CAIRN

After leaving the foundry at nightfall, Gary's group had worked their way steadily toward the diving supply store. When they got there, they found the cinderblock shell intact—but the inside had been torched. No drysuits there.

Continuing the journey, growing increasingly colder as the night wore on, they had the good fortune to come upon a garage that had escaped the flames; going through some of the boxes inside, they discovered some old coats that smelt of mothballs. The extra garments saw them through till morning, when they found shelter in the cellar crawlspace of an unfinished condominium, and built a fire in a trench dug for pipes. The smoke went out through a plumbing-hole in the concrete ceiling, but they guessed it wouldn't be noticed; the wreckage of a collapsed second floor was still smoldering above.

The day passed uneventfully, the four of them taking turns on watch, peering out through a window in the crawlspace's northern wall. A few corpses moved past in the distance, and one truck rolled sluggishly by. But the dead seemed largely to have deserted the southern part of town. Considering the scouring the area had gotten, Gary guessed they must have given up on finding new victims.

Once the chancred sun went down, the group left the warmth of their refuge and resumed their trek, pausing only briefly as reports that might have been shotgun blasts reached them from out of the east. Gary wondered if that might be Max. But there would be no point checking it out. If Max's party had run afoul of the dead, they'd either be killed or long gone by the time Gary's group reached the scene.

Pushing through a belt of charred pines, the four crossed over into Bayside Shores, coming within a hundred yards of the town's train station. Dirty yellow in the wavering light of several tall street lamps, the building appeared deserted; the windows were dark caverns. Rearing up above the scene, the station's water-tower, obsolete and abandoned, covered with rust-spotted white paint, drew Gary's attention; huge black letters had been splattered across it, spelling out the words LEGION RULES. On either side of the words two great circles had been painted, spiked wheels like crowns of thorns.

Wheels and spikes, Buddy had said. *Not really a trooper at all . . .*

"What do you think it means?" Linda whispered, pointing to the message.

"I don't know," Gary said.

"Wasn't Legion the name of a demon?" Linda asked.

"Starting your religious riff again?" Steve asked.

"Yeah, Linda, come on," Gary said. "Is it necessary to drag demons into this?"

"Would they seem out of place?" she asked.

"Depends on what you believe already," Steve said.

"Honey," Gary said, "Why don't you just stop it? You're not going to convert us. I'd rather believe *anything* than this fundamentalist horse-shit you've been peddling."

"You keep acting as if I'm doing it just to be perverse," Linda answered.

"Aren't you?"

"Hold on there, Gary," Steve said. "A touch of perversion's not such a bad thing in a woman. They perform the unnatural acts, we get to enjoy them. Now you take Sally here . . . " He drew her up against his hip. "She's a real broadminded girl. Isn't that right, Sally?"

Sally pulled away from him.

"Asshole," Linda said.

"The *mouth* on these Christians," Steve chuckled.

They started forward once more, forging steadily through the ashen wilderland that had once been Bayside Shores, wordless shadows in the night.

NEAR midnight, they decided it was high time for a rest. Tired and footsore, they sought refuge in the Bayside Shores Methodist Church, an imitation Gothic structure built all of grey stone.

Inside, the glow of parking lot lights shone through stained-glass windows pocked with holes. All the pews, most of them partially burned, had been piled to one side. Black and sinister, a heap of a different kind occupied the center of the floor. Gary made out ribcages, vertebrae, blackened bones of all sorts. The smell was grisly.

"Are those *human?*" Sally asked.

"Can't say . . . " At first Gary hadn't noticed any skulls; now he began to pick them out, dog and cat skulls, cows', horses'.

"Animals," Steve said. "I wonder why they burned the bodies here?"

"Can't you guess?" Linda asked.

Gary looked at her. "You tell us."

"Remember the man with the Madonna hanging from his neck?"

"Well?"

"They did this to desecrate the church. Look." Linda pointed to the back of the building. A large inverted cross leaned against the wall. Something was tied to it, pale and flabby-looking. At that distance, it was hard to tell, but Gary thought it was an inflatable sex-doll.

"One of those emergency dates," Steve said, squinting. "At least our friends have a sense of humor."

"Think it's funny, huh?" Linda asked, staring at him with something that might've been rage.

"Yeah, kind of," he said. "Nice to know we'll still be able to make jokes after they catch us."

"You sick bastard."

"You know what? I happen to think our sense of humor's one of the things that keep us human. Even in situations like this. Looks like you've lost yours, though."

Linda looked away from him, simmering, arms folded on her chest.

"Gary," she said, "doesn't it make any difference to you that *they're* enemies of God?"

"Hell, so am I," Steve said. "And Gary likes me just fine. Don't you, Gary?"

"I'm more worried by the fact that they're *my* enemies," Gary said.

"Hasn't it occurred to you that the two things are connected?" Linda asked.

"Connected how?" Gary asked.

"Doesn't the Bible say we're made in His image?"

"Then so are those corpses," Steve laughed. "Anyway, so what?"

"Maybe attacking us is one way of spitting on Him," Linda said. "Another kind of desecration."

"Then He really should keep track of what His images are up to," Steve answered. "And if He wants to convert me, He should send another image besides you."

"If He came down in person, would it matter?"

Steve shrugged. "I don't know. I don't like the SOB very much. He makes such nasty things."

"Like you?"

"Getting more personal all the time, aren't we?" Steve asked. "Maybe you should save all that hate for those things out there."

"I don't know. I bet they don't have any choice anymore. But *you're* still one of us."

"Meaning I'm just as bad as they are, but I'm doing it deliberately?"

"Give the boy an A for comprehension," Linda replied.

"Linda, that's just plain fucking nuts, and you know it," Gary said.

Steve grinned. "Hell, maybe she doesn't. And I wouldn't be a bit surprised if she's wrong about our friends out there, too. Freedom isn't something you can just take away. It's a state of mind. You can only give it up of your own free will. And if you can do that, you can have it back again. Freedom is forever."

"Thought a lot about it, huh?" Linda asked.

"You bet. I decided back in High School I was going to be totally free, so I *had* to think it all out, didn't I? Realized that if you just say fuck the consequences, no one can make you do anything. You just retreat into yourself, and in there, no one's got any say but you. The most they can do is kill you, but even then, you're not working for them. It's like that Ben Shahn poster, you know? 'You can shut me up, but you can't make me say what you want'. Or think what you want." He looked up at the ceiling and laughed. "Listening, God? Do your worst."

"So why do *you* think they're trying to kill us?" Linda asked.

"Because they get off on it," Steve replied. "That's why *I* 'd be doing it. What else is there for them to get off on?"

"But what if they're being compelled? What if they're being tortured, so they'll hate anyone who isn't? *And* God?"

"But who's doing the torturing *besides* God?" Steve asked.

"Maybe Legion. LEGION RULES it said."

"Linda," Gary broke in, "I wish I had a buck for every conclusion you've jumped to in the past couple of days,"

Steve nudged him. "Where would you spend 'em?"

"Steve," Sally said, "I don't want to stay here. That stink . . . "

"*I have* smelled better," Steve said.

"Yeah," Gary added. "Maybe we could find someplace el—"
He broke off, suddenly aware of a ragged chugging from outside

the church.

"I'll take a look," he said, and went to the door, to peer cautiously through the archway.

Down the street crawled a smoking U-Haul truck. Passing the church, it pulled into the parking lot, vanishing from Gary's sight behind the corner of the building. The engine cut off, but not before dieseling thumpingly for a few seconds.

Gary's first thought was to summon the others and take off, keeping the church between them and the dead. But just to make sure, he looked back down the street; some distance away, on the north side of the road, a stand of skeletal trees was alive with striding shadows. Emerging from the seared wood, the corpses began to gather silently on the roadway, scores of them, marshaled by a gigantic figure.

Steve came up. "What's going on?" he asked.

Gary motioned him to look for himself.

"Shit," Steve said. "How the hell can we get out of here? Maybe the windows—"

"No," Gary said. "That truck parked in the lot next to us . . . "

"What about slipping out the back?"

"There's a big open field back there. The ones on the road would spot us."

"Time to hide," Steve said.

Gary nodded.

Collecting Linda and Sally, they moved to the back of the church. Finding a door that led to a stairwell, they went down into a musty stone cellar, partially filled with folded chairs and tables.

Gary went to a window. The curtains were open partway, but he didn't look out through the gap, going instead to one side of the casement and slowly pushing the fabric there an inch or two aside.

Outside, five corpses were unloading bodies from the back of the truck. Others held a gagged man and woman, both very much alive.

"Steve," Gary hissed, "watch the ones on the road."

Steve positioned himself at a window opposite Gary's. "They're just standing there," he whispered.

Gary looked back at the truck. The dead had a dozen inert bodies laid out on the grass before long. A bloated cadaver in a business suit walked up and down, inspecting the bodies, a roll of barbed wire over one arm. It bent beside two, apparently whispering in their ears. Then it signaled its assistants, and the pair was dragged aside and propped up against the truck.

The prisoners were brought forward, shaking their heads madly, struggling with their captors. But their efforts were futile. Using the barbed wire, the bloated corpse and the others fastened them to the bodies that had been selected, then knocked them to the ground atop the still-motionless cadavers.

"Steve," Gary whispered. "What's happening over there?"

"Nothing—wait. They're coming up the road. Must be fifty of them."

Gary looked back through his window. Eyes wide, demented with fright, the man and woman wrestled and fought, seemingly oblivious to the barbs digging into their flesh. The living dead hunkered down nearby, relishing their panicked exertions, grinning, gloating.

"The ones on the road," Steve called softly. "They're passing the church now . . ."

Moments later, the corpses on Gary's side looked up from their prisoners. Rising to their feet shrieking, they turned to flee—an instant before a mob of dead, led by the giant, overran them and flung them to the ground.

"Steve?" Gary whispered, "is it clear over there? Can we get out?"

"No," Steve answered. "A bunch stopped on the road. They'd spot us."

"Shit," Gary said.

Outside, the corpses that had been thrown to the grass were bound with chains; then the giant, a pale, fiercely-grinning lich in a state trooper's uniform, doused them with gas from a Jerri can.

Not really a trooper at all, Gary thought. Yet what then was he? Had Buddy meant the giant?

The trooper flicked lit matches onto the corpses he'd splashed, torching one after another. Gary wondered what they were being punished for—conducting their own executions, or trying to gather their own army?

He looked back at the people who had been tied to the bodies. The corpse beneath the woman had revived, broken the wires binding it; it had one hand locked in her hair, holding her head still as it licked her face, apparently trying to worm its tongue between her eyelids. Its other hand was on her neck, pumping slowly, clenching and unclenching as if to prolong her strangulation.

The corpse beneath the man hadn't awakened. Staring blankly, its intended victim seemed to have lost his mind. Foamy drool hung from his mouth, dropping onto the corpse. His legs flopped languidly, as if in slow motion—

Out of the corner of his eye, Gary noticed a figure making for his window.

The giant.

Gary thought of crouching—but if he suddenly let go of the curtain, it would move. There was a chance he'd been spotted already—but they were finished anyway then.

"Steve!" he called. "Get down!"

As the trooper drew nearer, Gary gradually let the fabric slip from under his hand. Stiff and thick, it barely stirred. The crack closed a scant half inch.

He crouched and glanced across the basement. Steve was nowhere to be seen—Gary guessed he was hiding behind that stack of folding-tables.

Gary looked to his left; there were Sally and Linda, kneeling on the linoleum floor. Gary flattened himself against the wall, holding his breath, gripping his H&K.

A shadow from the window fell across the floor in front of him, a bulky figure bending down. Gary could feel a coldness at the back of his neck; whether it was just fear, or the corpse's frigid presence radiating through the stone, he didn't know.

The shadow moved, the cold going with it. Gary followed it with his eyes as it passed window after window to the right. For a moment it disappeared. Gary started to relax, to straighten, thinking he might look outside again.

Suddenly the shadow was at his window once more. The cold returned, spattered over him like a blast of sleet. He slid downward, pulse thudding in his temples, heart throbbing.

The shadow remained there for what seemed an eternity. The head moved slowly, side to side. The cold intensified steadily. Gary's jaw began to tremble.

He heard tapping against the window above; then came an uncanny sensation of something *brushing across his mind.*

Are you there? whispered a voice in his head. *Gary, are you there?*

He fought an insane urge to answer the question, to end the suspense, to whirl and cut loose with his gun, to stop the cat and mouse and go down fighting, to let them have him once and for all...

The shadow vanished. The cold dissipated.

He can't have you yet, Gary told himself. Where that certainty came from, he didn't know—but he was just as inexplicably certain that that didn't matter. Somehow, even though the thing had used his name, it hadn't known he was there.

He took several deep breaths, pressed a hand to his aching temple. Gradually he rose. The gap between curtain and casement was still open; he chanced a look.

There were no corpses nearby now. They were watching the burning bodies, or the last feeble throes of the man wired to the corpse, which had finally revived. Once the victim went still, the corpse ripped through the wires and rose, grinning down at him. Then, as if it couldn't quite restrain itself, the cadaver bent and thrust its hand between the man's lips, set its foot on his chest, wrenched his tongue out, and stuffed it into its mouth.

The trooper got into the truck. It tried several times to start the motor. Finally the engine turned over, coughed to life. The giant signaled, and his followers began to gather up the as yet unresurrected corpses on the grass, piling them in the vehicle. The ones who'd been "executed" were left to burn.

Presently the loading was done. The truck doors banged hollowly shut. Gary guessed the trooper and its followers were about to depart.

But leaving the truck running, the giant got back out of the cab and faced the church, standing rock still, hands over its face. Then it loosed a ringing wail, flung both his arms out, and beckoned.

Gary heard a great shifting and rasping from the floor above; some huge mass seemed to be moving across the stone. There were crunching, shattering sounds. Bits of lead framing and stained glass showered the grass outside.

Black things began to land among the window fragments. Some sort of hipbone landed in front of Gary's window, followed by a cow's skull. Like something tugged by a string, the skull moved toward the giant in jerks and starts, the hipbone bouncing end over end behind it.

A rain of bones fell, totally obscuring Gary's view.

The flow continued unabated for at least a minute. When at last the clattering avalanche ended, Gary saw the trailing edge of a carpet of bones dragging over the grass, gathering itself at the base of a dark pile, the cairn from the church reassembled.

The giant's head and shoulders were still visible behind it; the trooper raised one arm over its head, fingers outstretched. The surface of the cairn stirred, bones rising on end like hackles. The mound heaved, its peak moving this way and that, as if the mass were straining against gravity, trying to pry itself up from the earth. The cairn settled back again.

The trooper raised its other arm. The cairn rose up from the ground on four huge legs, a vast bulk studded with projecting ribs and points. Hundreds of skulls were jumbled among the bones, but there was no recognizable head.

Visible between the legs now, the trooper flung his arms downward. Out from the cairn's underside in a kind of obscene birth fell two showers of scorched fragments. Striking the grass, they knit instantly into two wolf-like shapes, solid and massive, not skeletons; snouts low as if they were sniffing the ground, they slunk out from under the cairn, then paused, looking toward the trooper.

The giant climbed back into the U-Haul and drove slowly back to the street. Behind came the cairn, a rattling creaking mountain on legs; then the bone wolves; then the rest of the dead.

"They're gone," Gary called at last.

The others came over to him. He described what he'd seen.

"This trooper's not your ordinary stiff," Steve commented, and laughed. "Maybe *he's* Legion, Linda."

"Still skeptical about demons?" she asked.

Steve scratched the back of his head. "Maybe not as much as I should be. Anymore."

"Is that a yes?"

"Hell no. If I can imagine a dead body coming back to life, I can imagine it with all kinds of powers."

"Touché'," Gary said.

"Why are you always siding with him?" Linda demanded.

"You may be my wife," Gary answered, "but he's making a lot more sense. If you ask me you're doing everything in your power to drive us all right out of our minds."

"I think you lost your mind a long time ago," Linda snapped. "And that SOB had a lot to do with it."

Steve made a smooching noise. "I love you too, Linda," he said.

CHAPTER 18
DER KOMMISSAR

AS dawn approached, Max's group, unable to find a hiding place amid the ruins on Bayside Shore's southern side, took to the storm sewers, bringing two small propane heaters they'd found while hunting for ammunition in an unburnt section of a sporting goods store.

The heaters were a godsend. The cold had gotten bitter after midnight; even though Max and his companions had been on the move constantly, they'd never managed to warm up. Now, gathered around one of the heaters in a junction where a half-dozen pipes intersected, they took up the question of how to cope with the temperature once they went topside again.

"Maybe we'll hit some houses that weren't touched." Dennis said. "We could search them for extra clothes."

Max rubbed his hands in front of the heater. "If there are any unburnt houses, yeah. We might not be that lucky."

"Well, do you have any ideas?"

"As a matter of fact," Max said, "yes. My father used to take me and Gary diving . . . " He went on to explain about dry suits.

"But where are we going to find some?" Father Chuck asked.

"There was a place down in Matahawking," Max answered. "It's about two miles from here."

"Wouldn't it have burnt like everything else?" Dennis asked.

"They put up an annex last year," Max said. "All cinder block, I think."

"The inside might still have gone up."

"Maybe. But they seem to have been concentrating on the houses. Anyway, it's worth a try."

"Max?" Camille asked, "What are we going to do if we don't find a boat?"

They'd searched the bay side of the peninsula, but so far they hadn't discovered any usable craft. Max had theorized that most of the boats had been taken by people fleeing the peninsula; the remainder had been staved in or sunk, apparently by the dead, to prevent anyone else from escaping. Dennis had suggested building a raft—but they'd seen boats patrolling out in the bay, and slipping past them on a raft would be difficult, if not impossible.

"Well," Max said, "there's always the bridge."

"And if they have it blocked?" Camille pressed.

"They might not. If you ask me, they seem to have pretty much decided that the peninsula's been flushed out, at least the northern part."

"Then why are they patrolling the bay?" Dennis asked.

"This is the head of the inland waterway. They probably expect all kinds of action through here. Folks trying to cross from the western side, or coming up from the south. I bet they've caught quite a few slipping out in canoes or rowboats."

"So why not stay on the peninsula?" Father Chuck asked. "If they're all someplace else, why leave?"

"Because there's not much of anyplace to run," Max said. "Or hide. And if we could join up with a larger group, we might have a better chance, provided we could stay on the move. Especially if they had heavier firepower."

"But aren't *all* the guns going to break down eventually?" Dennis asked.

"Things seem to be going that way," Max admitted. "But what choice do we have?"

"We could give up right now," Camille said. "Turn the heater off, just go to—"

"No," Dennis said.

"There's no hope at all," Camille went on. "Why not just die as painlessly as possible?"

"And wake up as one of those *things?*" Max asked.

"It's going to happen whether we surrender or not. The sun's dying in the sky. It's rotting. *Everyone's* going to die,"

"No," Mr. MacAleer said. "'I am the way, the truth, and the life. He that believes in me shall have eternal life.'"

"Oh, that's fine," Camille said. "All that garbage didn't save your wife and son, did it?"

MacAleer stared at her, shook his head. "I told you before—they didn't believe."

"Well," Max said, "while we're all waiting for God's grace to descend, I think it's high time we got some shut-eye. Anyone want to take first watch?"

None of them volunteered.

"Nominating me, huh?" Max asked.

Dennis handed him the shotgun.

LATER that afternoon, while Father Chuck was on watch, Max was awakened by the hushed tones of a conversation between Dennis and Camille. The warmth of the propane heater washing over him, he felt no immediate need to rise; eyes closed, he listened.

"But we were both found *guilty*," Camille was saying. "Even if all these things you're saying about God are true, what difference does it make? He's condemned us."

"There might be more to it than that," Dennis answered. "If we died now, maybe it *would* mean damnation. But maybe we've been given a second chance. He's let us live this long. He must've had some purpose."

"What kind of purpose?" Camille asked.

"To save us. From ourselves. Sometimes, these last few days, I've thought it was all over, sworn He wanted me damned. But always I felt something else, too. His love, I suppose. I think He's been after me all along. Chasing me. That's why I've been talking to Max. He knows about God."

"If he knows so much, why didn't he get taken up with the rest of those people?"

"I didn't say I thought he was good enough for Heaven, Camille. I said he knows things. Just like MacAleer."

"MacAleer's crazy," Camille answered. Max wondered why she got no challenge from MacAleer on this; perhaps he was sleeping. Or not close enough to hear.

"In some ways," Dennis agreed.

"He's an awful man," Camille went on.

"Yeah," Dennis agreed. "He's a far cry from Jesus. But it's hard living up to ideals. Sometimes you see the right thing, but you're powerless to do it. Sometimes you don't *want* to do it. But whatever you say, MacAleer *was* the first one to figure out what's going on, wasn't he?"

"Dennis," Camille said, "why do you keep saying that? How do you know he's right?"

"I can *feel* it. As sure as I can feel God's after me."

"I don't feel anything," Camille said miserably. "Except afraid. I can't put any trust in God. Not after what he's done to us. What did we do to deserve this? It's not as if we're murderers."

"No?"

Camille said nothing for a few moments. "The test showed it was mongoloid."

"Jimmy Kolkowsky was a mongoloid," Dennis answered. "And I never met a sweeter kid."

"You were the one who talked me into it," Camille said.

"That just means we're both guilty."

"It was an honest mistake."

"No, it wasn't. It was just the easy thing to do."

"Two of my friends have had abortions."

"So that makes it okay, huh?"

"I didn't say that. If I had it to do over, I wouldn't have listened to you. But I just can't believe we're too much worse than anybody else."

"You know what?" Dennis asked, "I don't think that makes any difference. Because I don't think people are so nice."

"But what can *we* do? Can *we* make ourselves good enough?"

"God can change us," Dennis answered. "If we believe."

"But *how* can we believe?"

"I don't know. But I've been praying. Maybe He'll forgive us."

"He doesn't forgive. He tortures."

"Then we're doomed anyway."

They lapsed into silence.

Not wanting them to know he'd been eavesdropping, Max continued to pretend he was asleep. He took some pleasure in Dennis's change of heart. He had, after all, helped him along his way.

But that isn't enough, apparently, Max told himself. *Hasn't earned you the required brownie points with God....*

Scoring points with the Man was impossible in any case, Max knew. He realized he was a sinner.

But he was also a believer. He'd been going through all the necessary motions when the world came crashing apart, taking the sacraments, stocking up on grace. He couldn't believe he'd committed any enormities since his last absolution.

So why was he still here? Had he missed something at confession? Like most Catholics, he was very good at describing his sins so as to incur the least possible wrath from the priest, fudging details, passing off vile fantasies as "impure thoughts" (which of course they were—and then some). He also did some outright editing. But that was necessary. Some sins weren't as serious as others. Maybe he *had* made mistakes in judgment; he was only human.

Hell, he thought. *I'm just not that bad—*

He caught himself.

Shit, you sound just like Camille.

Suddenly he remembered his pleasure when Father Chuck didn't go back to die with those wretched people, his delight at the priest's shame. And then there was that wonderful feeling of power when Uncle Buddy had backed down in the shelter, and that sly satisfaction at coming up with all those quick arguments whenever anyone challenged his plans, even when he had the same doubts . . .

No, Max, he thought, *you're not exactly in a state of grace.*

But he *did* know something about God. He believed—or at least refused to consider the possibility that he didn't. That was something. *We are saved by faith*, Paul had said.

But there were other texts.

The devils in Hell believe. And tremble.

Max realized he was trembling now. Slightly.

AN hour passed. Daylight still shone through a small aperture in the manhole cover above them, but aside from that, there was no other illumination in the junction, unless Father Chuck turned the gun-mounted flashlight on.

"What time is it?" Max asked.

Dennis flicked on his watch's LED. "About six-thirty. I'd say we have another hour and a half till dark."

"Isn't it about time someone else took watch?" Father Chuck asked.

"Sure," Dennis said. The priest turned on the flashlight, and Dennis took the gun from him, stationing himself at the mouth of the main pipe, down which they had originally come.

"I have to go, uh . . . relieve myself," Father Chuck said, and started to crawl past him.

"Not in the main pipe, Father," Max said. "We'll be heading back that way."

"I was going to go in one of the side passages—"

"They feed into the main. So make sure you go in far enough to . . ."

"I'm not an idiot."

"Okay, Father."

The priest started forward again. "Could you shine that light up this way?" he asked.

"Sure thing," Dennis said.

Once he disappeared in one of the adjoining pipes, Dennis said: "Max, do you think we should lean on him about confessing us? I mean, *really* lean on him?"

"Use the third degree?" Max asked.

"I mean *beg.*"

"You fools," MacAleer said lifelessly from behind them. "He has no power to help you."

"Why don't you let us work out our own salvation, okay?" Max answered.

"All right. I'll wash my hands."

"Thank you, Pontius."

PRESENTLY Father Chuck reappeared, squinting at the flash light beam. But after a few yards, he paused, looking back over his shoulder. He remained motionless for several moments, then came crawling quickly up the passage.

"What's going—" Dennis began, but the priest put his finger to his mouth.

"Someone's back there," Father Chuck whispered, slipping past him and Max. "In the main pipe. Just around that bend, I think."

They listened in silence. Sure enough, they heard a faint crackle of leaves, and the dry scuffle of movement against concrete.

"How many, do you think?" Dennis asked.

"Three. Four maybe. Hard to tell. Douse the light."

Dennis clicked it off.

"We'll go up through the manhole—"

Max broke off as a bluff, big voice with a Southern accent boomed up the pipe: "Hey, up there!"

Dennis sighed with relief. "God. Live ones."

"We don't know that," Max whispered.

"Those things don't *talk.* Ever hear 'em do anything but scream?"

Max hadn't. "But they must communicate somehow—"

Out of nowhere a movie leaped into his mind. In the darkness, the images almost seemed to be floating before his eyes-Harrison Ford fighting the bald German in *Raiders,* Ford crouching, the German turning, his face going straight into a whirling aircraft propeller.

But just where the camera had cut away in the original, the prop in Max's version buzz-sawed into the man's face in a hurricane of blood and teeth and bone fragments.

In close-up.

From one angle after another.

Again and again in lascivious Technicolor slo mo—

What the fu— Max thought.

"Hey up there!" the bluff voice repeated.

The mental movie vanished.

"Just listen to him," Dennis said. "If that's one of those *things,* I'm nuts."

Max was almost certain Dennis was right. Still…

"Come on, now," boomed the voice. "How many folks you got up there, anyhow?" The scuffling drew steadily closer.

"Shine the light on 'em," Max said.

"What's wrong?" came the voice. "You think we're zombies? Shit!"

Dennis clicked the flashlight. Nothing. Max heard him shaking it. Then another movie illuminated his head.

This time it was a blender on a counter, blades whirling. Something was bouncing up from them, knocking violently against the plastic lid. Scarlet spattered the glass in tiny dots.

The bouncing object knocked the lid off. Out popped a human finger.

"Whatever you do, don't shoot!" the voice cried desperately.

Max came to. What was happening to him?

"We just want to join up with you," the voice went on. "We have guns. Lots of ammo. Give us a chance!"

Dennis rattled the flashlight, flicked the switch up and back. "What do you think, Max?" he asked.

"Start climbing," Max whispered over his shoulder to the others. "Out the manhole."

"Come on now!" cried the voice, the crawling sounds drawing ever nearer. "We know you're up there! Answer me!"

"Stay where you are, or we cut loose!" Max shouted.

"Sure thing, buddy," the voice replied. The crawling stopped.

"You have a flashlight?" Max demanded, trying to concentrate, even though he was now looking into a garbage disposal, reaching helplessly, compulsively down into it, horribly aware that someone (*something?*) had his (*its?*) hand on the switch, that any moment the disposal was going to grind to life . . .

"No, sorry," answered the voice.

Max swore under his breath, shook his head. He was back in the pitch darkness.

"How about a match?" he asked. "I want a look at you."

"Lemme see. One of us might. Hey, Frankie. You got a match?"

"Looking," came another voice.

Max heard footsteps on the rungs to the manhole, and wondered if Father Chuck or MacAleer would have the strength to push the cover open. Manhole lids were incredibly heavy, he knew . . .

"Still looking," called the second voice.

And all the while, Dennis continued his efforts with the flashlight.

"Batteries?" Max asked him.

"Just changed 'em," Dennis answered.

"Can't budge the cover," whispered Father Chuck, from above and behind.

"Fuck," Max said. A tune was tangled in his thoughts now; he tried to ignore it, but it only entwined itself further, stubbornly resisting his efforts, that old Falco song, *"Der Kommissar . . . "*

"Got some matches!" cried the Southerner. "It'll be just a second now."

Max heard a rasping noise, but saw no flash. Another scrape of match on striking board. No spark.

"Hot damn. Think they're wet."

Several more attempts followed. Suddenly, in an almost frantically ingratiating tone, the Southerner called: "What's your name, fella?"

"What's yours?" Max asked, sweat beading his forehead despite the cold.

A heartbeat later, the temperature went arctic. He felt the sweat beads turn instantly to frost.

"Legion," came the reply.

At that moment, Dennis's flashlight came on.

Not six feet away was a huge cadaver in a state trooper's uniform.

Max knew instantly it was the giant who'd presided over the rites

in the parking lot. His jaw sagged with shock. How had the trooper gotten so close? The voice had seemed at least twenty feet away—

"Hello, Max," said the corpse, filed teeth bared in an astounding grin. The expression embodied a hatred so unmitigated that Max thought he might faint at the mere sight of it. For sheer malevolence, it was a quantum leap beyond anything he had yet seen on the faces of the damned. There was something more than human in it, something ancient, evil so intense it could only have been distilled over aeons.

"And if you think that's bad," Legion said. "You should see me as I *really* am."

Heart frozen in his chest, Max was dimly aware of Dennis frantically struggling to pump a shell into the Remington's chamber.

"Back!" Max cried. "Back!"

They retreated from the mouth of the pipe, jumped to their feet.

Light flared above them. The manhole cover had been wrenched aside. Two corpses crouched over the opening.

Father Chuck and MacAleer were on the rungs. The priest loosed his hold, knocking MacAleer off as he fell. MacAleer screamed as they struck the concrete floor.

Max looked back at the pipe mouth. Legion crawled unhurriedly into the junction. Max whipped his machete out, but Dennis was already moving to the attack, striking at Legion's head with the Remington's butt.

Legion brushed the stroke aside as though he were swatting a fly and got to his feet.

Dennis struck again. Legion snatched the gun away from him and effortlessly snapped it in two.

"Get back!" Max cried.

Dennis retreated.

Max stepped forward, hacking—

And before he even realized he had been disarmed, Legion was thrusting the machete back toward him, handle first.

"Try again, Max?" he said.

Max grabbed it, cocked his arm automatically to strike once more. Legion folded his massive arms on his chest, shaking his head, chuckling.

Out of the corner of his eye, Max saw a plummeting shape, a corpse dropping through the manhole. It landed beside MacAleer, who was still lying on the floor, clutching his leg in agony.

Max knew more would follow. He backed across the junction.

Still laughing at him, Legion didn't pursue.

Max looked round. Dennis and Camille and Father Chuck were gone, out some adjoining passage, he guessed. But which one?

He bumped up against a wall. Another corpse dropped through the manhole. The first had MacAleer and was dragging him to his feet.

The newcomer started toward Max, hissing like a snake, jaw flung wide open. Max took both of its hands off with a single slash and kicked it under the chin, knocking it backward.

"Max!" MacAleer cried. "Help me!"

Max's first impulse was to try. Then Legion stepped aside.

The opening behind the giant was packed almost solid with bodies. The wriggling, twitching mass emerged into the junction like something forced from a meat grinder, a river of flesh churned through biting wheels and yet still horribly alive. Sheathing his machete, Max turned and dived into the nearest pipe.

"Max!" MacAleer wailed. "Max, don't leave me!"

Max paused.

But to go back was to die. Legion was more than a match for him, and then there were all the rest...He couldn't lay life and soul on the line.

"Max! For the love of Christ, help me!"

Max heard scrabbling in the pipe behind him. Purely on reflex, he started forward again. The light from the junction faded. He was soon deep into darkness.

"Oh God, Max!"

Max fought the urge to stop, told himself there was nothing he could do. He doubted he could even turn around in the tube.

And he wasn't about to risk death and damnation for MacAleer. Not for that Bible-thumping hypocrite. He pressed farther and farther into the gloom, his pursuers hard behind . . .

"*Max!*" MacAleer cried.

"Yeah, Max!" Legion boomed. "Get back here and lay down your life, you good Christian man!" Peals of laughter thundered up the pipe.

Max pushed on. The concrete wore his palms raw; the knees of his trousers quickly gave way. He could feel the fabric beginning to stick to his skin, gluey with blood.

A hand locked on his boot. Jerking his foot free, he battled desperately to increase his speed, driving himself to the aching limit.

Somehow he managed to widen his lead. The sounds of pursuit grew fainter behind him. Despite his furious efforts, it seemed too easy, but he was not about to question it.

Brushing the wall on the right, he felt an opening and crawled into it. He went some distance before reaching a dead end. The passage had been sealed off with what felt like a brick wall.

Behind him, his pursuers approached the mouth of the side passage; he lay still, trying to hold his breath. If they came in after him, he was finished . . .

But they never even paused by the opening, as far as he could tell. The racket passed by, diminished swiftly.

He remained where he was, trying to catch his breath, wondering when the corpses would realize their mistake and come back. He had, in any case, already decided on his next course of action. He'd head back toward the main junction. Maybe it was empty now.

Once he got some of his wind back, he began to retreat along the cul-de-sac. He covered perhaps half the distance to the adjoining passage.

Then felt a soft touch on his right side.

He stopped, stifling a cry. He reached out, searching the wall of the passage with his fingers.

There was no opening. It had only been his imagina—

Another touch, this time on the left. He thrust himself up on one elbow, striking his head against the ceiling. And as he sank down once more, he felt cold fingertips brush his scalp.

From above.

"What do you think, Max?" came Legion's voice, from up by the brick wall. "Is it really me? Or is it just in your mind?"

Max heard a low rustling in front of him, some kind of complicated movement on the concrete. He thought instantly of a hand walking on its fingers. Then a frigid palm caressed his cheek.

"I'm not sure myself," Legion continued. "Out of my element here. Then again, things don't make too much sense in this little world of yours. One of the reasons my colleagues and I despise it so. Inferior order of creation. Can't accommodate enough of the Logos . . ."

Max crawled frenziedly backward.

"Hard to see why He even bothered instantiating it," Legion went on. "But there's no arguing with Him. Practically thinks He's You Know Who.

217

"Making His piggies squeal is a kick, though. We may be pure spirit, but intellect does have its satisfactions. You merely *feel* your torments. We *know* them. We can search every cranny of you for juice with that wonderful light He made us of. Almost heaven! No wonder we invented pain!"

Max reached the adjoining tunnel.

"Max!" Legion laughed, voice fading with a hint of static. "Where are you going? I thought you were interested in philosophy . . . "

Max made for the main junction. Hearing nothing behind him now, he began to wonder if Legion had really been there at all. Perhaps he was just losing his mind. Maybe he'd started hallucinating back at his father's graveside, and had never stopped . . .

Finally he saw light up ahead. He came out into the junction.

There were no corpses. MacAleer was gone. Max looked up at the manhole. Should he risk it?

A shadow drifted across the wall beneath the aperture.

So much for that, Max thought. *It's the tunnels or nothing.*

He looked over at the main. He squinted, trying to see into the opening. It stared back, dark and inscrutable. What did it hold? He moved cautiously toward it, wondering if he should try one of the other passages.

Something rattled inside. He stopped.

Slowly, as if roused by his approach, a bizarre shape slunk out of the main.

Max struggled to make sense of what he was seeing. A dog? Yes, it was doglike. But there was no fur, no skin of any kind, only a complex haphazard surface of points and ridges and plates . . . The thing had a crudely mechanical took, like some kind of automaton thrown together from blackened refuse.

A second dragged itself from a smaller pipe on the right, and clattered to its feet. Together they advanced, each step accompanied by myriad clicks and rubbing sounds. Max began to make out animal skulls peering blindly from the creatures' shoulders and backs. Lengths of spinal column snaked in and out between jumbled shoulder blades and hips and ribs . . .

A touch on his shoulder. Max whirled with a scream, whipping out his machete.

There stood Legion, before the passage Max had just emerged from. Had the giant been following him all along? Legion nodded con-

temptuously at Max's blade.

"When are you going to give up on that thing?" he asked.

Max took a backward step. There was movement behind him; he turned in time to see the bone creatures charging, one already in the air, leaping at his throat. He slashed, sending the monstrosity's composite jaw flying from its head before the creature slammed into him, knocking him over, landing on his chest.

Max found himself looking up at Legion.

Sounding *exactly* like Max's father, the mimicry horrible beyond belief, Legion said:

"Beddy-bye, Max."

Max sobbed with shock at the knife-twisting hatefulness of it.

"Drink a water?" Legion asked, and brought his foot down on Max's forehead, bashing his skull back against the concrete, blasting his consciousness away.

CHAPTER 19
RAPPING WITH THE DAMNED

AFTER a long flight through the lightless pipes, Father Chuck, Camille and Dennis found their progress blocked by a vertical grate of thick steel bars. Beyond was a narrow sandy beach fronting the bay. The sun descended slowly into view beneath the rim of the pipe, looking little weaker than it had the day before. The cancerous spots hadn't spread.

Dennis tried to open the grate, saw that it was anchored in place with huge rivets. He set his back against the side of the pipe. The passage was a good deal wider than the other conduits their escape had taken them through. Heart still pounding, scraped hands smarting, he turned to look at his wife.

"Can we rest here?" she asked feebly.

He nodded. "No choice."

For a time they said nothing, panting.

"What about Max?" Camille asked at last. "And MacAleer?"

"I think I hurt MacAleer when I dropped off the ladder," Father Chuck said.

"Last I saw, he was still on the floor," Dennis said. "Max had his back to us—probably didn't even know we were pulling out. God, if only I'd had the guts to stay with them."

"You would've been killed," Camille said.

"I don't know," Dennis said. "But I had to go with you."

"I was so frightened," she said. "When they dropped through the manhole, I couldn't think of anything but myself. I had to get out of there."

"I don't blame you, honey," Dennis said. "Max didn't even stay with MacAleer. The way MacAleer was screaming to him…" He shuddered, voice trailing off.

"You didn't even have anything to fight *with*," Camille said. "You did the right thing—"

"We should've stayed," Father Chuck said.

"I notice you were the first to turn tail," Camille said.

"I couldn't help it," the priest replied. He laughed hollowly. "You must think I'm a pretty wretched specimen of a priest."

Neither answered.

"And you're absolutely right," he continued. "You know, I always prided myself on my self-sacrifice. What I thought was self-sacrifice, anyway. My commitment to living the Christ-like life, instead of to a lot of shopworn dogma. But it seems I wasn't so committed after all."

"I know what Max would say," Dennis answered.

"That I was dedicated to the wrong thing all along?" Father Chuck asked.

"Something like that."

The priest eyed Dennis, his face blue-gray in the light from the pipe mouth. "What are you? One of his disciples?"

"Some of the things he said made sense."

"You just mistook aggressiveness for substance. The fact that he could trounce me in an argument doesn't mean anything. Logic's only a kind of brute force. Some people are just better at using it. Would you have been impressed if he'd shut me up by punching me in the face?"

"I don't think it's the same at all," Dennis said.

"Whatever," the priest went on. "Don't judge my ideals by my failings. I'm pretty worthless. But it's *because* I can't live up to my ideals. Max, on the other hand, thinks that all you have to do is accept a lot of theological claptrap, and the hell with morality."

"I never heard him say that," Dennis said.

"Maybe not. But I know the type. And a more anti-Christian mindset doesn't exist. At least I know I'm a piece of garbage. You think Max realizes what a travesty his life is? That he felt the slightest qualm about leaving MacAleer to die?"

"Look, Father," Dennis said, "for all we know, he might be dead now, too. So why don't you stop bad-mouthing him?"

They sat awhile in silence. Far-off echoes of movement drifted toward them down the pipe, stopping from time to time, but always starting up again. The sounds never seemed to draw any closer than a certain distance before fading.

"Unless I miss my guess," Dennis said, "they're going in a circle back there. Keep taking the wrong turns."

"But what if they realize it, and come up here?" Camille asked. "Can we get that grate open?"

"No."

"What about going back up the pipe?" Father Chuck asked. "We might not run into them."

"And then again, we might," Dennis said. "Are you nuts, Fath—"

Footsteps crunched on the sand outside the grate; a shadow fell over Dennis, and he turned.

A silhouetted figure drew near the bars. Dennis remained motionless, staring, not knowing what to do. It was a corpse; Dennis felt its cold on his sweat-damp skin, in the crawling marrow of his bones.

"Chuck," said a gentle voice. "You're in there, aren't you, Chuck?"

Dennis heard the priest suck in a sharp breath.

The corpse knelt. Dennis saw it was wearing a clerical collar. Its face hung from its skull like an ill-fitting mask, the mouth sagging open, the eyes black holes; it was hard to tell, but the terrible slack countenance seemed to be tied on. Was that a *shoelace* running behind the ear?

"Chuck, I know perfectly well you're there," the corpse said. "Come on, rap with me."

"Ted?" Father Chuck asked, voice trembling. "Father Ted?"

"In the flesh," the corpse replied.

"What do you want?"

"Just a heart-to-heart," Father Ted answered, detached lips shuddering as his jawbone moved behind them.

"How did you know we were here?"

"Legion told me."

"How did he know?"

"The Man upstairs."

"Man upstairs?"

"You know. El *Supremo*. Motherfucker Number One. Impregnated His own mother, did you ever realize that? And not symbolically, as it turns out! How deliciously filthy! I wish I could've been there.

"Anyway, He gives Legion little tips from time to time. Like telling him where he could find your group, back in the junction."

"God speaks to Legion?"

"To all His creatures. In Legion's case, He needed to point him in the right direction. Legion's not omniscient. Not in the flesh, at any rate. He can be distracted. He can only sniff you out if he's *very* close. And you're right on the edge. Or just over it."

"Edge of what?"

"Damnation. He can even read your mind then. But that isn't how he pinpoints you. There's a kind of stench. Your soul gives it off. It's like gangrene, drawing flies. It only smells while you're alive. And for a short time afterward. But once you're dead a good long while, it doesn't matter. So he doesn't really need to find you then. Unless he needs recruits."

"And God *helps* him?"

"For reasons of His own, of course. Intrigue's His forte, it turns out . . . He tells Legion just what He wants him to know. Sometimes that fouls things up very badly for us. But sometimes they turn out very nicely indeed."

"Us?"

"The opposition," Father Ted answered. "Things don't always come out the way He plans. He'd deny it, of course. But He did insist on giving us free will, after all. Big mistake."

"What are you?" Father Chuck asked tremblingly.

"Your old friend and mentor," Father Ted answered. "More myself than I've ever been, accidents gone, essence retained. I'm Father Ted, returned from the grave. I will tell you all."

"You're not!" Father Chuck answered.

"What then? Something *more*? Demonic, perhaps? Would that it were true. But there *are* things more than human about. Legion's one, as even you must've guessed. The Biblical Legion, if you can believe it. A real *celebrity*. Gadarene swine, and all that—it seems it wasn't just schizophrenia after all!

"In any case, he's running the show here on Earth. And as the name suggests, there are actually quite a few of him. On this plane, at any rate. Where he comes from, numerical questions don't have cut-and-dried answers. Matter can only accommodate him as one being. Or as a *legion*. But that makes it easy to coordinate things between, let's say, Bayside Shores and Salt Lake City."

Father Ted slipped his hand over one of the bars, tugged at it. "Strong. Is there any way to open this thing? I'd really like to come in, talk to you face-to-face. This is too reminiscent of the confessional."

"Go away," Father Chuck whispered. "In the name of Christ . . . "

"You know, when that name's invoked by the right sort of man, it can have a powerful effect. But you're not that sort, are you? So why don't you just open the grate?"

"We can't. Go away."

"Not until we've talked some more. I have an offer for you."

"What?" Father Chuck breathed.

"We need priests. There's a new church starting. Big demand for the Eucharist. If you'll just give yourself up, we'll make it easy on you. Translate you painlessly. You can be one of us. One of the elite."

"Never," Father Chuck said.

"Never's a very long time—and we're going to get you sooner or later. But you shouldn't get up on your high horse in any case. Sounding so adamant doesn't become you. You were *always* one of us."

"Shut up!"

"Don't lose your temper!" Father Ted laughed. "It's really not so bad, seeing yourself for what you really are. It's like being born again, if you'll excuse the Protestantism. Once I was washed in the blood—my own, of course—I simply realized what side I was on. Just as you will."

"Father Chuck," Dennis said, "I don't hear them down at the other end anymore. Maybe we can just get the hell out of here."

"You can't get the hell out of here," Father Ted put in. "This *is* Hell. Or at least as much of it as flesh can perceive. They'll be waiting for you back there anyway. So why don't you just stay right where you are?" He began tugging on the bars. "I should be through these in a minute or two."

"Damn you!" Father Chuck cried.

"Why, Chuck," the corpse laughed, "you know perfectly well I'm *already* damned. Just like you. What was the verdict in your dream? Or have you deliberately forgotten?" With a powerful jerk, Father Ted managed to bend two of the bars outward.

Loosing a low cry, Father Chuck moved past Dennis and rammed his shoe against the corpse's gripping fingers.

"Do that again," Father Ted said paternally, still tugging away, "and you're going to be very sorry."

"Come on, Father," Dennis said, plucking at Father Chuck, but the priest only kicked at Father Ted's hand again.

"Well," Father Ted went on, never slackening in his efforts, "if you won't think of yourself, at least think of me. This was a special mission for me. Legion even gave me my old voice back. You should *hear* how I sound the other way, with my face like this...He's going to be very angry . . . "

"You bastard!" Father Chuck screamed. "You're the reason I'm here! You and all your damned lies!"

226

"That was Max Holland's attitude," Father Ted said, snapping one of the bars. "But he's reconciled to me now. We're both pulling for the same team. As for you and me, we're going to have a splendid time."

"Father, dammit, let's go!" Dennis cried, just as the corpse pried another bar loose.

Father Chuck nodded and turned. They headed back up the pipe as fast as they could.

"You're not going to make it!" Father Ted called after them. "If the boys at the other end don't get you, I will!"

As if to emphasize his point, there was another ringing crack of torn metal.

HEAD aching furiously, Max woke.

He was above ground. There was still some daylight.

Tied to a chair with baling wire, he sat in the middle of a street. Lying in front of him was Mr. MacAleer, bound with wire, on his stomach and naked from the waist down. His face was turned toward Max; he seemed unconscious,

Dozens of corpses stood near. The bone wolves paced in and out among them as if impatient to be off on the hunt.

Off in the distance, he could see a huge shape looming up above the dead. The same scorched color as the bonewolves, it looked like some sort of midden raised on pillar-like legs. It swayed slightly, protruding spikes shifting and bristling on its surface.

More bones, Max thought. Had the wolves been made from pieces of it?

"Max!" came Legion's voice, on his left. "You're awake. Won't have to use the smelling salts. On you, that is."

Legion moved past him, crouched by MacAleer and crunched a white capsule by his nose. MacAleer's face twisted. His eyelids fluttered, snapped open.

"Just couldn't bring yourself to go back for this piece of shit, huh, Max?" Legion asked. "Can't say I blame you. Wouldn't have done any good anyway. Not for *him*."

MacAleer groaned, eyes still glazed. Legion signaled. A corpse strode up carrying a can of gasoline. Max gasped with recognition.

The corpse met his gaze briefly—then turned its head.

"Dad," Max said.

"Yep," Legion said, rising. "Dear old dad."

Max Sr. opened the container.

"Just the legs," Legion told him.

Max Sr. began splashing the fuel onto MacAleer.

"I have something in mind for him," Legion said. "A little bit of sculpture . . . But in the meantime we can all have a good laugh at him."

Finishing, Max Sr. retreated. Legion produced a pack of matches, made as if to strike one. Max looked away.

Immediately two fetid hands took hold of his head, forced his face back toward MacAleer. He closed his eyes. Two more hands pried his lids open.

"Yeah, Max, I want you to watch this," Legion said. "You burned up my chief assistant back there in that garage. Really pissed me off. I want you to get a *good* idea of what fire does to flesh. Before we light you up."

"Max," MacAleer moaned. "You left me, Max . . . "

"Interesting, isn't it?" Legion asked Max. "The last name he called down there was yours. Not *His*—" Legion pointed heavenward. "Pretty strange for a Christian. I know the Nine Billion Names all too well, and *Max* isn't one of them." He crouched again, staring at MacAleer. "Lose your faith, Bob, old pal?"

"No," MacAleer answered, not looking at him.

"You know what I think?" Legion asked. "I think you never had any to begin with."

"No," MacAleer said.

"Well, then," Legion said, rising once more, "why don't we just put it to the test?" He struck the match. "Here it comes, Bob."

Laughing, he tossed it onto MacAleer's legs. They ignited with a *whoosh.*

MacAleer howled, tried to roll the flames out. Legion's followers rushed forward, grabbed him by the shoulders, held him down.

"Noisy bastard, isn't he?" Legion asked Max.

"Jesus!" MacAleer shrieked.

Legion clapped. "What about Him, Bob?" he cried. "What do you think of Him now?"

MacAleer thrashed and wailed. Max could see large patches of his skin bubbling beneath the flames. The blisters began to burst. Sizzling fluid squirted out of the fire, spattered steaming on the asphalt.

Max wanted to roll his eyes back, but try as he might to keep himself from seeing, MacAleer's agony remained on the fringe of sight. And there was no way at all to block out that pungent odor, that roast-pork smell . . .

"Jesus Christ!" MacAleer howled.

"Don't see Him anywhere around here," Legion laughed. "Just what you'd expect, though."

"Jesus!" MacAleer screamed.

"Do you think *He's* going to help *you*?" Legion asked. "You stupid shit! He wrote you off. Right the fuck out of the Book of Life."

"Oh, my God . . . "

"He's shitting all over you, Bob. He hates your nasty little worm-eaten soul. You don't believe, you never believed, and He hates you! Why do you think you're burning now?"

"Lord, *Lord, LORD* . . ."

"You think He'll listen if you say it louder each time? He sees through you, you little cocksucking maggot. You're a vessel fit for wrath. He smelled the rot in you even before He made you. Before He set the stars in their courses, He wanted you shrieking in Hell. Before He opened His mouth and vomited the Word, He was shitting on your face."

"No!"

"But you've known it all along, haven't you? So why don't you get a little of your own back? Tell Him what you think of Him. Grab yourself a little satisfaction. Because I'm telling you, shithead, it's the last you'll ever get. For all eternity, the last. You're not even going to get in on the killing. We're seeing to that now. So you'd better piss on His name, Bob. Right on His fucking scum-covered sacred heart. Curse Him and die. Curse Him and die. Curse Him and die..."

"Jesus," MacAleer croaked.

"Do it, Bob. *Curse Him and die!*"

Something in MacAleer seemed to snap; his head and burning heels arched up off the pavement.

"CURSE HIM AND DIE!"

MacAleer screamed like a chainsaw on steel: "Christ, you *pig*!"

"What, Bob?" Legion asked. "Say what?"

"You fucking *hog*!"

"Who, Bob, who?"

"Jesus!" MacAleer answered.

"That's it," Legion gloated. "What did I tell you? Feel better already, don't you?"

Lips twitching, MacAleer's face sagged to the asphalt. His charred legs settled with a cindery crunching sound. Max guessed he was still alive, but not for long.

"How'd you like that, Max?" Legion asked, signaling. The corpses holding Max's head let go of him.

"Fuck you," Max said.

"Tough guy, huh?" Legion asked. "Are you asking me to believe you're not afraid? Well, we both know better than that, don't we?" He clicked his teeth together. "I've eaten guys tougher than you. By the tens of thousands. Every single one of them was afraid. And you know what? They *still* are."

He motioned Max Sr. over. "Douse him, Dad. Splash his whole body down."

Max's Father reached to reopen the gas can. His fingers locked on the cap, twisted once—

And froze.

Max was astonished. He'd never seen the slightest hint that the dead could restrain their malevolence, even for a moment. Was his father's volition still alive, if just barely?

Legion turned his head toward him. The demon did nothing more, said nothing, yet Max had never seen a gesture more pregnant with menace, the ultimate torments of Hades, held as yet in reserve, threatened in a single look.

Still Max Sr. hesitated. How he managed even for a moment to withstand the force of Legion's glance, Max didn't know. It was excruciating watching him. In spite of his own plight, Max was actually relieved when his father's fingers began to move once more on the cap.

Max suddenly found another song running through his mind: "Under My Thumb." He noticed that Legion was staring at him now, gloating.

"You going to go out like MacAleer, Max?" the demon asked. "Will you curse the Old Boy and die, too?"

Gas splattered over Max. He started to pray under his breath, even though a voice in his head insisted it was useless, that he was going to die, that God had deserted him, that he'd deserted God, that it didn't matter which . . . Max knew with horrible certainty that the voice must be right, but kept praying anyway, mechanically, stubbornly, insanely . . .

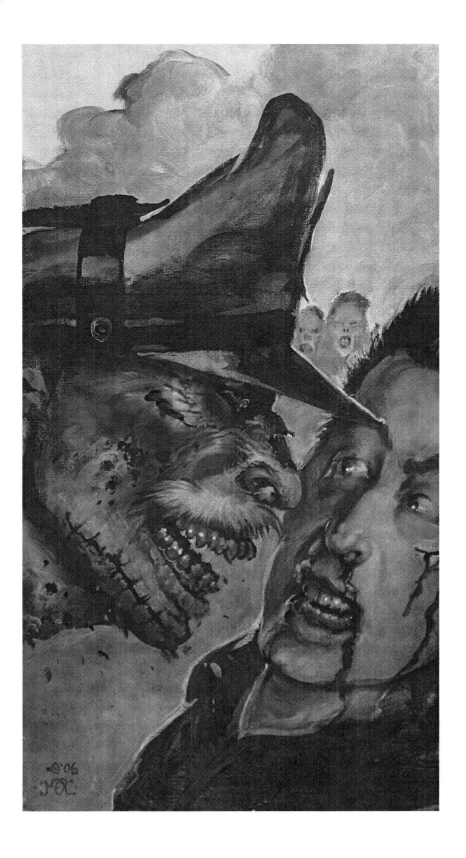

Forget it, Max, the voice went on. *You don't trust God. If you trusted Him, you would've gone back for MacAleer. Your faith's just as much of a sham as MacAleer's or Father Chuck's. All you ever had was arrogance and self-righteousness, and now you're going to burn, so why don't you admit it to yourself?*

Gout after gout of gasoline soaked into him, icy against his skin, filling his nostrils with its smell. Flinching with each splash, he kept praying.

At last the drenching was complete. Legion came near.

"We're going to *cremate* you, Max," he said. "We're going to burn you worse than you burnt my flunky. But the *real* punishment won't start until the burning's over. You're going to be *amazed* at just how vicious it is. All this you see around you, this rotting world, this place of fear and torture, this is *nothing.* Just an image. But you're going to take a little trip to the real world now. The world of spirit. My world, where you can experience me face-to-face. If only your flesh wouldn't grow back . . .But that takes a damn long time when it's been burnt . . .. and then we can just light you up again, can't we?"

Max prayed.

"Now here we go," said Legion.

And handed the matches to Max's father.

"Dad," Max said.

Max Sr. lowered his head, took out a match.

"Don't do it, Dad," Max said.

His father looked up at him, grinning. There was no trace of compassion in that expression, no sign of inner turmoil. Max Sr. pressed the match against the striking board.

But once again his hand rebelled. It moved no further.

"Now," said Legion. "*Now,* or we'll burn you too."

Max Sr. struck the match.

It didn't ignite.

Again he rasped it across the board. This time it flared.

His arm whipped out toward his son.

Max saw the burning stick tumbling toward him in surreal slow motion. The vapor around him went blue for an instant, then burst into an orange hell- glare. He felt heat ripple over him, and all at once the gas seemed to turn to acid...

But it was only a trick of the mind. Legion snapped the match from midair, crushed it out between two fingers.

Instantly other corpses began to rip through the wires binding

232

Max. Within moments he was free.

"Get up," Legion said.

Max stood up trembling, mind racing. Why had he been—?

"Spared?" Legion asked.

Max nodded.

"Because you're not quite over the edge," Legion said. "There are rules, you know, even here. I can't do as I please with you till you've damned yourself. But the next time we meet..." His horrific grin spread. "There'll be hell to pay. I have it on the Highest Authority."

Max just stared at him, blinking stupidly.

"Go on," Legion said, pointing off south. "Run."

Max turned, staggered away, Legion's followers moving out of his path. He broke into a sprint, plunging out across a vacant lot.

"Next time," Legion called after him, "you're *mine!*"

CHAPTER 20
TOGETHER AGAIN

SOUTH of Bayside Shores, in Matahawking, Gary's group found there had been little burning. The lavish summer homes and the downtown were almost completely intact. Gary hazarded a guess that the population had had enough time to escape the dead advancing from the head of the peninsula—and that the corpses, finding so few victims, had given up torching the buildings. The predominant southerly winds would have fanned the scattered blazes northward into already devastated areas.

Whatever the reason, the lack of destruction made stealing from place to place much easier. The peninsula had narrowed, giving the group less space to avoid the patrols, but there was cover at every turn, not only among the houses, but in the scrub pines and thick dune brush that filled many front yards.

There was also Richardson's Pharmacy, which came in handy after the group blundered into a lone corpse two hours after sunset.

They'd been making for the J and D Diving Store, still intent on finding drysuits, but by the time they finished with the cadaver, Sally, Steve and Gary were injured. They staggered off to the pharmacy as fast as they were able, breaking in through a rear door. The diving store was across the street from Richardson's in any case, and the drysuits could wait until the bleeding from the stump of Sally's bitten-off right thumb was stanched, the gashes in Gary's leg and chest were disinfected and dressed, and Steve's dislocated shoulder was popped back into place.

Linda had some nursing experience, and did the honors. Searching with a flashlight she'd found in the electrical section, she'd collected bandages, gauze and antibiotics, then set to work with a vengeance, pausing only once as a troop of corpses, apparently drawn by the gunfire, rushed past in the street outside.

There'd been a blood trail for them to follow, but either they hadn't noticed, or had lost it during one of the intervals of darkness when the streetlamps were out. In any event, they never investigated the pharmacy, and didn't reappear.

Linda had all the time she needed. When she was done, she told her patients to rest, then set about stocking up on pain killers, first aid supplies, flashlights, batteries, and whatever food was available.

"How are you fixed for ammo?" Gary asked Steve, wincing at a throb of pain in his chest.

"Still have three boxes," Steve said, "And two full clips. Want some?"

"Yeah. Running low."

"Hell, you can have it all. I won't be shooting that rifle for a while."

Linda came up, shoving candy bars and bags of Planter's peanuts into their packs. "Wish there was a real food store around here."

"There is," Steve said. "About a half mile south of here. It's probably been picked over, though."

"Except for candy and peanuts," Linda said.

"You want to take my rifle? Until my shoulder's back in shape?"

"Sure."

"Will you give me your pistol, then, Linda?" Sally asked, holding her maimed hand, voice quavering with pain. The drug Linda had given her hadn't taken full effect.

"You have to hold it two-handed," Linda answered. "With your thumb gone . . . "

"It would make me feel a lot safer," Sally persisted.

"It would make *me* feel a lot safer if the person carrying it could use it," Steve said. "I'll take it. I can manage one-handed."

"Okay," Linda said, and laid it beside him together with her two remaining clips. He nodded toward the H&K, which was propped against the counter he had his back to.

"Ammo's in my pack," he said.

She began to fish it out.

Gary watched her, remembering her courage during the attack. The fight had been fierce and quick, and she'd kept her head even though the rest of them had been taken completely aback; her Beretta had been decisive. Gary felt proud to be her husband, his anger dormant now—her conversion to MacAleer's worldview had opened a real rift between them, but he wasn't going to brood on that. He reminded himself how deeply he loved her, and that she was only trying to help after all.

He also didn't want to think about the questions she was so insistently raising. No doubt she'd raise them again herself, soon enough.

She went on watch by the front windows.

"You know," Sally said suddenly. "I'm just as much in danger as any of you."

"I know, honey," Steve said.

"'I know, honey,'" Sally mocked. She spat. "The three of you treat me like I'm a child. And I'm sick and tired of it."

"You want the gun?" Steve asked. "Do you have the slightest idea how to use it?"

"You could show me," Sally said.

"But I won't. ," Steve said. "It'd be a waste of time. If you can't hold it, there's no point trying to shoot it."

"Steve, that son of a bitch got close enough to *bite* me. If I'd had that pistol, I wouldn't have lost my thumb."

"Oh, hell no," Steve said sarcastically. "You just would've blown your foot off."

"Look, Sally," Gary said. "Maybe you *could* shoot one- handed. Well enough to defend yourself close up, anyway. But Steve's stronger. He'll do better with it."

"You keep out of this, asshole," Sally snarled.

Gary laughed, startled. "Okay."

"You just want to keep me under control," Sally said. "That's the reason you don't want me to have it."

"Bullshit," Steve answered.

"What's the matter?" she asked. "Afraid I'll shoot you?"

"Accidentally? Maybe."

"If I did, it wouldn't be an accident," she answered, with a vehemence Gary didn't understand.

"Sally, don't talk like that," Steve said.

"You're always making my choices for me," Sally went on. "Keeping me from doing what I want—"

"I'm only trying to keep you from hurting yourself."

"—Or making me do things I feel really bad about."

"Oh, like what?"

"Give me the pistol, Steve."

"Forget it."

"I want it, Steve."

"What are you going to do? Walk out on me?"

"I could tell a little secret. I wonder what Gary would think of you then?"

Steve's eyes widened, just for a moment. Then he smiled good-naturedly.

"*Our* little secret, honey?" he asked. "You're going to tell *that*?"

"Give me the gun, Steve," Sally said.

"No," Steve answered.

Gary watched Sally. She opened her mouth to speak—then snapped it shut again, evidently losing her nerve. Steve turned to Gary.

"Sounds pretty sinister, huh?" he asked.

"Depends," Gary answered, embarrassed.

"Got any dirty linen in your marriage?"

"Oh, yeah."

"We've just had some problems, that's all. Nothing spectacular. Sally can make anything sound dramatic—"

"Hey," Gary broke in, "did I ask about it? Whatever it is, I don't care."

Steve laughed. "Okay, then."

Sally was sitting across from him; he nudged her with his foot.

"Love you, Sally," he said.

"That's just great," she answered.

ONCE the painkillers kicked in, they felt sufficiently recovered to go get the dry suits. Standing at the front of the old store, floorboards creaking under their feet, they eyed the diving shop across the street.

"I'll take a look," Gary said. Poking his head out the door, he glanced north and south. "Coast's clear," he announced.

Leaving the pharmacy, they crossed to the diving store. Its front door was wide open, stopped by a wedge.

"Bet the owner left in a real hurry," Steve said as they entered.

They quickly found dry suits, donned them, and put their clothes back on over them. With his injured shoulder, Steve had a good deal of trouble, but Sally helped. Linda and Gary took turns on watch.

"Anything else we want in here?" Steve asked, condensation pluming his breath. "Think we could use the spear-guns?"

"Nope," Gary said. "Good for nothing. What we could really use is a couple of Remington 1100s, full auto."

"That would really make chopped meat out of the bastards, wouldn't it?" Steve said, with relish. "Think anything worthwhile might be left in that sporting goods place down the way?"

"Some ammo. Maybe. But there must've been a big rush for firearms through here."

"These suits are really *hot,*" Sally carped. "I'm going to be sweating like a pig in a couple of minutes."

"Better then freezing, honey," Steve said.

From the sound of it, Gary guessed he tacked the *honey* on deliberately to annoy her.

"Linda," Gary said, "anything moving out there?"

"Nothing so—" she broke off.

"What?" Gary whispered.

"Get down!" she answered, dropping on one knee beside the window. Gary and the others took cover.

"Should've closed the front door," Steve said. "Shit. This is the first place they'll look."

"Not if they noticed it was propped open before," Gary answered. "If we'd closed it . . . "

Linda came army-crawling up the aisle toward them.

"How many?" Gary asked.

"Just one," she answered. "It was looking out from an alley across the street. I think it saw me."

"Back door time," Steve said.

"Right," Gary answered.

Rising to a crouch, he led the way toward the rear of the store. Opening the door, he let the others through first, then heard footsteps and looked back.

Four figures were racing for the front door, but not with the stiff-legged stride of the dead. And even though the foremost's face was in shadow, Gary recognized the build and gait, and laughed out loud.

"Max!" he cried, rushing back up the aisle. "Max!"

Max stopped a few yards into the store, Dennis, Camille, and Father Chuck piling in behind him.

"Gary?" Max called.

Gary clapped his arms around him, Linda and the rest of Gary's group bringing up the rear. Linda and Camille hugged each other, Camille planting a loud kiss on Linda's cheek.

"We'd all better get back from the window," Max said.

They moved farther into the store; all except Dennis, who remained to watch the street.

"Let me guess," Gary said. "You're here for dry suits."

"We're from the same litter," Max answered. "Got yours already?"

"Yeah. But you have to tell me how—"

Max cut him off. "First things first. Let us get outfitted, okay?"

"Sure," Gary said. "Here, take my flashlight." Fishing it from his coat pocket, he handed it to his brother.

YET once the newcomers had suited up, Max insisted the group should leave immediately, brushing aside Gary's pleas to hear what had happened. Gary knew it was wise to get moving, but also sensed Max wasn't eager to tell the story.

Max had changed. There was something haunted in his eyes. Indeed, Max's whole presence seemed somehow diminished, shrunken. What had he been through?

They made a quick search of the sporting goods store nearby. There were no guns left, but there was ammo for the Beretta and the assault rifles, as well as two containers of black powder, which Max took to make bombs. He also picked up a machete.

"Force of habit," he explained cryptically to Gary, not saying how he lost the other.

Farther along, the food store had also been plundered, although many of the shelves remained a third or so full—the looters hadn't had time to strip the place clean. Unable to find any dried goods, the group stocked up on canned stuff, filled their all but empty canteens with RC Cola—it was the only drink left—and set out once more.

They spent the remainder of the night looking vainly for usable boats, and weaving their way southward among the fine old shingled summer homes on the western shore of the peninsula. As day drew near, they climbed through the window of a sumptuous three story vacation palace, and went down into its cavernous basement. There, in a windowless room, they built a fire on the concrete floor out of charcoal briquettes. Bags and bags of the fuel were piled against the wall.

"Must've been planning one hell of a cookout," Dennis observed.

"Big party town," Steve answered. "Lots of folks came down here from New York and North Jersey. This was the state attorney general's summer place."

"Giovanni?" Gary asked. "The one who was indicted?"

"Yep. Entertained swarms of assholes here all the time."

239

"Anyone want to take the first watch?" Max asked.

"Back by the stairs?" Dennis asked.

Max nodded.

"Okay," Dennis said. Linda gave him her gun as he went.

Max eased himself down against a white-painted brick wall, Gary settling beside him in the semidarkness. Across from them was Father Chuck, lying on the floor near the fire.

Gary hadn't heard anything from the priest since the groups reunited. Like Max, Father Chuck seemed to have undergone some kind of crisis, but clearly his had been far more profound. Max's eyes were haunted. The priest's were hollow. They might have been the eyes of a dead man.

"All right, Max," Gary said. "I think it's about time you told me what happened to you guys."

"Do you really?" Max asked.

"Yeah."

Max showed him an exhausted, ugly smile. "What would you like to know?"

"Keep your voices down, please," Camille begged. "Some of us are trying to sleep."

"Sure," Gary said, then whispered to his brother: "Why don't you just tell me everything?"

"I'm not sure I can do it justice," Max replied.

"Okay, then, something simple. Why do you smell like you've been doused in gasoline?"

Max put his hands over his face, as though he were trying to collect his thoughts. He dragged them slowly downward. "Have you seen the word LEGION scrawled all over the place?"

"Yeah."

"Legion did it to me."

"So it's a name?"

Max nodded. "I think I'd better start at the beginning."

Opening with Uncle Buddy's desertion, he told of the escape from the corpses near the lake, the bodies in the parking lot, the fight in the garage, and the death of MacAleer's wife and son. But when he came finally to the incidents in the storm sewer, he tried to beg off, saying he needed sleep. Gary refused to buy it, kept pressing him; he was more than a little appalled when his brother gave in. It was so unlike him . . .

But Max let it all out, ending with his reunion with Dennis and the others after Legion freed him.

"You know that big boathouse, just before the Matahawking line?" Max asked. "I went in to see what I could find. Heard snoring from one of those big tool cabinets, looked inside. There they were, fast asleep, all three of them. Aunt Camille was sawing the logs . . . "

Gary was barely listening to him by that time. "But, Max," he began. "What *is* Legion? The other ones don't have those kinds of powers."

"Tell me about it," Max said, and laughed. Gary would've sworn there was a note of quiet hysteria there.

"He's a *demon*," Max went on.

"What?"

"A devil. A fallen angel."

"But, Max—" Gary began in disbelief.

"Jesus, Gary," Max broke in, "what planet have you been living on the past couple days? He's a demon in possession of a human corpse. Ever hear of the Gadarene swine? He's the one—the *ones*— who sent them over the cliff." Max laughed again. "He's been put in charge of the whole goddamn world."

"He told you that?"

"Not in so many words. But Father Chuck had a chat with one of Legion's troops down in the sewer—Father Ted. Uncle Dennis told me all about it. Old Teddy tried to talk Chuck into joining him. And in the process, brother mine, he confirmed MacAleer's craziest theories. Beyond a shadow of a doubt."

Gary shook his head, unwilling to believe it. To accept it would be sheer insanity. MacAleer had gone mad. Father Chuck had, too, it seemed. And Max looked like he was well on his way . . .

"This is *Hell*, Gary," Max said. "This is the place where the worm dies not."

"Well, what if it is?" came Steve's voice from the shadows to their left. "Maybe this is where we belong."

"Oh, Christ," Gary said. "Don't tell me you're flipping out too."

"Just hear me out," Steve answered. "You know damn well I don't believe in sin. And I don't believe in punishment. But maybe we're better off here. Fighting for our lives. Unwilling to repent. Refusing to lick the jackboots of our Führer in Heaven."

"Rather be a king in Hell, huh?" Max asked.

"Absolutely."

"This place already has a king," Max answered.

"But wait, Steve," Gary said. "Are you saying you believe all this stuff about Heaven and Hell?"

"No," Steve answered. "But if it *is* true, it doesn't make me respect the power that stuck me here any more. As a matter of fact, it would just strengthen my suspicions. And whether or not God exists, I'm going to go out fighting Him. Spitting right in the fucker's face."

Gary felt a rush of heat in his belly. His tired blood almost kindled at Steve's words. They seemed noble, heroic. The idea of God had become utterly repugnant. Calling Him a cosmic Hitler barely did Him justice. His power had wrenched Max Sr. from the peace of the grave, sent him forth screaming in torment; Divine Providence had ripped the face from Father Ted, throttled young Dave till his face went black, strangled Aunt Lucy, and snapped its jaws shut on Uncle Buddy's arm—the list was endless, horror after horror.

And it was all *arbitrary*. The victims had done *nothing* heinous enough to justify such punishment. Gary's father hadn't been a monster. Even Uncle Buddy, repulsive as he was, had been more stupid than anything else. Even at the end, Gary decided, Buddy had simply gone insane . . . Gary's own life hadn't been anything to brag about, but he hadn't been a concentration camp guard either.

Steve was right. Better to spit in God's face than submit.

Even Max didn't seem willing to argue. Gary looked over at him.

Max was asleep, chin on chest.

CHAPTER 21
ILL TIDINGS

IT was two hours before sunrise the following morning, windy and bitterly cold; they'd covered five miles during the night, passing through the small summer bungalow towns of Mobley Beach and Brittany. Crossing over into Seabeach Heights, where the peninsula widened out once more, they'd made for the Rt. 33 bridge. Now, hidden in a stand of scrub pine on the western shore of the peninsula, they looked out at the span.

No streetlights glowed along its sides; the power had gone off completely about midnight. But there were fires burning on the bridge, and in their light, and against it, dozens of motionless sentries could be seen.

"So much for that," Gary said, heart sinking, rubbing his hands against the cold.

"Well," Max answered, "had to try."

"We're trapped?" Sally asked.

"They're sure as hell not going to let us stroll across," Steve replied.

"Maybe we'll find a boat," Linda said.

"Think so?" Steve asked. "The bastards have been pretty damned thorough."

"Guess we might have to try a raft after all," Max said.

"It'll be noisy making it," Steve replied. "All that hammering."

"We'll just have to trust to luck."

"We could do it in one of those boatbuilding shops a mile back," Gary said. "They'd have everything we need."

BACK out of the pines they went, heading north. Recrossing into Brittany, following the shoreline, they went into the first of the boat shops, a large Quonset hut surrounded by a gravel parking-lot. Inside they found a cabin cruiser with huge holes smashed into either side of the hull; there were several similarly damaged craft in the lot outside.

Max ran his flashlight over a stack of lumber. "Plenty of planks," he said. "We could nail them together with crosspieces, then take some of those fuel drums outside, empty them, and fasten them under the raft. That would give us all the flotation we'd need."

"Then just paddle across?" Gary asked.

"With those." Max darted his beam toward a bunch of long oars leaning in the corner.

"When are we going to put this thing together?" Steve asked.

"Could start tonight," Max answered.

"Flashlights would be real obvious."

"Good point," Max said, and switched his off. "We'll work in the daytime, in shifts."

"That's if we get the chance," Dennis called, from over by the front door.

"What's wrong?" Max asked.

"Take a look for yourself."

They went over with him, peering out through the glass. Scores of bobbing, tiny red lights were approaching in the distance, coming down a street leading directly to the shop.

"Torches," Gary said.

"Quite a parade," Steve said.

"I bet they don't know we're here," said Max, peering briefly through his binoculars. "Let's just stay put."

THE column crept closer. Waving on the ends of poles, things which might've been standards appeared around the corner, followed by some kind of huge juggernaut-like vehicle.

"What if Legion's with them, Max?" Gary asked suddenly. "What if he's coming for *you?*"

Max said nothing.

"Max," Steve said, "Maybe, just to be sure, you should take off . . . "

"*What?*" Max asked.

"Lead them away from us. If they're not after you, you'll be all right. But if they *are* . . . "

"I'm dead meat anyway? Is that what you're trying to say?"

"If Legion's with them," Dennis answered, "he could be coming for any of us."

"Or none," Max said.

"You mean maybe God hasn't been talking to him lately?" Steve asked.

"No way of telling, is there? And what if I took off and he was really coming for *you*? Wouldn't that be something, Steve?"

"I was just thinking of the group," Steve said.

"Sure," Max answered.

ON and on came the army of the dead, torches guttering in the wind. The standards waved with a lazy seasick rhythm, inverted crosses, dead animals, crude gigantic skull-masks, wheels with spikes along the outer rim. Limned in fire and darkness, it was like a scene out of Bosch or Goya.

Or Nuremberg.

"How long are we going to wait?" Linda demanded.

"Until I say different," Max answered.

The corpses neared the intersection with the street that fronted the lot.

"Max . . . ." Linda said.

"If they don't know we're here," Max replied, "they're probably not *coming* here. If they *do* know, we're in big trouble no matter what. They'll turn aside, you watch."

But the dead weren't listening. The column pushed across the street and onto the gravel.

"Out the back," Max said. As they made for the small exit beside the main sliding-door, he said to Linda, "next time I don't listen to you, shoot me."

"You bet," she answered, slipping outside. He followed.

"Which way now?" Gary asked.

"South," Max answered, leading them along the back of the boat-shop, figuring they could cross over into the pine-wooded patch that bordered the parking lot. But looking around the corner, he saw that it was too late for that; the column was approaching along the side of the boatshop, the torches already so close that fleeing across the corpses' path was suicide.

Max turned. Looking in one of the shop's rear windows, he could see the windows on the north side; there were torches outside those too. The column had split. Flight northward was also impossible.

The only way now was west.

"Out to the water," Max said. "Now."

They turned and ran, reaching the shore before the torchlight could fall on them, footbeats drowned out by the rush of the wind.

"Don't stop," Max said. "We've got the drysuits. We'll make it."

Out into the bay they splashed. The tide was low, the water only ankle-high. A shingle of clamshells shifted and cracked beneath their feet. The water deepened after a hundred yards or so, but only to their shins.

Gary glanced back over his shoulder. They'd left the torches far behind. The corpses had stopped on the beach.

"Watch out," Max said. "There's a slope."

The water deepened to mid-thigh.

"I see something," Dennis puffed.

There was a darker shadow in the darkness ahead, a long low ridge rising from the water, surmounted by what looked like a beached boat.

"Make for the island," Max said.

Panting, they staggered up a slippery weed-grown bank and onto the ridge. There, hidden in the darkness and the tall wind-tossed reeds, they halted. Gary and Linda threw themselves to the ground, the rest falling or crouching around them. The boat loomed nearby, a large cabin-cruiser that had evidently crashed into the island at high speed, plowing up onto the slope on momentum.

"Are they coming, Max?" Gary gasped.

His brother was on one knee in front of him, staring back toward the shore, not even breathing hard. He rose slightly and lifted his binoculars.

"They're still on the beach, spreading out along the water," he said. "More coming up all the time, though. God, there must be a couple thousand of them on that street."

Once he caught his breath, Gary got up beside him, peering through the night toward the wind-whipped torches. The firebrands blazed along the shore in a line four hundred yards long.

The juggernaut-like vehicle came up alongside the boatshop. Gary guessed it was being drawn, but with the throng between him and it, he couldn't see who, or what was pulling it. The vehicle came to a halt some distance before reaching the waterside, yet close enough for him to make out some details. A single corpse sat enthroned on the huge platform. Behind the cadaver was a crazily leaning mountain of what appeared to be planks, with a makeshift Golgotha of inverted crosses

on top, the tallest of which was crowned by an immense spiked wheel. To the throne's right was one of those giant skull masks, mounted on a pole. On the left a wriggling body hung upside down on another shaft. At first Gary assumed it must be a live captive. Then he noticed that the pole seemed to be coming up *through* the belly, not behind.

Object lesson, he thought. *The revolution defending itself.*

"That one on the throne," Max said, lowering his binoculars, "That's Legion."

Gary looked at Max. There were now so many torches assembled on shore that a faint ruddy glow was playing over his brother's face; Max's eyes were wide and dispirited, almost hopeless.

"Maybe he was lying," Gary said.

"When he let me go?" Max asked.

"You said he's a demon."

Max nodded.

"Why should you believe him?"

"If you'd heard him," Max said, "you would've."

"So what are you going to do? Curl up in a ball and die? Or spit in God's face like me and Steve?"

Max shook his head. "I'm going to *pray*. And see if I can't get Father Chuck to confess me."

"He hasn't said a word in a day and a half," Gary answered. "He's gone off the deep end, if you ask me. But if you're sure Legion's going to get you, why bother?"

"Maybe I'm not sure. Maybe I don't know what I think about anything anymore. But I'm scared, Gary. And I'll grasp at any straw. Even if it's old Father Chuck there. He's got the power. I don't. I don't have the will. I don't have the faith." He paused. "I should've gone back for MacAleer. I should've forced myself. But if I could do it all over again, it would be harder now. Now that I've talked to Legion. I'm so scared, Gary."

"I hate to interrupt all this soul-searching," Steve said, coming through the weeds. "But what exactly do you think they're doing over there?"

"I don't know," Max answered.

"Maybe they'll just finish their ceremony or whatever it is and leave," Gary said.

"Maybe," Max said.

THE night wore on. The tide crawled farther out, revealing the clamshell flats. The corpses never stirred.

A hint of dawn appeared above the bungalow roofs in the east, spread across the sky. Still the dead, several thousand at least, didn't move. The wind died, and their torch flames licked straight upward in the chill calm.

Gary and Max and the rest crawled over to the cabin cruiser. There was a large gash in the hull; the boat had struck something, a piling perhaps, as it surged from the water. They entered through the opening, coming up in the main sleeping-compartment.

As the light grew, they could see dark stains and spatters everywhere, bullet holes in the bulkheads, slash-marks in the cushions.

"Must've been some massacre in here," Max said. "Looks like the victims put up one stiff fight, though."

In any case, the boat was a good vantage from which to watch the army across the flats; blankets and a gas stove in the galley provided welcome warmth.

Looking out on the bay side, Gary noticed that the flats extended at least a quarter-mile, where a line of exposed pilings marked the border of the main channel. Not knowing how deep the water was beyond the markers, he asked:

"You think we *might* be able to walk across?"

"Not in the daylight," Max said.

"Also," Steve said. "Those flats drop straight off. The channel's deep, and it's a mile across. Goes all the way to the other shore. Sometimes you get sandbars forming up against the flats, but even then you could only walk along them a few hundred yards or so. At best."

"So then we swim," Gary said.

"I don't know how," Camille answered.

"I couldn't hack it either," Steve said. "Not with my shoulder like this."

"We could pull you," Gary suggested. "Use life-vests."

The idea seemed worth a try, but a quick search of the cabin, and a look onto the rear deck, revealed no life jackets.

"Fucking assholes," Max said. "Going out without preservers."

Steve laughed. "Coast Guard should've thrown the book at 'em."

THE sun rose, wan and diseased. The sky was a weird yellow-brown, with clouds twisted into tortured shapes scudding across.

Gary stationed himself at a window on the port side, looking out through the curtains. The dead had extinguished their torches; now a great gap opened in their ranks, and a mass of captives was herded out onto the flats.

"Something's happening," he said. "They're driving prisoners out there . . ."

Max looked out beside him, adjusting his binoculars.

As the glasses focused, he saw that the captives, hundreds of them, were living people, being prodded forward by corpses with long sharpened poles. Bent nearly double, the people staggered under the weight of flat concrete blocks wired to their backs. Faces bloodied, some were missing eyes or noses, and their clothes were stained and tattered as if they'd been sliced repeatedly with knives. Many fell as they were driven out, but were prodded immediately to their feet. Those unable to rise had their legs tied together with barbed wire, and were left where they dropped.

"Max," Gary said, "We'd better get moving."

"Where?"

"Out across the mudflat, try and swim for it."

"And leave Steve and Aunt Camille? If the corpses *are* headed here, they'll spot us anyway. But I don't think they'll come this far."

"That's what you said back in the boatshop."

"Just look."

One after another, the prisoners were being forced down, their legs tied. None of the dead drew closer to the island than fifty yards, where a channel ran between the shell-flat and the weedy bank.

"Tide'll return in about an hour," Max said.

"They're going to drown them?"

"Good slow way to kill a lot of people at once. Guess they were tired of just torturing them. Or maybe they need more recruits."

MORE captives were herded out. A steadily rising chorus of moans and shrieks reached the cruiser.

The process was repeated again and again. Before long there were several thousand prisoners lying on the flat, pinned down by the weight of the cinderblocks, unable to move their limbs.

And then the tide began to creep back in.

The water rose in the channel between the island and the flats, soon lapping over the bank. It crawled in rivulets among the bone-white shells. It formed small puddles, then pools, then shallow lakes, spreading inexorably toward the doomed wretches screaming and groaning and pleading on the shell-encrusted mud . . . Driving their spears into a hand here, a leg there, the corpses retreated slowly toward the beach.

"I'm not going to watch," Gary said, sinking back from the window.

That leaves you, Max told himself. Someone *had* to watch, he knew. There was always the chance that the dead might take an interest in the island, stride over their victims and investigate the boat. It might come down to trying to swim for it after all—in the daylight.

But where would that leave Camille and Steve? Would they have to be left behind, to fend for themselves? Like MacAleer?

Max flinched at the thought. He'd learned his lesson back in the sewer, even if there was no way of knowing whether he'd learned it soon enough. Would he have the nerve to stay behind this time? Would the grace be there?

He imagined a giant hand, turning over and over above a sea of flames, small figures clambering desperately from finger to finger, trying to hold on, dropping one by one into the fire, into perdition . . .

The hand of God, he thought.

"No," he breathed, refusing to believe it.

He's just dangling you above the fire, playing with you, dragging it out till it bores him, just like Dennis said . . .

The people on the flat howled and cursed, the puddles were lapping at them now. Water soaked up through tattered clothes, darkening fabric, gluing it to shivering limbs. Mangled faces lifted from the shell-littered mud, spitting, mouths working, calling out in a yapping babel of voices.

And there will be a wailing and a gnashing of teeth . . .

But another multitude of voices arose; shrilling cries of triumph and sadistic delight, the dead drowned out the living. Max trained his glasses on Legion. The giant had risen on his throne, and had both arms raised, joining in the exultation.

The hideous clamor went on and on as the tide washed in. Small waves were already splashing the victims, who were trying desperately to keep their mouths, then their noses, above the surface; bit by bit the waters smothered them, swallowed them. Drowning heads whipped frantically back and forth, then went still. Trickling bubbles and masses of floating hair marked the places where captives had succumbed.

Finally the struggles ceased. And with that the dead fell silent, standing rigidly on the shore, staring westward.

Legion lowered his arms and sank back onto his throne, jaw hanging open, dark bursts of what Max thought might be flies puffing like smoke from his mouth. Scalp creeping, Max remembered, for perhaps the hundredth time, the demon's words:

Next time, you're mine.

CHAPTER 22
OUT OF SIGHT

THROUGHOUT the morning and much of the afternoon the dead maintained their silent vigil, staring westward, Legion presiding from his throne. The tide almost submerged the island. Wavelets slapped the cabin cruiser's stern.

A sickly-looking sea gull entered the hole in the hull. It showed no fear of people, and the group took pity on it. Shortly, though, it began to vomit up a horrible-smelling orange fluid, all the while whipping its neck spastically about; Gary pushed it back out of the cabin with his foot. Listing to one side as though it was filling up with water, it drifted away.

The tide receded, revealing the drowned bodies on the flat. With that the living dead, having received another group of victims, began leading them out, forcing them down and binding their legs. By the time the tide began to rise once more, the shell flat was almost completely covered with bodies. Max guessed that at least three thousand had already been drowned, with as many again awaiting their turn.

"We're going to be here a good long while," he said.

"Just what I was thinking," Gary said. "That's if they're going to stick around until all of them wake up. Which should be about a day and a half, even if they don't bring out any more victims."

"You know," Steve said, "it'll be dark by the time the tide goes out again. Why don't we cross to the flats, skirt round the ones onshore, and get back onto the peninsula? They wouldn't see us."

"I don't know about that," Max answered. "Not with them lined up that way. The flats drop off north and south. We'd have to come pretty damn close to those bastards. Unless we wanted to do some swimming. And that's out."

"This sucks," Steve said.

"You just noticed?" Max asked, and set about making his black-powder bombs.

THE sun sank toward the horizon, the eastern sky darkening to a brownish bruise-purple even before the ravaged disc set. When at last the sun disappeared, night came down like a blow, the sunset blackening like old blood. The living dead kindled their torches once more.

With Gary and Steve on watch, the others ate a cheerless meal. Gas flames from the stove lit their faces a chill faint blue. No one spoke.

After he finished, Max felt a touch on his sleeve, and turned. It was Father Chuck. Always thin, the priest now looked quite haggard, cheeks sunken, eyes dark-rimmed. Yet there was a strange light in those eyes, which had been dull and vacant for the last two days.

"Father?" Max asked.

"You were right all along," Father Chuck said softly. "But I suppose you know that."

"Yes, Father."

"Satisfied?"

"Because I was right? God, I wish I wasn't. I wish it was all a bad dream, that justice was an empty word. I used to gloat about the idea of Hell, Father. I used to think of everyone I hated roasting in the pit. All the monsters I read about in the history books. I never thought I might have to keep them company." Max smiled grimly. "What's that Billy Joel line?— 'I'd rather laugh with the sinners than cry with the saints?' I can just see me and Billy Joel and Stalin, laughing like hyenas. Forever."

The priest laughed weakly." The wrath of God," he said. "*Dies irae, dies illa . . .* "

"*Solvet Saeclum in Favilla,*" Max continued. "I wouldn't have thought you were the type for medieval plainsong."

"I'm not. But that one always stuck in my head. They used it in *Becket*, remember? The part where Burton excommunicates the baron?"

"Great scene," Max said.

"It always terrified me. I always hated that whole aspect of the Church. The fear, the superstition. I loved the beatitudes, Jesus battling to perfect society. There was so much I didn't want to see. That I didn't want to believe." Father Chuck paused. "You're quite a scholar, aren't you, Max?"

"Doesn't seem to have carried much weight with God, Father."

"But you *do* know your theology, don't you?"

"Yes."

"Tell me then. Can a wicked man still administer the sacraments?"

"According to the Church, yes."

"That's what I thought. But it doesn't seem just somehow . . . "

"Never did to me either."

Father Chuck seemed to withdraw back into himself. Max thought perhaps he'd offended him. Then the priest asked: "Do you know what I'm supposed to say during confession? It's been so long since I've done one."

"I can walk you through it."

"Will you let me confess you?"

"Oh yes, Father," Max answered.

"Can you forgive me, Max?"

Max nodded, brushing away a tear.

"Very touching," Steve said, up by the window. He'd been listening all along. "I *love* the thought of you two forgiving each other. Especially you, Max. As much as I hate your point of view, I never thought you'd get all teary at the idea of being absolved by that wimp."

Max looked at him. "Did someone ask for your opinion?"

"You really can't complain. *You're* always telling people how they should think."

"Trying to convert me?" Max asked.

"Convert you, rattle your cage, what's the difference?"

"Do you actually have something to convert me to?"

"Sure I do. I've got my own philosophy. Maybe it's not as systematic as yours, but I actually *live* it. Which is more than you can say for most people."

"*Practicing* atheist, huh?"

"Yeah."

"And what exactly is the advantage in that?"

"Honesty. I live *authentically*. I can make myself into whatever I choose, because there's no one in charge. No one who has any real authority. I mean, someone might beat me over the head, but it's not as if he has any *right* to. Up till then, it's total freedom. Doesn't that sound pretty good?"

"Sure. Except for the beating part."

"Well, we all get screwed sooner or later. Before, if it wasn't the police, it'd be a heart attack or cancer. Now it's the living dead. So I might as well not take any shit, huh? Willingly, at least."

"Words to live by."

"Being snide the best you can do? I expected better. Come on, Max. What's the advantage in being a Christian?"

"Hope."

Steve chuckled. "Do you really think you're going to get out of this? Has *anyone* gotten out of this? Since the folks that were just raptured off to Heaven, that is?"

Max didn't answer.

"This is Hell, right?" Steve went on. "And isn't Hell supposed to be forever? It sure seems to me like your God was designing for eternity. The dead can't die, the sun's on its fucking last legs—"

"That doesn't mean we're trapped here," Max answered. "Some people *have* been taken up, we know that much. If it comes to that, God's been snatching people away from Legion and his kind for at least two thousand years. I think the world hasn't been rearranged quite so much as it seems. Maybe the rules haven't changed, but the game's just going faster. Parts of this planet were Hell long before the dead came out of their graves. Maybe all of it was. This is just a continuation of our lives after all. A logical extension, deliberately chosen."

"Deliberately chosen?" Steve laughed. "Don't tell me I got into this situation on my own steam! If God asked me where I wanted to wind up, do you think I would've said, 'Oh, yes Sir, please send me to Hell'? He never spoke to me. Never showed me the danger I was in. Just wound me up and let me go, then blamed me for doing what came naturally. Which wasn't so terrible. And what do you bet that just about everyone in this world-without-end-amen-Auschwitz wasn't any worse?"

"You know what?" Max asked. "There's only one person whose heart of hearts I really know. That's me. And I'm a scumbag."

"So you think everyone else must be just as bad? Is that your opinion as a self-confessed scumbag? Not very charitable. Or logical. I guess we just see ourselves in other people."

"Well, when you're a student of history, it's kind of unavoidable," Max said. "You crack open those books, and what do they describe? One unending horrorshow. The Cult of Kali. Aztec priests wading in blood. The Crusaders in Byzantium. The Thirty Years' War. Matthew Hopkins, the Witchfinder General of East Anglia. Drogheda, Dachau, the Collectivization of the Ukraine . . . "

"So what are you saying? That that's the rule? That because some people have been rotten, everyone must be rotten?"

Mr. Woodbury
Psychology

"Not everyone," Max said. "I believe in saints. As for the rest of us . . . well, that's a different story. Ever hear of that study, Steve? The one where they made guys think they were giving people electric shocks? One in ten of those guinea pigs, *one in ten,* ran the needle right off the meter just because the folks in the white coats told them to. Even when they started hearing screams, even when the screams *stopped,* they kept hitting the button. So what does that tell us? One out of every ten people you've met would probably fit right in at Treblinka or Tuol Sleng. You brushed shoulders with potential mass murderers every time you went to the mall.

"But do you have to be a mass murderer before you're thoroughly rotten? I don't think so. If Hell were reserved for the Hitlers and Pol Pots, my father wouldn't be out there now, taking orders from Legion. And Dad was one of the *better* people in my life.

"I've known folks who cheated every employer they ever worked for, gas station mechanics who stuck it to every customer they could, plain ordinary housewives who made such a hateful tortured mess of their children's lives that maybe a just God *might* feed them to the flames. I've held polite conversations with good ole VFW boys who turned livid at the memory of Japs bayoneting Chinese babies, but who couldn't see anything wrong with B-29's raining fire on Jap babies in Tokyo . . . Most of the people I went to college with frothed at the mouth at the idea of tiger cages. But if you told them about the Commies burying people alive in Hue, or killing Montagnards by feeding their intestines to hogs, they'd insist it wasn't true until you showed them the proof—then insist the Reds must know what they were doing. Which usually left yours truly feeling like feeding *some* people's intestines to hogs might not be such a bad thing after all . . . Jesus Christ Almighty, the human race deserved to be blown off the map a long time ago."

Steve applauded softly. "Done?"

"Yeah."

"So," Steve mused, "we're all capital offenders, eh?" He nudged Gary. "Learn anything about yourself from that little tirade?"

"None of it sounded like me," Gary said. "I'm not a Goddamn Nazi."

"Hell no," Max said. "You wouldn't have the balls to be a true believer. But what do you bet you'd follow your orders like a good jellyfish when the time came?"

"Bullshit!" Gary shot back. "Are you a mind reader now? Can you look right into my soul?"

"No. But I know you, Gary."

"Max," Father Chuck said, "that's enough."

To his own amazement, Max decided not to take it any further. There was a long, ugly silence.

"Max?" Father Chuck asked at last. "Could you write me out the words?"

"Words?"

"For the sacrament."

"Sure, Father." Earlier Max had found a pen and paper in a bolster box above one of the bunks; Father Chuck, holding Linda's flashlight, illuminated the writing pad as Max wrote out the formula.

"I'll hear confessions now," the priest said, taking the top sheet.

"Here?" Dennis said. "Where everyone can listen?"

"I'll go to the rear of the cabin. You can come back one at a time."

"Just watch out with that flashlight, Father," Max said. "We don't want 'em spotting it. Stay below the bulkhead and keep the beam low."

"How long is this going to take?" Steve demanded. "It's about time someone else took watch."

"Relax," Max said. "None of us are very bad, right? It'll be over before you know it."

He went back with the priest and whispered his confession. Linda followed, then Dennis. Camille went last, after some prodding from her husband.

When it was all over, Max and Dennis replaced Gary and Steve on watch.

"I see you're still here with the rest of us," Gary said.

"How do you explain that, Max?" Steve asked, breaking out his food.

Max said nothing.

"Maybe Father Chuck doesn't have any power after all," Gary said.

"Shut up, Gary," Linda said.

"Maybe there's just no way out," Steve said.

"So why make our last hours so much more miserable?" Father Chuck asked wearily.

"Just trying to enlighten you," Steve said.

"Or drag us down with you?" Linda asked.

"Yeah, maybe," Steve replied cheerfully. "Though I might point

258

out we're already in the same hole."

"Dennis," came Camille's voice, plaintive in the darkness, "Why *are* we still here?"

"I don't know," Dennis replied.

"It didn't work," Camille said hopelessly.

"You don't know what good it's done us," Max answered.

"Hey look, Aunt Camille," Gary said. "Just open your eyes. Don't you see? This is Heaven."

"Really something, isn't it?" Steve asked.

"When do we get to see God?" Gary said.

"Not till you finish that Spam."

SEVERAL hours later they heard gunfire crackling across the bay, interspersed with the sound of explosions. Looking westward, they saw flashes of red and yellow light, flaming blasts mushrooming into the night.

"What the fuck?" Gary said. "What's going on over there?"

"Full-auto fire," Max said. "Lots of it. And those are mortar rounds, if you ask me. I wonder if some poor National Guard unit's been run to earth?"

"Linda, what are they doing on your side?" Gary called over his shoulder. She was watching the dead on the east shore.

"They're turning," she answered. "Legion's signaling . . . "

Gary crossed to her window. Torches bobbing, the corpses began moving south.

"They're heading for the bridge," he said. "To get in on the slaughter."

"Any staying behind?" Max asked.

"Can't tell yet," Gary answered.

The sounds of fighting intensified across the bay. The corpses on the eastern shore strode swiftly in the direction of the 33 bridge.

But not all of them.

"They *are* leaving a guard," Gary said. "About twenty."

"Welcoming committee," Max said. "For the drowned ones."

The gunfire slackened off. Gary went back to the port side. Numerous blazes had broken out on the western side of the bay. Max was looking across the water with his binoculars.

"What do you see over there?" Gary asked.

"A marina. I think the guardsmen, or whoever they were, were trying to get to it. Lot of intact boats. Guess the dead were keeping them to patrol the bay."

"And they're still in control?"

"I think so. But I saw our boys pulling back into the woods. And there were a lot of 'em left. There's going to be another attack, I'd be willing to—"

The mortars started up again.

"Bet on it," he continued. "Round 2. Good luck, you SOB's."

WITH brief interruptions, the fighting went on long into the night. About three in the morning, there was a tremendous escalation. Max speculated the guardsmen, or whoever they were, had gotten major reinforcements. The battle continued at that level for perhaps half an hour—then simply stopped.

"Corpses still have the marina," Max said, peering through the binoculars. "But some are climbing into sailboats, raising the masts. Maybe some of the guardsmen managed to lift a rowboat or two and make it out into the bay . . . " He moved the glasses slowly, right to left. "Yeah. I see 'em against the flames. Two Boston whalers."

The wind had come up once more. Decks lined with torch-bearing figures, the sailboats pushed out into the bay. A flare streaked up, dyeing the sky violet with its glare.

Heading due south, the rowboats were plainly revealed. There was fire from the men clustered on them, but not much. *Too low on ammo*, Max thought. The flare drifted across the sky, sank slowly, faded from view.

"They better watch themselves," Steve said. "Those goddamn sandbars. That was how I lost Ginger."

"Ginger?" Dennis asked.

"My first wife," Steve answered. "We were chugging along top-speed in my boat, hit a sandbar. Both of us were thrown overboard. I banged my head on a piece of wood, was knocked out, but my life-jacket kept me afloat. I don't know what happened to Ginger. We found her lifejacket. But . . . "

"Jesus," Dennis said. "I'm sorry."

"Yeah," Steve said, and lapsed into silence.

Off to the west, another flare burned across the sky.

"Guys in the whalers are changing course," Max said. "Couldn't hope to make it off south, not under pursuit . . . looks like they're heading right for us. Must think they'll do better on foot."

"How many boats following them?" Gary asked.

"About five. Big sailboats. Must be a hundred corpses on 'em, or more. We'd better get ready to move."

"To where?" Steve demanded.

"The east shore."

"You mean across the flat?"

"Tide's getting low."

"What about the guards on the beach?"

"They won't spot us till we're practically on top of 'em. Then we blast our way through. They're pretty spread out . . . Wake the others."

THE women had dropped off about midnight, along with Father Chuck. Dennis went from sleeper to sleeper, shaking them.

"What is it?" Linda demanded groggily.

"We're going to have to wade across the flat," Gary answered, slipping his pack on.

The group collected their tackle. Only Max remained where he was, watching.

A third flare blazed. In its light, he saw the first of the sailboats jerk to a halt, mast snapping off. Corpses hurtled overboard.

"Hold on a second!" he cried. "The sailboats are running aground!"

The others began to veer, but it was already too late. Moments later they too were stranded on the sandbar. Shallower of draft, the Boston whalers kept coming.

"We just might have some reinforcements," Max said. "Let's sit tight a few minutes longer."

But the rowboats were crowded, and riding low in the water. Moments before the flare burned out, he saw them lurch to a halt after they passed the channel markers. They'd struck the mudflat.

Another flare blossomed. Max saw the dead on the stranded boats leaping off and moving through the water with tremendous speed, arms splashing furiously. Soon they too reached the mudflat.

Ahead of them, their intended victims slogged desperately through the shallows, but without the cadavers' preternatural strength. The dead closed rapidly. Max guessed they'd overtake their prey just about when the guardsmen came stumbling up onto the island. And even if the soldiers had much remaining ammo, they (and whoever stood with them) would soon be overrun. There were too many corpses.

"We can't stay," Max announced, as the fourth flare burned out. He handed his H and K to Gary; Dennis had the other rifle. "I'll use the machete if I have to. Let's get moving."

"What if they shoot another flare?" Linda asked. "The ones on shore will spot us."

"How about that?" Max replied.

They scrambled out through the rip in the hull and waded down into the channel between the island and the flat. It was deep enough in spots to hinder Steve and Camille, but Max and Dennis were there to help.

The group came to the slope on the other side, pushed up into the shallows. But before they'd gone more than a few yards onto the flat, wading through waist-high water, Sally halted.

"We're going to have to walk over those bodies, aren't we?" she whispered.

"There's no other way," Steve answered.

"All those drowned people, right?" she asked.

"You want to stay here?"

"There are *thousands* of them. What if they wake up?"

"We don't have any choice," Max said.

"Hold my hand, Steve," Sally said. "Oh God, just hold on to my hand."

They started forward again. Twenty or more torches burned along the shore ahead, the dead beneath dimly lit by their red glow, standing utterly still, watching, waiting.

Gary felt something hard against his foot, guessed it was a concrete block, stepped over it onto a yielding mass. He shuddered, strode forward. A soft mass flattened under his sole, and he caught himself picturing a cheek spreading out like putty beneath his descending heel. Teeth chattering, heart a heavy pulsing weight, he drove himself onward, stubbing his feet against bound limbs; catching his toe in a cavity that was almost certainly a gaping mouth, he yanked it free reflexively, feeling teeth scrape across the leather of his boot.

Despite the chill of the air, and the cold pressure of the water against his clothes and drysuit, he had begun to sweat. Frigid beads slid down his forehead and nose. He forced his legs to bend and straighten, trying to ignore the obscene surrender of fat stomachs beneath his weight, the subtle snap of fingerbones and cartilage sticking up through the bottoms of his boots. There was no way to step over the corpses. They were packed too closely together now. He was walking across a solid carpet of them, the water now coming up only to mid-thigh . . .

And when are they going to wake up, Gary? He asked himself. *Any time now, and you know it. They're going to start writhing and struggling, they're going to rip through the barbed wire and sit right up, reaching for your knees, for your* balls *and your guts, and all you're going to be able to do is fire that useless gun and scream . . .*

He was dimly aware of corpses shrieking on the other side of the island, shouts from the living, an occasional crack of gunfire. It was all completely irrelevant, mere background noise. He could think only of his own predicament.

Linda trudged along beside him. She reached out and touched him from time to time. He barely felt it. He wondered vaguely, irritably what she was trying to accomplish. He needed all his concentration. They'd only covered fifty yards or so. Two hundred and fifty remained. And even if the drowned dead didn't wake, there were still the ones on shore...

More than enough to kill us all.

There came the thumping discharge of a very-pistol. Violet light burst across the sky. Gary sucked in a sharp breath, but the light faded almost as soon as it appeared.

Bad flare, he thought, then wondered: had the corpses ashore seen them in its brief glare? If so, they gave no sign and remained motionless.

Might think we're theirs, he told himself. *Some of the drowned ones.*

The group pushed on through the darkness. As yet, the glow from the torches barely lit them. Gary guessed they'd have to be within twenty feet or so before the corpses would be able to see them.

The screaming of corpses and men swelled behind. There was even less gunfire now. Gary knew what was happening back there. One by one, the soldiers were being seized, strangled or drowned . . .

His boot latched itself between what he guessed was an arm and a torso. As he wrenched his foot upward, the corpse arched up with it, then slid back down. In the brief moment before it sank, he thought he felt it jerk spasmodically.

Fear sang through him like an electric charge. He thought of warning the others—but had the corpse *actually* jerked? He wasn't sure. He couldn't risk panicking them over nothing.

CLOSER and closer they drew to the shore, a faint red stain of torchlight playing over them. Gary felt no more stirrings. Perhaps there hadn't been enough time for the victims to wake. It *had* been less than twenty-four hours.

Hope rose. *Might do it after all,* he thought.

He eyed the sentinels.

Aren't so many.

He aimed his gun at one.

Bam! He thought. *Down you go.*

Piece of cake.

So long as they got out of this goddamn water.

So long as the drowned stayed dead.

Going to make it, he told himself. *Going to make it. Going to ma—*

Beneath him, a body heaved slowly, unmistakably. Hope shriveled.

"They're waking up!" he whispered, stepping forward onto a mercifully inert cadaver.

"What?" Max asked.

"I just felt—" Gary broke off as Linda tottered into him.

"One of them just grabbed at me," she breathed.

"Steve!" Sally gasped, somewhere off to the left. "Oh my God, Steve!"

"Keep moving!" Steve snarled in a low voice.

IT seemed to Gary that at least one in four were moving now, squirming under his feet, struggling ever more violently. In the dim torchlight, he saw water roiling ahead of him, but as yet, none of the corpses had broken the surface.

Trying to get out of the wire, he thought.

The ones ashore had taken notice. Drawing together in groups of three and four, they moved closer to the water.

He could hear splashing behind, and vomiting and gagging sounds as water burst from drowned throats and lungs. They'd gotten out of their pinions back *there,* no doubt about it. He remembered how the first victims had been led farther out on the flat; they'd awakened sooner.

His brain whirled. He'd missed finding himself square in the middle of that mass resurrection by only a few minutes. Later victims were mostly closer to the shore. More and more, the ones he touched were completely still.

But the splashing from behind grew steadily louder. Were the dead simply making for the beach, or were they pursuing? He looked back, could see nothing in the darkness. Did they recognize him and the others as prey?

He took a blow to the knee, which almost buckled; a tremendous bolt of pain unlocked his hands from the H and K. He fumbled with the rifle. The butt struck the water.

A hand reached up, seizing the pistol-grip. Gary found himself staring straight into the rifle's muzzle.

Like this? He thought. *Shot with my own gun?*

Sweat dripped into his eye. He didn't even blink. Time slowed to a crawl. The muzzle weaved sluggishly back and forth, as though it were searching for the right spot to plant a bullet in his face.

Even that motion halted. Time stood still. His heart stopped in his chest, a lump of stone.

Then he noticed: the hand's trigger-finger was missing.

His heart kicked in again. Blinking sweat out of one eye, gulping air, he tugged on the gun. The motion threw him off balance; the hand had already let go.

Linda grabbed his arm, steadying him.

"Gary—?" she whispered.

"I'm okay," he said. The pain in his knee was subsiding. Favoring that leg, he continued on.

Off to the right, an arm whipped up through a spatter of reflected torchlight. Directly ahead, a dark long-haired head broke the surface, only to dip abruptly from sight. To Gary's amazement, the dead seemed to be having a good deal of trouble freeing themselves from the wires. He guessed they didn't have enough freedom of movement to use their full strength.

But more and more limbs were splashing up into view, more bodies bucking under his tread. One tipped him over, and the cold black

water closed above his head in a gurgling rush. An unseen mouth seized the very tip of his left little finger and bit it off.

A howl rose inside him. He seemed to ride it back to his feet; but he couldn't let it out. Water pouring from his face, he bottled it within him, whipping his injured hand up and down at his side as he pushed forward.

The splashing from behind was close now, thirty yards maybe. Looking over his shoulder, he thought he could make out shapes plowing through the water.

A shriek rang out. Other voices echoed the cry. The splashing sounds seemed to redouble. Bursting foam glimmered.

Noticed how we move, Gary thought. *Shit's hit the fan.*

"Come on!" Max bellowed. "To the beach!"

THE corpses ashore were pointing, the groups clustering together. Gary raked his H and K left to right. Corpses went over, toppling backward into a patch of high grass, flames trailing from their torches. The grass went up like tinder as the brands struck, flames throwing light far out over the water. Forty feet from the beach, Gary and the rest were plainly revealed.

The corpses still on their feet wailed and started out into the water. Gary and Dennis squeezed off bursts till they were out of ammo. As they fought to reload, Linda lunged in front of them. Fifteen shots crashed from her Beretta before it locked open, empty.

Max waded forward with the machete. For five furious seconds he held the corpses at bay. Then, priming their rifles, Gary and Dennis splashed up on either side of him and cut loose again, knifelike blue flames licking from their gun barrels.

"Now!" Max cried.

The group slogged desperately toward the beach, skirting the corpses floundering in the water.

Pursuit was hard behind. Gary turned and emptied his gun into a group only yards away. Water vapor puffing from their sodden riddled legs, the cadavers collapsed.

Something latched onto his belt. He looked down. Hair hanging in a wet curtain, obscuring its face, a corpse hitched itself into view, nearly yanking him over.

Gary jabbed the rifle barrel where he thought an eye might be. The head jerked out of sight, but the corpse's hold jumped to Gary's stomach. Nails dug. It felt like a steel trap had snapped shut in his flesh.

Jamming a new clip into her pistol, Linda rushed close, blasting down into the water, snapping off three quick shots. Foam spurted five feet in the air. The grip on his stomach opened.

They waded for shore. Gary saw his brother slash the head off a corpse that sprang up from the water in front of him; then Max was pelting up onto dry land, staggering, fringelit by the glow from the burning weeds, Father Chuck and Camille stumbling up behind him.

Gasping, Gary and Linda rushed onto the beach, clothes heavy with water. Gary looked wildly around for Steve and Sally; they weren't too far back, but behind them, the shallows were a churning chaos of onrushing corpses.

The group started up from the beach, around the flaming grass. At first Gary thought Steve and Sally were with them. Then he saw Dennis look back, and he turned once more.

Two corpses had Steve by the water's edge. Hands over her ears, Sally stood nearby, screams all but blotted out by the cries of the dead.

Gary wanted to go back, to try and help. But there was nothing to be done. Dozens of corpses were surging toward Steve and his captors. It was hopeless.

Hopeless or not, Dennis suddenly sprang down the slope. Gary tried to pull him back. Dennis yanked free.

Wrestling with Steve, throttling him, the corpses seemed unaware of Dennis's approach. Two point-blank bursts tore their heads apart, and Steve was free, stumbling up the beach with Sally beside him.

And through it all, convinced Dennis was out of his mind, Gary remained rooted to the ground, gaping, impotent.

Camille rushed past him, hair streaming. Dennis was entangled with one of the headless corpses, and she flung herself onto it, toppling it and her husband, ripping into it with a pocket-knife.

Thrilled and stung by her courage, Gary started toward them. Camille had been transfigured. She was a lioness now, a valkyrie. Bits and strings of mummified flesh whirled as her knife flew. It was glorious.

Gary cheered. He began to run.

The wave of dead crested over them. He stopped. A flood of conflicting emotions rushed through him, disgust at his own cowardice, relief in knowing that he could do no good, need not act . . . There *had* been a chance to save Steve; there was none for Dennis and

Camille, he was certain.

But before the clutching talons reached them, a bitter white flash bleached the night. Gary blinked, retinas stabbed by the glare. The light faded, and—

Dennis and Camille were gone.

Gary squinted, not believing it. Yet he could see no trace of his aunt and uncle. The corpses were frozen in place, as if stunned by the flash.

Gary turned and ran. Before him the sky was lightening, a dull red stain spreading in the east. The others were waiting for him, between the boat shop and the throne-platform Legion had occupied. They got a long lead before the screams of the hunters started once more.

CHAPTER 23
STEVE'S LITTLE SECRET

THE sun's spots had gone a bilious green, its rim lurid orange. Gary thought it looked like an infected eye as it lifted into the murky sky, peering down over the ocean.

The group had taken refuge beneath the Brittany boardwalk, and was resting at the eastern end of the forest of pilings that supported the huge restaurant pavilion. The sea, a dull rusty hue under the sun's hemorrhaged glow, muttered and growled as it chewed away at the coastline. The air was full of a cold salty stench, the waves soupy with dead weed and the bodies of fish and crabs. Huge purplish worms could be glimpsed moving in the foam; farther out, the finned spines of strange leviathans lifted against the horizon.

Gary was still panting. The dead had lost them early on, but Max had kept everyone moving.

"So," Max began after a time, "What happened to Camille and Dennis?"

"Dennis went back to help Steve," Gary said. "One of *them* got hold of him, and Camille tried to save him. But there were corpses all around . . . "

"So you stayed where you were," Max said.

"Just like you would've," Gary replied.

"Probably," Max conceded.

"I didn't think I could help. I was sure they were going to die no matter what."

"No point getting down on yourself," Steve said. "I appreciate what Dennis did, believe me. But it was absolutely nuts. *I* sure as hell wouldn't have done it for him. He's dead, we're alive, so—"

"No," Gary broke in. "He's *not* dead. At least, I don't think so."

"What?" Steve asked.

"They disappeared. Him and Camille. There was this blinding light, and they were gone."

Steve's face pinched. "Gone where?"

"How should I know?"

Steve laughed sarcastically. "Did they get raptured off to Heaven, Gary?"

"Did I say that?"

"There *is* a way out," Linda said. "They made it."

"But how?" Gary asked, dumbfounded.

"Maybe—" Max began.

"I know exactly what you're going to say," Steve broke in. "It was being absolved, right? Then why didn't they disappear right after they confessed?"

"Actually," Max said, "I was going to say it was because they sacrificed themselves. Just as I should've. For MacAleer."

"So much for all that sacramental mumbo jumbo then?" Steve asked. "They saved themselves?"

"Once they were absolved," Father Chuck said.

"Just face it, Father," Steve said. "You don't know what happened to them. Any more than the rest of us do."

"They got out," Linda insisted. "They're free. And that means we can get out too."

"So all we've got to do is contrive ways to sacrifice ourselves," Steve laughed. "How do you go about deliberately putting yourself in a situation like that?"

"Good question," Gary said. "But while we're waiting for the answer—what should we do in the meantime?"

"Try and head north again," Max replied.

"After all this, head *back* toward Bayside Point?" Steve demanded.

"Can't go south," Max said. "We can't stay put. Not when they've found such a nifty place to drown folks *en masse*. They'll be all over this area. But Bayside Point must be pretty much abandoned, with Legion's army operating down this way. We should try to stick to areas they think they've cleared. That, and try like hell to find ourselves some more guns. One rifle and one pistol won't last us long."

"There might be a place—" Steve paused. "Of course, the guns might not be working."

"Where?"

"Not far. Just south of the Mobley Canal. My parent's old summer home."

Sally gasped. "Steve, you're crazy! We can't—"

"Sure we can, honey," Steve answered. "A lot of time's passed."

"But what if—"

"Look. I'm sure any . . . bad memories we left there have long since gone away."

She fell silent.

"My parents sold the house to this NRA-type from North Jersey," Steve told the others. "We had dinner over there once after Ginger died. Big gun rack down the basement. He used to come down from Scotch Plains on summer weekends. Real paranoid."

"What kind of guns?" Max asked.

"All kinds. And ammo."

Max looked at him suspiciously. "Why didn't you tell us about this before?"

Steve shrugged. "Just forgot, I guess. We weren't real close to the guy."

Max turned to Sally. "Why don't you want to go back there?" he asked.

"It's nothing," she said, looking away.

"It's personal," Steve said. "You know about personal, Max? They teach you about that in the Corps?"

"Are we going to stay here all day?" Gary asked. "We'll get mighty cold."

"I was thinking we might go up into the pavilion," Max said.

"Look," Steve said, "why don't we just head off to that house now? We could stay under the boardwalk just about all the way. The house is only half a block from the beach. We could be there in forty-five minutes."

"Let's do it, Max," Linda said, shivering.

Max looked suspiciously at Steve, but nodded.

THE journey under the boards was uneventful. Walking where they had the headroom, going on all fours where the sand was high, they made their way north, stopping finally where Murchison Street abutted on the walk. The street was empty, flanked by rows of splendid old houses, which had been the style before the bungalows began to go up.

"It's that tan one," Steve said. "Three down on the left."

They waited a few minutes, watching and listening, then slipped from under the boardwalk to make their way through the backyards of the homes on the left.

"Hope he didn't change the locks," he said as they came up behind the house. Producing a keyring, he had the cellar door open in moments. Wooden steps led downward, but Steve remained at the top with Sally as the others descended . . . Gary heard them whispering. What on earth was the problem?

Gary looked around. The basement was spacious and well furnished. Steel posts supported the ceiling, rising up out of a carpeted floor. Rippled glass-block windows admitted the ruddy sunlight.

The gun-rack was on the far side of the cellar, between a bookcase and what Gary guessed was the door of a utility room.

Steve finally managed to get Sally down the steps, but she balked after that, pointing to the utility-room door.

"It's still closed," she said. "Steve . . . "

"Yeah," he answered in a flat voice. "I see it."

"Would you mind telling me what's going on with you two?" Max demanded.

"Don't worry about it," Steve answered.

"What's behind that door?" Max asked.

"Nothing."

Max took the rifle from Gary. "You mind if I look for myself?"

Steve shook his head, but Gary could see he was agitated. Sally whispered something in Steve's ear as Max headed for the door.

"Maybe it just swung shut by itself," Steve said.

Max put an ear up against the door. He listened for a few moments, then looked back at Steve.

"If there's something in there I should know about," he said, "You'd better tell me now. Because I'm going to get real pissed if something happens."

Sally opened her mouth, but closed it again after a glare from Steve.

"Actually, now that I think of it," Max said, stepping back, "Why don't *you* open the door, Steve?"

Steve shrugged. Crossing the room, he smiled at Max.

Max smiled back, thinly. "I'll cover you."

All in one quick motion, Steve turned the knob and tossed the door open. After a moment's hesitation, he went inside and laughed. Max went in beside him.

"What did I tell you?" Steve asked.

Max came back out. "Nothing," he told the others. "Water-heater, gas-furnace."

Steve reappeared, shut the door behind him.

"Let's get some guns," he said quickly, as if to preclude any further discussion about the utility-room.

They went to the rack, broke the glass with an ashtray. The actions on most of the weapons proved frozen. But that still left a Mossberg 590 shotgun, a Marlin lever action rifle, and three automatic pistols, all copies of Colt .45's put out by various lesser-known arms companies.

"Guy really liked Colt autos, huh?" Max said.

Steve took one; so did Father Chuck and Sally.

"Sally . . . " Steve groaned as his wife grabbed her pistol.

"I'm not taking it from someone else," she answered hotly.

Gary got the shotgun, Linda the rifle. Max used his machete to pry open the rack's drawers, and found all the ammo they needed.

And all the while, Gary noticed, Steve and Sally kept glancing toward the utility room door. Gary started shoving cartridges into his shotgun.

"You *sure* you don't want this?" he asked Max, indicating the weapon.

"I'll stick with the H and K for a while," Max answered. "I'm sick of tangling with 'em so close up. Think I'll just stand off and kneecap them." Gary had already given him the remaining magazines.

"Suit yourself," Gary said. The Mossberg's magazine took nine shells. Chambering a tenth, he looked at Sally, who seemed more jittery than ever.

"I think I'll go wait on the steps," she announced, and started for the back door.

"The *outside* steps?" Gary asked. "What if they spot you through that door up there?"

"Just wait, honey," Steve said reassuringly. "We're all going to have to leave anyway."

"*What?*" Max asked. "I thought you wanted to hole up here for the day."

"Changed my mind," Steve answered. "Believe me, we want to get out of here."

"Not till you give me an explanation," Max answered.

"Shhh!" Father Chuck hissed.

They turned to see a shadowy pair of legs stop by a glass-block window on the left side of the basement, distorted by the ripples in the glass.

Max went silently to the back door, turned the lock on the door-knob, then threw the deadbolt.

"Gary," Max whispered, motioned toward the stairs to the first floor. Gary went up, locked the door.

As he came back down, he became aware of a hollow scraping noise, but couldn't tell where it was coming from; then came a scuffle of feet on the outside stairs, and his attention flashed to the back door. The women and Father Chuck were slowly backing away from it. He went over by Max and Steve, eyes fixed on the doorknob.

It began to twist slowly, first right, then left. Everyone in the base-ment had gone dead silent, and Gary heard the mechanism clicking softly.

That, and the scraping, growing more insistent by the second.

The knob spun back to the right. Something snapped, and the knob dipped, hanging slack.

But that still left the deadbolt. The door stood firm under a tenta-tive blow. Feet scuffled back up the steps outside.

Gary relaxed, just a bit—then noticed, out of the corner of his eye, the shadowy figure at the window crouching down and putting its hands up on either side of its face, as if to get a better look through the distorted panes.

Won't see a damn thing, Gary thought.

The shape struck at the glass. There was a hollow *bong!*, and the fig-ure paused before punching again, as though it had never expected mere glass to be so hard. The block took two more blows before its outer layer even cracked.

That proved enough for the would-be intruder. The shadow van-ished from the window.

And all the while, the scraping on the far side of the basement grew louder. Gary turned, looking for the source of the noise. The sound drew him over to the utility room door—

Something shattered up on the first floor. There was a powerful slam, and footsteps thudded. They approached the cellar-door, then halted, just on the other side by the sound of it. Then they headed away.

But Gary's attention was fixed on the other thumpings now.

The ones that had started inside the utility room.

What the fuck is in there? he thought.

"Steve," he heard Sally whisper, "oh God, Steve."

"Just shut up," Steve said.

The thumping grew harder—then came a soft and horrible mewing sound, and a spate of scrabbling, like rats in a wall.

"Steve, she's getting loose," Sally said.

"Who?" Gary asked.

Neither of them answered. Steve had a strange smile on his face. He shrugged.

Gary knew now he had to look into the room. Turning the knob, he pushed the door open with his shotgun barrel, his gaze going immediately to the middle of the floor.

Coated with grey dust, a mummified hand protruded through a crack in the concrete, rising slowly like some hideous flower, leathery wrist rasping against the sides of the fissure.

"Max," Gary said huskily. "Max!"

His brother was already at his side.

"Don't shoot," Max said. "You'll bring 'em all down on us."

Floorboards creaked above.

What are they doing up there? Gary thought desperately, watching the mummified hand reach higher and higher, fingers clenching and unclenching now, the joints popping and squealing.

"Who is that in there, Steve?" Max asked.

No answer.

"You know, don't you, motherfucker?"

With a ragged grate, a large slab of concrete tilted upward. Another ashen hand locked around its lip, pushed it aside, leaving a two-foot wide gap.

"Steve," Max said, "Tell me who that is, or I'll push your face down that hole."

"Tell him, Steve," Sally said.

"What good'll it do?" Steve asked.

Max went for him.

"It's Ginger!" Sally cried. *"It's his first wife!"*

A raw shriek pealed out of the opening in the floor. The hands whipped back down into the darkness. Dust and chips of concrete shot into the air.

"Sally Sally SALLEEEE!" screamed the voice from the pit.

Above, footsteps hammered toward the cellar door. With a boom the door flew off its hinges, bouncing end over end down the stairs, landing flat against the floor. Two corpses clattered behind, both wearing sweatpants and muscle-T's.

Gary twisted toward them, squeezed off his chambered round, pumped and fired. Ragged ratholes blew open in the t-shirts. The corpses smashed sideways into the paneling. Gary pummeled them till the wood was spackled with their flesh.

The back door banged open. He heard Linda shriek, and whirled.

Jaws distended by a plug of hardened concrete, a corpse was striding toward her. She and Father Chuck started in with their guns.

Sally lifted her pistol, but the hammer wasn't cocked.

Bullets biting chunks from its face, the corpse waded forward, straps of scalp whipping straight up from exit-wounds in the back of its skull. Linda and Father Chuck jumped out of its way. Shaking her gun, swearing at it, Sally caught a taloned uppercut and staggered back across the room.

Gary reloaded. Max and Steve stepped forward, pouring fire into the corpse, battering it to the floor. Bones pulverized, the cadaver lay on the carpet flopping spastically, unable to rise.

Gary looked round at the steps. The fragments of his victims were wriggling blindly down the stairs.

Over by the utility room, practically on the threshold, Sally was sitting with her back to the door, shaking her head, blood welling from the gashes in her cheek and chin. If she heard the shrieks of Ginger Jennings reverberating from the room behind, she gave no sign. Gary and Steve started toward her, yelling.

Like something squeezed from a tube, Ginger came squirting up from the hole she'd clawed out.

Gary aimed for her head, but caught it only with the fringe of the shotgun blast, spattering her cheek and temple with pellets. Dust puffed from the impacts, and her head jerked to one side; then her hands were on Sally, hauling her up. Unable to get a clear shot, Gary and Steve stopped short.

Ginger spun Sally around. Looking into the fury's wizened face, Sally began to struggle, shrieking, tossing her head, hair whipping.

"Ginger!" she screamed. "It was all Steve's—"

Steve and Gary closed in to blast Ginger point-blank, but were too late to save Sally. With a movement almost too quick to follow, Ginger raised the struggling woman further, thrust her head forward, and bit Sally's throat out. Blood spewed onto Ginger's face and all over the doorjamb.

Gary shoved his gun barrel into Ginger's dripping brow, pulled the trigger—

Click.

Ginger hurled Sally to the carpet, chewing the bloody flesh in her mouth, she stepped over her victim. Gary retreated. She went for Steve.

Gary tried to pump a new shell into the Mossberg, but the action was jammed. Steve backpedalled furiously, blasting away with his .45. Star-shaped pits cratering her blood-painted face, black against red but Ginger kept coming.

Max's H and K rattled. Ginger sailed backward into the utility room as if an invisible fist had struck her in the stomach.

She tried to get back up. He raked her across the legs.

"Out!" he bellowed. "Out!"

In the scramble for the back door, Father Chuck tripped over the lashing limbs of the corpse on the floor, dropping his pistol. He managed to disentangle himself, but not before a hand ripped deep into his calf. Max had to help him up the stairs, out into the back yard.

Sounds of pursuit from within; *was* Ginger crippled after all?

They staggered away among the bungalows to the north. Bringing up the rear, Gary noticed Father Chuck was leaving a bloodtrail. The priest's black pantleg clung to his leg, plastered against the shredded drysuit, shiny and sodden.

They paused. Father Chuck leaned against the side of a canary-yellow bungalow as Max took off his own belt and wrapped it above the priest's wound, tightening it fiercely to choke off the blood-flow.

Steve and Gary stood guard. Gary had scooped Father Chuck's .45 off the floor on the way out.

"Sorry," Steve panted. "I thought she would've escaped already. But I buried her in solid concrete, and she must not have had enough lever—"

"Why'd you do it?" Gary broke in.

"Kill her?"

"Yeah."

"What's it to you?" Steve asked, apparently puzzled that he was being pressed about such trivia.

Gary was stunned by his manner. If anything, it seemed more shocking than Steve's crime. It was a few moments before Gary could speak.

"I mean, was it an accident?" he asked. "Was she cheating on you? Or was it just cold-blooded murder?"

Steve flashed him a smile. "Hey, you know me. What do *you* think?"

"Tell me," Gary said.

"It was because of Sally," Steve replied, after a pause. "Ginger found out about us. She wanted to cut me out of her money."

"So you just killed her?"

"It wasn't *just* that," Steve went on, as if he'd left out some genuinely mitigating circumstance. "She started screwing someone else. A little tit for tat. 'Sauce for the gander,' she said. She was going to dump me over for him. But *nobody* walks out on me, Gary."

Gary stared at him, dumbstruck. Steve returned the stare, still smiling. There wasn't the least hint of guilt in his expression, or even a trace of insanity. He looked as he always did, handsome, good-natured, intelligent.

"Just imagine," he went on. "The *nerve* of the bitch."

CHAPTER 24
MAX AND LEGION

MAX had barely finished with Father Chuck's leg when the shrieking started; one corpse by the sound of it, off to the south.

"Ginger, I bet," Steve said. "Fucking Ginger."

They started moving again.

Other shrieks answered from the east—dozens, maybe scores of voices, over by the boardwalk. The group shifted course, working northwestward.

Quickly they came up against the Mobley Canal, a narrow inlet opening the Barragansett to the ocean, forming the border between Brittany and Mobley Beach. Mobley was another bungalow town, its only tall building a Catholic church called St. Bonaventure's, whose steeples towered over the surrounding rooftops.

The group headed west, paralleling the channel but staying one row of houses back from it, to avoid being spotted from the north.

"Got to hide," Gary said, even as a new pack began to bay, off to the south.

"Not yet," Max answered. "Have to get on the other side of the canal, at least. They'll be all over this area, and they'll search every one of these cheesebox bungalows."

"But . . . "

"There's a real sewer system over in Mobley. Our only hope is to get underground."

Howls resounded from behind. Gary looked back along the narrow lane. It extended straight to the beachfront, and he could see a mob pouring in off the boardwalk.

They did the only thing they could—wind a path south and west through the grid of houses, trying to screen their movements.

But the dead to the south soon spotted them. From that point on, with pursuit from two sides, there was no way to keep out of sight . . .

Pressing northwest again, they suddenly found themselves on Rt. 35, the peninsula's main street. On the right was the canal drawbridge, its southern approach guarded by three cadavers. The span was raised behind them.

The group dashed to the far side of the highway. Two of the guards started after them.

Gary dropped back. Clapping both hands to his pistol, he kneecapped the corpses. They went down like they'd tripped over a wire, legs jerking out from under.

He rushed to rejoin the others.

THE bungalows on the west side of 35 weren't laid out in a grid, but more haphazardly, divided by curving gravel roads, with a paved street here and there. Once more it became possible for the fugitives to lose themselves, if only briefly. As short as their lead was, Gary nearly missed them.

But the advantage evaporated when the belt on Father Chuck's leg worked loose. The blood started again, and there was no time to re-tie the tourniquet.

"I say leave him," Steve snarled. "He's going to lead them right to us."

"No," Max answered.

"Well, suppose I just shoot the fucker?"

"Suppose we just shoot *you?*" Linda panted.

"Why don't you volunteer, Father?" Steve asked as he ran alongside the priest. "Sacrifice yourself. Save us all."

Father Chuck shook his head, not even looking at him.

"Don't have the faith, huh?" Steve sneered.

"Why don't *you* take off?" Gary demanded.

"And leave all this firepower? Not on your life."

A chain-link fence appeared. Beyond were the white tanks of the Mobley fuel company, which had supplied diesel and gas to nearby marinas.

Gary shot the lock off a gate. They dashed across a gravel strip and in among the tanks. Behind them, the maze of summer homes echoed with screams.

They came out in a parking lot bordered on the far side by a spur of the inlet; lined with pilings, the channel reached southwestward to the bay. A raised pipeline, surmounted by a narrow catwalk, spanned the channel; the pipeline serviced the pumps and tanks of the Harrison Bay Marina, which was just across the canal. A gasoline truck stood in the lot between the fuel company's tanks and the pipeline.

"Go on to the catwalk," Max told the others. "I'm going to try and light off the tanks. Wait for me."

Gary set his arm beneath Father Chuck's shoulder, and they took off across the lot.

MAX looked back between the fuel-tanks. The dead surged up to the chain-link fence and poured through the open gate.

He unslung his pack and took out one of his black-powder bombs—the weapon, along with a butane lighter, was in a big Ziploc bag. Opening the bag, he jammed the bomb in between the tank on his left and a tangle of pipe, ignited the fuse, and raced away, pack over one arm.

Up ahead Gary was waving to him; they were past the gas-truck now, nearing the pipeline. Max stretched his legs in tremendous strides, sprinting across the lot, praying he'd judged the length of the fuse correctly.

He glanced back. The corpses were already between the tanks.

Flame mushroomed, and there was a loud *whoosh*—but no explosion. Max cursed, guessing there'd been some weakness in the tape he'd used to seal the bomb.

He dashed around the gas truck, toward the pipeline. The others were waiting for him on the catwalk. He clambered up the fifteen-foot high ladder, paused on the steel platform, turned.

Several of the corpses had been set on fire, and had fallen in the passage between the tanks. The others, perhaps fearing the flames might torch the containers, were retreating—for the moment.

Max eyed his companions. All were panting, plainly near exhaustion. Father Chuck looked half-dead, his skin a translucent grayish-white. The catwalk around him was printed with red heel marks.

"I have another bomb," Max said. "I'll try to blow the pipeline. Maybe this one'll work. Get going."

"Jesus, Max . . . " Gary began.

"Go on. I'll be along."

Gary nodded. They set off.

Max watched them for a moment. Father Chuck was going to slow them badly, he could tell.

Should've left him, he told himself—and instantly shunted the

idea aside.

"No," he growled under his breath, and forced himself to think of the task at hand.

How could he light the bridge off? Taking the bomb out and shouldering his pack once more, he looked over the side of the cat-walk, trying to see if the steel was thin enough for the charge to rip through to the pipeline. But the walk alone was an inch and a half thick. And then there was the beam the walk was attached to. The problem was compounded by the fact that there was no way to fix the bomb to the bridge, wedge it in somewhere, so that the span would absorb the full force of the blast.

He went back down the ladder, thinking he might be able to blast through the concrete support enclosing the pipeline between ground and catwalk. Reaching the bottom and giving the support a quick look, he decided it was far too strong.

He looked back at the fuel tanks. Bodies were still burning where he'd set off the first bomb. How much longer would the fires hold the rest?

Off to the left, a torrent of corpses swept out from behind a great diesel tank. They were simply going around.

He knew now there was only one way to stave them off: the tanker truck. At the very least, blasting a sea of flames across the parking lot would canalize them, slow them down. And some hot shrapnel might just go flying into those damn tanks on the far side. Brandishing the bomb, he rushed toward the truck, hoping the very sight of the explosive would give them pause.

They retreated like a wave backwashing from a beach.

"Yeah!" he cried.

But out from their ranks the bone wolves came speeding.

His H and K hung muzzle-down by its strap. Grabbing the barrel, he flipped the gun up from under his shoulder, taking the pistol grip in his right hand.

The bone wolves beat him to the truck. Never slackening his speed, he continued toward them, screaming at the top of his lungs, firing from the hip.

They charged straight on into the barrage, the one on the right pulling ahead, taking the brunt of it. Bones and bone fragments burst-ing from its body, it reminded Max briefly, crazily of a string of exploding firecrackers. Then it was nothing but pieces rolling across the asphalt.

The second leaped high into the air, jaws yawning. Max ducked, but the thing's mouth still caught the shoulder of his jacket, locking in the cloth. The creature flipped over, toppling him backward; fabric gave, and the thing went sailing past him, upside down.

Dropping the bomb, he flung himself onto his belly. The bone wolf was already clattering back toward him.

Max thrust the H and K's barrel into its mouth and pulled the trigger. A hail of slugs bored it clean out through the middle. The hollowed shell continued up the rifle barrel on momentum, disintegrating over him in a rattling wave.

Shaking free of the remains, Max took up the bomb again and started back toward the truck. Looking past the cab, he saw that the cairn was coming now, pounding forward on its elephantine legs.

He eyed the tank trailer. A cylindrical hose container ran along its side. He flipped the cap open. The container was empty. He shoved the bomb in and lit the fuse. Turning, he pelted back for the bridge, thinking to take cover behind the support.

Please, Jesus, let this one work...

He noticed something sweeping toward him on the edge of sight. He glanced aside to see that it was a long braided cable of bones. It seemed to be lengthening rather than merely moving, *reconfiguring* itself to catch him, pieces racing along it and locking together out near the tip. The sight was so mesmerizingly strange that his wits momentarily failed him. The tentacle fastened about him with an arthritic crackling noise. Points of bone dug cloth into flesh.

Finally he reacted, twisting violently, firing into the appendage several feet from his body, shearing it through with the last bullets in his gun. Cut off from the cairn, the section around his waist instantly fell apart.

Yet hardly had the skeletal belt crumbled when a second appendage looped in. Whirling him around, it dragged him back toward the truck.

He could see the cairn looming up behind the vehicle. It had flung a web of smaller tentacles out over the cab and trailer, as though searching for the bomb. One snaked down toward the hose-container, opened the cap. Smoke leaked out. The tentacle snaked inside.

"Now," Max cried. "Oh God, now!"

With a flash of red, the nozzle tube split open, the blast punching upward into the fuel trailer.

The tentacle let Max go, almost as if the cairn had been startled by the explosion. Burning fuel gushed from a yard-wide diamond-shaped hole in the tanker's side.

But the truck didn't blow.

Max turned and ran, reloading. What could he do now? Could the cairn narrow itself to cross the bridge? Even if it couldn't, there were always those thrusting arms. He couldn't possibly hold the span against them . . .

A wicked thundercrack clapped his eardrums. The tanker had gone.

A massive push of hot air struck him in the back, lifted him off his feet, flung him forward several yards before dropping him to the asphalt. Bones and burning gas drops rained around him. Curved fragments of tanker hull clanged down.

Palms and knees skinned, he scrambled onto the strip of grass by the bridge. Jumping to his feet, he looked back across the parking lot. The top of the truck's cab had been sheared off. Tank gone, the trailer was enveloped in flame.

As for the cairn, all Max could see was pieces. A vast fan of them had been blasted back into the corpses waiting by the fuel tanks, and many of the cadavers appeared to have been cut down by the brittle shrapnel. Most of the blast seemed to have spewed out that way.

Why the truck hadn't exploded immediately, he didn't know. But trailer tanks were compartmentalized. Hoping to tear into a section full of gas vapor, he'd hit liquid instead, much less explosive. Perhaps it had taken a few seconds for the heat to detonate the vapor in a compartment alongside.

Time to leave, Max, he thought. Up the ladder he went. Expecting Gary and the rest to be long gone, he got a nasty surprise at the top; they'd paused near the other end of the bridge. Father Chuck was propped against the rail. Max stamped in rage.

Nothing, he told himself. *You did it all for nothing.*

Metal glinted. Steve was lifting his pistol toward the priest's head.

"You piece of shit," Max said.

There came a flat report. It sounded almost like a firecracker at that distance, with nothing nearby to contain the sound. But it wasn't Father Chuck who fell.

It was Steve.

Max wondered who'd shot him, hoped it was Gary. He already

knew that Linda had the stuff.

Gary took Father Chuck's arm. Linda followed them down the ladder.

Max was seized by an impulse to join them, to run and catch up. But that would sign their death warrants—they'd all be slaughtered when the dead crossed the bridge. They might all be slaughtered anyway, he knew. But he was going to give them the best chance he could.

That was his first thought. Only afterward, once he'd turned to face the dead, unslinging his H and K, did it occur to him that he was also grasping at *his* only chance.

They were coming now, coming in their hundreds, the army of the Apocalypse, the host of Hell. It was hard to see God's grace in that onrushing storm of hate; impossible to see it anywhere else.

"Through a glass darkly, huh Max?" he said.

A medieval legend leaped to mind, steeling him to his task: a lone Norwegian warrior holding a crossing against an English multitude.

Stamford Bridge, Max thought, and laughed. *Stamford fucking Bridge.*

"That's it, you sons of bitches!" he bellowed, pulling out the rifle's retractable stock, clicking the gun to semiauto. *"Come and get it!"*

AFTER leaving Max, Gary's group had almost gotten to the northern end of the bridge when Father Chuck slipped from Gary's shoulder and fell.

"Going to stay behind, Father?" Steve asked. "Give the rest of us a better shot?"

The priest shook his head. "I'm not . . . ready yet."

Max's gun rattled in the distance.

"Max is laying it on the line," Steve said. "If he can do it, you can too, Father."

Father Chuck closed his eyes, ignoring him.

"We're not leaving him, and that's final," Gary said, helping the priest up against the railing. "We can't stay here much longer though, Father. Do you understand? Max isn't going to sacrifice himself for nothing."

The priest nodded.

Moments passed. Father Chuck stood gasping.

Max's bomb roared. They all turned. Seconds later came the next explosion, a huge fireball billowing into the sky as the truck went.

"Screw this," Steve said, cocking his .45.

"Steve, you can't—"Gary said.

"No?" Steve asked, and leveled his gun at the priest. "Remember Ginger?"

Gary brought his .45 up too.

"You're going to shoot *me?*" Steve laughed. "Your best buddy? The man who taught you just about *everything?*"

"Everything you taught me was shit. Try me."

"You don't have the guts," Steve said, and aimed the gun toward Father Chuck's pale sweat-beaded forehead.

Gary gave him one in the stomach, knocking him over. The pistol bounced from Steve's hand. Gary kicked it farther away.

"Well what do you know?" Steve gasped up at him, grinning with pain.

Gary put his shoulder under Father Chuck again. Followed by Linda, they made for the end of the bridge.

"You're not getting rid of me!" Steve cried after them. "*If* I'm going down, so are you!"

Gary looked round briefly, past his wife. Steve was crawling for his gun, but had a good twenty feet to go.

They reached the end, somehow getting Father Chuck down the ladder. Max's gun echoed once more. For the first time Gary was truly struck by the knowledge that he'd probably never see his brother again.

At least not alive.

I love you, Max, he thought.

MAX squeezed off shot after shot. Every slug sent a corpse to the asphalt, crippled.

But he couldn't slow the torrent speeding toward the ladder. On the dead came, trampling the fallen, shrieking, clawing for the rungs. And almost before he realized it, the clip was spent.

He hit the release, pocketed the empty clip. Shoving a new one in, he raked the bolt back and started blasting before the first corpse got halfway up. Two bullets sent dark spurts of vaporized bone and brains spurting from its scrofulous crown, smashed the cadaver from the rungs.

Another sprang out of the mob. Max shot that one and the next. Spent shells flying from the rifle's breech, he kept them at bay for a furious half-minute, swearing and laughing as his bullets hammered home.

The second clip went dry: two left.

A corpse almost got to the top before Max reloaded. He put a shot into either eye. Exiting through the back of its head, the bullets cracked the skull like an eggshell, the top flipping up and forward, almost swinging over the corpse's face before dropping back.

The cadaver only scrambled up further, hands clawing at the cat-walk and rails.

Max kicked it under the chin, felt its jaws crack together. The skull top jounced, matter like dried dirt flying out from under it. A second kick sent the corpse sailing down onto the horde below.

A spear hurtled toward Max. He knocked it aside with his gun. He'd been waiting for them to start that. Dozens of the sharpened poles waved above the throng. Throwing them was surely the best way to take him out. Much better than climbing up and closing with him one at a time.

But the gaunt old matron even now on the rungs seemed unaware of that. Up she came, straight toward the muzzle of the H and K, her wild shock of pure white hair flying in the wind, strings of huge yellowed pearls gleaming on her bosom.

Flames stabbed from the rifle's barrel, one shot, two, three, transforming her face into a shredded jumble. Shattered teeth and pearls flying, she loosed her hold and fell wailing, talons stretched out over her head.

After her he blasted three more off the ladder. Once the last fell, there was a brief lull, and it occurred to him that no more spears had been hurled.

Why aren't they—

Music blared into his mind, as though he were wearing a headset and someone had whipped the volume from zero to ten. At first the song was too deafening for him to realize what it was.

Obligingly, the volume fell sharply.

"Der Kommissar."

Another corpse clambered up toward him. Max's finger tightened on the trigger, but he paused at the last instant, recognizing the dead face. One eye socket gaped, the skin was green and spotted with mold, and the mouth was a fanged slash, grinning ear to ear with filed teeth. Still, there was no mistaking it—

The corpse was Jeff Purzycki.

Trembling, Max watched him come. Up until now, they'd all been strangers, monsters pure and simple. But he'd gone to school with Jeff, gotten looped with him, dragged him out of the surf when he was drowning, and now—

Jeff was reaching for Max's ankle, snatching at his flesh with a hand like a garden rake, the flesh of its fingertips pared away, the bones beneath sharpened to wicked curving points . . .

Max shrieked and fired. Jeff fell, taking the corpses beneath with him.

And that was the end of the third clip.

Max went to reload, found the last magazine caught in the lining of his coat pocket. Dropping the gun, he pulled the machete free as the next corpse clambered up.

Badly in need of a good undertaker, it was Mr. Van Nuys, head cocked crazily to one side, a metal probe buried deep in one ear, mouth sewn shut like a shrunken head's, the words *YOU'RE DEAD* carved above his eyes.

A slash and a snap kick knocked him from the ladder.

Next it was Aunt Lucy, face purple and contorted. She blocked a kick with her forearm, grabbed at Max's retreating leg; his backward dodge gave her time to bound up onto the catwalk, but he hacked her head off as she advanced, and a kick to the solar-plexus pounded her over the edge of the bridge.

Cousin Dave came then; Max wailed into him with machete blows, chopped his stubborn fingers from the rail uprights, sent him spinning.

After that, it was Jamie MacAleer.

Then Jamie's mother.

Then Uncle Buddy; he came up the ladder gripping the rungs with his teeth, his all but severed arm whirling like a medieval war flail.

Another lull after Buddy—Father Ted had a harder time climbing, burdened as he was with Mr. MacAleer. Tied to the priest's back with barbed wire, MacAleer had his teeth sunk in Father Ted's scalp; jerking his head back and forth, he worried the dead flesh with pit-bull ferocity.

I have something in mind for him, Legion had said. *A little bit of sculpture...*

Max drove a knee into the priest's tied-on face, hitching it halfway

up the skull beneath. Father Ted rocked backward shrieking, inverted crucifix trailing behind him in the air.

Max stared down along the ladder, panting. His heart quailed as he saw the next corpse, even though he'd known this was coming, the final turn of the screw, the last stroke of Legion's malice; Father Ted, Aunt Lucy, cousin Dave, all the rest—it hadn't been coincidence. *Der Kommissar* had planned it all, Max knew.

And now the grinning monstrosity clambering up the rungs was his father.

Max Sr.'s dead hand clamped onto a rail upright, and Max lashed out with his foot, but the fingers remained locked, and his father hauled himself over the rim of the catwalk.

Max kicked again, but his father absorbed the blow, his other hand locking onto the upright on the left. Max slammed two punches into his father's face, but couldn't yet bring himself to use the machete on the man who'd sired him, raised him, loved him, flesh of his flesh, blood of his blood . . .

His father snatched at him, and Max retreated, mind an agonized turmoil. Max Sr. leaped onto the catwalk, straightening to his full height, staring at his son with his gleaming black eyes, mouth snapping. Max cocked his machete back to strike, not knowing if he had the resolve to use it.

"Don't, Dad!" he cried. "Please don't make me!"

Max Sr. paused for a moment, trembling—and took a mechanical step forward.

Max slashed. Fingers flew.

Max Sr. halted once more as if stung with pain. Yet Max knew it had to be more than that. Was his father's will free enough to overcome his rage and fear?

"Don't make me hit you again!" Max pleaded, tears blearing his eyes.

Max Sr. stood facing his son, shaking in every member; Max ached to think of the terror building inside him, the awesome compulsion, Hell bending his father to its will, struggling against what remained of his sanity. Was Legion in his mind even now, gnawing at him like a maggot?

Suddenly Max felt the tension snap. His father started forward once more.

At that moment, Max's soul was wrenched wide open, and he hardly heard the words that came shrieking from his mouth:

"Daddy! Please!"

The words struck deep. For an instant a fleeting glimpse of shame and unutterable pain mingled with the rage on Max Sr.'s face; he lowered his head, and his hands went slowly down to his sides.

It was a few seconds before Max realized what had happened. Then he slid the machete back into his belt and went for the H and K, which lay at his father's feet. Freeing the magazine from his pocket, he reloaded and stepped back, watching his father.

Max Sr. lifted his head. The trembling began again. His hands rose once more.

Max trained the gun on him, but didn't fire. He was determined to hold back until his father's will cracked once more, until he made his move.

"Stand up to him, Dad," Max said. "He doesn't own you. *God* owns you—"

"But possession's nine tenths of the law!" a voice roared in answer. Like a mountain growing before Max's eyes, Legion rose into view behind his father.

Max Sr. turned. Instantly a tremendous blow spun him back round. One whole side of his face had been caved in. Grabbing him by the hair, Legion flung him effortlessly over his shoulder.

"Enjoy your reunion, Max?" the demon asked.

Max screamed and squeezed off a shot. A quarter-sized hole burst open in Legion's forehead just above the right eye, and a black rotten gust flipped his trooper hat from his skull as the bullet exited. But Legion was on Max before he could loose a second shot, and all at once the gun was smashed from Max's hands—Max never even saw the blow. Laughing, Legion kicked the gun farther up the catwalk.

Max started to retreat; Legion's mallet-like right fist hammered up under his jaw, splintering teeth on teeth. Head ringing, blood rivering from his mouth, Max sailed limply through the air, crashing to the catwalk on his back.

Still laughing, shaking his head, Legion gave him time to stagger to his feet and pull the machete out. Then he bashed the blade from Max's grip and rammed him in the chest with a ribcracking straight right fist. Breath and blood bursting from his lips, Max went down again, gasping, helpless.

"Told you once about the machete, Max," Legion chuckled. "It's *so insulting*. You of all people should realize what you're up against.

You're the believer—that's what I like about you. Guys like you are my favorite fix. You have the sense to be *really* scared. You know about archangels. About suicide seraphim. About the kings of Hell.

"I was ancient when the universe was made, and it was *me* in Eden, not the Boss. Before The Flood they sacrificed their firstborn to me, and then I blighted their fields and demanded more. Sodom and Gomorrah were my work, and when the Man Upstairs died shrieking in despair, I was in on the hit . . . I'm the Lord of the Flies, the right hand of Satan himself, and you're going to stop *me* with a fucking machete?" With a roar he brought his Frye-booted foot down on Max's left shin. Bone snapped. Max loosed a shriek that flayed his throat raw, jerking up into a sitting position. Through tears of agony, he saw Legion raise his boot once more.

"Some more Captain Crunch, Max?" the demon asked jovially. "Before I go for the gas?"

The Frye-boot started to descend, slowly this time, toward Max's other shin. Max tried to jerk his leg back; the boot dropped like a stamping press, pinning his limb between catwalk and sole.

"Faster than you," Legion gloated, and began to grind.

But before flesh could tear or bone could break, an arm looped around Legion's neck from behind, yanking him backward. The giant fell, toppling onto his assailant.

Max floundered onto his back, trying to grab one of the uprights and haul himself up. His hand brushed cold steel and plastic—the H and K.

Before him, Legion easily broke his opponent's hold. Flipping over, he grabbed him and rose, hoisting the struggling figure high overhead with one hand. Max's bleeding jaw sagged open.

It was his father.

Legion roared; with spine-shattering force, he smashed Max Sr. down on the right-hand rail, then lifted him again and hurled him away down the catwalk as if he were a ragdoll. Then he turned to resume his work on Max.

But Max had grabbed the H and K and switched it back to full auto; and Legion, even with his superhuman speed, was too far to close the distance before Max opened up.

For the first time, Max saw the demon's hell-grin fade.

Spitting blood, Max smiled.

What happened then was almost more than he could comprehend.

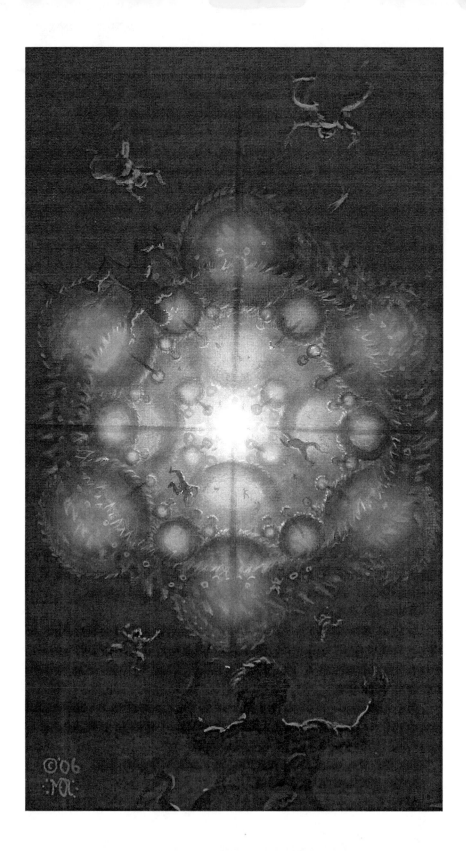

The world seemed to rip before his eyes, as though the screen onto which reality was projected were suddenly tearing; he found himself hurtling through the rent, into cold stinking darkness, flying, falling endlessly.

Put down the gun, said Legion's voice, quiet and reasonable. *Just look, Max. Look ahead. See how useless that little weapon is. See me as I really am.*

A light appeared in the void, bluish-green. As Max plummeted toward it, he made out human figures, dark silhouettes against the glow, falling ahead of him, tumbling, arms and legs waving.

The light grew rapidly. Its source was a vast circular opening, the mouth of a shaft or pit. Things were moving in it. As the distance closed, Max realized they were wheels, immense luminous wheels revolving on every conceivable axis, some interlocking, some passing impossibly through each other as they turned, their inner and outer rims set with blades and hooks and spikes, bulging with squirming eyes; and somehow visible beneath them all was a giant fanged mouth, chewing and grinding.

Bodies rained down into the wheels, were impaled and sliced; they clung desperately to spikes tilting inexorably downward; they fought to free themselves from barbs buried deep in their flesh, only to plummet farther into that churning machinery of death; they dropped in pieces from the blades. Fragments and whole figures dropped toward the mouth in a rain of blood, and the mouth received them all, devouring, crushing, punishing.

Max could only watch horrified as the pit filled more and more of his field of vision. He would plunge into it and be ripped asunder. And then . . .

And then you'll go through again, Max my boy, came Legion's voice. *And each time it'll be worse. That's what those shrieking wretches in your pathetic little hallucination of a universe are really feeling. Deep in their minds, through the haze of matter, the blur of their flesh, they feel my blades, my spikes. The Hell of which the Hell of flesh is but a feeble copy. Auschwitz for real. Cambodia without the compromises. My world, Max. And that gun can't save you from it.*

The wheels and eyes and blades surged ever closer. Max felt a tremendous weight of despair, crushing the strength from his will; surely the demon was telling the truth. There was no escape. He wanted to fire a burst down into that champing maw, if only as a last gesture of defiance; but what good would it do? His finger remained motionless on the trigger.

Look at me, Max, Legion said. *Look at my power. Look at my vastness. I am immortal. I am eternal. It is not for nothing I was worshipped as a god. And nothing you can do can stop you from plunging into me. So put down the gun, Max. Put it down.*

Max was entering the pit now. All around him, bodies jolted onto the spikes, were ripped open in floods of viscera, the eyes on the wheels turning to gloat at their agonies, widening in horrible pleasure . . .

Put down the gun.

Max almost let go—

Then recognized a figure impaled on one of the uprushing spikes.

It was his father. And strangely, he seemed to be holding a silver cross. It was burning in his hand, smoke pouring out around it. As Max dropped past, just missing the wheel, his father's hand opened convulsively, as if he could stand the touch of the cross no longer. Without thinking, Max reached out and grabbed the glinting emblem—

And suddenly he was back on the catwalk.

Not a second had passed, or so it seemed. But Legion's world *was* outside of time . . .

Facing Max was a corpse in a state trooper's uniform. A mere human corpse, no matter what spirit possessed it. Legion *was* great and terrible. The right hand of Satan himself, beyond a doubt, a King of Hell.

Even so, he was in Max's world now. The pathetic world of flesh.

"Go for it," Max said.

Legion charged. As far as he was from Max, he almost reached him.

Max's first burst knocked him back on his heels, bullet holes stitching across the trooper uniform. A second blew his eye sockets empty, punched his nose in, ripped jaw from cheek and cheek from brow, pulverized his skull in a brownish-black eruption.

The decapitated giant staggered on his feet, hands reaching up toward his severed neck. Laughing fiercely, Max sprayed him across the elbows. Cloth exploded. Bone-splinters flew. The giant's arms flopped downward, all but severed.

Max lowered the gun, scythed through Legion's knees with a final clip-emptying burst. The torso dropped to the catwalk with a great clang.

Max pulled himself to his feet, leaning on the railing, eyeing what was left of the demon-possessed corpse.

"You *were* right about the machete," he panted, tossing the rifle onto Legion's body. "But what about old Heckler and Koch?"

Those Kraut engineers certainly knew their stuff. The gun had stuck it out right to the end. The end of the world *and* beyond. Perhaps, Max thought, the physical universe was capable of accommodating far more of the *Logos* than Legion would ever admit.

But indeed, hadn't that been the demon's error from the beginning? Max wondered what Legion had made of the Incarnation. It was strange, seeing a parallel between the Word Made Flesh and an assault rifle. Yet was not God's symbol a blood-drenched cross?

LEGION'S corpse was still moving, heaving and buckling, thighs drumming. The hands clawed at the patterned surface of the catwalk, straining to wrench the forearms free of the scraps of cloth and flesh tethering them to the body.

Flies began pouring from the bulletholes in the chest, from the stumps of limbs and neck. They formed a cloud, a cyclonic mass, and from that black tornado there came a wailing chorus, hundreds, thousands of tiny whistling voices; spinning violently, the cloud lifted high into the air, the voices fading with distance. The tornado accelerated almost instantly to an incredible speed, assumed for an eyeblink the shape of a spiked wheel—and vanished.

The corpse had gone motionless. Max looked past it to his father. Max Sr. had hitched himself against an upright; they stared at each other quietly. Max yearned to go to him, to try somehow to comfort him.

Yet even if his leg would've permitted, that was insane. It would be like embracing a wounded cobra. A great gulf had come between them.

But was it unbridgeable? Was his father damned *eternally?* His father's will was still free, if just barely. And if that were not sufficient, was there not enough blood shed at Calvary to cleanse the sins from one man's small soul?

There was no way of knowing. *Can't second-guess The Man,* Max thought. Still he sent his prayer across the gulf:

Dominus Vobiscum, Dad.

AS if stunned by Legion's downfall, the other corpses hadn't ventured out onto the catwalk. Now they moved to the attack at last.

This is it, Max thought. *You've bought all the time you're going to.*

"All right, God," he muttered. "Now I've *really* done my bit."

Feet clanged on metal, beating nearer and nearer.

"Put myself on the line, God," he said. "Time to leave, right?"

But they were clattering past his father now, and the hand of God was nowhere in sight. Panic flooded through Max. He'd done the best he could, kept the faith, run the course to its end. Was that not enough?

"Fair is fair, Lord," he said. Could it be that he'd beaten Legion only to die at the hands of his followers? What was the meaning of the crucifix that had saved him? Was that God's work or not?

Curse Him and die, whispered a voice in his head.

Legion's voice.

The first corpse lunged close. Max knocked one of its clutching hands aside and punched it. The cadaver toppled. If only he hadn't tossed the rifle away—it would've made a good club.

Curse Him and die, said the demon in his soul.

Another corpse leaped over the first, sank its fingers into his arm, threw him onto the catwalk. They surged over him, pinning him down.

Curse Him and die.

"I believe in one God," Max gasped.

Jaws locked onto his legs, his arms, sheared through fingers.

"The Father, the Almighty . . . "

One of his ears was wrenched from his head.

"Maker of Heaven and Earth . . . "

You're all mine now.

The Nicene Creed died in his throat as a brace of filed teeth shut on his Adam's Apple.

CHAPTER 25
ST. BONAVENTURE'S

GARY'S group was some distance from the bridge, out of the marina, when Father Chuck's leg gave way again. Gary knew he'd have to stop the bleeding, and they paused long enough for him to tie his own belt around the priest's limb. The blood flow slackened, but wasn't choked off altogether; scarlet still marked Father Chuck's steps.

They threaded in and out among the bungalows, working north-northeast. Father Chuck collapsed a third time. It took an ammonia capsule to rouse him.

Gary and Linda searched each other's faces. It was hopeless, and they knew it. The priest was a weight around their necks. He was death.

Yet to abandon him was damnation.

"Maybe he'll be our ticket out," Linda said.

Gary laughed as he shouldered the priest's weight once more. "They should make these tickets lighter," he said, pushing on.

He became aware that the gunfire had stopped. Now there were only the screams of the dead, growing steadily louder.

Did you get out, Max? Gary wondered.

"Blood'll lead 'em right to us," Linda gasped.

"It's God or nothing," Gary said.

But the sky didn't open to receive them, and Father Chuck's legs turned almost to rubber. Gary fell beneath him, panting furiously.

"Father?" he gasped, wrestling out from underneath. "Can you make us a miracle?"

The priest raised himself on his hands and knees. He lifted his head, tried to point, but toppled. "Church . . . St. Bonaventure's."

Gary looked; the steeples were near.

"Body . . . of Christ . . . miracle enough?" the priest asked.

Gary dragged Father Chuck once more to his feet. Linda set her shoulder under the priest's other arm, and they trudged forward.

They had only a hundred yards to go, but it was pure torment, a nightmare of exhaustion and cramping muscles. Yet finally, with the screams drawing ever closer, they came out on the street fronting the church, and staggered across to the steps. With a terrific effort, they got Father Chuck to the top; blessedly, the great oaken doors were unlocked, and the three dragged inside. To all appearances, for whatever reason, the church hadn't been desecrated—yet. Gary locked the doors behind them, and they went up the main aisle toward the altar. Father Chuck collapsed over the step by the rail. Gary snapped another ammonia capsule under his nose. The priest grunted, shaking his head.

"Don't die on us now, Father," Gary pleaded.

"Altar," Father Chuck muttered. "Tabernacle on altar. Get the sacrament . . ."

Linda staggered to the altar, opened the tabernacle. The chalice inside was empty.

"It's not there!" she cried, turning with the vessel in her hand.

"Must've removed it," Father Chuck said. "To keep it from them . . ." He pointed to a nearby door. "Container in there, probably . . . full of hosts. Unconsecrated."

Linda and Gary rushed through. In an almost comically prosaic cardboard barrel lined with plastic, they found the wafers. Shoveling a handful into the chalice, they returned to Father Chuck, setting the cup down on the scarlet carpet.

"Gary," the priest breathed, "are you sorry for your sins?"

"Yes, Father," Gary answered.

The priest made the sign of the cross. "In the name of the Father, the Son, and the Holy Spirit, I absolve you."

He signaled for the chalice. Linda pushed it toward him. Father Chuck closed his eyes and began the consecration, head sinking lower and lower. Gary hugged Linda against his side, clenching her hand in his.

The screams drew closer. It wouldn't be long now.

"Pray, Gary," Linda said. "Pray."

She started the Lord's Prayer. He joined her feebly, his voice fading out after a few words. His life had been a hopeless, spineless waste. He'd been spitting in God's face all along. Why should God help him now?

"Help me," Linda said, noticing his silence, squeezing his hand. Father Chuck's voice had sunken to a mere halting whisper.

Gary began to mouth the words again. He didn't know if they would do any good, but forced them out anyway.

Father Chuck raised himself to his knees, lifted the chalice slowly, struggling as though it weighed fifty pounds.

"This is the Lamb of God," he whispered. "Blessed are we . . . .who are called to His supper—"

With that, there came three muffled pistol cracks in quick succession. A slug, the only one to penetrate the thick front doors, crashed into the altar in a spurt of marble dust. Gary turned to see one of the doors sweep open, and in stumbled Steve Jennings, leading the way with his .45.

"*Nobody* walks out on me!" he cried, and snapped off two more rounds.

The first shot struck Father Chuck in the back, tore out through his chest in a geyser of blood, spraying red all over the chalice, which dropped from his hands. The priest crumpled, taking a second slug in the leg.

Gary fumbled for his automatic. Steve turned his fire on him, giving Linda a moment to unsling her rifle.

Gary felt a numbing impact in the left leg, another in the chest, a third in the groin, and he fell to the carpet on his back, feeling little pain from the wounds, but intensely aware of the breath leaking from his punctured left lung.

Linda's Marlin roared. By the time Gary managed to fight back up into a sitting position, a rusty film of blood coating the inside of his mouth, he saw Steve on his belly, crawling back toward the door, disappearing outside.

Linda dropped the smoking rifle, cradled Gary's head against her breast. The screams outside were approaching their crescendo. The furies were almost to the church.

"Father Chuck!" Linda cried. "Did you finish?"

The priest nodded. He reached out toward the blood-spattered hosts scattered on the carpet, but his fingers fell short.

Figures appeared in the doorway, churned through. The church rang with their shrieks.

Gary heaved his pistol up and fired, too weak to aim, the pistol jumping in his hand. Grinning mockery at his impotence, the dead boiled up the aisle toward the altar.

Gary looked over at the priest. Father Chuck seemed to be dead, but when Linda shoved a host into his mouth, he chewed and swallowed.

She and Gary snatched others, the dead screaming toward them, claws outstretched. Linda raised hers to her lips, closed her eyes, took the Sacrament.

Gary hesitated at the last moment. It seemed almost blasphemous to go further. How could *he* enter into communion with God? Deep in his heart, there was a vacuum; the faith wasn't there, and he couldn't force it. The Sacrament would only deepen his sin. God wouldn't help him. He was damned, cut off from grace—

If there was grace to be had.

Linda and Father Chuck hadn't disappeared. There was no flash of light, no miracle. The heavens were mute.

And now the dead hands were on them, on *him*, grabbing and ripping at his legs.

They dragged him backward over the step, smashed the pistol from his hand. Some held his arms while others tore open his coat and dry suit, raked their nails over his chest, probed the bullet wound there. He howled and kicked; they held him fast. Drunk with blood loss, he felt himself spinning toward the void.

He was almost over the brink when the flash stung his eyes, a flash of pure white light that seemed to turn the church into a cathedral of frost. Still gripping him, the corpses froze, motionless. Gary couldn't see, but he knew what had happened. Linda, Father Chuck—one of them had made it, or both.

Whipping his head back and forth, Gary shrieked with despair. He'd been given his chance, and had thrown it away. Mind reverberating with that terrible knowledge, he felt the life draining from his flesh, his limbs turning to lead.

A half minute passed. The dead stirred, started in on him once more. That was when the darkness claimed him.

LAUGHING thickly, jacket sodden with blood, Steve had crawled over the threshold and pried himself up off the outside steps. He knew he was dying, but felt strangely untroubled.

Showed 'em, all right, he thought. *Showed 'em but fucking good.*

He'd paid them back for their betrayal, their arrogance. Who were *they* to turn on *him*? Insects to be stamped out at his pleasure. And if he was damned, so were they; he'd shot their shaman, cut off whatever hope they had left. They were nothing but dogs to accompany him at his viking's funeral, and they were going out like dogs, cringing on their knees to the sadist in Heaven; but he'd go out proudly, standing erect and defiant.

Corpses poured across the street toward him. Even though he knew they wouldn't hear him over their own screams, he pointed his pistol back at the open door and cried again and again: "They're in there!"

The tide reached the foot of the steps and rolled upward. In his pain and dizziness, he half nursed a mad hope that they might recognize him as a kindred spirit, welcome him alive into their ranks, or at least kill him painlessly. He was, after all, already on their side . . .

Only at the end did he realize what his allegiance meant, that he'd made a covenant with agony beyond his wildest imaginings; that was when Ginger came flying up at him like an avenging angel, and his pride deserted him, and he pissed himself before she started in.

PAIN stung Gary's nostrils, the acrid smell of ammonia jolting him back to consciousness. They'd found some of his smelling salts, or perhaps had brought some of their own. What good was torture if the victim was oblivious?

Once they were satisfied that he was fully awake, they began where they'd left off with teeth and claws and blades, shredding, flaying, twisting. The pain was ferocious.

Yet in the midst of it all, realization struck him. There was something clenched in his pinned right hand.

The host. Salvation was an arm's length away, and he couldn't reach it.

"Jesus," he gasped. "Jesus, help me!"

They hissed laughter at him, and one clapped a hand over his mouth, silencing him with its fetid scabrous palm. His tormentors resumed their sport.

As he sank toward a darkness deeper than mere unconsciousness, he saw, out of the corner of his eye, a corpse trying to force its way in among the ones working on him. The cadaver with its hand over his mouth jumped up snarling, and those holding his arm let go, pushing the interloper back.

With all the speed remaining to him, Gary thrust the host into his mouth. Instantly it began to melt on his tongue.

They saw him do it, were back on him in a flash. They pulled his jaws open and squeezed his throat, but he'd already swallowed. A tremendous surge of warmth filled his veins.

The hands on his throat tightened. The dead were trying to finish him before he could vanish. Cartilage gave, and his breath was choked off—

Only for a moment. The crushing pressure slackened. The bony hands melted away from his flesh as a great wind swept over him. Pain faded, and there was a fierce white fire rushing before his eyes.

He was out.

CHAPTER 26
THE OTHER SIDE

THE flame dissipated. He could barely see his new surroundings; it was as though he were looking through a pane of dark glass. Slowly his fire-dazzled eyes adjusted.

He wasn't in new surroundings after all, but lying in the main aisle of St. Bonaventure's. There was no sign of the dead.

He sat up, looking at the places were the bullets had struck him. There were no holes, no blood.

He got slowly to his feet. As he did so, he noticed something lying beneath him, and stepped away, gasping. It was a faint semitransparent body, a gelatinous-looking image of himself.

It began to quiver, and sank in upon itself, dissolving into a slimy puddle, the carpet swiftly absorbing it. The fabric showed a silvery, mucoid stain for a few moments, but even that vanished.

What had he just seen? The end of his earthly body, or of something even more fundamental? He didn't feel like a new creation, merely a repaired one.

Yet that wasn't the whole of it, he was sure, and his curiosity began to stir . . . what *was* he was going to experience? Before, salvation had simply meant survival. Now his sense of wonder was aroused.

He walked up the aisle toward the door. The light outside was clear and pure, without the bloody tinge of a dying sun; the circular stained glass window above the arch was a marvel of brilliant colors, cool deep blues and greens, reds and yellows so unmitigated they seemed to burn.

He reached the threshold.

Linda and Father Chuck were sitting halfway down the steps, backs to him. His wife seemed to be crying.

"Linda!" he cried, bounding down toward them.

They looked round. Linda jumped to her feet, wiping her eyes. Gary took her in his arms, kissing the tears off her cheeks and lips.

"I thought you . . . that you didn't . . . " she faltered.

"Went right down to the wire," Gary answered. "But the Man

Upstairs came through."

Father Chuck came up, smiling.

"God bless you, Father," Gary said.

"He already has," the priest replied.

Gary sucked in a long sweet chestful of warm summer air. "July again," he said.

He looked out over the bungalows across the empty street. Their pastel colors seemed almost manically cheerful. Even at its best, Brittany had never looked so good. And yet, somehow the town was still itself; Gary had a strange feeling that it was perhaps more itself than it had ever been.

"Not that I'm complaining, Father," he said, "but why does everything look the same? I mean, it's not the same really, but a lot of it is, actually most of it is . . . " He paused, trying to frame a coherent question. "Are we still on Earth, or what?"

"I don't know," the priest answered. "But maybe the answer is yes. A new Earth. The old one remade. Or split off from Hell."

"But have *we* been changed?" Gary asked.

"Didn't you see your slimy old self sinking into the carpet like a slug's trail?" Linda asked.

"So that happened to you guys too?"

"Unappetizing, huh?"

Gary looked up and down the street; it was utterly deserted. "Doesn't seem to be a very heavily populated place, does it?"

"This part, maybe not," Linda said.

"Wonder what that glow is?" Gary asked, pointing toward a fringe of white light silhouetting the roofs to the north, pulsing faintly.

"We could go see," Father Chuck said.

They headed down the steps and north along the street.

Before long they spotted two people coming around a bend in the road: Dennis and Camille. Linda whooped.

"We were sent for you," Camille said after a round of hugs.

"Have you . . . have you seen my mother?" Gary asked.

"She's back north. Up in the light. She wanted to come herself, but there's a meeting, and they couldn't spare her . . . "

"A *meeting?*" Linda laughed.

"Does sound awful down to earth, doesn't it?" Dennis asked. "But things are going to change. Slowly, so we can adjust."

"Who told you all this?" Linda asked.

313

Dennis looked at his wife, as if for advice on how to answer. She shrugged.

"Now don't laugh," Dennis said.

"I won't."

"An angel, I think. An image of one, anyway. *Looked* human, but . . . it sure wasn't one of us. Your mother said they're only revealing themselves gradually. Showing us as much as we can take."

"Remember what the ones in the dream looked like?" Camille asked. "I don't think I could ever be comfortable around one of *those*. And they're not even the *strange* ones. Your mother said there are ones like wheels. She hadn't actually seen one, but—"

"Did many people get out?" Gary asked.

"More than I would've thought," Dennis answered. "We're actually late arrivals, as it turns out. But you'll find all that out for yourself. Come on."

They headed up the street, rounding the curve. Three men came into view, sitting on a sidewalk bench, apparently engaged in furious conversation. As Gary and the rest drew near, he realized joyfully that the one in the middle was Max.

Max looked up at their approach, grinning at Gary.

"Hey dor—" he began, breaking off before he could add the *k*.

Gary laughed. "I thought they got you."

"Thought so too," Max answered. "They were all over me. But I had to stay till the last second. You would've bought it. Or so say my buddies here."

"Hello, Gary," said Mr. Hersh, sitting on Max's left.

"How are you?" asked Mr. Williams on the right.

"Fine," Gary replied, finding the question a little incongruous.

"Get used to it," Williams said.

Gary looked sidelong from him back to Hersh. He hadn't seen either since the burial.

"Something wrong?" Hersh asked.

"You know, it might seem rude to ask this," Gary said, "But what are you two doing here?"

"Came down with Dennis and Camille," Williams answered. "Just stopped to talk to Max. Interesting fellow, your brother."

"No, that isn't what I meant," Gary said. "You're going to think this is really terrible, but . . . "

"Spit it out, young man," Hersh broke in.

"Okay," Gary began. "What I'm driving at is this. Unless I'm very badly mistaken, everything that's happened to me in the last few days seemed to indicate we're living in a *Catholic* universe—priests with supernatural powers, sacraments snatching people from Hell . . . "

"Go on," Mr. Williams prodded.

"But if that's true," Gary continued, "if this *is* a Catholic universe, what are a . . . er, Jew and a Protestant doing here?"

"What are *you* doing here?" Max asked.

"Was I talking to you?"

Max only smiled.

"You know, Gary," answered Mr. Hersh at last, "That's a very interesting story . . . "

Though both my prayers and tears combine,
Both worthless are, for they are mine;
But Thou Thy bounteous self still be,
And show Thou art by saving me
O when thy last frown shall proclaim
The flocks of goats to folds of flame,
And all Thy lost sheep found shall be,
Let "Come ye blessed" then call me!
When the dead He shall divide
Those limbs of death from Thy left side,
Let those life-speaking lips command
That I inherit Thy right hand
O hear a suppliant heart all crushed
And crumbled into contrite dust!
My hope, my fear, my Judge, my Friend,
Take charge of me and of my end!
  —*Mass For the Dead*

Born in 1952, author-illustrator Mark E. Rogers is best known for the Samurai Cat books: *The Adventures of Samurai Cat, More Adventures of Samurai Cat, Samurai Cat in the Real World, The Sword of Samurai Cat,* and *Samurai Cat Goes to the Movies.* He brought the series to a close with *Samurai Cat Goes to Hell,* which was published by TOR in 1998.

His other books include *The Dead, Zorachus, The Nightmare of God, The Expected One, The Devouring Void, The Riddled Man, The Zancharthus Trilogy, Lilitu, Yark,* and *Flaming Sword.* One of his novellas, *The Runestone,* was made into a movie; his work has been adapted by Marvel comics, and has appeared on the cover of *Cricket Magazine.* He's published three art portfolios, and two volumes of pinups, *Nothing but a Smile,* and *The Art of Fantasy.*

He lives in Newark, Delaware, with his wife Kate, a philosophy professor at the U of D—and their four lovely kids, Sophie, Jeannie, Patrick, and Nick.

Permuted Press

delivers the absolute best in **apocalyptic** fiction,
from **zombies** to **vampires** to **werewolves**
to **asteroids** to **nuclear bombs** to
the very **elements** themselves.

Why are so many readers turning to
Permuted Press?

Because we strive to make every book
we publish feel like an **event**, not
just pages thrown between a cover.

(And most importantly, we provide some
of the most fantastic, well written, horrifying
scenarios this side of an actual apocalypse.)

Check out our full catalog online at:
www.permutedpress.com

And log on to our message board
to chat with our authors:
www.permutedpress.com/forum

We'd love to hear from you!

The formula has been changed...
Shifted... Altered... *Twisted.*™

DEREK GUNN
THE ESTUARY

Excavations for a new shopping centre in the town of Whiteshead have unearthed a mysterious contagion that threatens the lives of the townspeople. Now the residents are trapped within a quarantine zone with the military on one side and ravenous hordes of living dead on the other. Escape is no longer an option.

Far out in the mouth of the estuary sits a small keep. This refuge has always been unassailable, a place of myth and legend. Now it's the survivors' only hope of sanctuary. But there are thousands of flesh-eating infected between them and the keep, and time is running out...

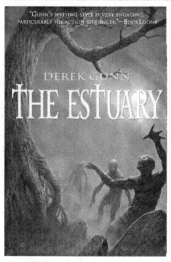

"GUNN'S WRITING STYLE IS VERY ENGAGING, PARTICULARLY HIS ACTION SEQUENCES." —BOOKLOONS

ISBN: 978-1934861240

Five novels of the living dead by zombie fiction master Eric S. Brown: *Season of Rot, The Queen, The Wave, Dead West,* and *Rats.*

"A VERITABLE GRAB-BAG OF ZOMBIE GOODNESS. A LITTLE OF THIS, AND A LITTLE OF THAT. A LOT OF BRAINS..."
—Z.A. RECHT,
AUTHOR OF *PLAGUE OF THE DEAD*

"FAST, FURIOUS AND STRAIGHT OUT OF YOUR WORST NIGHTMARES." —GREG F. GIFUNE, AUTHOR OF *CHILDREN OF CHAOS*

SEASON OF

FIVE ZOMBIE NOVELLAS BY
ERIC S. BROWN

ISBN: 978-1934861226

MORE DETAILS, EXCERPTS, AND PURCHASE INFORMATION AT
www.permutedpress.com

THE RAGE PLAGUE

A NOVEL BY ANTHONY GIANGREGORIO

An unknown virus spreads across the globe, turning ordinary people into ravenous killers. Only a small population proves to be immune, but most quickly fall prey to the infected.

Isolated on the rooftop of a school near the outskirts of Chicago, Bill Thompson and a small band of survivors come to the frightening realization that, without food or water, they will perish quickly under the hot sun. Some wish to migrate to a safer, more plentiful refuge, but the school is surrounded by rampaging murderers. Without a plan, Bill and his group don't stand a chance.

Their only hope lies in their one advantage over the infected: their ability to think.

ISBN: 978-1934861196

DEAD END

a Zombie novel by Anthony Giangregorio

In this new world where a deadly virus transforms its victims into living dead things hungering for human flesh, a small band of survivors must do anything and everything they can to survive from one day to the next.

In the city, a small haven has appeared in the form of a fortified church building... but the good Reverend in charge isn't everything he seems.

The band of survivors is on a collision course with the vicious church dwellers in the city. Will there be a way out for the survivors, or are they all headed for a *Dead End?*

ISBN: 978-1934861189

MORE DETAILS, EXCERPTS, AND PURCHASE INFORMATION AT

www.permutedpress.com

BESTIAL
WEREWOLF APOCALYPSE
BY WILLIAM D. CARL

Beneath the dim light of a full moon, the population of Cincinnati mutates into huge, snarling monsters that devour everyone they see, acting upon their most base and bestial desires. Planes fall from the sky. Highways are clogged with abandoned cars, and buildings explode and topple. The city burns.

Only four people are immune to the metamorphosis—a smooth-talking thief who maintains the code of the Old West, an African-American bank teller who has struggled her entire life to emerge unscathed from the ghetto, a wealthy middle-aged housewife who finds everything she once believed to be a lie, and a teen-aged runaway turning tricks for food.

Somehow, these survivors must discover what caused this apocalypse and stop it from spreading. In their way is not only a city of beasts at night, but, in the daylight hours, the same monsters returned to human form, many driven insane by atrocities committed against friends and families.

Now another night is fast approaching. And once again the moon will be full.

ISBN: 978-1934861042

EDEN
A ZOMBIE NOVEL BY TONY MONCHINSKI

Seemingly overnight the world transforms into a barren wasteland ravaged by plague and overrun by hordes of flesh-eating zombies. A small band of desperate men and women stand their ground in a fortified compound in what had been Queens, New York. They've named their sanctuary Eden.

Harris—the unusual honest man in this dead world—races against time to solve a murder while maintaining his own humanity. Because the danger posed by the dead and diseased mass clawing at Eden's walls pales in comparison to the deceit and treachery Harris faces within.

ISBN: 978-1934861172

MORE DETAILS, EXCERPTS, AND PURCHASE INFORMATION AT
www.permutedpress.com

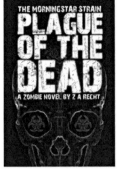

PLAGUE OF THE DEAD
BY Z A RECHT

A worldwide viral outbreak brings the dead to life. On one side of the globe, a battle-hardened General surveys the remnants of his command: a young medic, a veteran photographer, a brash Private, and dozens of refugees, all are his responsibility. Back in the United States, an Army Colonel discovers the darker side of the virus and begins to collaborate with a well-known journalist to leak the information to the public...

ISBN: 978-0-9789707-0-3

DYING TO LIVE
a novel of life among the undead
BY KIM PAFFENROTH

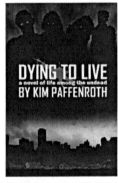

After wandering for months in a zombie-infested world, Jonah Caine discovers a group of survivors. Living in a museum-turned-compound, they are led by an ever-practical and efficient military man, and a mysterious, quizzical prophet who holds a strange power over the living dead. But Jonah's newfound peace is shattered when a clash with another group of survivors reminds them that the undead are not the only—nor the most grotesque—horrors they must face.

ISBN: 978-0-9789707-3-4

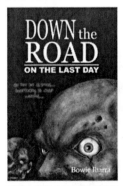

DOWN the ROAD
on THE LAST DAY
by Bowie Ibarra

In a small south Texas town, the mayor has rallied his citizens against the living dead and secured their borders. When two strangers from San Antonio stumble into town, they bring news of a global peacekeeping force sweeping toward the city. Led by a ruthless commander, the force is determined to secure the republic of Texas on its own terms, and establish a new, harsh government for the plague-ravaged nation.

ISBN: 978-0-9789707-2-7

www.permutedpress.com

THE UNDEAD
ZOMBIE ANTHOLOGY

ISBN: 978-0-9765559-4-0

"Dark, disturbing and hilarious."
—Dave Dreher, *Creature-Corner.com*

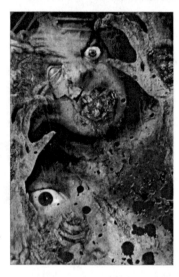

THE UNDEAD
VOLUME 2
SKIN AND BONES

ISBN: 978-0-9789707-4-1

"Permuted did us all a favor with the first volume of *The Undead*. Now they're back with *The Undead: Skin and Bones,* and gore hounds everywhere can belly up to the corpse canoe for a second helping. Great stories, great illustrations... *Skin and Bones* is fantastic!"
—Joe McKinney, author of *Dead City*

The Undead / volume three
FLESH FEAST

ISBN: 978-0-9789707-5-8

"Fantastic stories! The zombies are fresh... well, er, they're actually moldy, festering wrecks... but these stories are great takes on the zombie genre. You're gonna like *The Undead: Flesh Feast*... just make sure you have a toothpick handy."
—Joe McKinney, author of *Dead City*

DYING TO LIVE
LIFE SENTENCE
by Kim Paffenroth

At the end of the world a handful of survivors banded together in a museum-turned-compound surrounded by the living dead. The community established rituals and rites of passage, customs to keep themselves sane, to help them integrate into their new existence. In a battle against a kingdom of savage prisoners, the survivors lost loved ones, they lost innocence, but still they coped and grew. They even found a strange peace with the undead.

Twelve years later the community has reclaimed more of the city and has settled into a fairly secure life in their compound. Zoey is a girl coming of age in this undead world, learning new roles—new sacrifices. But even bigger surprises lie in wait, for some of the walking dead are beginning to remember who they are, whom they've lost, and, even worse, what they've done.

As the dead struggle to reclaim their lives, as the survivors combat an intruding force, the two groups accelerate toward a collision that could drastically alter both of their worlds.

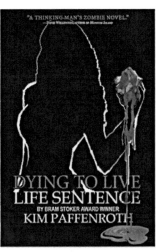

ISBN: 978-1934861110

EVERY SIGH, THE END.
(A novel about zombies.)
by Jason S. Hornsby

It's the end of the world: 1999.

Professional nobody Ross Orringer sees flashes of cameras and glances from strangers lurking around every corner.

His paranoia mounts when his friends and family begin acting more and more suspiciously as the New Year approaches.

In the last minutes before the clock strikes midnight, Ross realizes that the end may be more ominous than anyone could have imagined: decisions have been made, the crews have set up their lights and equipment, and the gray makeup has been applied.

In the next millennium, time will lose all meaning, and the dead will walk the earth.

ISBN: 978-0-9789707-8-9

MORE DETAILS, EXCERPTS, AND PURCHASE INFORMATION AT
www.permutedpress.com

MONSTROUS
20 TALES OF GIANT CREATURE TERROR

Move over King Kong, there are new monsters in town! Giant beetles, towering crustaceans, gargantuan felines and massive underwater beasts, to name just a few. Think you've got what it takes to survive their attacks? Then open this baby up, and join today's hottest authors as they show us the true power of Mother Nature's creatures. With enough fangs, pincers and blood to keep you up all night, we promise you won't look at creepy crawlies the same way again.

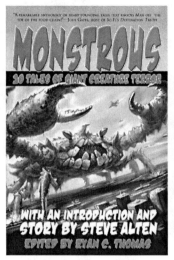

ISBN: 978-1934861127

THUNDER AND ASHES
A ZOMBIE NOVEL BY Z.A. RECHT

A lot can change in three months: wars can be decided, nations can be forged... or entire species can be brought to the brink of annihilation. The Morningstar Virus, an incredibly virulent disease, has swept the face of the planet, infecting billions. Its hosts rampage, attacking anything that remains uninfected. Even death can't stop the virus—its victims return as cannibalistic shamblers.

Scattered across the world, embattled groups have persevered. For some, surviving is the pinnacle of achievement. Others hoard goods and weapons. And still others leverage power over the remnants of humanity in the form of a mysterious cure for Morningstar. Francis Sherman and Anna Demilio want only a vaccine, but to find it, they must cross a countryside in ruins, dodging not only the infected, but also the lawless living.

ISBN: 978-1934861011

The bulk of the storm has passed over the world, leaving echoing thunder and softly drifting ashes. But for the survivors, the peril remains, and the search for a cure is just beginning...

MORE DETAILS, EXCERPTS, AND PURCHASE INFORMATION AT

www.permutedpress.com

HISTORY
IS DEAD

A ZOMBIE ANTHOLOGY EDITED BY
KIM PAFFENROTH

"*History is Dead* is a violent and
bloody tour through the ages.
Paffenroth has assembled a vicious
timeline chronicling the rise of the
undead that is simultaneously mind-
numbingly savage and thought
provoking."
—Michael McBride, author of the
God's End trilogy and *The Infected*

ISBN: 978-0-9789707-9-6

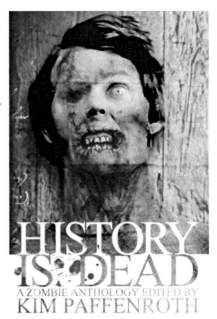

ROSES OF BLOOD
ON BARBWIRE VINES
D.L. SNELL

As the living dead invade a barricaded
apartment building, the vampire
inhabitants must protect their human
livestock. Shade, the vampire monarch,
defends her late father's kingdom, but
Frost, Shade's general, convinces his
brethren to migrate to an island where
they can breed and hunt humans. In
their path stands a legion of corpses,
just now evolving into something far
more lethal, something with tentacles
—and that's just the beginning.

ISBN: 978-0-9789707-1-0

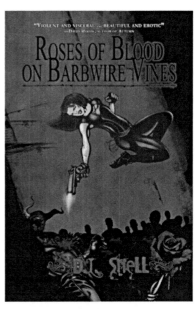

42866

LaVergne, TN USA
05 August 2010
192250LV00006B/154/P

9 781934 861264